# GEMINI

## ANTHONY TYE RODRIGUES

# GEMINI

By

ANTHONY TYE RODRIGUES

*Gemini*
By Anthony Tye Rodrigues

ISBN: 978-1-64594-218-4

Also available in a hard cover edition: 978-1-64594-217-7
And as an e-book: 978-1-64594-219-1

Published by GutenBookPress. Copyright, 2023.
All Rights Reserved

www.gutenbookpress.com

# TABLE OF CONTENTS

# Names of Towns and Fortifications

| Ancient Name | Modern Name | County |
|---|---|---|
| Banna | *Birdoswald* | *Cumbria* |
| Calcaria | *Tadcaster* | *Yorkshire* |
| Colanica | *Croy Hill* | *North Lanarkshire* |
| Coria | *Corbridge* | *Northumberland* |
| Corinium (Cironium) | *Cirencester* | *Gloucestershire* |
| Curia | *Traprain Law* | *East Lothian* |
| Deva | *Chester* | *Cheshire* |
| Durobrivae | *Rochester* | *Kent* |
| Durovigutum | *Godmanchester* | *Cambridgeshire* |
| Eburacum | *York* | *North Yorkshire* |
| Glevum | *Gloucester* | *Gloucestershire* |
| Iatubriga | *Otford* | *Kent* |
| Isurium | *Aldborough* | *North Yorkshire* |
| Lagentium | *Castleford* | *West Yorkshire* |
| Lindum (Colonia) | *Lincoln* | *Lincolnshire* |
| Londinium | *London* | |
| Luguvalium | *Carlisle* | *Cumbria* |
| Onnum | *Halton Chesters* | *Northumberland* |
| Petuaria | *Brough-on-Humber* | *East Riding* |
| Segolocum | *South of Littleborough* | *Nottinghamshire* |
| Trimontium | *Newstead* | *Scottish Borders* |
| Uxelodunum | *Stanwix* | *Cumbria* |
| Vagniacis (Five Temples, Quinque Templa Pempe Dewoi) | *Springhead* | *Kent* |
| Villa on Oak River | *Lullingstone Villa, Eynsford* | *Kent* |
| Villa on the Hill | *Great Witcombe* | *Gloucestershire* |

# Names of Rivers

| Ancient Name | Modern Name |
|---|---|
| Abona Derwentiu (Oak River) | *River Darent* |
| Abos River | *River Ouse* |
| Bodotria River | *Forth River* |
| Derwentio River | *Calder & Aire Rivers* |
| Tamesis River | *River Thames* |
| Tueda river | *River Tweed* |
| Verbeia River | *River Wharfe* |

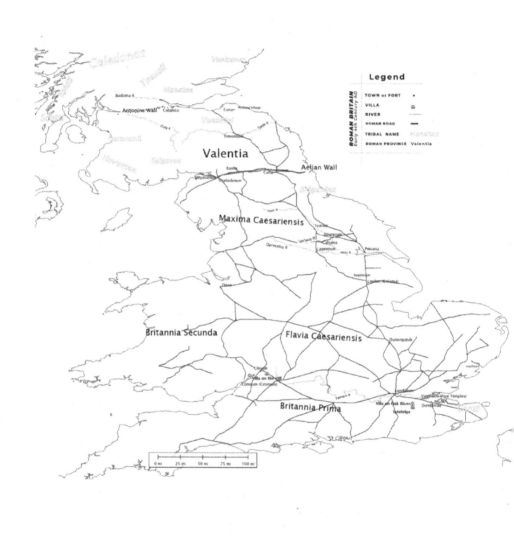

# AUTHOR'S FOREWORD

*Gemini* is the second book of a trilogy, *The Villa at Oak River,* which offers a fictional history of the Roman family, the Vindexes, who lived at Lullingstone Villa in Kent.

The villa was discovered at Lullingstone near the village of Eynsford in Kent, when, in 1939, a tree blew down and revealed fragments of a mosaic. It was excavated in the period 1949–61, and a remarkable find occurred: a Roman temple had been built on the hill above the villa, and under its floor were the bodies of a young man and a young woman. This was very unusual: Romans usually buried their dead along roads, well away from their dwellings and temples.

The skeleton of the young man is visible to this day at the villa, which is administered by English Heritage Trust.

The first volume of the trilogy, called *Storm before Sunset,* tries to explain that mystery. It is set in the years 275-286 AD, a period in which seven emperors fought their way to power, and were, until the very last, murdered one by one. Between civil war and recurrent barbarian invasions, the upheaval was so extreme that some fled the chaos in the mainland provinces for safer ones, such as Britannia. The Vindex family was one such.

The current volume, which is a stand-alone story, follows the second generation of this British family. It is set in a new period of growing uncertainty. The Roman empire had been divided into two realms by Diocletian, ruled by subordinate Emperors and their seconds, called Caesars. But now, as Diocletian's health fails, they begin to vie for supremacy. Their plans are complicated by rebel emperors such as Carausius, who had seized power in Britannia. One of the Caesars, Constantius, sent to deal with the rebellion, has now become Emperor of the West. His untimely death in York, and the prevalence of a new religion, Christianity, threatens to plunge Britannia into chaos again. His illegitimate son, Constantinus, seizes power; but he commits an outrage which compels the Vindex family into the dynastic conflict, and, unwittingly, into the religious one as well.

# CHAPTER 1

## Licinianus: The Emperor

It surprises me that I once saw Flavilla as just my beloved aunt, happy, sweet and kind. And so she was: a lovely, delightful woman, who took me in her arms and danced singing with me down the paved path to the river, whirling in and out of the flower beds that her mother so carefully tended. She loved us dearly, my twin sister Severiana, and me. I learned why, when I got older: we were all that was left of her twin brother and his wife, and she had loved him as life itself. But I never understood it as a child, for children don't understand loss. It's unfathomable to them, until they experience it themselves.

But there was more than that: Flavilla taught me the names of the plants, and if she didn't know one, her mother was there to ask, even as Aelia grew older and older. And that taught me a little about death, for I saw that plants had a cycle of life, and if I found that hard to relate to men and women, it lay there waiting for me to find one day, and not much later, either. I was nine years old when that happened.

I was dressed early by my nursemaid, and she was talking excitedly to me as she dressed me in a purple-bordered toga praetexta.[1] I didn't know why I was being dressed in such an uncomfortable piece of clothing. I usually ran around in a short tunic, which allowed my legs the freedom I needed to climb trees, skin my knees, and get muddy on the bank of the river. But not today. It was special, she told me: the Emperor was coming.

I knew of the Emperor, but not as a real person. I had thought he was a god, and so could never actually be seen. But now I was to see him, and the slave was brushing my hair firmly, telling me to be a good boy and not mess it up before the time.

"It shines so, little master," she said. "Like red gold it is!"

And that was the first time I learned what color my hair was. I said: "Is it the same as Severiana's?"

"Of course, sweetheart! You're twins, like two sides of a halved apple!"

"Then I know what it looks like!"

She smiled and kissed me, and took me by my hand. "Come, Lady Flavilla

---

[1] A garment with a purple border worn only by young boys and some magistrates.

1

and Lady Aelia are waiting. Put your bulla on! You are too young to be without protection. What if one of the Night Hags saw you and decided to choose you for hers when the sun goes down?"

I put the charm on quickly, for sometimes I feared that might happen. I knew I should always wear it, against the supernatural world that might wish to harm me.

We went out onto the veranda, and then down to the garden, with me shaking my hand free from the slave-woman's, for I was a man, I believed; and there the family was waiting for the Emperor to arrive. Flavilla, Aelia... both came to kiss me as I was led there, and, of course, I hated it, for everyone could see. And Aetius, Flavilla's husband, was there, and Catigernus, a freedman, yes, but someone I loved. I did not look at Numerianus, my half-brother, who, though a little younger than I, was always ready to say something embarrassing. Cassianus, Flavilla's son, who was only seven, had been pushed by one of Catigernus's sons, knocking down Catigernus's daughter in the process, and both were sitting on the tiles crying, with the women trying to calm them, and Catigernus promising retribution to his offspring. I saw Numerianus grinning, and I grinned back. My stepmother Aurelia Paulina looked at me sternly, but then I saw that she had suddenly hidden her mouth behind her palm, and knew she was laughing.

That was the beginning of my introduction to mortality, with children laughing, children crying, and boys with their hair brushed until it shone.

As I look back on this scene, and the week that followed it, from a distance of sixty years, I recall that there was a sudden murmur that came from the family and the gathered slaves, for, off to our right, riding towards us, we saw the head of the column. The standards were bright red and purple and gold as they came along the road, the vines in neat rows in the field to their right, the orderly trees my grandfather had planted to their left. As it passed, the slaves in the fields fell to their knees and prostrated themselves. And then they were right in front of the stairs leading to the Villa, and we, gathered before it, fell to our knees and bowed our heads.

It's hard to talk about this, because I'm not sure what I actually remember, and what has become part of my memory because I was told it later by my aunt and stepmother. I remember that there was a standard with the words "*Redeunt*

*Sāturnia Regna, Iam Nova Prōgeniēs Caelō Dēmittitur*[2] written in gold on its red face, but I think this must have been told me, for, though I could read at nine, I doubt I would have known or remembered this myself: I had not then encountered the Eclogues of Virgil. And I certainly did not understand its significance. But yet I do remember seeing it, and demonstrate thereby the falsity of memory.

Now, the man, him I clearly remember. He rode a large bay, but one whose coat was redder than most, with a mane and tail of the purest black. It shone in the low sun, and the man on its back seemed huge, though I know he was not, and his hair and curled beard somehow mirrored that of the horse's: red-brown, combed, and glowing. His head was bare: no helmet on it, or even the broad-brimmed hat that most used in travel. I was on my knees, almost prostrating myself, but I could not help trying to look up and see him more clearly. And at that instant, Carausius's eyes met mine, and he grinned.

Those who knew him much better than I ever did, more than once told me that Carausius, the Emperor of Britannia and Gallia, was a man who was easily loved. I can't speak to that. But I know he got down off his horse and walked to where my family knelt in obeisance, and it was not the adults he addressed, but the little crowd of us children. He looked down at us, as we gazed in paralyzed fear at this man, and said, "Now who are all of you? The children of the house? Tell me your names."

None of us could speak, but he came to me, and said: "Your nurse will tell you that you were a bad boy to look at me sidelong, but you tell her from me, you were not. You were just being what a boy should be at your age! And maybe when you're older, you'll be one of my soldiers!"

And to each of us children, scared though we were, he stopped and talked with such kindness, until he had spoken to all. Then he looked up at the adults, called everyone to their feet, and apologized for leaving them kneeling.

"As Allectus will tell you," he said to them, and gestured to the man by him, "I have always had a soft spot for children. I lost all but two of mine to the blood-plague, and I miss them dearly."

I've always thought that somehow Allectus should have made more of an impression on me, considering the huge damage he was to do; but on my nine-year-old mind, he had very little effect. Even his name I never remembered until told it later. I only saw him vaguely: he was overshadowed by the glow that was

---

[2] "The Golden Ages are back, now a new generation is let down from Heaven above."

Carausius. So, what I remember most is that the Emperor turned to that man, his treasurer as I later learned, and took from him a pouch, and gave to each of us children a gold coin. As I took mine, he said, "Now don't ever spend this. Just keep it to remember me by. See, my head's on it?"

I looked down at it, saw it was new-struck, and read "Expectāte venī"[3] I have it still. But the irony of those words I certainly did not see, for I did not know that he had just been defeated in Gallia by Constantius Chlorus, who had been sent by Maximinianus and Diocletianus to take back Carausius's provinces. I was more interested in the boy who rode just behind the Emperor, older than me, certainly, but not much older.

The slaves were now busy setting up tables in front of the house to serve the emperor and his men, for they were far too many to use the dining room; I and my sister Severiana were watching, fascinated, she drawn to the lavish silks and clothes, I to the shining armor and shields of which, even then, I had read so much in the classics. I wanted to talk to the boy, but I was hesitant to do so. It was probably a good thing, for there is no gap in age as big as when a nine-year old tries to engage a boy two or three years older. Severiana, however, had no such reticence, and showed me for the first time that girls can get away with things that a boy cannot, for she walked up to him and asked him who he was. She has never been shy.

I followed in her wake, interested to find out more about a boy who traveled with the Emperor. He was already talking to her, and I understood his name was Mausaeus Carausius Artorius. "Why are you with the Emperor?" Severiana was asking. "Is he your father?"

He hesitated, as if he was about to say no. But then he said stiffly: "Yes. I'm his son. But my mother was just his concubine." And at that point, drawn by the smell of the delicious food now being served, I walked away.

+ + +

It seems to me astonishing that I never noticed the strangeness of Carausius coming to our villa, or spending the night there, after a lengthy day spent with so many important British landowners and military officials. The road between Dubris and Londinium did not pass by the Villa on Oak River: to reach us meant a detour, for we lived perhaps seven or eight miles south of it. But what do children know or care about distances? I thought nothing of it for years. I

---

[3] "Come, expected one."

was far more excited by the fact that my stepmother Aurelia Paulina had promised the three of us – me, Severiana and Numerianus – that she would take us with her when she went to Londinium a few days later.

I knew that she was immensely rich, for she had been the daughter of the Emperor Carus. She was also very good with finances, and so looked after our holdings as well. And that meant regular visits to Londinium to talk to our agents and factors. We wanted to see the city: we had heard so many things about it... its amphitheater, its theaters, its shops, its port... All of us were excited.

It was a very frustrating journey. We rode with Aurelia Paulina, and asked again and again whether we had come to Londinium yet. Since the journey took many hours in the slow carriage, she left us to the ministrations of the two slave women who looked after us, and devoted herself to her papyrus rolls and tablets, frowning at the accounts as she familiarized herself with the figures. I seem to remember that she had discovered some discrepancies, which she was not happy with. Flavilla was also with us, for her husband, Aetius, who was a legate, was in Londinium at that time, and she played a game of tabula with us. But at last, we came to the area south of the Tamesis, and crossed the bridge into Londinium. The family owned a house that overlooked the river, not too far east of the bridge, and there we stopped to spend the night. I thought I would never sleep; but darkness fell over my mind no more than a minute or two after we were put to bed. The rising sun woke me to the one day I will never be able to forget in all my life.

My stepmother went off to do her business, while Flavilla took us to see the city. I and Severiana were two over-animated nine-year-olds, and the two slave-women were busy keeping us in check. To ensure that we were safe, two male slaves accompanied us, bearing thick wooden staves, and from their hard faces no one would have doubted they would use their clubs if they had to. We went first to the market, and though I, like so many boys, had no great taste for shopping, the sheer number of stalls and the size of the selections made me open my eyes wide. I said, in awe: "You must be able to buy anything you want here!"

Flavilla laughed. "No, not quite, but this is the biggest city in Britannia, and all the traders come here. But if you ever go to Rome, you'll see so much more for sale!"

We spent a while buying a dress-length for Flavilla and another for Severiana, one lavender for my aunt, the other a very pretty pink. Then Flavilla bought some honeycakes from a pastry-seller carrying his wares on a wooden

5

tray hung from his neck, and we stopped at a caupōna to enjoy them at the bar with some heavily watered wine. They were delicious, and I wished for more; but we were led off to see the sights. We went first to the Governor's Palace, and there was the first time I heard the story of my father's fight there, as he and the assassin of Ignotus the Pretender struggled to stay alive until rescue came. "He fought there," I said, more than a little awed. "Yes," said Flavilla. "He and his father… my father too, because we were twins, just like you and Severiana. Your grandfather died there, and that is so sad… you would have loved him. But he died to save the Empire from another civil war, and that was a very good cause."

I wanted to know more; but I could see from her eyes that she was almost crying, and when she shook her head, I knew that this was not the time.

We walked some blocks to the west, and came to a place by the river where there were many temples, some big, some small. There were two temples side by side, built in the native style, so I knew that they were there to honor two of the gods of the land.

"Now, stay here, said Flavilla. 'I must sacrifice to Litavis… here she is called Matrona. You know her from our little temple. She is the goddess who has blessed our family ever since we were in Gallia, with her husband Camulus, as Cicoluis is called here, so our family always needs to honor them. When you are older, you will do so too."

She haggled with the sellers outside the precinct and in the end bought a hen and a cock, one for each god, and took them inside to each temple. I sat down on a low wall with Severiana, and we played at fingers, where we tried to guess what the other meant by the shape of our hands. We were so absorbed in our game, laughing loudly, that I never even noticed Flavilla's return until suddenly she was joining our game. We walked back the way we had come, then turned north and east to head for the Forum and the Basilica, where the Emperor Carausius was to sacrifice for the wellbeing of the Empire. There was a man running through the street, a brush and paint jar in hand, writing with amazing speed on the walls every few yards. "What is he doing?" I asked, fascinated. Flavilla glanced casually at them. "Writing a notice of some games to be held, I'd suppose." She looked closer. "No, it's a play that's being held next week. They're paid to advertise things, you know. It's how they make their living."

The day was a beautiful one, with a clear blue sky, but no birds flying, which was strange. So often in Britannia the sky is cloudy, and the sun muted behind a pale cloak, as if shy; but today none of that was true, and as we walked, we could hear the birds' quavering calls in the bushes and trees. Beauty had not yet come to me as a concept at that age; all I knew was when I felt good, the sun warm on my skin, or my belly full. A bad day was when it was too cold for me to go out, or too wet. And on that day, I felt very good indeed.

The Forum was packed, for Carausius had ordered that all who came should be fed and given free wine. There were stalls along the sides dispensing all this, and people were milling around them, enjoying what they had not paid for. The two male slaves went ahead, forcing the crowd aside so we could get close to the dais; and if anyone thought to oppose our progress, they changed their mind when they saw whom they were dealing with or received a blow from a staff for their hesitance.

We made our way until we were very close to the front, and then we waited. There was no set time for the Emperor to appear. I think it was just supposed to be somewhere around noon, though I can't really remember. We were looking at the Basilica: everyone expected him to appear there. But he did not, though there was a large group of soldiers there on the steps, and with them, though I did not recognize his face, was Allectus. Instead, we heard a commotion from behind.

I was too little to see over the heads of the people behind us, but I heard the whisper start, and then grow into a roar... the Emperor was coming up behind us. I could see glimpses of his purple robe between the people who masked him from me, and the swinging kilts of his soldiers. And then he was walking right by us, and I could see all of his party clearly. It never occurred to me that there were far too few of them.

My memory tells me that he looked at me, waved, and smiled. But I can't imagine that he singled me out. How could he have remembered that brief meeting at the villa, when I was just a little boy without the distinctive angles that adulthood gives, or see me in the crowd? But that's what I remember.

It happened right in front of me. The group of soldiers on the steps suddenly broke and were running down, drawing their swords. It happened so fast that I was bewildered at what they were doing. Even when I saw them hacking down the soldiers with Carausius I did not understand. And then they were all around the Emperor, and their swords were stabbing and hacking at him, and the blood was spattering everywhere. One of them stabbed into his throat, and I felt something wet strike my face, and when I blindly reached up to wipe it, my hand was red. Everywhere men were shouting and women screaming; and then they started running. One such I recognized: it was Artorius, Carausius' son, and behind him a soldier who slashed viciously at him. Artorius was right in front of us, running towards us, then amongst us, and the soldier behind him. Severiana was right in front of him, and he raised his arm to slash at her.

I believed my sister would die then, and I knew terror. I began to cry out for her.

But a slender arm moved with blinding speed, and blood bubbled from the soldier's mouth as he choked on the blade that Flavilla had driven into the side of his neck. Her face was like nothing I had ever seen in my beloved aunt, the face of a lioness, the face of someone not quite human. She shouted: "Away! Get them all away!" And I was lifted off my feet, as my aunt and her woman ran with the children in their arms behind the slaves who forced the way open for us. But Severiana was not with us. I saw her running away screaming, with Artorius behind her.

+ + +

There was little time spent making ready to leave Londinium when we reached the family's town house. My stepmother was already there, having finished her business, and she and Flavilla talked hard together. Everyone was agreed: we must leave at once, if we could, for who knew what would happen now. Then the two women came to us, and gathered the three children around them.

"You're so young to have to learned about these things, Licinianus, Numerianus... so young," said Aurelia Paulina, as the slaves ran around collecting our belongings in the house. "But the times we live in... My own father was murdered just as you saw Carausius murdered, and for the same reasons. Someone wanted his throne. My own two brothers were killed just in this way. One day I will have to tell you the details of all this, for you deserve to know where you come from. But that can wait. For the moment, all you need to know is that Carausius' friend and treasurer Allectus did this terrible deed, and has declared himself emperor. And all who were linked to the emperor are in danger. So we must go, and try to leave the city."

"Where is Severiana?" I screamed, and I was crying, for I was filled with terror at her loss. To be without my twin was an icy stone in my throat, and the thought that she might die, as I had just seen men die, was unbearable.

"We are looking for her, Licinianus," said Flavilla, and came forward to hug me. "We will find her, and we will not leave without her!" But I hung back, not comforted at all, for I remembered what she had done to the soldier.

She knelt down, and took me in her arms. "What is it, my sweet boy?"

I could hardly speak. "I saw…"

"You saw what?"

"The soldier…"

"Oh, my poor little soul." She hugged me. "Never fear me, my sweet brother's boy. What I did was to save you and your sister. I would do *anything* to keep you from harm. Our family… we have a gift, which is both beautiful and terrible. When you become a man, and your sister a woman, you will understand it too, for you may have similar gifts."

"But Severiana…"

"We will find her."

And then we heard a noise at the door, and the ostiarius's voice. There was the sound of a young girl calling and crying, and I knew at once it was Severiana. I ran to the door and threw my arms around my sister. For the first time in my life, I knew immense relief, as if I had been saved from a nightmare.

Artorius was behind her. "She ran from me…"

"I know," said Flavilla. "But you brought her here. Thank you. Thank you!"

"I couldn't leave her! She told me a little of where she lived, and then I asked in the street…"

He put his chin up. He was trying to be a man; but he was still a boy. "I must go. Allectus will kill me if he finds me. He will want no Menapian to live, and especially not me. Carausius' daughter has already been killed! My sister is dead in the palace, and what harm could she offer, what possible harm? I will die too! They cannot let me live!"

Tears were running down his cheeks.

"Where will you go?" asked Aurelia Paulina. "Do you have somewhere?"

He shook his head. "No. There's nowhere to go. I have no one anymore. But I can't stay in Londinium. Too many know me here."

She looked at Flavilla, who nodded. "Then I know where you'll go. The Vindex family owes you a debt. You will come with us, to our villa on Oak River, and then I will write to a friend I know, far from Londinium, where you'll be safe."

That was the beginning of almost everything that was to be of importance in my life. All that followed flowed from the events of those few days. I never realized it for many years.

# CHAPTER 2

## Severiana: Invasion

When I think about my life, sometimes I find myself laughing at how little I understood. I didn't know all I believed I did about my family's gift, really, and so I was inventing something for myself. I just knew that my beloved Aunt had shown such power after Carausius's murder, and I saw no reason why I too should not have it, for I was a twin, as she was, and to twins in my family great gifts are given.

I didn't know the limits of that gift.

I was going to learn all about it, though, for what happened when I was twelve years old was momentous. After three years of rule by the usurper Allectus, Constantius invaded in the Spring.

Numerianus, Licinianus, and I had started building dams and channels. At first, they had tried to exclude me, just because I was a girl, and I got angry, and told them I would kick over their constructions if I wasn't allowed in. When I proved my threat by doing it, they rolled their eyes, but let me into the task, having no choice. We had not allowed Cassianus, our eight-year-old cousin, to join, and he had left crying to find his mother Flavilla, saying we were mean, and that she would make us. It seemed unlikely. She was involved with Faustina, Cassianus's sister, who had just been born, and was not feeling well.

So here was what we were doing. Fortunately, our river – the Oak River – Abona Derwentiu as it is called in the British tongue – was very high with the winter run-off, and the small skiffs and boats that the villas along the river used to transport materials and people were moving freely. The water, then, was right up to the highest level on the bank, and we were building into it, digging a pit about six feet from the river, and three channels leading to it. Don't ask me why we were doing this, for there is no good answer. But the logic was that we were building a canal from the Mare Nostrum to the Erythraean Sea, just as the Emperor Trajan had done. Being interested in engineering projects, Numerianus had been reading about this, and Licinianus and I had agreed that this was a good project. We had failed to build a canal across the Corinthian Isthmus – a small bend in the river – so we were happy to find something new, as we reminded ourselves that the Emperor Nero had failed at this project too.

It might sound as if my brothers were mean to me, but really, they were not. We loved one another dearly, even Numerianus, who was a half-brother to me and Licinianus, and a year younger. Of course, there was a special bond between the two of us who were twins, and we all fought on occasion; but we knew that the father of all three of us was Licinius, who was buried with my mother below our temple, and was dear to our family gods. And that was our special thing, and our special bond.

It was a lovely day, and we were happy, digging in the sun. We were all filthy, and mud-covered, and none of us cared, for the channels were moving along, and soon, we hoped, we would be able to open the gates and fill the deep pit. This would be a great satisfaction, we were sure.

We heard the horse's hooves in the distance, but no one was very interested. The estate was large, and many came and went on horseback. Only the speed of the rider was perhaps unusual, and we didn't care about that. We had more important things to do.

"Stop that, Severiana!" Numerianus was shouting at me, claiming I was digging too near the water. "We want to open all three channels at once!" I readied myself to indignantly deny that I was doing anything wrong when I heard my aunt call.

"Children! Come! You must come quickly!"

We looked at one another. Urgent calls were usually a sign that we were about to be scolded, or that the adults had found out something we would rather they had not. But we could not think of anything bad we had done recently, so, reluctantly, we got up and began to walk towards the villa.

As we hove into sight at the top of the bank, I heard the intake of breath as stepmother Aurelia Paulina saw the state we were in. In her shock she forgot the urgency of the moment, and said, "Mater Mea! What were you doing to get so filthy?" She shook her head. "Horaea!" She said, calling the slave whose unfortunate task was to see to us. She was a sweet, middle-aged woman of 40, yet somehow of indeterminate age, in whom kindness ran strong; but we were more than a handful for her. "Clean them up! And do it quickly!"

"What's wrong?" said Numerianus to his mother, and in his surprise, he spoke in the British we children used almost all the time amongst ourselves. His mother did not understand him, for she was a Roman of Rome, and spoke British badly if at all. So he repeated it in Latin. "What's happened?"

Aurelia Paulina was already turning away. "The Caesar Constantius has landed on the coast, and is heading towards Londinium. His army will march right through this area, and Allectus will try to stop him. We have to leave!"

We were still very much children, and knew rather little of the world. And we did not see why someone coming to deal with a murdering usurper should be a problem for us.

We were soon to find out.

+ + +

By the afternoon, we were headed up into the hills, away from our home and away from any road. The herdsmen were driving our cattle, sheep, and horses up into the higher, rougher country, where lay valleys they could hide in. Everything was being moved that could be carried; even the household cats that we could catch were in baskets and the dogs were following on. Everyone was either walking or on horseback. Where we were going, no carriages could travel. Each of the children was held in the saddle before one of the family or a slave. I was in front of my stepmother, for Aunt Flavilla held only her baby, and was only a month or two past childbed.

I remember asking Aurelia Paulina: "Why? Why are we running away? Aren't these men Roman soldiers who are coming?"

"They are," she said. "You are very young, sweetheart, but armies when they come take everything, and we're only ten miles from the Londinium road. They will seize our sheep and cattle and pigs to feed themselves, and steal everything they can. And what they will do to people... especially to girls..."

"Especially to girls?"

She shook her head. "Just know that it's not safe for anyone at the villa, even though we're not on the road. We must run and hide, and hope they don't find us."

She paused. "And we must hope we still have a home to go to when they have passed..."

We pitched camp as the sun was going down, in a little cup of a valley surrounded by tall oaks. The sun slanted through the leaves and turned everything golden. To us children it was beautiful, not frightening at all. Rather it was just a wonderful adventure, and we ran around the fires as the slaves started them from dry bushes and fallen branches. But then we were called harshly to order by our grandmother, Aelia. This shocked us. She was always so kind.

The slaves unloaded the pack-horses, and then set about making our dinner. There was not a great deal of food offered, for we had no idea how long we would be here, and we had to husband it, but it was sufficient: bread and cheese, and a little salted pork that they cooked over the fires, with watered wine for everyone in the family, and barley-ale for the estate workers. I liked watching the fire making the green wood hiss and then burst, and I was glad to be there.

The sun set, and one of the herdsmen's wives began to sing, quietly, as if she was afraid that she would be heard. "Look!" said someone, and silence came. "Look!" He was pointing to the east. Far away, there was a glow, hardly visible against the darkening sky, yellow and blended red, shining dully against the clouds.

"Fires!" someone said. "It's like the land is burning! They're burning everything!"

"Tomorrow," said Aunt Flavilla to Catigernus, who was also the estate overseer, swaying her baby in her arms. "Light no fires. They'll be too close, and they'll see them."

Constantius's army was in Britannia, and we could see its campfires.

+ + +

We went higher in the hills the next day, and there we stopped, for there was nowhere to retreat to anymore. We had gone as far south as we could; if we went further, we would encounter the road from Anderida, and we had been told a contingent of Constantius's army had already landed there, and was advancing west. We were between the two wings of his attack. All we could do was wait.

We spent three days there, and on the second it began to rain, and turned colder. We had tents, but we were still afraid to light fires, so life began to be miserable. It did not stay that way long. Instead, it became frightening.

As the sun was setting that day, we were sitting huddled together, I against my aunt Flavilla's shoulder, her child on her thigh. Catigernus suddenly sat up, and started gesturing to the men who guarded us, but saying not a word aloud. They were all old soldiers who had served under my father, I knew, and stayed with us because we gave them a good life. They talked to each other with their hands, silently, in the most amazing way; and then they disappeared into the trees and bushes around us, and in the fading light, they were invisible in seconds. I could see from everyone's stillness that there was danger; but I had no idea what it was.

Now I heard horses and voices coming down to us from the heights above the valley, their edges black against the fading light. The sounds were coming closer... and then from the darkness came the shapes of six mounted men, soldiers all, as I could see from the last of the light shining on their helmets and mail.

They came forward, and everything in their approach said confidence. They were not afraid of us. Indeed, they rode towards us as a hungry man would ride towards a feast. They reined in, smiling, even laughing, some of them, looking about them. No one in the camp spoke, and I had the strangest thought: since they found us anyway, I wish we had built a fire, for I wanted to be warm.

The lead man rode up to where my aunt and stepmother stood, and looked down at them, almost like a father would look at his children.

"So," he said, "what are you doing here, ladies?"

"And who are you?" asked Aurelia Paulina. "What are you doing here? And what business do you have with us?"

"Why, we are of the First Cohort of the Frisii, auxiliaries to the most illustrious Caesar Constantius. And you are?"

"I am Aurelia Paulina of the Vindex family, and these are our slaves and animals. You need to have no more business with us. We wish merely to be safe up here from the armies which are now fighting."

He was laughing at her now. "Well... from *our* point of view, you are just British rebels, and since we are here to deal with the usurper Allectus, I think we'll deal with you first." He grinned, and swung himself off his horse.

He looked around, caught sight of a ewe with its lamb, and smiled. "That will do for dinner." He walked up to Flavilla. "And you will do for dessert." And as he said that, he grasped her hair and twisted her face towards him, and began to kiss her mouth.

That was when I realized that, though she had saved me from the soldier in Londinium, here she was incapable of saving herself. I saw her struggle, and I saw her drawn inexorably into the man's embrace. She could do nothing to stop him. I wanted to cry out to her, to tell her to fight as she had in Londinium, but all I saw was her useless resistance. He was so much stronger than her, and she could not stop him. I saw her try to kick him, and he laughed, pushed her away, and slapped her. And that was when he died.

I never saw who threw the javelin, but I think it was Catigernus, though I don't know why I say that. It was just that he was not a man to tolerate behavior like that to the sister of the man he had followed, and who had freed him; and I once saw him throw three spears into a hand's breadth from forty feet away. The shaft struck the Frisian in the throat, missing Flavilla by inches, and that took great accuracy. Others of Catigernus's men were suddenly at the edges of the bushes, and firing their bows into the group of auxiliaries. Many had been Cataphracti, and the composite bows they used were designed to penetrate mail.

The auxiliaries were falling; but one, though there was an arrow in his shoulder, was riding away. He almost fell, and I saw another arrow take him in his arm, but he kept on. His blood trail showed black in the fading light.

"*Merda!*" said Flavilla. "One got away."

"Yes," said Catigernus. "We'd better move, my ladies, and at once."

"I don't know where to," she said.

"There's nowhere safe, I know… but not to move is our death, and worse for you and the lady Aurelia Paulina. We must live until the battles are over. Then…"

"How did they find us?"

"As your brother used to say, my lady… in war you must expect luck, both good and bad."

She walked up to the man who had kissed her, and kicked him viciously in the face as he lay in the dirt. I heard his nose break. That was my dear gentle laughing Flavilla, my beloved aunt. I think I loved her even more then. No man should treat a woman as he had. She had such laughter in her; but she had the Vindex steel as well.

+ + +

We moved two valleys over, where there was an abandoned round-house. The fire circle inside it was still warm, so the inhabitants had clearly left not too long ago. But the walls of the valley were steep, covered in trees that clung precariously to the slopes, and, except at each end, it would be hard to get to us. In that place we stopped, and hoped we could round up the livestock who had strayed in the morning. Catigernus set guards around the valley, and we waited. We could only hope that Constantius's army would have to move on, and the auxiliaries with them. But even I, a child, was starting to be afraid. What would they do to us? I hoped for comfort from my aunt and stepmother; but instead I heard Aurelia Paulina whisper to Flavilla: "They won't pass us by. We killed five of their men."

Flavilla shook her head.

They found us in the early afternoon of the next day. I couldn't see how many of them there were, for the news was brought by the lookouts and we could not yet see the riders, but I knew by the still looks on the others' faces that there were many… too many for us to fight.

"Can we save the children?"

"We can try," said Catigernus. "And you too, my lady, with the Lady Aurelia Paulina."

"They'll kill everyone left behind!"

He nodded. "They will. That's why we must try to save you two and the children."

"I can't just leave all these people of ours behind!"

"You have to. Look at the children." He pointed at us. "Where will they be without you to look after them? They are all that is left of your brother, my lady."

I saw tears appear in Flavilla's eyes.

"Tell everyone to run," she said. "If we all go in different directions, some of us might escape."

"I agree, my lady. And it's no use trying to fight this many soldiers. Will you let me try and get you and the children and the Lady Aurelia Paulina away?"

She nodded. "I must. It breaks my heart to abandon our own, but we must all try to survive."

It's odd that the thing I most remember about that day was how beautiful the weather was. The cold had gone, and the sun was out; the valley was so green with trees and grass, and the steep hillsides with their rocky gullies threw shadows that gave an edge of enticing mysteriousness to the place. In the valley grew what they call Dog's Mercury, with their tiny flowers, and white-flowered ramsons. In the shaded areas there were white and yellow wood anemones and wood sorrel. With grass I had made myself a wreath of all of these, a wreath that I thought looked so pretty, and I was happy in a way, yet strangely disturbed. I could not even hear the sound of the approaching troops. But I could, even at that age, understand the grim faces of the adults. What I could not understand was why they seemed so afraid of what the soldiers would do to *me*.

"Come children. Come now!"

It was Catigernus calling, and with him my aunt and stepmother. Each of the adults was holding the hand of one of the children, and we were running. I tripped on my skirt, and fell; and I felt myself scooped up into Catigernus's arms, as we ran on, towards the trees at the end of the valley. Behind me I heard Numerianus crying as one of our men grabbed him and ran with him.

Carried in Catigernus's arms, looking over his shoulder, I saw the soldiers sweep into the valley. Their swords were out, and they were cutting at our people, crying out as if with joy at the delight of slaughter. Why did they want to kill us all for what we had done? Those who had attacked their fellows were few. Those they were killing now had done nothing but witness the fight.

We reached the end of the valley, and started to run uphill towards the trees, where the horses following could not go without danger. The men at the head of the column saw us, and they called out to their companions to pursue us. I could not take my eyes off them, as their galloping horses came closer and closer, and now I could see their faces clearly. I saw the leader raise his sword for the cut that would kill Catigernus.

But now there was another noise, and it seemed as if there were hoof-beats not just behind us but in front of us. I turned awkwardly to look behind me, my eyes passing over the set whiteness of Catigernus's face. And if I had been older, I would have known how hopeless our plight was, for, spilling from the end of the valley towards which we were fleeing, was a dense mass of heavily armed men, men wearing not just the light mail of the auxiliaries, but the heavy armor of the cataphracti.

Catigernus did not stop running towards them, nor did any of us; but I could see in the way we ran that hopelessness went with us. There were imperial soldiers, not just behind us, but in front of us. And then the cataphracti were around us, and I heard them shouting at the Frisian Auxiliaries to stop.

All of us thought we were certainly dead, and worse, for we were surrounded. But then I realized that the cataphracti had passed us and were using their armor and horses to form a barrier between us and the Frisians. They were shouting, but their cries were not for us to be killed, but directed at the Frisians, telling them to stop. One voice in particular was from a young man, his voice like a bull bellowing. "Stop, you bastards! Harm one of these people and I'll have you on a cross before nightfall!"

It seemed we had been saved; but I could not understand why.

I heard Aurelia Paulina's voice, calling loudly to know who they were. One man shouldered himself forward, and his armor and helmet were different, finer. I only knew later that that was how a Roman officer went to battle.

"May I ask who you are, my ladies?"

"I am Aurelia Paulina of the Vindex family, and this is my sister Flavilla, and our people and children."

He smiled. "At last. Do you know how long we have been chasing you?"

"Chasing us? To rob us?"

He laughed loudly. "No. To protect you. I have a personal message from the Emperor Diocletianus, Dominus of the Empire. 'I told your husband I would never forget what I owe him,' he said. I'm sure you know what this refers to, though I do not. Now you must forgive me: I have to deal with this scum, who, it seems, meant to kill you."

17

"They had some cause."

"And I am equally sure that they were the ones who began it by trying to rob you. And worse. I will deal with them as they deserve. They were told to look for you, and guard you, and instead…"

"What is your name?"

"Julianus, my lady, son of the Magister Militum Julius Asclepiodotus, Dux of this wing of the army, by the command of the Caesar Constantius."

He started to ride forward, then paused. "We'll help you try to gather what you can, but I think some of your people are dead, and your stock scattered. I wish I had gotten here sooner. But your villa is safe, and well-guarded by my men. We'll take you back there."

He was wearing a helmet, but a curl of light brown hair had escaped, and fluttered by his left temple. His eyes were grey, there was a small scar above the right one; his nose was a little hooked. But he had a face that seemed to me full of smiles, even as he turned to grim business. That seems silly. Yet that was what I thought.

It took a while for them to gather everyone, and some of the females were weeping with relief or with grief for their dead ones. We had lost stock and slaves, but we were not poor. More could be bought.

They put us on horses, then, and in a long cavalcade, we rode off, heading for our home. I tried to look back, but Flavilla stopped me. "Don't look," she said. But I had, and far behind I thought I saw men kicking at the end of ropes from tree-branches. My eyes flew to hers, and I started to ask. "It's nothing, my sweet soul," she said, "It's nothing."

And that was how I met the man who was to be my first husband.

# CHAPTER 3

## Severiana: Dedication

So... what do you do when a sick grey and white kitten spends the whole day on your shoulder? I know what Licinianus would say: bump it off onto the ground and let it live or die as it chooses. But that was just him trying to be a boy. When no one was paying too much attention, or so he hoped, he was getting a bowl of cream for the little thing, and trying to settle it in a basket on the heated floor with a warm blanket, for it was late winter, and cold outside. And I would leave something of mine on my brother's bed, to let him know that I knew and loved him for what he was doing, without saying anything more.

The kitten's mother was nowhere to be found, and we thought perhaps an owl or wolf had taken her. But at least she was old enough to eat on her own, even if she was not much larger than the size of my hand. And every chance she got, she would purr, climb up my tunic, and settle herself against my neck, as if I were her mother. But I knew that the purring was just her need for my warmth, and all I could do was hope she would recover. I doubted she would survive, but resisted all suggestions that one of the slaves drown her. We all need our chance to live.

So I went to bed that night with the little furry creature on my neck, and fell asleep to the sound of the wind driving the icy rain against the roof and the small glass window in my sleeping cubicle. When I woke, she had moved to my side, and it seemed to me she was better, for she stretched out on her back and put her paws up for me to stroke her stomach. But when I got up, I saw that there was a red patch in my bed, and my heart missed a beat, for I thought it was from the cat, and that she was bleeding. But it was not. It was me, as I saw when I looked down.

It is an odd thing to be expecting something, for I was now thirteen years old, and had been awaiting this for the past year or more. But to have it actually happen... I was afraid. I was suddenly convinced that I was bleeding to death, and I think I screamed, and the slave who slept just outside my room came running in. I pointed at the blood, and she looked horrified at first. Then she started laughing, took me in her arms, and held me. I would never normally allow a slave to do that, but she had been with me since I was very little, and I cried on her shoulder as she comforted me. "You are a woman now," she whispered to me, "Be happy, my dear lady! You are a woman!"

And I knew that in a week we would be going to the temple, I and my brother, to be made known to our household gods, Cicoluis and Litavis. We still call them that, in the Villa on Oak River, for those were their names in Gaul, where our family comes from.

It is never planned. It's always decided by the girl's body, if she is a twin with a brother, and in the Vindex family that happens often, for Litavis's chosen children are always twins. When the girl first shows the blood of her womanhood, it is the sign that she and her brother must go to our temple, and make the sacrifice as soon as she is pure again. As everyone knows, a woman cannot enter a sacred place of the Gods Above during the time when her monthly cycle shows, though it is the best time for her to meet the Gods Below.

I had been waiting for this for years. Yes, I know, that sounds strange, but when you live in a family that has a secret, even if rather an open one, you want to be part of it. So when I became aware of its effects when the Emperor Carausius was murdered, I wanted to become a woman. I saw what it meant, to see such a slender, kind woman as my aunt Flavilla kill a soldier with one blow of her knife, all to save a child. I wanted that kind of power too, and perhaps I would get it when I went to the temple. That, at least, was my hope, and my belief. Licinianus acted as if he were laughing at me, but I know that he found what he had seen in Londinium frightening too. That was why I ran away, and Artorius following me was really all that saved me, I suppose. I could so easily have been taken up as a slave, killed casually… anything, perhaps. And I didn't want to be someone who could be hurt so easily.

Romans don't usually celebrate this time of a girl's life. But my family, though Roman, comes from Celtic stock in Gallia, and girls there and in Britannia too have a ceremony of dedicating their dolls at this time to Argantorota, the Goddess of the Silver Wheel of Life. And our twin family gods are even more special to us, for at this time we ask them to bless us; so this is a great ceremony for the family whose name is Vindex.

But this first menstruation is particularly important. Everyone knows the magical power of a woman at this time. As Plinius Senior has said, if such a woman strips herself naked while she is menstruating, and walks round a field of wheat, all vermin will fall from the ears. And the blood of a woman can guard against any magical spells if placed on the doorpost of a cursed house.

So I had to wait a week; and then, after I had bathed to remove all traces of my body's function, we assembled for the short walk up to the little temple behind our house where stood the images of our household gods.

Every time we go to that temple it is as if we mourn, for beneath its floor lie my mother and father, at the feet of Cicoluis and Litavis. Other Romans call this a sacrilege: bodies should not be buried in a temple, but decently along a roadside. But we are different, our family, for we belong to these gods, and these gods, too, are different.

Whenever I say, "I am an orphan", I feel a wrench, but a wrench that goes both ways. I don't think any child could have people caring after them as well as my stepmother and my aunt did, let alone my dear grandmother. And sometimes I even guiltily wonder: would my real parents have been this good to us?

When I was quite young, I once asked my aunt Flavilla this question, and when she had overcome her surprise, she took me on her lap and told me of my mother, the daughter of the Great Aurelianus, and a woman as kind as any you could find; and my father, her brother, who loved his wife so much that he had no will to live after she died bringing us into the world. "Your name is Severiana, and so you are named after her, for she was called Severina," she said, "and that was so that you would be as loving as she was."

"And my father?" I said.

"He loved you, though he lived only a short two years after you were born. He carried you around in his arms, and his great sadness was that your mother was no longer with him. But you made him happy, for she lived in you."

We stood together in the garden in front of the villa, and then Aunt Flavilla led us away, for she was the only twin in our family still living. So with Licinianus and me close behind, we walked around the villa and made our way to the path leading up the hill to the temple.

A low wall marks the temenos of the temple, and around it are beds which in summer burst with many-colored flowers. Now all but the hardiest had died back, and only the rosemary and box were still green, as they marked the sacred area, ever-living as are the gods.

All of us wore loose clothing, with no knots or bindings; even the straps on our sandals were free, so that nothing could hinder the acts of the gods. A slave held a pitcher of water, drawn from a running stream, not a well, and poured some of the icy water over our hands and feet. My toes were already cold, and now they were icy. But I was too excited to care, for now we could now walk into the temenos, and then to the temple. Over its entrance was its dedication:

## CICOLVI.ET ·LITAVI
## QUI ·IN ·HAC ·TERRA
## CAMULUS ·ET ·MATRONA
## APPELLANTVR [4]

It was a small building, for it was meant only for the family. But the low wall around the ambulatory carried polished pillars of marble holding up the roof that covered it and the square cella inside. It was finely decorated, with the floor of polished limestone, and the roof of red tile, and the walls of the cella were carved in the swirling style of this land, the design picked out brightly with many colors of paint. Nothing had been stinted. We went forward into the cella, which was full of light: there were lamps everywhere, and now we could see the statues of Cicoluis and Litavis.

In some places they make the old gods in the fashion of the Roman: perfect and human. But we had kept the old way, and both of the two statues were human only as a gesture, for the gods have no clear shape. They are what they choose to be, and so Cicoluis was almost like a man, and Litavis almost a woman; but only just.

I had been here many times before, but never had I been so filled with knowledge of the divine as I was now. I felt the shiver in my body grow, and I saw Licinianus's hands shaking. As if by agreement we held each other's hands, and my fingers were trembling. For underneath our feet was the stone that marked the grave of our mother and father.[5]

---

[4] For Cicoluis and Litavis, who in this land are called Camulus and Matrona.

[5] To the spirits of the departed, Galerius Vindex Licinius son of Caelius and the wife of his soul Aureliana Domitia Severina, two of one mind. Tears are of no benefit. [His] mother and sister undertook to make [this monument].

The priest and priestess began the ritual, speaking Gaulish so that I could understand only a little of it, for British was the tongue I had grown up with, and Latin was what we spoke when we were all together at home. Aunt Flavilla knew Gaulish, for she had grown up there; but we, the children, could only understand it when it was like British, which some of it was.

It was not a long ceremony, but all of us were anxious. If a single mistake is made, it must all be begun again. This was the time when we were dedicated to our family gods, and that is not the time for mistakes to happen, for it is a very bad omen.

It was done, and done right; and now the sacrifice. I was shocked when I saw it led in, for it was an ox, and a young one. I suddenly realized how very important this rite was to my family, for an ox is a huge thing to offer. But would it come willingly? If it did not...

It was willing. As the priest cut its throat it made barely a sound, collapsing onto the altar, its blood spilling over it and into the trough that surrounded it. It had been a good sacrifice.

Now we were led forward, Licinianus and I, to stand in front of the altar and the gods. I knew that if I were asked to speak, I would not be able to. I reached out, and held Licinianus's hand again. We were both trembling now. I was first, and the priestess led me to the blood. She dipped both my hands in, just the fingers; and it was warm. I wanted so to recoil, for the warmth seemed to speak of a life gone, fading. But I did not. With a horsehair brush she smeared the blood on my shoulders, left and right, on my heart, on my cheeks, on my forehead, on my belly. It ran down, and for a second my vision was blurred. Then it was Licinianus's turn. We were both so scared, and, without a word, our hands sought each other again.

There was blood on the face of both the priest and priestess, for they too were joined by the sacrifice. And they drank together from the cup, and began chanting, one for me, and one for Licinianus. I heard our names called.

"Severiana!"

It was the priestess's voice. "Litavis gives her gift to you unreservedly! It is yours."

Then it was the priest's voice. "Licinianus! Your father gained Cicoluis's gift for what he was! But you... you must earn it."

He turned to Flavilla. "As long as you keep faith, the two gods will be your protectors. But remember that times of change are coming. And if you abandon them, they must abandon you."

We went back to the villa. And instead of the satisfaction I had expected after this day, all I felt was a confused mind. None of us, I think, slept well that night. There was too much unease at the gods' words, and what they might mean for my brother.

The kitten slept with me again that night. I was grateful for it.

# CHAPTER 4

## Severiana: Loss

I was seventeen. There were so many things that happened that year, good things, and bad things too. It's hard to disentangle them, so far in the past. Julianus, son of the Dux Julius Asklepiodotus, who had commanded the force that saved us those years ago, came to visit us.

There was nothing strange in this. His father had stayed for four years to restore order in Britannia, and he had stayed with him. Then, when his father had grown ill and returned to Rome – he was quite an old man who had even served the Great Aurelianus – Julianus had stayed in his own command. And he came to the villa often, to be welcomed by us all as our savior, and as a very decent young man too.

I loved his grey eyes.

He was only nine or ten years older than us, but he had been a soldier for years now, and he told us stories. I liked most his tales of Rome and what it looked like, and the people there, and what an Emperor's household was like. But he also told us about his campaigning, and the boys especially loved that. He had been there when they pursued the usurper, for he was then with a part of the army that had been separated from the rest by fog during the crossing of the British sea. They caught up with Allectus and his men at Londinium. There was a battle, and after it all the survivors had been beheaded, and their heads thrown into a river. Allectus was hanged the slow way, his body left for the birds without rites, and I was glad for their cruelty to him… I remember that terrible day when he betrayed the laughing Carausius, and I was almost killed. I hated him.

The story had made me shiver, nevertheless, though Julianus was a fine-looking young man, with a voice I loved, and I was at the stage of a girl's life when those are very important things.

My aunt Flavilla's husband Aetius was also there, on leave from his position as Legate of Legion XX *Valeria Victrix*, stationed at Deva, so we had lots of people, and the villa was full… so full, in fact, that we had to eat dinner outside, in the garden, sitting up in chairs.

No one minded, for the weather was delightful, and it was not raining, or even drizzling, as it so often does in Britannia. We sat among the flowers and bushes my grandmother had planted, with acanthus close by, their spikes yet not fully formed. What everyone wanted to do then, as we ate, was to hear the gossip from those who knew things to tell, for news travels slowly when you live in the country.

Everyone knew that trouble was brewing, for the Picts, the Attacotti and the Scotti had been raiding across the Wall.

"We should never have let Valentia go," said Aetius. He was looking older now than when I last saw him, though he was only in his middle forties then, I think. His hair was rapidly turning grey. "It just provides a good base for the tribes to attack us from."

"I'm told it's a miserable, cold place, sir," said Julianus respectfully.

"It is. But if we want to stop these raids on the north, we're going to have to retake it. The base on the west end of the Wall can't stop people coming around by boat: it's too short a distance. Just wait for a dark night or a mist, and it's an easy crossing. And the Scotti are flooding across into Caledonia from Hibernia, and driving tribes down south against us. They raid all the west coast of Britannia, they even raid the coast east of Deva. White shields they call them, for that is what they carry."

"So you think there'll be a campaign soon?"

"I do. Either this year or the year after. We'll have to do something. The raiding is just causing too much trouble."

Aunt Flavilla was eating nuts, for it was the end of the meal, and the sun was very low. No one ever knew how she stayed thin, for she ate lavishly, a word she loved. I had often seen envious looks from Aurelia Paulina, who struggled with food's subtle temptations, and worked hard not to get fat. "All I know, Aetius," Flavilla said, "is that I hardly see you anymore. Deva is a long way away!"

"You could come to live with me..."

"You know I can't leave this place to itself! It was my father's and my brother's! I must safeguard it for Licinius's children!"

"Aurelia Paulina is not only a good manager, she is also Licinius's widow. And she loves the children. She could do the job without you."

She looked at him with the long-suffering look of a mother about to address a very young child, and I giggled.

He leaned back in his chair. "Well, you may not have to come to Deva."

Her eyes opened wide. "What? Have they taken the legion from you?"

He nodded solemnly. "In a manner of speaking."

"Tell me, you teaser!"

"You know that Diocletianus has broken up Britannia into four provinces?"

"Of course. Everyone knows that. Aurelia Paulina gets all that kind of news from her agents."

"Exactly. But do you know who the new Praeses of Britannia Maxima Caesariensis is going to be... with its capital at Londinium?"

Her frown grew. "Are you going to be on his staff? That would be wonderful!" Then, as she saw his sly grin, she jumped up and threw her arms around him. "Oh, you horrible man! It's you! You're going to be Praeses! You knew this yesterday, and you didn't tell me! Oh, I could hit you. Except I want to kiss you. So I think instead..." And she took his face in her hands and pressed her forehead against his. "We can live together for the first time in years!" And she lifted her skirt and danced a little. And everyone laughed, for that was our aunt Flavilla. She was a middle-aged woman then, but who would have known it?

"Well, I'll have to be in Londinium a lot, but we can go back and forth. It's not a long journey. I suppose I'll be the first governor to live here too!"

"No, you won't," said Flavilla. "This used to be a Governor's villa, a long time ago."

"It was?" said Aetius, surprised.

"Yes," she said, matter-of-factly. "Pertinax's, before his troops rebelled and drove him out, sacking the villa behind him. Escaped by the skin of his teeth, I believe. They really hated him. Ran in his loincloth to escape, the workers say, which a woman running after him snatched off trying to get at him. Arrived at the highway stark naked."

"Is that true?" he asked cautiously. She was renowned for her wicked sense of humor.

She nodded, inclining her head to the side. "Absolutely."

His eyes widened. "Thank you for that encouraging story," said Aetius. "So, am I to see this as an omen? Will I too one day be chased naked from this villa by enraged soldiers? I thought all I'd have to do was deal with insane Christians."

"We can but hope," she said, her eyes crinkling. And everyone started laughing as they rose to applaud Aetius's new appointment with a cup of wine and water.

A man was running down the hill to us. At first, I didn't notice him, but then I heard his voice yelling, and Catigernus got up and shielded his eyes. The man came closer, and he was shouting. "Saxons!"

We were suddenly all alert. We were starting to have more and more trouble with those pirates, though the Saxon Shore forts and their fleets worked well. I was glad we were inland. But every so often a ship would slip through, and loot a villa or a village.

Catigernus and Aetius were talking to the man. They turned. "A ship sneaked up the estuary at last night and landed near Durobrivae," said Aetius. "They tried to enter the town, but the guards caught them. They're still in the area. Look that way."

Durobrivae was no more than 15 or 16 miles away, so the danger was all too near. And I could see that a thin plume of smoke was rising to the northeast from a beacon.

"Half an ala of cavalry is after them. But messengers have been sent to warn all the villas around, and we should be careful."

Aetius turned to Catigernus. "This is your job, old friend."

"Thank you, sir." Catigernus had been my father's slave, until he was freed for bravery, I'd been told. "I'll get the men out on watch." He stood up and began shouting orders.

"I wish Carausius were still here!" said Aetius. "We never had so much trouble with the Saxons when he was in charge!"

"Careful, my love," said Flavilla, laying a finger on his lips. "That's treason you know."

"Well, I can't help it. Rome doesn't care much about Britannia anymore!"

I stood up from the table, and my aunt came over to me. "I don't think we need to worry. They're a long way away."

I was a little offended. I wasn't worried at all. This was exciting, unlike the time when Constantius invaded, for I felt safe with my uncle the Legate, and Catigernus and his group of old soldiers. But then I looked over to my grandmother Aelia, and saw that she was leaning forward holding her chest. I rushed over to her. "My soul, how are you?"

She put her arms around me. "Oh, you sweet girl. How you remind me of your father now! It's like someone put him and your grandfather together and made you both from them!" She kissed my hair. "I am just a little tired, and sometimes I miss my husband so much…"

"I wish I'd known Grandfather…"

"Yes. My beloved Caelestius. I too wish you had met him. He was such a nice man! I think I'll be with him again soon…"

"Oh no! I want you here. Who else will tell me the names of flowers? Who will we read romances with?"

I was trying to make her laugh. But I was afraid.

She laughed. "Your aunt loves them too. And I hear she's just received a whole parcel of new ones." She leaned back, touching my shoulder. "Don't worry… I'll be fine."

I heard a commotion, and saw that Julianus and the house slaves were looking towards the south. There was smoke rising there too, but this was not a beacon. This was much bigger than that.

"That's near Iatubriga!" said Flavilla.

That was the villa and hamlet about five or six miles to the south of us near the headwaters of the Abona Daruentiu: the name meant Hill of the Ford in British, because it was near a place where the Daruenta was easy to cross. We had bought it and its lands when the whole family there died of the bleeding sickness, and now used it mainly as a base for shepherds and the slaves who farmed the lands around. But my breath caught, for I had always loved going there, ruined as now it was. It must once have been the most beautiful place, for it was much larger than our villa. We had once talked about making it our home; but we could not leave the temple of our gods, still less the graves of my father and mother.

"Well, it makes sense," said Aetius. "If you go from Durobrivae and keep to the lowlands, that's where you'll end up."

"They must have stolen horses to have gotten here so quickly," said Julianus.

"Yes." He shook his head. "Well, the buildings were in bad shape. But we'll lose animals, and our people!"

"How many Saxons, do you think?"

Aetius lifted his hands helplessly. "I don't know. I've never been stationed on the Saxon Shore. But from what I've heard, anywhere from twenty to sixty men on a ship."

He turned to a slave. "Get Catigernus back."

The big Briton appeared in ten minutes. I suddenly noticed that his red hair was also greying. All the people I loved were getting old.

"Do we dare do anything?" Aetius asked.

Catigernus looked up at the sky, as he so often did when he was thinking.

"Well," he said at last, "we have twenty-two old soldiers, and at least thirty slaves who can look after themselves. We could leave half of those behind, and take a look. Most of the Saxon ships tend to be small. Let's hope this one was too."

"Hope!" snorted Aetius. "I hate going into an area I haven't had scouted!"

"I think we'll be fine, sir. Iatubriga is so close. And if they come in this direction, we'll see them. In any case… they must be hot to get back to the sea. They surely know the cavalry is on them, and being crucified is to no man's taste."

Aetius grasped his shoulder. "You should have been a soldier, Catigernus."

Catigernus smiled. "I more or less was, sir, for years, and with a very good one."

"Yes. I too was there." Aetius looked down. "And I do so miss Licinius! Fine. Let's go. Come on, Licinianus! You can start to learn your father's craft!"

I looked at my brother, and saw that his face was pale. He was afraid. I wanted to go to him and comfort him, but I knew he would not want his sister to know. So I looked up, and commented on how pretty the sound of a bird was, as if I were just an oblivious young girl. But I saw Aunt Flavilla's expression. And suddenly she too was commenting on the bird.

These are the things women learn to do, to smooth the rough world around them, and not shame their men.

+ + +

All the men of the family had ridden south to Iatubriga, leaving us guarded by the old soldiers they had left behind. They would arrive there in the dark, but they seemed to think this was a good idea. I was no soldier, to know why this should be so. But I was worried for Licinianus.

I found Aunt Flavilla upstairs, in the room that had once been my grandfather's library. She was surrounded by lamps, reading a book, their light playing on the red-painted walls. At her elbow was a silver cup of watered wine, and beneath her feet, the mosaic of Orpheus playing to the animals my grandfather had commissioned. I thought I would see her with one of the romances we all enjoyed. But instead I saw that she was reading an old scroll of Sappho's poems. I looked over her shoulder, and tried to decipher the difficult Aeolic Greek.

> *Kyprian and Nereids, I beg you*
> *to bring my brother home safely,*
> *and let him accomplish whatever*
> *is in his heart.*
>
> *Let him amend his former errors*
> *and be a joy to his friends but*
> *a terror to enemies- though never*
> *again to us.*

30

*Let him do honor to his sister,*
*and be free of the black torment*
*which in other days of sorrow*
*ravaged his soul.*

"You are afraid for him too, my loved aunt."

"Yes," she said. "I read this poem when your father was lost over his love for your mother, and went to war. I was afraid for him, but it was good... he did well." She shook her head. "But your brother... I fear for him, Severiana. You know the gifts of our family... the gift given to the women who are twins, and the gift given to the men who are their brothers. We don't have the option of refusing it. If we do, we cannot live on. If we are not worthy of it, it destroys our soul in our hopelessness, and our body follows. And I fear that Licinianus..."

"...might not be worthy of it," I whispered.

"Yes."

I started to cry. "I love him."

"We all do. He is the kindest, nicest boy. But that is not the gift boys are given in our family."

Beyond my tears, I heard a voice crying. "Mother! Aviola!"

"What is it?" called my aunt, and began to run into the corridor. At the far end Numerianus was standing, looking distraught. "What is it?"

"Aviola can't breathe, amita![6]"

Flavilla ran to him, and into my grandmother's bedroom. My grandmother was heaving in her bed clutching at her chest, and, even in the low yellow light from the oil lamps, I could see her lips were blue.

Flavilla was at her side, and lifting her up as if to make her breathe by sheer force; and then my grandmother went limp.

"Matercula!" Flavilla was screaming. "Matercula!"

But she was dead.

+ + +

Nothing useful can be said on the death of a beloved family member. There is a sense of unreality in it, a feeling that somehow it will all have been false, and the person will soon be back among you, smiling and telling you not to be silly. It's a horrible thing to admit, but I had forgotten about everything else; about

---

[6] Aunt (Father's sister)

31

Licinianus and my fears for him, for the men who had gone to Iatubriga and were certainly in danger from the Saxons. All I could think of is that I would never see my grandmother's dear face again and her pure enjoyment of the romances we all loved to read together. And her flowers. Oh, how she loved her flowers... Whenever I thought of that, or looked at the garden she had planted I started to cry again. I'm crying as I write this, so many years later.

We all gathered around the bed, slaves and family, and Aunt Flavilla, as her closest relation, kissed her to seal the passing of her spirit, and closed her eyes. Then the lamentations began. I could not stand it, for we must call on the dead by name, and the calls of "Aelia Honestia! Aelia Honestia!" broke my heart. Four of the slaves carried her body out of the house, and laid her on the bare earth, to be washed and anointed with oil, for from the Earth she had come, and to the Earth she was now to return. A coin was placed in her mouth, and then she was brought in to lie in the atrium, her bed a bier, until she was buried. Though it was late, the priest and priestess of Cicoluis and Litavis had been called, for the house and all in it were polluted, and must be cleansed.

I went to bed, and cried as if every fragment of me would leave my body. I did not sleep until the sun was rising, and then not for long, for I heard Licinianus's shouting from below: "Aviola! What has happened? What has happened? Aviola!"

He had come home, and was calling our grandmother by the pet name we had used ever since we could barely speak. I heard Aunt Flavilla's voice, trying to comfort him.

I ran downstairs, and found them in the atrium, all of my family, around the bier. Licinianus and the women were crying openly, but none of the other men, except Catigernus, who had tears in his eyes. But he was a Celt too. Aetius's face was frozen, but he was trying to comfort my aunt.

No one spoke for a while, until at last Catigernus did. "How did she die?"

Aurelia Paulina gathered herself. "We don't know for sure... but we think her heart failed."

I spoke: "She said she wanted to go to be with our grandfather. She said she was unhappy without him!"

Had she said that? I couldn't remember. But that was what I thought I remembered, true or not.

"How are we to bury her," asked Aetius. "The old way, or the new?"

"The old," said Aunt Flavilla. "She wanted her ashes to be beside her husband's."

It was only then that anyone thought to ask what had happened to the men who had ridden south. The truth was that my grandmother's death overshadowed all, and none of ours seemed to have been harmed.

"All went well?" said Aunt Flavilla, who had already half turned away, her voice shaking. "None hurt?"

"They burned a byre, and took some sheep for food," said Catigernus. "Two slaves were killed. But the cavalry caught them, and were already nailing them up when we left."

"Ah," said Flavilla. "Good." She turned away, as if she had hardly heard. "I need to prepare for the funeral."

+ + +

The seven ritual days that followed before my grandmother could be sent to the Shades were torture to us all, and our house seemed somber even though the sun shone brightly outside. But that is the way of it, and no one can move on before those days are done. On the eighth day as the sun set the men of the household, their heads covered, carried her out to the pyre by my grandfather's tomb, followed by the women with their hair loose to the sky. As the sad music played and the hired mourning women screamed, the sacrifice and libations were made. Then Licinianus, the eldest male of her body, set fire to the pyre, being careful not to see the flames take, for otherwise her soul might not leave. On the next day, her ashes and bones would be gathered up, and placed in the tomb next to her long-dead husband, and her name added to its inscription.

The funeral feast was done, of which I ate and drank just enough to honor her; and then we went back to the villa, to sit in a group, knowing her loss was complete. No one was crying anymore. We had cried too much during the week before.

No one wanted to be the first to leave, for it felt as if it would be disrespectful. Then Aunt Flavilla stood up, and said: "I am going to bed. I urge you all to follow me. There's no further good to be had here. We'll meet in the morning again."

That broke the gathering up, and we all went our ways.

I had been sleeping badly this whole week, and this night was no exception. I tossed and turned, and thought of calling a slave to bring me some syrup of poppies. But I always had a headache after I drank that, and I hated the idea of a sleepy slave trying to be solicitous when I was so unhappy. So I got up, drew a cloak around my shoulders, and walked into the garden, along the xystus[7] overlooking the lower garden. There was a shrine to Pan there, and I saw his broad-smiling face as he played his pipes.

The moon was full, and the carefully tended beds and shrubs stood out clearly, though all their color was gone. Suddenly it came upon me that this must be exactly how death would be, and with that thought came the remembrance that this had been my grandmother's pride: the mulberry trees so carefully placed, the marigolds that shone in summer, and the hyacinths between them. Every plant had been chosen by her, every bed carefully planned so that the slaves knew exactly where to plot it, and in what shape each bush should be grown. Who would do that now?

That was when I heard a distant movement to my right, as if leaves were being moved aside, or a branch was scuffing the ground in the distance; but there was no wind; the night was still.

Now, I don't see myself as a brave person, though I've had to be brave so often in my life despite myself. But on that day, with my grandmother's pyre still glowing, I felt as if I cared for nothing, even my survival. And so I walked towards the noise, along the river bank, past the bath, hearing now only the sound of moving water. Then I saw movement ahead of me, and suddenly I was at the edge of a little clearing, in which there were three women and two men. The women were kneeling, and I saw one of the men pass something to them, and then a cup in the light to the moon, and words being murmured. I was by then close enough that I heard the last words so clearly: "This is the blood…" I felt myself recoiling in horror at what they were doing; and in the dark, at first, I could recognize no-one. Then one of the women turned just a little, and moonlight shone full on her face. And I knew who she was: she was one of the slaves who worked in the laundry.

It was so clear that this was a religious rite I was witnessing, but I had never seen anything like it. The kneeling women, the blood… and the prayers were being said with the hands raised as they should be, but the head bent to look down! How could that be for any but the Gods Below?

The women had been raised to their feet, and now all were kissing one another on the cheek, even the men and women! And this was happening on the day of my grandmother's funeral!

---

[7] A long and open portico often lined with trees.

"Stop," I shouted, fury overcoming me. "What are you doing here, making a black ceremony on my grandmother's day!"

The women began to scream, and then all ran, men and women. I made no attempt to catch them, for there were too many. But I knew one of them. She would tell us what evil thing had been going on, or suffer the consequences. If a curse had been leveled at my grandmother, she would pay the price, and tell who else should as well. The whip and hot irons would ensure that.

# CHAPTER 5

## Licinianus: Departures

I heard the commotion in the night, but I pulled the blankets over my head, and somehow managed to go back to sleep. When I woke at dawn, everyone was up, and angry, or distressed, or both... I could hardly tell the difference. They were all in the small dining room, and there was oil, olives, wine, water, and bread for those who wanted them. But no one was eating.

"What is it?" I said as I entered.

"A ceremony!" said Severiana, and her voice was unsteady, she was crying with anger. "At night, looking down, drinking blood as they prayed! On the day of our grandmother's funeral!"

"We can only surmise that it was a ceremony for the Gods of the Underworld... and that could not be good," said Aurelia Paulina.

"I recognized one girl there," said Severiana. "A laundry slave. She's locked in one of the rooms below."

"Are you sure this was a ceremony for the Gods Below?" said Julianus. "It might have been nothing to do with your grandmother."

"Why do it on that night?" said Aunt Flavilla. "And drinking blood? Heads bowed? That's how you talk to the underworld! No, let's find out. If there was a ceremony against my mother, we must act quickly."

"Why would they?" persisted Julianus. "Everyone adored your mother!"

Aunt Flavilla's face was implacable. "We still need to find out!" She turned to the majordomo. "Bring her here."

The girl was so frightened that I felt pity for her. I doubt if she were more than 15, and her frailness made me wonder how she had endured the hard work in the laundry. Aunt Flavilla spoke to her:

"You have one chance. Explain what you and your fellows were doing last night in that grove. Was that a ceremony to the Gods of the Underworld?"

The slave screamed. "No, no! It was nothing like that! I swear, domina, it was nothing like that!"

"Then what was it? Tell me, if you wish to save yourself!"

The slave threw herself down. "Please, Mistress! I can't tell you!"

"Tell me, or take the consequences."

"Please..."

"The whip," said Aurelia Paulina to the majordomo, and even Aunt Flavilla stood, implacable.

"Your last chance now," said Aunt Flavilla.

The slave sobbed, but shook her head.

"Begin," said Aurelia Paulina. And the majordomo raised the whip.

"Wait," said Julianus. "I think I know." He faced the girl squarely. "You are a Christian, aren't you?"

"What?" said Aurelia Paulina. "A Christian? You're saying that's what it was? A Christian ceremony?"

The girl was sobbing helplessly. "Answer, girl!" said Julianus.

Her head was nodding. "Please," she cried. "We were praying for the old lady, that she should be allowed into heaven, despite that she was a pagan! She was so good! And one of us was baptized!"

I had never seen my Aunt Flavilla so angry. "Baptized? What is that? Christians? In this house? Do you know how much we depend on our household gods, and you pray to this... this dead creature, who rejects them?" She slapped the slave girl so hard that she fell sideways onto the floor, screaming and sobbing.

Then Flavilla too was crying, and I could see how bad she felt about her action. She was a kind woman, and this was not the sort of behavior she admired, even with slaves.

"We cannot have Christians in this household," said Aurelia Paulina. "They will destroy our family if we don't protect ourselves from them! And the Emperor Diocletianus has declared it a superstitio![8] All Christians are to be turned over to the authorities in the nearest town."

I heard the slave scream with terror. She knew she was not worth the trouble of trying to persuade. It would be her death sentence.

"We can't do that," said Aetius. "They won't trouble with a slave; they'll just send her to the beasts."

"We can't let those who follow that vile faith stay here!" said Aurelia Paulina, and she was implacable. "Very well. If we can't turn her over, we have no choice. She must be sold away."

"Who will buy her?" said Julianus.

"I don't care. We can't have them here, worshipping the dead. They will drive our gods away and the house will be cursed!"

He shrugged. "I don't care about them. I'll buy her."

---

[8] An irrational religious belief.

"That's foolish. If someone in your position harbors Christians, it could be very bad for you. But that's up to you. Take her for free," said Aurelia Paulina. She turned to the Majordomo. "There must be others. Find them, if they are slaves sell them away. If they are free, send them off our land! Get her out of here! We will not have Christians here!"

I sat down. I could not help feeling pity at the plight of this girl. And I knew my family. They were not cruel, not unmovable. But we were constrained by our two gods. We could not betray them.

A slave entered, and walked towards me. I could see how disturbed he was by the atmosphere in the room, but he had his task. He handed me a sealed letter. "Dominus," he said. "There is a messenger come. His letter has the imperial seal on it."

"What?" I exclaimed. "Imperial seal? Ridiculous!"

"No, Dominus."

A man walked in behind him, one I had never seen before. He was dressed in the traveling clothes of a soldier. I heard my stepmother call out to him: "Milo!" she said.

He nodded to her. Clearly, she knew him; but how I did not know.

He handed the letter to me, and I saw the purple wax.

My hands shook. How could they not, to get a letter such as this? I suddenly thought how like I was to the plight of the slave girl sobbing before us. Just as she was helpless to anything we did, no matter how cruel, so was I helpless before an Emperor. I broke the seal, and read the text. Finally, I spoke:

"The Emperor Diocletian has appointed me a Tribune, to serve at Eburacum, until Caesar Constantius arrives."

How does one explain to others what I felt? All around were clasping me in their arms, kissing me, applauding me; and all I felt was terror. I knew how I had felt when we went south to confront the Saxons: I was afraid. I knew that if we met them, I would shame myself, and my family. And especially my father, who had had no fear in battle, so they said. But that was not me. This was a great opportunity... for someone else.

Only one man was looking at me as if he understood, and that was the newcomer. His mouth had on it a wry smile, and he half shook his head.

Flavilla was hugging me. "This will open great opportunities for you, Licinianus! This is the Emperor rewarding you for the things your father did!"

I felt as if I were in a mist. "But what did he do?" I said.

She looked at me as if she were talking to an idiot. "Hasn't anyone told you yet?" she said harshly. "Your father is the reason Diocletianus is Emperor! He killed Emperor Carinus at the battle of the Margus!"

Aurelia Paulina spoke up, and her voice was both angry and defiant. "Yes. He killed my brother. And then I married him, for my brother was an evil man, and deserved to die. Surely you've been told of this?"

My grandmother used to shake her head at me, commenting that I seemed to walk in a kind of obliviousness to the world, lost in my books. It struck me at that instant how right she had been. I knew the stories of my father's prowess, I knew how much he had been admired in battle, and I knew that he had helped Diocletianus become emperor. I knew, too, that my stepmother Aurelia Paulina was the daughter of the Emperor Carus. Why then had it never occurred to me that she must therefore be the sister of the Emperor Carinus, *damnationis memoriae*,[9] who had been killed when Diocletianus had become emperor? And if she was that, how had she come to marry the man who had helped destroy him?

I turned away to the table, and poured myself some of the wine. I watered it not at all. With my back to them all, I said: "I don't want to be rewarded. Reward Severiana, if any of my father's children! She deserves it."

I heard a gust of breath from behind me, and smelled my sister as she put her arms around me. No one else smelled like her. "You don't want this," she whispered. "This is not the life you want..."

"No," I whispered back. Then we had to stop, for Aunt Flavilla was there by us. "Poor boy," she said, and her voice was again the lovely kind voice I knew so well. "Now I understand what the god meant."

I turned to face her. "I've never wanted to be a soldier. I know all the men of my family have been... but surely not all of us have to do this?"

Now it was her turn to hug me. "You dear, sweet boy...I know. I understand. But you understand too, don't you? To turn down this gift of the senior Augustus? Can you imagine what might happen?"

"It would harm us."

"No, it could destroy us. For your family, you have no choice."

My stepmother's voice broke the tension. "Sit down, Milo, and eat a little. You can bathe later."

He thanked her. "I have some messages for you too, Domina."

"So I would have thought. But sit down."

---

[9] Of accursed memory.

39

I never thought to think how odd it was that the two knew each other. I was too lost in my misery.

I went that night to the temple, and stood for hours above the tomb where my mother and father lay, my arms raised, and begged Cicoluis to speak to me, and help me to know what I should do. But there was only the mocking sound of night birds and owls, and no answer came from the darkness that could help in any way.

+ + +

I left six days later for Eburacum, traveling with a body slave my aunt Flavilla had given me, each of us riding one horse, and leading another. He was older than I, but still in his twenties. I discerned my aunt's hands in this disparity: she thought I was too young, and needed some restraint. Milo went with us, for he too was headed to Londinium, and it is always safer not to travel alone.

At first, almost nothing was said between Milo and me, but then, as the day wore on, he started up a conversation, and I was forced, out of politeness, to respond. I hated him for those words he aimed at me: I felt like I was going to a funeral... my own. I could see nothing before me but failure and shame. And I wanted to be alone with my misery.

Some pleasantries passed between us, and then the focus of the matter: "Your stepmother and I have known each other a long time. She's told me about you."

I felt angry. This was a total stranger to me. What was she doing saying anything to him at all about me?

"The life that you are going to... from what I hear, it's not one that you want or were made for. And there's no way of living that's harder, crueler, or more brutal. You are going to have a very difficult time. I hope you'll pardon me, then, if I say some words to you.

"I met your father once. I poured a cup of wine for him. I was very young, and I never even spoke to him: he had such a reputation that I would never have dared. But I heard him say to a friend who asked him how he had come to be what he was: a man with such extraordinary gifts. He answered: 'It only came to me when I had nothing else to lose, when I knew I was going to die, and didn't care if I did.' That might be useful to you. Remember it, if you wish."

To myself, I thought what a useless thing to tell me.

Months later, I had a very different view of those words.

We left Londinium on the second day, I taking the road north, he the one to the west. I had almost reached Durovigutum before I thought to ask my new slave's name.

I felt ashamed, for I remembered my grandmother's words about how heedless I sometimes was, and knew that was not the way a man should be, oblivious to his servants. His name was Lugobelenos.

# CHAPTER 6

## Severiana: Ceremonies

Is there any way to describe a girl's marriage that a male can truly understand? To a girl, this is fulfilment of a desire that has encompassed her since she was little. And yet... why is it? We don't know the man we marry... we don't understand him. He is a mystery. Yet we go to him, thinking, "This is what I dreamed of."

I was in my way lucky. I knew Julianus. I had known him for years. I saw him as a friend. And I liked his eyes.

They play music, all through the days of marriage. The time of signing the agreement, the time when we retreat to our homes, the time when they bring the bride to the house of the man. And we are carried in to him, and our body is offered to him. And then? We know. But we've only seen it in pictures and statues and animals, for a well-born girl must marry as a virgin.

I was twenty when I took off my lunula[10]. I put it aside to give to my daughter, if I had one, for only an unmarried girl wears one.

The decision was not imposed upon me. Rather, the way it came about made me think of a comment of Grandmother Aelia's: "Some things in life," she said, "are like a rosemary bush. If you water it too much, it dies. If you leave it alone, it grows all by itself. And then, one day, all of a sudden, the scent of those neglected leaves overwhelms you as you pass by."

Julianus had been coming to visit us for so many of the years after he saved our family. When he had first brought us back, he had stayed for some weeks to ensure our safety; and even after he rejoined the army, he had come back periodically. He was the son of Julius Asklepiodotus, who had been Governor of all Britannia, and no man with such powerful connections could have been rejected lightly. In any case, we had no desire to. He was a friendly young man, with a taste for amusing stories, and no arrogance at all that anyone could see. He was good to have around.

I first met him when I was very young, of course, my body with as many

---

[10] A lunula was a pendant in the shape of a crescent moon worn by girls in ancient Rome. It was the equivalent of the boy's bulla. Both were designed to ward off evil.

curves as a well-planed plank, and he treated me as I was, a child. It was he who argued that I, like my brothers, should be taught how to ride a horse. Upper-class girls usually don't, going by coach when they need to travel, for one can only ride astride, which is not modest. Eventually, my stepmother agreed, for, unusually, she had herself been taught, and could hardly object to me learning too. But Aurelia Paulina insisted I should wear a tunic with an extra-long skirt, so as not to expose myself. Licinianus and Numerianus laughed hard at this, for, although they were my age or less, they were trying to be men, and knew that girls were an attraction, even though I'm not sure if they felt any such thing yet. All they knew was that no one, surely, could be drawn to their sister.

So Julianus taught me and my brothers how to ride, and all of us had falls enough to worry our stepmother and the slave women who looked after us. He showed us some of the tricks used by cavalrymen in battle. He even taught us how to shoot a bow, and at a gallop from the saddle too, though none of us could yet bend the compound bow the cataphracti used. But once we were well enough trained, he took us all riding, and even hunting, and we loved it. It was one of our greatest treats, and even when he was gone, we managed to get my stepmother to allow us out on horseback, provided we took one of the old soldiers with us. We lived in a lovely area, with hills and rivers and streams, and it was such fun to trot, or even better, gallop, through our lands.

During all this time, he was kind and generous to us all, but treated us simply as a man who likes to be around happy children. I was hardly a lovely child. My legs seemed to me too gangly all of a sudden, and I hated thinking of how I looked, which seemed to me so unattractive. But then, perhaps a year or two before the time I and Licinianus were dedicated to our family gods, my body began to change in other ways. No longer was I as flat as I had been... I began to show breasts, and my hips seemed to have a mind of their own. And, slowly, I realized Julianus was starting to look at me in a different way.

I didn't like it at all, for when he looked at me, I felt both shy and demure and even a little angry, which is not my nature at all. I didn't like being looked at like that, and I missed the ease we had had. I was resentful of his change. So I started to avoid him, and our pleasant, easy, childhood relationship began to fall apart.

There were perhaps three years when our friendship was quite distant. He still visited us, but I treated him coolly, and when he tried to make a joke and revive our old easiness, I did not respond. I still went riding with my brothers, but not when Julianus was with them. By the end of those years, I was a young woman, no longer the hoyden I had been earlier. I tried to pattern myself on Aunt Flavilla, who I thought was a perfect example of what I wished to be: a happy, laughing woman who loved to joke and play with words, but always someone to be taken seriously, with steel hidden in her, waiting to be bared if needed. But when Julianus was there, I did not act much like her at all. I was, I must admit, more sullen than pleasant.

Aurelia Paulina was not pleased. "You are acting so rudely to an old family friend, Severiana! What is wrong with you?"

I answered defiantly... I can't remember now what it was, and she walked away shaking her head in exasperation, muttering: "Young girls should be hit on the head after they reach their time!"

I started to make an angry comment to the effect that I was sorry someone hadn't done that to her, but managed only a word or two before she turned, completely the Emperor's daughter, aimed her finger at me, and said, "Don't you dare!"

I ran to my cubicle, and cried.

Julianus came to our villa less and less during those years, but never broke his visits off entirely. When he left after my grandmother's death, I found I really missed him, and wished I had been kinder. But it was almost two years before we saw him again, and when he came, he brought letters from Licinianus for us. One was for Aunt Flavilla and one for my stepmother Aurelia Paulina. And one was for me.

My aunt and stepmother read the letters to us at dinner that night. Since we had a guest, we ate more elaborately than normal, and reclined in the triclinium instead of sitting in chairs, as mostly we did of nights. It was a chilly evening, but inside the hypocaust was at full blast, and it was warm and pleasant. We lay down to a gustatio of green and black olives, hard-boiled eggs with garum for dipping, and boned fig peckers rolled in sesame seeds and honey and grilled over charcoal, along with fresh bread. The joke in the household was that if ever we saw slender Aunt Flavilla off her food, we would know she was pregnant.

We all took a cup of wine, watered it to our taste, and settled down to hear the letters. Aunt Flavilla read the Latin. It was as perfect as I would have expected from my scholarly brother:

*Galerius Vindex Licinianus Galeriae Vindici Flavillae Severianae Carianae Aureliae Paulinae plurimam salutem d. Si valetis, bene est. Ego valeo.*

*I have been at Eburacum now for a year and many months, and I have been well-trained to my new task as Tribune to the XX Valeria Victrix. I cannot say that things have been perfect here, for the life of a soldier is no easy one. But I have made friends and I am accustoming myself to what is needed. There are rumors that we are to move north against the Picts and Votadini, who have leagued themselves against us, and raid us incessantly. But of that I have no proof: that may only happen when the Caesar Constantius joins us. You may tell Aetius that he was absolutely right: the food is terrible, but one becomes accustomed even to the porridge and the vinegary wine that they call posca. It is vile, yet strangely thirst-quenching after a hard day. Nor can one love these northern territories: it is far more often cold and miserable, drizzling when it is not raining, and with an edge to the wind that makes me glad of my barbaric breeches. I am reading Plinius the Younger these days, for I find his moderate voice calming. But I am also reading Sappho, for I came across an old scroll that contains works of hers I have never read before. What a divine poet she is. She'll never be lost or forgotten. I wish I were home.*

We sat there silent, as if waiting for someone else to speak. We knew Licinianus well, all of us; and this was not the happy boy we knew.

Aunt Flavilla turned to me. "Severiana, you know your brother best of all. What is going on?"

"He's not happy," I said weakly.

"Life as a soldier is very hard at the start," said Julianus. "I said I wanted to kill myself at first." He smiled as if he were joking.

I had so often avoided saying anything to him, but this time I spoke. "Did you really say that?"

"No," he said. "Not really. But I thought it."

"Do you have your letter, Severiana?" asked Flavilla. "What did he say there?"

I don't usually lie to my family. I love them. But this time I did.

"There was nothing in it," I said. "Just a pressed violet and a little note that he loved me."

I could tell Julianus didn't believe me. He may not have opened the letters, but he had carried them. He knew there was more there. I felt a rush of gratitude that he said nothing, for he so easily could have, and I had been so cold towards him. I knew a wave of remorse that I had treated him like that.

The dinner seemed interminable, and all joy had gone from it. We were worried about my twin, though no one would say a word. When it ended, I went back to my cubicle to read my letter, for I had not even opened it.

I was so unused to getting letters on papyrus that I tore it before I could get it open. But I could still read it, and it made me feel like death. There was none of the usual introduction.

> *Severiana, I cannot do this more. It is destroying me. I see from my fellows only contempt. They tell me about my father, and what a soldier he was; and they compare me to him, and I see the curl of their lip at the coward I am. I have been a failure here. They trained me as a soldier, and the hardship I can stand, but not the reality of a soldier's life. I am worthless as a fighter. I don't have any of the talents needed for it, Severiana! And, though I can barely write this, I am afraid! I was born to read books and be a scholar. Yet I can't escape. Can I tell Diocletianus that I reject his gift, that I would rather be anything else but what he wants me to be? That would shame my family before the Emperor and the world. I've decided that I will take the only choice that will free me. When you hear, please forgive me, my dearest lovely sister, light of my soul.*

I threw the letter down, and began to sob, for I knew exactly what he meant. And I knew I could not stop him.

I heard a tentative knock on the door; it opened a crack, and I saw Julianus's face, glowing yellow in the light of the lamp he held. "Severiana… Are you alright? You were crying…" he said.

I put my face in my hands. "He's going to kill himself."

He came in, though I was an unmarried girl, and sat by me. With such gentleness he took me in his arms, and held me until my sobbing was done.

Then, my head on his shoulder, he stroked my hair and asked: "Can I see the letter?"

I had let it fall to the floor, and he bent and uncrumpled it, to read it.

He was silent so long, I wondered what he was thinking. But his arm held me tight, and I felt safe.

He stood up suddenly, and it was as if he was resolved.

"Your family gods give gifts. They gave them to your father and your aunt. You too are twins, you and Licinianus. There is only one thing to do: to go and sacrifice to them, and hope that they'll help."

"What?" I said. "It's night!"

"What better time, when we fear that the darkness will take your brother's life?"

46

I threw on a cloak, and we left the villa, and walked up the hill to our family temple, the place where my mother and father were buried, and woke the priest in his little hut beside. We had no need of the priestess I thought; this was for Cicoluis alone. But the old man shook his head, and said this must be a prayer from me, and so the priestess of Litavis was needed, and she was woken.

The sacred fire was stirred, and from its ever-living embers the flames broke. And then the call came from the priest to the god, and then from the priestess. She turned to me, and asked: "What is your sacrifice?"

I had brought nothing, and panic struck me. A god demands proof of deep desire, and that is a sacrifice. I had nothing. Then I thought... Yes, I do! And I shouted it aloud. "Yes, I do!"

"Give me your knife!" I said to Julianus. "Give it to me!"

I think at first he believed I intended to kill myself with it, sacrificing myself for my brother. But I shouted: "Give it to me!" And he did.

"Cicolui! Litavi!" I called. "Here is my gift! Save my brother!" And I slashed my arm hard again and again until the blood poured from it, and held the stream over the altar.

"Cicolui! Give him the gift so he can live! I implore you, as your daughter and your wife Litavis's! Nothing else can save him! I promise: he has earned it by suffering, and will earn it through his loyalty!"

The priest turned to the altar, and poured wine on it. And it flared up, in a spire of green and gold and red.

"The god has accepted your sacrifice. The gift will be given if he does one thing to earn it."

It was the best we could do.

I was exhausted as we walked away, down the hill to the villa. Julianus was binding my arm with a piece of his tunic. His eyes were moist, and he was shaking his head. "Your arm," he said. "Your beautiful arm. It will be scarred forever."

I looked up into his face, and said, "It's my signum, my signum of honor. It will be my pride forever."

He looked at me, as if he were seeing a person he had never met before. "You are so beautiful, dear little Severiana, and so brave, and so full of love. Do you know how much I've thought of you, since you became a woman?"

"I think perhaps I do," I said. "Perhaps that was why I withdrew, too..."

"Will you marry me?"

"Yes," I said. "Yes, I will. You, too, have earned it. I will marry you."

# CHAPTER 7

## Licinianus: Valentia

The wind was cold, but not icy. Yet with the mizzle falling around us, and the need to stay absolutely still, I was chilled to the bone as I lay in the autumn-flowering heather. I often felt hot in my mail coat and steel helmet, but not today: the temperature was going down, and it was as if winter was about to overcome us too early. I would have loved to be warm today. Instead, I let my face rest in the purple-covered bushes, and breathed in the woody, mossy, honeysuckle smell of it. It gave me a moment's peace.

We were in the old province of Valentia, north of the Wall, and in the land of the Votadini, who were all around us. But that was not the worst thing. It was not just the Votadini; there were Picts here, and Scotti. All the north was against us, and Rome had withdrawn so many troops from the Wall that all feared it could fall.

We had heard too many reports, reports so dire that in the end the only choice was to send out our own men to see what was being planned. What we had found was frightening. There were groups of armed warriors moving south from every direction, and where previously they would have fought, tribe against tribe, instead now they came together and merged into a river of armed men. We were only twelve strong, if that: one of the men had vanished. We were awaiting our death, a death that would come if we tried to move. All we could do was stay until night, hoping that we could slip away in the dark, and that no one would find us before then.

I dreaded what was to come. I had asked myself a hundred times if I was a coward, and I had no answer. I was not at all afraid of death, so I didn't think I was; but when the time came for me to act, it was as if I was paralyzed, and had no idea what to do. All I seemed to know was how to hold my shield up, and make feeble blows back, trying to avoid being hurt. During training I had been laughed at so many times, and had received smashing blows across my head and shoulders from the centurion in charge. Yes, in theory I was a tribune, and his superior. But that counted for nothing then. "Hit him, you little shit! What are you, an actor playing a girl? Hit him!"

My muscles had strengthened, my arms and shoulders and thighs grown from the brutal work; but so had the contempt from everyone around me. I was worthless as a soldier, and everyone knew it. They called me Diocletianus's bum-boy, and worse things, and not always behind my back. There is nothing a soldier despises more than someone who won't fight.

"This is reconnaissance," said the Primus Pilus, "not a raid. Do what the explorator tells you: he knows the land beyond the wall far better than you ever will." I thought his lip curled. "I don't have to worry about you doing anything foolhardy, do I." He shook his head. "Look, boy. I knew your father. A better soldier there never could be. When he was in battle, and the dream took him, no one could face him. But some are just not born for this life. You are not. Find a way of getting out of this, or you'll die for nothing in some worthless skirmish, killed by a tribesman out for his first blood. You just aren't made for this."

"I can't leave," I said. "The Emperor…"

He shrugged. "Then you're going to have to die. Just try not to take good men with you when you do."

We waited in the dusk, and shivered. As the sun was setting, the explorator crawled over to where I lay, and spoke in British, for he was of the land too.

"As the sun goes down, we should move. We need to move south-west, and the setting sun will make it hard to see anything west from them. Tie your cloak around you so the armor doesn't catch the light. And take your helmet off. Leave it behind. If they catch us, it won't help you, and it's too easy to see. When I say go, we go, right Tribune? And keep low!"

We crawled for what seemed like far too long, and then we got to our feet, and ran southwest, bending so as not to silhouette ourselves against the skyline. We had ten miles to reach Banna on the Wall, and we had to do it all by night, through rough land and streams and heavy growth. There was thick cloud covering the moon, so it would be hard for our pursuers to see us; but this also meant that we had no idea where we were walking, and our legs were cut and bruised from falls and thorns. I fell, and I felt my wrist twist. I could only hope the explorator had enough of a sense of direction to bring us home; I had no idea which way we were running.

I thought, as I picked myself up yet another time, that if I died here that would be a solution. I might be a useless soldier, but to lose my life on such a mission could only redound well to my family. No one would feel that the family's honor had been lost, or the Emperor's gift shamed. And no one would whisper the word suicide, which was the only alternative.

There was a slight red glow on the horizon now, and I knew it was the signal fires of a fort. "Five miles or so away," said the explorator. "When we go down into the valley we won't see it, but we know which way!"

There was a murmur from the men, though not from me... survival would just make my life more miserable. We ran on. We were no more than two miles away from the northern wall of the fort when the moon came out from behind the clouds.

We abandoned all effort at concealment and ran. But we could hear voices shouting behind us. They had seen us. If they had horses, we were dead men.

We could see the signal beacons on the walls clearly now, not flaring, for that would destroy the night-vision of the sentries, but red, dull red, and yellow embers. But the tribesmen now were behind us, nowhere near as exhausted as we were, and suddenly an arrow flicked by, falling to the ground before it could touch us. They were almost in range. Then we were in a valley, and briefly hidden from our pursuers. I heard a voice, and the words as clear as if someone stood at my elbow: "You are braver than this," it said. "Show me how that is true."

And I suddenly felt joy, for suddenly I knew how I would die.

"Go east, along the wall," I shouted. "Lie down in the gorse until they're past. Then double back! I'll go ahead so they'll see me! They'll follow me, and you'll be able to get to the gate!"

They hesitated, and I shouted, "Go! Go!"

And they went. And I felt such joy. I was going to be free, and my family would not be shamed. I stood up and began to run.

The arrow hit me when I was no more than a hundred yards from the northern gate. It felt as if I had been slapped on my shoulder by a sharp piece of ice, not hard; I didn't even know what it was, and I ran on. But when the spear struck, I was thrown forward, and fell. I tried to get up, but there was no strength in me suddenly, and I failed. I waited for death, hearing the howls behind me.

I felt the world recede; all pain and suffering had left me. My shins no longer throbbed where I had fallen, the wrist that I had sprained was quiet, and for the first time in six months, I no longer hated myself. I was at peace.

I knew I was dying.

There was no voice that I could hear, but it was as if I someone were whispering in my ear. "You have earned it."

I heard the voice receding, as the silent speaker went away.

I heard other voices, but they didn't seem to matter.

"Shit, spear right through his back, right through his lung I'd guess. He won't last."

"Didn't think this little *cinaedus* had it in him."

"Well, seems he did, didn't he. You two. Pick him up. Leave the spear in him. You, standing there gawping: hold the spear so it doesn't rip him apart as you carry him. Don't pull it out: it's all that's stopping him bleeding out. Come on. He can die in the fort. He's earned it."

# CHAPTER 8
## Severiana: To Eburacum

The letter that destroyed my life came the day after I married Julianus. It was a simple thing, a wax tablet held together by string and an army seal. It had not even come from the prefect of my brother's legion. The hand was crude, as if he hardly ever wrote, and the message was blunt.

*Fulgentius Acer Caluentius, Primus Pilus Leg II AVG Dominae Galeriae Vindici Flavillae Dominaeque Severianae Carianae Aureliae Paulinae salutem plurimam d.*

*Trib Ang Galerius Vindex Licinianus while scouting with exploratores in Valentia was discovered by the tribesmen as they fled south to the Aelian Wall. Bravely, he sacrificed himself for the well-being of his comrades as they tried to escape. He is to be commended by the general with the Civic Crown. The Divine Diocletian has been notified of his loss and his award.*

*Hail and farewell.*

I began to scream, smashing my hands down on the table in front of me: "Useless, useless, useless!"

I should have dissolved in tears. The tears would come, but now I felt betrayed. Now I felt fury. I felt angry at our Twin Gods, and that sent fear through me as well.

I found myself shouting, "You promised me! I gave my blood, and you promised me! It can't be! I would have felt it!"

Then I began to cry and scream. Julianus heard me, and came running to calm me; but that was impossible, and I saw the blood drain from his face as he finally read the letter. The tablet had broken as it fell to the mosaic floor, and I saw him holding the pieces together to make them legible.

I sobbed into his shoulder. "I would have felt it! Why did I not feel it?"

+ + +

Two days later Julianus told us he had been ordered north to Eburacum.

I mourned my brother. Or rather I *tried* to mourn my dead brother. But to be in the Villa at Oak River was a torment. Everything reminded me of him. There was not a place untouched by memory. Even the pit we had made in the riverbank as children was still there, though so eroded by years of flooding that only its shadow remained. But that was in so many ways fitting, for my brother too was now a shade, an eroded ghost from the past, just like that pit.

Julianus told us about his assignment as we sat at dinner in the winter triclinium one chilly night. There was no one but the four of us; my aunt Flavilla, as was often the case, was in Londinium with her husband. We did not recline: the custom of using couches was in any case starting to be more and more old-fashioned these days, reserved for special occasions.

"I've been called north," he said. "The army is going to move on Caledonia in the Spring, and I am to take over as second in command of a legion."

The comment came out of the blue, none of us expecting what he said. I, lost in my depression, at first hardly heard him: that was how far I was from the world I lived in. So it was Numerianus who responded first.

"Going north?" he said excitedly. "I wish I'd joined the army! I'd love to fight!"

His mother snorted. "Unless you intended to revolt against your emperor, and win, you're better where you are now, as a notary. That's where the safe path to success lies."

He shrugged, and took a pull at his wine. "I know. And I do like my work. I like figures." He grinned. "I suppose I inherit that from you. But sometimes I think of just a *little* bit of glory."

"My father and my brothers tried for glory," she said. "All are now dead."

She turned to me. "How do you feel about this, Severiana?"

I was so lost in myself that I had barely heard what was said. But then a deep sense of determination struck me.

"I'll go with Julianus."

I could see how surprised everyone was. Wives only go with their husbands on military assignments when they are stationed somewhere for a long time. This was just a campaign.

Julianus leaned across to me and touched my arm. "Wouldn't you be better staying here, my love," he said so kindly, "at your childhood home?"

Anger rose in me, furious anger, overwhelming and sudden. "Stay here? In the home I and Licinianus grew up in? Do you think I want to? Do you really think I want to stay in this place without my brother, where everything reminds me of him?"

I controlled myself, though I hardly knew how. "I need to go north. I need to get away from here!"

+ + +

I'd seen snow before, but never snow like this. I had heard that the north was a bitter place in winter, but it was still Britannia, and surely, I thought, it could not be that much different from our villa amongst the Cantii in the south.

I was wrong.

I had wanted to ride there, as the men did, but Julianus had convinced me that for a woman of my class to ride on her estate was one thing; the roads were another matter. And I will admit, that on this journey I did not envy the men, for they rode out in the rain and sleet and snow and even hail – we had all four on the way up – while I journeyed in a closed carriage with the two female slaves my stepmother had given me on my marriage, with braziers and furs to keep us warm.

I knew a mixture of emotions. One part of me was bereft to leave the Villa behind, and still more bereft at the people whom I would not see for many months, if not more; and another part of me so grateful at the thought that I was away from everything that could remind me of Licinianus.

Twins are special, especially twins like us, who are the same in every way. We have a bond with one another that others can never understand. I still felt tied to him, and I could hardly believe that he was dead. Each night I woke up from First Sleep, and felt a sense of relief as my mind told me I had just been dreaming of my brother's death. But then reality overcame me, and I realized he was indeed gone. It was as if I had lost the love of my life.

That sounds strange for a married woman to say; we are supposed to know strong emotion only for our husband. But I had married Julianus, not for love, but because of that very special night. I felt, deep in myself, that he had tried to save my brother by urging that offering on me, and thus to save me. No one, I thought, could have done more for me. But now? Now I looked back and saw that it had all been for nothing. And, even though this was not Julianus's fault, I could not restrain my anger at him, as if he had cheated me into marriage.

Yet, I had great affection for Julianus, and the more I knew him, the better I liked him. I liked him to hold me, and kiss me, and I liked to sleep by him. I even liked it when he took me. It was comforting and pleasurable and fulfilling in a way I had not before experienced. I thought I was coming to love him. But he was still not my brother, to whom my soul was bonded as steel is bonded to steel in the making of a sword. And – though how could I ever be sure? – I looked at my scarred arm and knew pride. Licinianus and I were bound even in our bodies, in the useless sacrifice I had made for him, even if he was now gone.

So, in the next few months, I learned to be a wife.

Julianus was a high-ranking officer, and so we had a house all to ourselves in the city near the Basilica, with everything that provides the comforts of life: slaves, hypocaust, even a private bath. He was, after all, his father's only son, and so a rich man. As a wedding gift, Julianus had bought me dozens of the romances the women of my family loved, as well as a complete set of the poems of Sappho we often read, and brought them secretly north with us. He unveiled them in a special room set up as a library, with shelves to hold them, whether scrolls or the new codices. I think there must have been over three hundred of them, many of which I'd never read. He had been sending to all the booksellers in Londinium, and even into Gallia, to ferret out every one he could. The act was so sweet that I cried with mingled affection and sadness when he revealed them to me, his face so proud at how he had managed to find something which really pleased me. I hugged him as hard as I could, and tried to act as if the only sorrow I knew was the thought that my dear grandmother would never be there to read them with me. But really it was the ghost of my brother, which never left me.

So the northern winter passed as well as it possibly could in such circumstances, when a young married girl is far from her family for the first time, aided by the letters I received regularly from my aunt, stepmother and half-brother.

The days were scarcely idyllic, for bitter cold and snow does not make for Arcadia; but at night we always slept together, not separate as some do, and I would lie warm in Julianus's arms as we talked in the dark. Most of the time we would compare stories of the day, and he would try to make me laugh at foolish things that had happened when he had visited the villa, the times we had enjoyed, and the times we were sad. Indeed, I was sad all the time, though I tried to hide it. But on one night he asked me a much deeper question, for he said, "Would you like to have a child?"

I had thought about having children, for how could one marry and not do so? But I was young, and before I left, my stepmother had shown me how I could stave off pregnancy if I wished, and given me enough of the extract of wild carrot to last me for a considerable while. I had been using it, for I thought that I was very young yet, and pregnancy scared me: my mother had died giving birth to me and my twin. I had no idea how to answer, so I said: "Do you want a child from me?"

He pressed his face into my neck, and his voice came muffled to me. "More than I can ever tell you."

I hugged him, and kissed his head, thinking that perhaps I might have a son like my lost Licinianus. "Then I want it too..."

"When the Caesar moves north, I'll go north with him. And..." He hesitated. "War is not a thing to be faced lightly. If I don't come back, I would be so much happier to know that I was leaving something behind that is you and me joined together, for I love you."

There were tears in my eyes. "Then," I said, "Let's see if the gods will give us that gift."

He took me in his arms, and we made love more than once that night. And I did not use the wild carrot then or after that.

# CHAPTER 9

## Severiana: Constantius

In Spring, Constantius arrived in Eburacum, now no longer just a Caesar, but an Augustus. I hardly noticed that his son Constantinus was with him too. That indifference would change, very soon.

I had come to an acceptance of my brother's death, though I doubted the wound would ever fade entirely. But one cannot fight the past, and to reject the future because of it struck me as weak, and beneath me. So I resolved not to let the loss destroy my life.

Since our house was along the road that led to the Principia, I stood with my women on the balcony and watched the procession. Julianus was not with me: he was with the party of officials waiting at the steps in the distance to give welcome and obeisance to the imperial party. I could see quite well, and I have always had sharp eyes: the Emperor had a rather long face and nose, I thought, and no beard, which emphasized his features. But that was not what struck me most, for it seemed to me that the man rode his horse tiredly, and though he was trying to sit upright, I had the impression of an exhausted, sick man. I wondered how he would deal with the campaigning to come. And I wondered if he was ill, and not just tired.

I didn't see him again until the next evening, when Julianus took me to the banquet that was being given to honor the new Augustus in the Praetorium. Eburacum was an important city, and the Basilica had been repainted just in time for Constantius's arrival. I had only seen it before in its previous somewhat disreputable state, but now it glowed in the hundreds of lamps, the walls bright with images of winged Victory, her spear high, banquets being prepared, and gardens from the south with golden fruit hanging from branches. The mosaics were huge, one portraying an underwater landscape, one a pastoral scene, and one a scene showing musicians playing pipes, symbols and drums. All were bound together with the recurrent sign of the crux gammata, to bring luck, peace and prosperity.

Wives were invited, which told everyone that this would be a staid affair. I had learned never to ask what happened during the men-only affairs: these, I had heard, could range from the hilarious to the horrendous as soldiers who spent their lives with violence ever at their elbow got drunk. But today, everything was apparently intended to be, as they say, *familiaris*.

Perhaps it was intended to be so, but when we arrived, the hushed whispers among the women portended scandal. And, indeed, that there was: Constantius had with him, not his wife Theodora, but the woman Helena, who had been his concubine before his marriage, sitting in the chair of honor to his left, next to a man I guessed was her son Constantinus.

I had no idea who she was when I arrived, trying to be more pleased with the lovely gold-figured emerald stola I had found for the night, trying, indeed, to hope that someone would notice it and compliment me on it. But I could not ignore that the sadness in me made feelings like that seem false and illusory, and I felt ashamed at my vain thoughts.

A hissed whisper from Quintina, the wife of a fellow-officer of Julianus's changed that, and I suddenly realized that I was seeing something extraordinary. Theodora was the Augustus Maximinianus's daughter, and to replace her like this was an insult. It was more than that, in fact: it was a political statement that Contantius no longer cared about Maximinianus's approval. And why should he? Maximinianus had stepped down as Augustus, and Galerius had taken his place. And Galerius hated Constantius. And, thus, apparently, his son Constantinus. What was there to lose?

I learned this from a whispering Quintina: "Galerius was so angry that the Emperor Diocletianus wanted to make Constantinus a Caesar that he kept Constantinus at his court! But Constantinus ran away!"

I had to be satisfied with this fragment of gossip, as we moved into the hall. But I wanted to know more. Who would not?

In the old days a *cena* always took place in a triclinium, or at least on couches to which dinner was served. But when so many people attend, that is often not possible, and of course fashion is changing: nowadays many eat seated. But before such a large gathering, slaves circulate among the guests with wines and tastes of various kinds; not quite a *gustatio*, but reminiscent of it.

Julianus had vanished by now, called away by the Legate of his Legion, and I was left alone, if one can be alone amongst more than a hundred guests. And I learned what it was like to be a young, lone woman amongst dozens of military officers.

I am pretty, I know, and I will not deny it. Both my brother and I have fine features, I had been told, and my hair, red-gold from the Celtic side of my family, had been brushed till it shone, and done up in ringlets that fell around my ears and forehead in a way I had enjoyed seeing in my mirror. But now, all of a sudden, there were men around me trying to talk, and it seemed that the stola which showed my married status meant nothing to them, for just talking was clearly not all they wished to do. I was not at all used to flirting, so of enjoyment there was none, in that moment. With my brother's death still fresh, I felt uncomfortable, even angry, at the very idea, and I tried to move away.

Then, all of a sudden, a man pushed forward, and instead of trying to crowd him out, his fellows gave way before him, and he stood before me. He smiled at me, and said to those near him: "You are being impolite. Can't you see this lady does not want to talk to you?"

Before me there was a tall man with a square face, a long nose, full lips, and thick, dark-brown hair. His eyes were too prominent, it seemed to me, and I was not sure I liked his looks at all, for there was an edge of brutality to them. But I was thankful that he had saved me from the other men, and so I smiled at him, and showed my gratitude.

"Thank you," I said. "I'm not used to these big gatherings."

He nodded, and I was, even at that age, not unwary: people do not give way that easily to anyone. "May I know whom I'm talking to?" I said.

"My name's Constantinus…Flavius Valerius Aurelius Constantinus."

My breath caught in my throat. "You are… you're the son of the Augustus."

"Yes. The son of pale Constantius[11] himself."

I was silent for a minute, with no idea what to say. Though this was an epithet given to the Augustus because of his unnaturally white complexion, it seemed almost a mocking comment now about his father, for he used the Latin *pallidus* to describe his father, not the Greek term *Chlorus* that made up his usual nickname. And everyone had heard he was not well. I did not like it. There was a callousness there, despite his smiling face.

"What's your name?" He asked.

Reluctantly, I told him.

"You're from Britannia?"

"Yes. My family has a villa in the south. I'm Julianus Asclepiodotus's wife."

"Ah… Yes… I know the family. It's served the empire well."

Another man walked up, and by the way he clapped Constantinus on the shoulder, he knew him well. "You're talking to this lovely young lady! I had to come over and see who she was."

I can only describe him as elegant, in a way that Constantinus, in his square, heavy-featured way, never could be. He was tall, with a nose that verged on the

---

[11] Constantius Chlorus

aquiline, and his hair and beard were midnight black. He looked, to me, as if he were from the eastern provinces, for where Constantius Chlorus was pale, this man was sallow-skinned.

"Let me introduce you," said Constantinus. "This is my dear friend Valerius Avilius Apollinaris."

I looked up at the tall man. "You are from the east, sir?"

He laughed loudly. "My accent gives me away... Yes, my family comes from Berytus. That is a city on the coast of..."

"Of Syria. Yes, I know."

"My pardon. I am unused to ladies who know much geography."

He was certainly sneering at my sex. Was he sneering at me too? I had the distinct impression that he was, but I ignored it. All I wanted was a way out from a conversation which made me feel so uncomfortable.

"Have you met my mother and father?" asked Constantinus, and his expression was odd, his mouth twisted just a little.

"No," I said, and I could barely breathe.

"Then come and do so."

I was young, but not a fool. Why would such a person take me to meet the Augustus and his beloved concubine? What purpose was to be served in that except to flatter me?

But what could I do? Could I refuse to meet the Augustus? People have died for less. I followed, as Constantinus made his way through the crowd to the uppermost couch.

He bowed before his parents, and I had no idea what to do. In audience, you prostrate yourself before an emperor. But did women do that too, even in a new stola? And should you do it in such a place?

I bowed low. Somehow the idea of casting myself on the floor in front of them didn't seem very appropriate. And I saw something very strange: Helena started laughing, and I knew she understood exactly what I was thinking. I could not help myself. I laughed back. And it had been a long time since I laughed.

Looking back in time I realize how well Helena knew her son. She loved him dearly, and she was the greatest influence in his life; but she had no illusions about him.

She beckoned me forward, and Constantius looked at me with a smile both friendly and weary as Constantinus introduced us. I bent over her hand, and I saw the single emerald ring she wore on her middle finger. So many women festoon their hands with rings, two or three to a finger. There was just one ring on hers.

Constantius looked up, as if he had suddenly recognized my name. "Vindex…" he said. "Is that the family of Galerius Vindex Licinius? Who was at Margus?"

I nodded, afraid, but replying. "Yes, Dominus. He was my father."

He leaned back. "Ah… The Emperor Diocletianus has talked about him more than once. He owes him a great debt." He smiled at his wife. "Do you realize, my dear, that you are looking at the granddaughter of the Great Aurelianus himself, the *Restitutor Orbis*[12]? Her mother was his daughter."

Helena looked at me with sudden interest, but I was afraid. To be the granddaughter of such an emperor might seem like a great thing; but all know the danger of such a relationship, and I found my fists clenching in my stola. I wished so hard that I were elsewhere.

She spoke, and her eyes were narrowed on me. "I've heard of your father too. A very special man, I'm told."

She gathered her robe around her. "You are very pretty! And clearly, you've captivated my son: he introduces very few girls to me. What a pity you're married! You must come visit, and we'll talk! And you can tell me more about your brother too! He did great things at Coria, the reports say!"

It was like the world stood still. Why was she bringing him up? I did not want to talk about my brother to her. What would that serve except to bring forward all the misery I felt about his death.

I stammered. "I have little to say about my brother. He died bravely, and while I feel such grief at his loss, at least that is some compensation."

I backed away, after that murmured reply, and hoped desperately that I could get away from Constantinus to collect my thoughts. But a gesture stopped me.

"What?" she said. "Why do you think he's dead? We just saw him an hour or two ago! He was with the troop that was sent to welcome us! He is a hero!"

This felt like a nightmare to me. The cruelty of this denial almost made me lose my breath. I do not know why she was playing such a vicious trick on me! I struggled to stop myself rounding on her in a fury. Then I thought that perhaps there was a reasonable explanation: perhaps she had mistaken another Licinianus for my brother.

She turned to the guard beside her. "Bring the Tribune Caelius Vindex

---

[12] Restorer of the World.

Licinianus here, at once."

That was the right name. I felt breathless. I could not believe this. Was there any truth in this madness?

Then I heard his voice speaking from behind me. "Domina? You wanted me?"

That is when I felt my legs give out, and I screamed so loudly that everyone turned to look.

My brother caught me as I fell, and I knew it was him just from the feel of his hands. I was sobbing, and trying to turn in his arms to kiss his beloved face.

"I thought you were dead," I said, again and again. "I thought you were dead!"

He hugged me tightly. "I almost was, but I had good doctors! Who told you I had died?"

"A Centurion sent a letter! I think his name was Caluentius!"

He had tears in his eyes too.

"Oh, gods! He is the stupidest officer I know! Trust him to have sent a letter before he knew for sure! I was very sick, very injured, and everyone thought I'd die. But I didn't!"

We hugged each other as if we would die if we did not. I was trembling. "You must come home with me! I need to have you near me, to *talk* to you!"

"I'll have to ask the Dominus Constantius," he said, looking at Constantius and Helena, who were laughing at our emotion. At that point I realized that I was entirely ignoring an Augustus and his concubine. I turned in terror to look at them. But Helena was laughing.

"Of course," said Helena. "You must let him go, my love, this is too great a thing to pass without lots and lots of talk!"

Constantius smiled. "Go. You can come back tomorrow."

As we left, I saw Constantinus looking at me, his lip curled as if in contempt. I shuddered

"I don't know what it is," I whispered to Licinianus. "There is something that I just don't like about him!"

"You're not alone," he said, in as quiet a voice as mine. "I've only been here a day, but I've been hearing stories about him and his friend."

"I don't like him," I said. "And I like that other man even less!"

"Don't say that loudly... Constantinus may be emperor next..."

But such thoughts passed rapidly from my mind, and I clung to him. "Oh Lincinianus..." I said, again and again.

Julianus never returned that night, I was so glad! I wanted my brother to myself. "What happened, my dear brother? Tell me how you came to live!"

And he told me.

# CHAPTER 10
## Licinianus: Coria

"What is this place?"

"Coria. You're in Coria."

My mind was in a fog… But I slowly remembered where I had been. "We were trying to get to Banna."

"Yes. And all of you succeeded."

"I thought I had died."

"You almost did. The orderly at Banna got the spear out, gave you mandrake to slow the bleeding, and packed the wound, but couldn't do more. So they brought you here."

"To die."

"That was what everyone expected."

"So why am I alive?"

The grey-haired man shook his head. "No one knows. You should have died. You had an arrow in your shoulder, and a spear that went through your chest. It missed your lung, but I've never seen a man with a wound to his chest wall like yours who lived. You must have a god looking after you."

I let my head fall back on the hard army pillow, remembering a voice I had heard as I lay in the heather stained with my blood. I said: "You're a cheerful man."

"I'm sorry, tribune. But I've been a military doctor for a long time, and I don't have the graces my civilian colleagues do."

"It's alright. Well, it seems I do live… though the pain in my chest when I breathe almost makes me wish I didn't."

"The spear broke two ribs. They'll take some time to heal."

He handed me a cup. "Here. Opium poppy. It will make you sleep."

I drank it.

"Your name," he said. "Vindex. Does your family have a house not too far from Londinium?"

"Not quite," I said. "Not too far south of Vagniacis. Perhaps 10 miles."

He nodded. "I was there once, then. When Carausius visited. My name is Flavius Poenicus Vegetius."

"You were there? I remember that day very well, though I was very young. And I was in Londinium a few days later when he was murdered. We almost died, too."

He looked at me in a strange way, a calculating way. If I had not been so exhausted, I would have wondered what was going on. "There are still friends of Carausius in Britannia, gone though he is. You have a stepmother, Aurelia Paulina. I know her well."

"What?" I said.

"Go to sleep."

As he left the cubicle, I heard myself ask, as if to the air: "I wonder they bothered."

My eyes were closed, but I heard his reply as the poppy took me.

"Because you're a fucking hero, boy! Didn't you know that?"

+ + +

Recovery took weeks, but I was young. Looking back now from my present age, I wish I had that talent now. Instead, every time I hurt myself, or fall, it stays forever. Nothing did then. And in the end, as Spring started to give signs of its coming, the Doctor said it was time to exercise. I laughed when I heard how he thought I should, for I knew the brutality of the centurions who trained soldiers. "You want me to do arms training? Now?"

"Yes," said Vegetius.

I shook my head. "Do you know about me? Do you know how my fellows saw me, before this?"

"Yes. Everything. But then I heard what you did. You drew the tribesmen away, and you expected to die. Is that the behavior, I asked myself, of a coward... of a *cinaedus?* And I thought: *There's something wrong here. Let's find out what it is."*

"I don't want to stay in the army. I want to leave!"

"Not unless the Emperor lets you go... And the Prefect of this fort is not minded to write that letter to him, just yet."

He cocked an eyebrow at me. "Don't worry. The centurions have been told not to deal with you as harshly as they might. But military training... well, there is no equal to bringing a young man who was wounded back to his proper strength."

I laughed bitterly. I knew how much that promise was worth.

It took me over two months to come back to my full strength, and the strangest thing happened: the centurions were almost gentle at the start, though as days passed their gentleness decreased, until their natural brutality could manifest itself in its full, luxuriant flowering.

I was able to handle it, and consoled myself writing letters to Severiana, though I was not at all sure how they could possibly be delivered, for we were isolated by the war here. I thought of how sometimes she would put flowers on my bed when I was a child, and the warmth of that memory made life somehow more livable.

But there did come a day when everything changed. And it didn't happen peacefully at all. One night, just a few miles northeast of us, the attack finally came: the tribesmen broke through the Wall where it had been weakened, and never repaired, and, surrounding Onnum on all sides, took the fort. They killed everyone and everything in the place, even the dogs and goats. That year was not a good one for Rome, but we had brought it on ourselves by our neglect.

The fort was only five miles away, and we could see the flames as the buildings burned. We hardly needed the exhausted remnants of the Ala I Pannoniorum Sabiniana who rode at a gallop through the southern gate to tell us. It was obvious.

We stood on the wall, and looked to the west, and to the east. We could see sparks of flame in every direction, much smaller ones than at Onnum: these were beacons. The whole Wall was being attacked.

The Prefect sighed. "Well, no surprise. We were expecting it, from what we learned from your little excursion over the Wall." He pointed at me. "We only have 300 active soldiers here. There'll be a lot more than that coming at us. Thank Fortuna that we built a wall around this town, or we'd have to run." He shook his head in anger. "Carausius would never have allowed the Wall to be so weakened!"

He turned to the Chief Centurion. "Tell everyone to get their girlfriends and children and whatever into the walls and bring all the supplies and animals they have. This could last a while. Arm everyone who can fight." And he looked at me. "I believe that includes you. Let's see if the doctor is right."

To look down from the ramparts was as if to see a river flood a meadow filled with leaves, picking them up and carrying them forward, one by one or clumped together. The leaves were men in their many-colored tribal dress; and, unlike Romans, they did not come in anything that could be called a formation. But there were hundreds of them, surpassing many times in number our small garrison. If we met them in battle, they would overwhelm even our veteran Roman troops. There were just too many of them.

+ + +

Being besieged is surely one of the most boring experiences a soldier experiences, and yet also one of the most nerve-wracking. By the nature of things, you can never know when an attack is about to happen, so vigilance is important. But how can you be vigilant when, day after day, nothing happens?

Until one day it does.

They came moving silently in the night. I know why they chose that time: there was no moon, and a wind, gusting back and forth, hid the rustling as they moved through the brush. They reached where it had been cut back around the walls to destroy cover for attackers, and then they crept forward. As we found out later from their dead, they had wrapped their weapons so that no sound of metal on metal would reach the sentries.

They would have made it to the wall with their ladders except for one small thing: one of the cats the fort kept to keep down vermin seemed to know unerringly when the sentries had been given some meat or fish, and he would go up to the ramparts, and entice them to give him some. He was there that night, sitting in one of the crenellations, having been well fed. And suddenly he looked down into the darkness outside the wall, arched his back and hissed and hissed, his eyes blazing. One of the sentries looked down, and could still see nothing; but he knew that cats are supernatural creatures and can see in the dark as we cannot, and he shouted: "There's something outside the wall! Crispus can see it!"

Now, Crispus was the cat's name, used by the soldiers in mockery of a fearsome centurion who had grey hair the exact color of the cat's. But no one took it as anything but the centurion himself who was being referred to, and in panic the guard grabbed their weapons and piled out of the guardhouse in the nearest towers. They started lighting balls of tarred wool, throwing them down into the ditch and out towards the bank beyond. And in their flaring light they could see both were full of men.

Silence was now of no use to the attackers, and with a roar they ran forward with their ladders. All through the town alarms were being blown, and troops were rolling from their beds and arming themselves as fast as they could. I was one of them. I think I felt happy. This was the day I would die, and my family's honor would be safe. I know I was not afraid.

A night attack on a fort is strangely mysterious. Until you get to the walls, all you can hear is the shouting of men, screams of pain, and the indescribable sounds of the torsion artillery firing missiles, the wood creaking and the sinew and hair releasing itself in one sudden thumping surge. You can see little: there are no torches on the walls, for these will outline the defenders, and make them targets. But when you get to the walls, suddenly your eyes are filled with images, for the flaming balls thrown down light the ditch below.

The soldiers were hurling their javelins down into the mass of men as they struggled to get their ladders up against the ramparts. The noise was so great that an ordinary voice could not be heard. There were shouts of men's voices, and screams as a missile struck home in flesh. On both sides of me archers and manuballista[13] men were firing into the attackers, and slingers were sending lead bullets smashing into faces.

There were barrels of javelins and plumbata[14] ready on the rampart, and all on the wall, no matter their rank, took from these and hurled them down. I threw until my arm ached. "Well, at least," I thought, "I can do this."

We were keeping the ladders off the walls, using long forked poles to force them sideways, so that they and the men trying to climb them fell into the ditch, some never to move again.

The noise from the West Wall suddenly rose as trumpets there blasted the call that told us that there had been a breach. One out of every four men turned and ran in that direction, leaving the rest of us to fight off the attackers.

It seemed we were succeeding, and then they managed to get two ladders up, and a huge fair-headed man swinging a sword reached the Ramparts, and a soldier fell back as he tried to stop him, dead from a single blow. He swung himself over and stood there, fending off the legionaries attacking him from both sides, his shield bright blue and yellow swirls, his kilt a mix of the same colors. He was not one of the Scotti: I could understand him, though the dialect was strong and raw and archaic. He was calling his men to come up. And come they did. Quickly they climbed up and gathered behind him in a growing ring, forcing the soldiers back, and I knew that if he were not stopped, the fort would fall. Soon there would be enough of them, and they would attack, and each few yards would mean another ladder, and more of the throng outside would be inside.

I cannot recall when or how I made the decision, but I knew that this was my time to die, and I threw myself forward. In my head was a kind of song, a new one, one I had never known before, and I felt the world recede. I struck,

---

[13] A mounted crossbow.

[14] A short fletched dart with an iron head weighted with lead.

and a man died. I hardly noticed. The sword felt light in my hand, the shield a feather to ward off death with a casual ease that I had never conceived before. I realized how happy I was, and I moved and struck without thought and without fear. I hacked into the circle of men and they fell before me. One tried to attack me, and a single quick movement brushed his sword aside, and my right wrist flicked, and his throat opened into a gouting mouth. My wrist took the sword back in a smooth swing, and a tribesman screamed as his face opened up and his brains spilled grey. And then I was facing the fair-headed man. He towered a full six inches over me, and I am a tall man. We faced one another, pausing just a little, and I said in British, "Now is the time." His eyes opened, for he understood me, and he answered: "Yours or mine, Roman." And he settled back, his shield high, for we knew one of us would not see the next sunset.

A tribesman came at me from my right, and I crouched, and swung without even thinking, and there came the sound of wood hacked that always come when you destroy a man's knee with a sword, more felt than heard. His scream was agonized as he fell back, and the fair-headed man came at me. I took the blow on my shield, and the edge hacked through the metal edge and was fixed a hand's breadth in the leather and wood. I threw my left hand outwards, and the sword was almost wrenched from his hand; but he got it free just in time. And now, if I had cared, I would have seen that he was afraid. But he came at me anyway, for this was no coward.

The fighting was all around us, and we circled one another, just one time; and then he came at me and his shield smashed against mine as he tried to force me back. I let him, I let my sword fall too, and as I did I grasped my pugio, and in one movement, drew it and drove it up under his mail into his stomach. I saw his mouth open in a gasp of agony, and I drove the dagger into his neck to finish the matter. And he fell back, dying.

I heard a roar of triumph from behind me, and the tribesmen were being thrown off the wall, and archers were at the crenellations, shooting down into the ditch. It was a massacre now. We Romans build our ditches so that they are hard to get out of both ways, attacking or retreating. The vallum, in a failed attack, is a killing field, and we killed and killed.

But for me, when it was over, I hardly noticed that. I sat down, suddenly tired and strangely disoriented, as if I had been elsewhere. I looked up to see the Prefect looking down at me.

"So," he said. "The doctor was right. Not a cinaedus at all."

I nodded. "It seems so."

"That was the battle dream, wasn't it? Your father had it too."

I shook my head. "I don't know."

"Hmm. Go and rest. We'll have some more of this before the Empire sweeps them back. And then… we'll have to go north, to teach them to stay where they are."

He turned away, and then stopped, turning. "Your father would be proud of you. I met him at Margus. Be proud too. You saved the town."

I remembered the voice that I had heard north of the wall, and I shivered.

# CHAPTER 11

## Severiana: United Again

And so, after Licinianus had told me, we sat together in my room in Eburacum, talking to one another about what had happened to both of us. We spoke in British, as we always did when alone, and I realized as we spoke that the name of the city we were in, Eburākon, meant "Place of the Yews". It made me think of the name of our villa.

"You heard the god's voice…"

"Yes," he said.

"And everything changed?"

"Not then. Not until I fought. Then suddenly I was not afraid, not clumsy anymore. It was like playing an instrument that I knew very well."

I looked down at my arm, thinking remorsefully that I had not trusted our gods, and should have. He had seen the scars and was shocked, of course. They were healed, but still red and angry, and very visible. I didn't tell him what I had done to cause them. Sacrifices given secretly are better gifts. I lied, and said that it had been an accident in a horse stall. I knew he didn't quite believe me, for the wounds didn't look like accidental tears from nails in wood, but he didn't pursue it, except to ask: "Just tell me it wasn't Julianus, was it?"

"Julianus?" I said, shocked. "Never! He is as kind as any man could be! He would never hurt me!"

He looked at me measuringly, then, reassured, nodded. "If he's good to you, then I'm glad you married him. I've always liked him."

I changed the subject. "What happens now?"

"You mean with the army?" He laughed, curling his lip a little. "Well, after years of neglect, they've finally realized that Britannia will be a wasteland unless something is done. So the Augustus Constantius is here to lead us, along with fresh troops who should have been here all along! We have to respond to the northern tribes. Everything on our side of the frontier has been laid waste, our people driven north as slaves! As any fool could have predicted when they took so many troops away to fight on the Rhine! Only the walled towns held out, and not all of them. To do nothing is to ask for it to happen again. So Diocletianus has finally ordered that the army prepare to march north in Spring or in Summer at the latest."

"Constantius has been so sick…"

"Yes."

"How will he handle the campaign?"

"I just don't know."

I reached out with both my hands and took his forearms in them. I felt, in the back of my mind, a sense of shock at how thick and powerful they were. I could not get my fingers around them, and they were more like wood than flesh. This was not my bookish brother any more.

"Will you be all right?" And I was crying. I couldn't help it.

"This is war, and nothing is certain... but it seems now I have our family's gift, and that will help me live..."

"That wasn't what I meant!" I knew my voice was shrill, but I felt absurdly angry that he had not understood me. "You never wanted to be a soldier! You wanted to be a scholar! Can you be happy doing this?"

He sighed. "We all have to do what fortune calls us to do. And I will serve the family well by this... perhaps better than I could any other way."

"We don't need it! We have lands, wealth, standing... we don't need any of this!"

"I don't have a choice, my sister soul. And in these times, to be a soldier is the path to advancement, and the ability to help those you love. Maybe one day I'll leave and lose myself in my books, as Aviola said grandfather did. He too was a soldier before he left to lead a peaceful life."

"Yes," I said bitterly, "before dying fighting in Londinium!"

As he turned to leave, he suddenly stopped and said, "Severiana, have you ever heard of something called 'the friends of Carausius'?"

"You mean the Emperor Carausius?"

"I believe so."

I shook my head, shrugging. "I don't think so... though it seems a little familiar ... Wait! I heard our stepmother once talking to someone and using those words!"

"Aurelia Paulina? Well, that fits."

"Why do you say that?"

"Because I think she was much more involved with Carausius than we know. We were just children, but now it seems remarkable that an Emperor – even a rebel one – would go out of his way to come to our little villa."

"But who are they?"

"I don't really know. When I was recovering, a doctor treating me seemed to know her and he said there were 'friends of Carausius' still. I have the impression that there are people who don't like what's been happening in Britannia, and remember Carausius with great fondness. Perhaps with enough fondness that they might want to turn time back."

I shivered. "Oh, no! Not another revolt! Things are bad enough with the neglect by the Emperors! Carausius is dead and gone, and it's better to leave things as they are."

"Perhaps. But since then I've been keeping my ear open for comment on these people. I've heard quite a bit. I've even heard talk among the men about his son."

My breath stopped. "And we know who that is," I whispered. The boy who had rescued me so many years ago in Londinium… Artorius.

He looked down at the mosaic floor. It showed two lions tearing at a boar whose tusks were red with their blood.

He gestured at the floor. "Well, those are the times we live in. Fitting, isn't it, this scene?"

He offered to leave, for it was late; and surely I needed to sleep. But I would not let him.

"No. You must stay here tonight. I can't bear to have you go. We'll have breakfast together!"

But a fearsome thing happened next morning. Before we had even broken our fast, the majordomo came and told me that an imperial slave was at the door, bringing with him an invitation from the Lady Helena. I was to come and eat the midday meal with her that very day.

But first I had an urgent task that morning. I needed to sacrifice to our family gods to show my contrition at doubting them.

# CHAPTER 12

## Licinianus: Starlings

There is nothing that easily describes a Roman army on the move. It seems to stretch forever, and the sound of boots and horses is constant and, when you are near, overwhelming. Consider, after all, what twenty thousand men marching in unison sound like, for Romans never just walk. We march. It's more than that, in fact. It's very hard *not* to march at the same pace as one's fellows. It's as if their steps draw you. In any case, anyone who falls out of step will get a blow across the head or shoulders from a centurion's vine-staff.

I was a tribune, so I could ride all the time if I wished. But, after Coria, I was no longer mocked, and I was given my own command. And so, because I did not want to be separate from them, I often marched with them.

It was summer, and summer in the north is not like summer in the south. There is often rain, or at least a drizzle. But not this year. It's hard to imagine a drought in Britannia if you come from the south, but this came as close to it as it could in this cloudy land; and since the army was so large that horsemen had to ride alongside the beaten earth road, not on it, the dust was a thick cloud of peaty particles. I could smell it. I had smelt it in many fires since I came north.

We were now at the Aelian Wall, as we call it after Hadrianus. There was a northern wall, of course, but Romans had not manned it for decades. And I remembered my last time when I had entered the old province of Valentia, and how close I had come to dying there.

We were not the only column entering Valentia. We had left Luguvalium, and were now about to cross at the fort of Uxelodunum under the command of Constantius. The other column, under the command of Constantinus, was to cross at Onnum. Then we would march north, and herd the tribes between us.

The first watchword was given out. It was *Severus*.

I doubt that many of the soldiers knew what that could mean. The Emperor Septimius Severus, one hundred years before, had attempted to conquer Caledonia, and almost succeeded. On his first campaign, despite great losses, he had brought the Caledones and Maeatae to their knees so that they sued for peace. They broke their word, and on his second campaign, he launched a very different kind of war. Every living male the soldiers met, they killed, even the children. His words are famous: "Let no one escape sheer destruction, no one our hands, not even the babe in the womb of the mother, if it be male; let it nevertheless not escape sheer destruction." And for two generations the land was unable to resist us: it was desolate.

Which campaign was that name meant to gesture towards this time? I didn't know. No one knew. It was not even clear to me that we were fighting the same people, for the most northern tribes were now called Picti because of their painted bodies, and there had been very few Scotti back then. Names change in the north, for all of the land beyond the southern wall is in a constant ferment, and peoples come and go like the foam on a wave from the sea, rushing to attack the land, and vanishing as it withdraws to the water.

We were at the fort, and we started to cross.

The forts are intentionally designed not to allow large numbers of people through at once, and the entire wall is protected by a deep ditch on the south, and a second to the north. All crossings, then, are funneled through the bridge across the ditch to the south, then the southern and northern gateways in the fort, and finally the northern bridge across the ditch and glacis that faced the barbarians. It took two days to get the men, horses and supply wagons through, and so we camped within sight of the wall. The next day we would march much faster. In fact, we would move like lightning, for that was the plan.

We had only a few heavy cavalry – Cataphracti – with us, for this land was not inhabited by people who were susceptible to attack that way. It was heavily wooded, except where the natives had cleared fields for their staple, barley, and there were mountains further north. We leveled huts as we found them, feeding our horses on the young crops in the fields, and burning the rest. The aim of this attack was simple: punishment for their attacks south of the Wall. Constantius wanted this land to starve when winter came, for nothing could teach them a better lesson than that. But we held back from the wholesale massacre that Severus had ordered in his second campaign.

We met almost no one as we moved north, but we were not so foolish as to think this was a result of cowardice or reluctance. Our scouts had seen them withdrawing to the north, and we had no doubt that they were massing ahead of us. The reports from Constantinus's column were the same: the tribes were all pursuing the same course. This boded ill, for it told us that our attack had been expected. But then: how could it not be, with an Augustus in Britannia? We would have to take what Fortuna gave us. That they were certainly planning a coordinated response was daunting.

I had very little taste for this kind of warfare. To be honest, I had little taste for any kind. But burning the homes of the few women and children left behind, their men nowhere near to protect them, destroying their hoarded food, killing their animals… you have to be a hard man to do that with either indifference or, even worse, pleasure. Rapes happened often, and the officers did nothing about them, nor did they constrain the men from them. Constantius wanted these people punished, and women are always an easy target, for the act sends their men into a rage at the humiliation. It all served a purpose.

Julianus and I shared a tent, though he was much my superior. But we were relatives, and, as he put it, "It's silly for you to sleep in a tent with 3 other tribunes when I have one big enough for two."

I was grateful. I now had something of a reputation, and my peers were wary of it, and thus wary of me. I did not receive hostility from them, but I did sense a pervasive coldness. They were waiting to see for themselves. Time in their company was not all that pleasant.

We sat in Julianus's tent that first night north of the wall, and he brought up what had happened at Coria. He did it with considerable hesitation, but, still, he did it.

"Do you remember how it came upon you, Licinianus?"

I tried to think back. But really, I hardly needed to. I had thought of that time more often than I could remember, and had never come to a conclusion. I shook my head. "It was just there… as if I were in a dream, and what was happening wasn't real."

"You felt no fear?"

"No. None at all. And it was as if I knew exactly what to do. But I didn't know how I did it."

"And this was the first time you felt that…"

"Yes."

He poured neat wine into two cups, one for me and one for him. I had learned to drink the vinegary posca the army was issued, and even found it refreshing on a hot day after a hard march. But liking it was another matter. We drank.

He spoke slowly. "I've been thinking a great deal about whether I should tell you something. But now that I've married your sister, and love her so dearly, I can't stand for you *not* to know."

"What?" I said.

He reached up and rubbed his forehead. He was tired, as were we all. Apart from those on guard duty, there were not many awake now.

"I know your sister doesn't want you to know… So you must promise me you won't tell her?"

I felt a sense of foreboding, for I was afraid that I would hear something dreadful about her, and the bond between us is so intense that to hear anything bad would be a pain hardly to be borne.

But I said, "Go on. I won't tell her." Of course, I lied. My sister and I kept nothing from each other.

"Severiana got your letter, and I heard her crying as I passed her room. She believed you were intending to commit suicide."

I took a deep breath. "Yes," I said. "I was. That was why I wrote to her, so she would know."

"We went to the temple of your family gods, to ask for their help for you."

"And they gave it?"

Julianus nodded. "I believe they did. Do you see that terrible scar on Severiana's arm?"

I felt cold inside. "That… that was her offering?"

"It was. She slashed herself again and again until the blood poured from her."

I drank more of my wine, swallowing it with a jerk. "What did the god say?"

"The exact words? I can't remember exactly. But he said that you would gain your family's gift if you earned it."

"When was this?"

"It was the last month of autumn, when the moon was full."

I remember that month, and thought of me and those few men running back towards the Wall with the tribes behind us, and the voice asking me to show my bravery.

"I think – I can't know for sure – but that could have been the night we reached the wall as we ran. The moon was full, when the clouds had parted…"

Julianus nodded. "It could be. Did something happen?"

"Yes. I was called upon to show what I was worth."

He looked up questioningly, but I said no more.

+ + +

From the next day on, the days were hard, everyone moving at a fast pace. Constantius sent light cavalry curving to the northwest, with our few cataphracti following close behind. The aim of these troops was not to do battle, but to get around the tribesmen where they were massing, and stop them from retreating farther to the north, where, beyond the abandoned wall Antoninus

Pius had built, the ground became mountainous and broken. That part of Caledonia had been the cause of many of the difficulties that Septimius Severus had faced in his campaign a century ago: he could never bring the tribesmen to battle when there were so many places for them to hide in, and he was constantly beset with small bands attacking his flanks. This was not a trap Constantius was going to fall into. My command was infantry at that time, so I marched behind with the rest of the army, moving straight north.

In the late afternoon of the second day, I was marching with the senior centurion of my command, and we had become quite friendly. He was curious, I think, about the "Dream" as it was called, though too polite to say so. All of us were eager for the signal to make camp; by the time we did so, it would be dark, at this rate. But it was still hot. I took my helmet off and complained about it. He started laughing, and then straightened his face. "Born in Britannia, I understand, sir?" he said.

"Yes," I said warily, knowing he was laughing at me.

"Well, sir, I grew up far south on the coast of Dalmatia. Now, this is what we'd call a mild summer where I come from."

"Well, we call it a drought!" I said stiffly. I was still unsure of myself then, having been an object of contempt for so long, and was therefore for an instant humorless. But then I grinned too, and we laughed together. Then I heard some of the soldiers calling out and pointing upwards. I looked too, and saw something amazing. In the sky thousands of small birds, tens of thousands, were collecting from all over, wheeling and turning, as if they were all of one mind. It seemed almost as if someone was swirling smoke through the air, except these were living creatures doing it, so many that the red light of the setting sun darkened as they wheeled. It was a dance, a dance of birds, to the music of their calls and the sound of their wings, as swirls of them broke free, and rejoined the others, and it was the most beautiful thing I had ever seen.

And the army stopped. No one gave the order. It was as if we joined the birds, needed to become their audience, to stand and watch in wonder.

"Sturni!" someone called out.

Starlings…

Someone called out in British. "I've seen this before! But it always happens in winter! It shouldn't happen now!"

Those who knew the language started to talk loudly. And then when someone translated this into Latin, and as it spread, the hubbub broke out all across the army.

We all knew then that this meant something, that this was a message from the gods. And we thought about Constantius, now being carried in a litter, as if the winter of his life had come.

+ + +

There was not a soldier in the army who was not afraid that this was a bad omen, not just for Constantius, but for the army. Those who had been in arms for many years were fearful, as much as a soldier can be, for an army which loses heart very easily becomes an army defeated. And defeat by these tribesmen was a destiny that sent chills down a man's spine. They enjoyed torturing their captives to death, or burning them alive as sacrifices to their gods.

On the seventh morning we came out of the uplands, and saw the lower land before us. There we learned from a messenger that the cavalry had been successful in keeping the tribesmen from escaping into the Caledonian highlands, and in the afternoon, we saw the first scouts of the tribes. We stopped beside a river, and built our marching camp, even though it was early. There was no need to hasten now. Was it a good omen that where we were, once Romans had been, but no longer were? There were ruins of a bathhouse inside a turf-walled fort, and only we build things like that. We included the walls into our defenses, though it was only large enough for perhaps 500 of our men. The rest slept outside, behind the outer defenses. We rolled ourselves up in our cloaks and blankets, and many did not sleep well as they thought of what the morning would bring.

By noon the tribesmen were forming up further north, away from the river where the land rose to a low hill. The trumpets called and we rushed to arm ourselves. But no orders were given to leave the marching camp. Constantius clearly wanted to see what he was facing before acting.

They were a long way off, but I have always had very good eyes. I could make out that they were forming up in discrete groups of men, each of which had a difference in shield-colors and decorations. Just as each of our legions and cavalry alae have shields of their own, so it seemed did these tribesmen. And when I counted the number of groups, it was daunting: there were at least 14 of them. Many of the northern tribes had united against us, even some of those in the highlands far away, who must have come south before our cavalry cut them off. By the time evening fell, the lights of their fires made the sky glow.

In the night before a battle it's common for men to exchange letters with their friends for their loved ones, in case they fall the next day. I didn't write one, for there was no need. All my family knew my great love for them, and especially my twin. If I died, she would know without being told: we were one being. Instead, I closed my eyes and thought of all those at the Villa on the Oak River: staunch Catigernus, my sweet aunt Flavilla, my stern but loving stepmother Aurelia Paulina, my grandmother... and at the thought of her, my eyes filled with tears. How I wished she were still at the Villa, waiting for me to return.

But Julianus did bring a letter, written on expensive papyrus, so I could easily carry it, and his face was filled with emotion as he sat by me.

"You must tell her, if I die, Licinianus, how much I love her. I felt like my life was completed when she agreed to marry me, and it's just grown as we have lived together. I so wanted to make a child with her that would bring together both of us in one creature. But it has been such a short time... Look after her in every way you can, if..."

"There's no need," I whispered, though I don't know why. "I would die to keep her safe."

He nodded and gripped my arm. "I'm sorry. I know."

He lay down. "Let's rest, and sleep if we can."

+ + +

I slept well that night, surprisingly, and was woken at dawn by the sounds of the Diana being played by many trumpets, and the shouted calls by the centurions to get up: "Exvigilate! Exvigilate!"

I rolled from my cloak, and stood up to throw water into my face, trying to wake up as Lugobelenos brought us a morning meal of barley porridge. There was no time for anything else: we were sure we'd fight today. Julianus and I faced one another, saying nothing, as our slaves helped us into our armor. He was wearing one of the new-style helmets, with a steel nosepiece. I still had the old style.

"Don't lose your nose," he said, smiling.

"It's too beautiful for that!" I joked.

He laughed, and came up to me. We embraced, metal ringing against metal. "Are you afraid of the battle, Licianius?" he whispered. "I always am."

"I used to be. But since Coria... no. I won't be allowed to die, until the time comes."

"Are you so sure the gift you were given will stay? You really have faith in your family gods, I see."

"No. I just know that they keep their promises. In any case... what if I died? It would just free me from all this..."

"You don't love war."

I smiled and shook my head. "No. You know what I really wanted."

"They say your father never cared whether he would die in battle either."

"That was perhaps for another reason. He thought he'd lost my mother."

"Ah... One day you must tell me the story. But we have no time today..."

A Roman camp when it prepares for battle looks like utter chaos. But nothing could be further from the truth. Everyone running around has a purpose and a task, and you can see order gradually forming everywhere, until in the end the cohorts are in their places, fully armed and in formation. And we waited for the command. But when it came, it surprised us: "Ad laxare! Ad laxare!"

We were to rest in place?

I turned to the centurion behind me: "Any idea what's going on, Manlius?"

He shook his head. "If I had to guess, either the Augustus is waiting to see if they're stupid enough to attack us in a fortified camp, or there's going to be a parley."

"A parley with these people? Look what happened when Severus tried that!"

We soon found out. I heard my name called: "Tribune Licinianus!"

I stepped out of formation, and went forward to the Senior Tribune, who pointed me to the Legate. Julianus was beside him.

I saluted. "Legate!"

"The Augustus has heard about you, and once saw your father in battle. That impressed him. So you are to go with him. The British have asked to talk terms."

"What?" The exclamation came before I could control it. "Sorry, sir!"

He was almost an old man now, I noticed. I had never been so close to him before. And he laughed. "Yes, I don't believe it either. But we do what we are told."

I took a deep breath. "I understand, sir."

+ + +

The good thing about droughts is that many days are lovely, before they get too hot. The soldiers from other parts of the Empire laugh at us British, of course, for they have a different view of hot weather. But we can all enjoy the mornings, as the sky shows such a deep blue, and birds sing.

We rode out, a group of perhaps 30 men, and the Augustus was amongst us, all of us dressed in the heavy armor of the cataphractus: clearly, I was not alone in my mistrust. The Augustus's presence was a surprise; he had seemed so ill. But he rode his horse determinedly today, and I understood why so many admired Constantius's bravery and determination, for he showed it that day.

No one spoke as we rode, and all we heard was the sound of horses' hooves on the yellowing grass, sometimes a stumble as a hoof met a rock, and slid off, and bird calls. There was a line of trees to the left of us along the river, and a troop of cavalry had already been sent to investigate it, to make sure that no ambush was planned. To the east of the river, most of the land had been cleared to make way for fields, though it looked as if the harvest from these would be very poor this year unless the rains started again. There was no danger there.

A group of horsemen rode over the hill before us, and then we were close enough to see each other. That was the first time I saw Picts.

I'm remembering back so many years, but the impression they made still stands stark in my mind. Not all the men in front of us were Picts of course; some were Votadini, Selgovae, Damnonii, even Epidii, though I didn't know enough then to tell them apart. There may have even been some Scotti, judging by the white shields I saw, despite the enmity the Epidii felt towards them for their invasion of their lands. All of them were painted for war, but what made the Picts stand out was that they were not just painted, but tattooed, with the woad hammered into their skin to make patterns. The patterns were lovely in themselves; but there is something about seeing a man's face covered with whorls and curlicues, beautiful as they may individually be, that makes him frightening. And that was what I felt as I looked at them: an edge of fear. They did not seem to be fully human. And there were more redheads than I had ever seen in the south. Most of the tribesmen lacked armor, and what they wore was largely bronze, of their own making I thought. Some of their helmets were of horn. Some even wore very old Roman armor no longer used by us.

"Picti indeed," someone whispered behind me.

The interpreter rode forward, a broad-shouldered man with the same red hair. Suddenly I noticed that he had the same tattoos as the Picts did, and for some reason that made me uneasy. He looked so like the Picts, even if he did wear a Roman coat of steel mail and a Roman helmet, not just in his hair color but in every way. Suddenly I felt very uneasy, and without realizing it, I was kicking my horse forward until I was right beside Constantius, so I could hear better. He looked at me frowningly, for this was not a polite act.

Our interpreter began to speak. And I realized with a shock that, though his accent was very strange, and gave me considerable difficulty, I could understand him. I was very surprised: his speech was much more archaic than the British I knew, with some words almost beyond recognition; but it was still British. And as he spoke, it became easier and easier to understand him.

"Greetings to you, Vipoigos of the Caledonii, and to you, Canutulachama of the Novantae." He turned to the right: "Greetings to you, Cunedda of the Damnonii." He turned to the left: "Greetings to you, Niniavos, of the Epidii."

I stood as if uncomprehending. But I realized that the four of the most powerful kings of the North were here.

But the reply from Cunedda astonished me.

"So, Cunogobannos? Do these fools really think that we will surrender our land to them?"

The interpreter smiled, and nodded, as if pleased with what he had heard. "They do indeed believe they are here to parley."

And he turned and, in Latin, said: "These are four great kings of the North, and they do not wish war with you. They ask what they can do to make peace."

Constantius replied: "They have attacked our land and if they do not wish war, they must allow garrisons of our soldiers in the north, reparations for our losses, and send us one man in ten as recruits to our armies."

Cunogobannos translated: "Don't laugh, but this is what they want…" and he listed Constantius's demands.

Only Vipoigos smiled, but there was no contempt to accompany it. He was a careful man. "They are mad," he said.

"I agree," said Cunogobannos. "But we are here to turn their foolishness to your advantage."

"They are not happy about this, Augustus," he said in Latin. "But they will consider this, and perhaps there can be a compromise."

"There will be no compromise," said Constantius. "Tell them we will attack if they resist, and destroy them."

"Have you made the plans we discussed?" said Cunogobannos.

"Yes," said Cunedda. "We have no choice. Their cavalry has locked us off from the high lands, where they cannot touch us easily."

"So, you must fight. Good."

He turned to Constantius: "They promise that if you withdraw, they will not attack Britannia again."

Constantius shook his head. "They've heard my terms."

"You are sure that if Constantius is killed, his army will withdraw?" said Cunogabannos.

"They must," said Cunogobannos. "Constantinus, his son, will need to secure his place as the new Augustus. He will go to claim that. He won't stay to fight us. Everything's ready?"

"They're coming now, as you see, in Roman armor, riding as if from the Romans' camp," said Cunedda.

"Kill everyone here," said our interpreter. "Leave none alive."

"Except you?" said Cunedda with contempt.

I turned, and saw a group of what seemed to be Roman cavalry come over the rise, and start to trot towards us, with no haste, with no urgency, as such cavalry would do in such a situation. They even carried a Roman standard.

I knew I had no time left. "Run!" I called. "Augustus! All of you! Turn and run!"

Constantius looked at me as if I was mad. I shouted: "I understand British! They are lying to you! Those are not Romans!" And his mouth set. He understood. "Go, go!" he shouted.

"The men coming up are not Romans!" I shouted, trying to ensure that all knew. "Kill them! Get past them! Don't wait!"

And we turned, and ran. Behind us was a group of thirty British tribesmen breaking into a gallop, and in front of us their allies, every one wearing Roman mail and helmets and carrying Roman cavalry shields.

+ + +

What is one to do when you are outnumbered two to one, and no path to run away? You fight. You fight, and without mercy, for anything else is death.

I was riding the horse I had been given when I left the Villa on Oak River, and it's good horse country down there. The animal was fast, very fast, and powerful to handle a man in the heavy armor of the cataphract. And as I rode, I felt the Dreaming growing in me. I had started with resignation: I had no choice. But as I approached the riders, joy grew in me, and I knew that, though perhaps I had not been born for this, it did not matter, for just as no one is born for the love of a particular woman, when you meet her, she overwhelms you. I started to draw my spatha, my wrist feeling for its hilt, and then it was as if someone was shaking his head, and saying: *"No... the mace..."*

I lifted it from where it hung on my saddle, and now I was a lover racing to an assignation with a gift in his hand.

The first of the masquerading tribesmen came up on me, his teeth bared, and a black beard reaching to his eyes. His sword was pointed straight at me, as if to stab; but I was not fooled, and I leaned sideways and backwards, as it changed direction with lightning speed, and slashed at where my throat had been. My mace smashed at the horse's head, and it went down with not a sound in splinters of bone and blood; my hand lifted and swung again, and I felt the satisfying sound of metal buckling as the man's skull was crushed by the wrecked helmet as the dying horse catapulted him from the saddle. The battle joy overtook me. I was lost in it, now.

Two men were racing at me, one from each side; my knees drove the horse sideways, and it reared as it tried to stay on its hooves. They smashed one of the riders out of his saddle, and I turned and came at the other from his sword-side. The mace smashed the blade aside and crushed his shoulder as he bellowed in agony. There was nothing in me now but the desire to kill and kill; and the enemy column split around me, turning away from me, their faces looking shocked at the ferocity I was showing.

There were men behind me, and these were real Romans, driving their horses into the break I had made, forcing the column apart. But I wanted more, and as they turned, to left and right, as I drove on hard between their paired riders, the mace struck left and right, and men screamed, their arms breaking as their shields yielded, as their helmets collapsed, as their ribs were shattered under mail that could stop a sword, but were helpless to hinder the bone-breaking power of a mace. As men fell, spears stabbed at the faces and necks from the riders who followed me. I roared the barritus, that supernatural sound that grows from a low murmur to a gigantic roar, and the men behind me echoed it, so that it reverberated across the hills. And the tribesmen fled. They fled, and they were not cowards.

I looked for people to kill, and now there were none. I was not quite sane at that instant; but then I heard Julianus's voice calling my name, and the god drained from me, and the mace fell down by my side, held only by its thong. I was exhausted, I realized, and I let my head fall. I heard a voice, the Dalmatian-accented Latin low but clear. "They were not mistaken about you."

I did not look up. I simply said, "Who are they who know me that well?"

"The men who saw you at Coria."

Now I raised my head, thinking to meet the eyes of a centurion or senior Tribune. But instead, I found I was looking at Constantius himself, Augustus of the Empire.

"Dominus," I said, confused now, and made as if to dismount to prostrate myself before him.

He reached out and touched my arm. "No," he said. "Stay there. Let's ride back to the camp together. What warned you?"

"I grew up in Britannia, Dominus. I could understand them."

He nodded. "We have not done well by your homeland. It has been too much neglected. But that ends now." He paused. "You fight like Achilles. Using the mace was brilliant. You trained in the cataphracti?"

"No, sir. It just seemed right."

"Even better then. You saved my life, I think, all our lives, in fact. And all because we had the good luck to bring you with us." He smiled crookedly. "My son will not be pleased."

My eyes widened in shock, and he was suddenly overcome by uncontrollable, coughing laughter at my expression.

"Now," he said, even as he coughed, "Now they will pay."

Cunogobannos was unlucky enough to fall off his horse as the three kings fled, taken by an arrow. Constantius had his wound bound up so that it would not bleed too much, and crucified him in front of the camp.

# CHAPTER 13

## Licinianus: Colanica

I thought that what we had done before was cruel; but what followed the failed betrayal was brutal beyond belief. I couldn't blame Constantius; there should be no mercy for those who break oaths as the northern tribes had done. That is the rule of war and always has been. So now, when we met any of the tribespeople – man, woman or child – if they were young enough, and fit enough they were sent back to the slave-traders who always followed an army. The rest died.

The aim of this was not just vengeance, though there was certainly some of that in this. The intent, rather, was to drive the tribes into a state of anguish in which they would have no choice but to fight us in a desperate struggle to save their people rather than running away. And if they fought us, we would destroy them. Meanwhile, the two horns of the attack, as we call them, closed on them, one led by Constantius, the other by his son Constantinus.

Here was where they made their mistake. They should have attacked us before the horns could come together, and they should have attacked on our flanks. That was their only chance. But they did not. They were very willing to attack us unawares, but they knew that in a pitched battle they were rarely our equals. Even the story of the legendary Ninth Legion was not enough to embolden them. That legion had supposedly marched north beyond the Wall almost 200 years before, and was never seen again. The story, I'm told, is not true; but it hardly matters, for everyone, especially the men of the northern tribes, believes it, and what is believed is true for all purposes.

They finally stood and fought no more than seven or eight miles from the shore of a great inlet of the sea, towards the eastern end of the Wall of Antoninus, near the ruins of a fort. I was told it once had been called Colanica. We called the battle after it.

They had been trying to move north, towards a valley to the northeast beyond the turf wall, through which flows a broad river called the Tavum. From there escape to the highlands would be easy. But to do that they would have to cross the river Bodotria; and the cavalry attacked them constantly, running in to strike with swords and lances and maces and then running away, the cavalry firing their bows at the native army over their shoulders as they fled after each sally. The tribesmen's passage was slowed to a snail's pace; and eventually, they had no choice but to stop and fight, 20 miles or so short of their goal.

We marched out in mid-morning, as the tribesmen assembled before us. They had chosen a rise to stand on, which gave them something of an advantage, and if there were any of us who were not touched by unease at the mass of men that faced us, they did not make their feelings known. I was still with my legion, but I had been put in charge of three cohorts of the XX Valeria Victrix. That in itself said that I was favored by Constantius, but I was not so foolish as to believe that I was supposed to overrule the seasoned centurions who led each of them. I would do what I was told. I was in the first formation, too, formed of new recruits: the seasoned cohorts would form the second, behind us.

We approached in three columns from the south, and Constantinus's army approached with three on the west. The northerners would be attacked from two sides, though there was a ravine in front that we would have to negotiate to reach them.

There were a lot of them. I estimated that their army outnumbered us by almost two to one. But we were Romans, I told myself, and marched on. We formed up, facing them, hearing the trumpet calls to fall in with the old double three-line formation. This surprised us, and my chief centurion commented: "He expects a slog. This is not going to be quick."

We took up our positions, and stood silent. Anyone who spoke or called out received a blow from an optio, or even a centurion: we are silent before battle.

The same was not true of the British tribesmen. They were screaming taunts at us, shaking their weapons. And then three men rode out and laughed at us, and hurled in our direction head after severed head. The heads still had the wolf-skin caps our scouts wore. There was not a sound from our soldiers, but this action was not wise on the tribesmen's part: we had just received notice of what would happen to us if we lost, and that tends to encourage a soldier.

There's a point in a battle formation where you wonder who is going to start it. You'd rather have them attack, for that is safer than you doing it. But you know that you are going to have to obey, whatever the call.

The command came, and everyone's left foot met the ground at once as the advance began. That is always the way. We were marching through grass, but it was so yellowed and crumbling and dry from the drought that it hardly softened our step, and the steady sound of thousands of military boots hitting the ground at once was as loud and regular as a drum beating.

I've been told by some who have faced us that our silence as we advance is frightening. I can't say, but I know that many among us wish we could shout or voice the war cry as our enemies do, for that would comfort us. But we do not.

We were getting close, and now there were missiles starting to fall around us, flung from too far to do damage: the tribesmen are not disciplined enough to wait. We could hear also the strange whistles of sling stones as our slingers began to let fly at the barbarians. I was glad our enemies had no slingers: any old soldier fears those bullets more than an arrow, for they smash what they strike, leaving terrible wounds. We marched on, and the command came: "Heads down, shields up!"

We all bent our heads as if contemplating the ground, and our shields kissed our helmets. Seconds later, the storm of arrows came, skittering off our armor. Those who had obeyed the command too late fell with an arrow in the eye, or earned a scar that would never leave their face. Those who cried out in pain, and lived, received a blow from a centurion's staff, and those who died were stepped over as men filled the gaps in our line. We were now almost at the ravine, just yards from our enemies.

A trumpet blew and men ran out on all sides carrying bundles of brush, rushing frenziedly to throw these into the ravine to give us passage. They wore armor, but had no shields. All these were men who faced capital charges for crimes in the army. If they lived, they would be free to rejoin their comrades. If they did not, they would be better off than facing death by being beaten to death in the fustuarium. Some died under the rain of missiles. Some did not, and ran back, exultant, free of their crime.

We marched on.

"Iacite pilaaaa!"

As one man, the front row leaned back and threw, and the pila flew into the defenders on the hilltop. I saw them falling back as the steel heads smashed through their flesh and into their shields, rendering them useless, for the pilum cannot be withdrawn easily once embedded.

"Charge!"

And we ran, still in line, but now moving as fast as we could, no longer silent, the barritus growing as we ran to get beyond the ditch and establish a front of attack. I heard the soft sound of the second line hurling their pila over our heads, then they charged too, and then the third line. As we approached the enemy line, men began hurling their plumbata, short barbed darts that caused wicked wounds when they found flesh. The air was filled with the distinctive whistling of the slingers whirling their shaped bullets into the tribesmen.

I felt the bundles of brush under my boots, and I felt the dreaming start in me. I had a second to think: *"This is my first real battle..."* and then it overcame me, and I was no longer concerned about anything but the need to fight and kill.

A man with red moustache and beard was stabbing down at me with a boar spear as I climbed the hillside, with nothing but a leather tunic to guard him, and an ancient helmet. At another time I would have thought that this was just a poor man who had been called by his lord to fight. But now it meant nothing. I caught the spear on my shield and stabbed up into his stomach, my sword's point piercing the leather easily. His mouth open in agony, he fell back, and I forced myself up onto the hilltop.

At first I was alone, and then the line reformed around me and we began to move forward. In my strange state I realized instantly that the tribesmen's swords were not designed for stabbing, for their points were, while not blunt, poorly suited for anything but slashing. But slashing they were very good at, and the first blow I received on my shield chopped deep into it. I twisted the shield to loosen the blade and force the man's arm down, and struck into his throat. I heard my voice, as if far away, "Stab them! Keep low and stab them! Kill them!" And with a roar my men surged forward, shouting "Kill them, kill them!" and the line of Celts recoiled at our ferocity.

Battles with such odds are never quick, for unless terror overcomes a large army, it will stay and fight, and only when exhaustion and death have overcome them will they give in. I could see to my left as Constantinus's columns rushed up the hill and smashed into the northerners, that they were now fighting on two fronts of a triangle. And behind, I knew the cavalry would be riding up and loosing arrow after arrow from their bows, bows of such a weight that the arrows could pierce the mail on an enemy's back, if not full armor. But these were brave men, and they would win, or die, and fight they did.

When I look back, I feel an edge of anger, for the leaders of these brave men were fools, who had let their army be trapped in a battle they could not win against Roman soldiers, and in a place that was not to their advantage. Their leaders knew nothing of how to maneuver their forces so that they could win. Their idea of a battle was simple: brute force, until one side won. Why not? They had twice as many men as we had.

Except that does not matter when a general knows his business, and has steady troops. And Constantius did. And these soldiers were some of the best in the Empire.

I was told the battle lasted for over five hours. I can't vouch for that: when the Dream takes me, time has no meaning. In the Roman way, each line of troops fought until exhausted, and then fell back to allow the next line to take their place... then the second line... then the third... and then back to the first. This meant that the tribesmen always faced troops who were fresh and rested, and they died in numbers that were hard to count.

I never fell back, but I take no pride in that. It's the dream that takes me, and it never wishes to stop killing and fighting. So I fought for all that time, and I don't know how many died under my sword, or whose faces were smashed by my shield rim or my shield boss. I had the god in me, and the god needs sacrifices.

Towards late afternoon, I felt the change. I could see it in their faces, a look of hopelessness and of terror. They knew they had lost, and so we pressed harder, killed more, drove forward more. And then they turned, and started to run... at first only a few, then hundreds, then thousands. And we pursued them implacably, no mercy in our hearts, and killed and killed.

When all was over, there were 22,000 Caledonians and more dead on the field. We lost 540.

And as the Dream left me, I fell to my knees onto the ground in an agony of exhaustion more complete than any I had ever known, the setting sun warming my cheeks with a loving, bloody caress. It was over.

# CHAPTER 14

## Licinianus: Desolation

When I could stand, I got up and cleaned my sword on the tunic of a dead tribesman. The place was a charnel house... so many lay dead, bodies as far as the eye could see. We had given up our pursuit not from lack of enemies to kill, but from sheer exhaustion. There is a point when men can go no further. And already the murderous work of the battle's end had begun. Doctors were working through the field, looking for Romans whose wounds were not beyond help. The others got a quick slash across the throat, for it's no use trying to help a man whose guts lie in the earth beside him, or whose lungs are both pierced by a spear, even when he's one of your own.

The wounded tribesmen were another matter. If a man's wound was light enough that he would easily recover, and he looked young and strong, he was sent back to the slave-pens. All the others had their throats cut, and their bodies searched afterwards for valuables. We had no resources to look after prisoners, even if we had had the inclination. Everyone remembered the desolation they had wrought when they broke through the wall so recently, and there was no mercy for them. All gold and silver was supposed to be turned in, to be shared equally, after the Emperor took his share; but most soldiers manage to slip a gold torc or silver ring into their breast without being noticed.

I stayed with my men until it was late, and the time came to return to camp. We marched in fair order; but we were so tired that I doubt many would be awake for long after the evening meal was served. The chief centurion walked beside me, silent for a long time, and then, as if he could not contain himself, he said: "I've never seen anyone fight like that, sir. They say a god takes you in battle?"

I nodded wearily. "Yes. It's a gift my family has, if gift you can call it."

"Well, sir, a lot more of our men would be dead if you didn't have it."

I made no answer, and left him to deal with feeding the men. As the custom was, tonight, after a battle, they would be given a sextarius and a half of wine each... not posca, but real wine, the same wine given to wounded soldiers in the field hospital. Not enough to make them very drunk, but enough to make them sleep happily. They deserved it. This was a great victory.

When I went back to our tent, Julianus was not there, but I was too tired to notice or care. He was a staff officer, and they kept long hours. Lugobelenos helped me off with my armor, brought the evening ration of dry spelt bread and boiled salted pork, and I drank a cup of wine. Then I lay down, still in my bloody red tunic, intending just to rest a little. The next thing I knew, the Diana was being played and the centurions' voices were rousing the men from their sleep.

As I ate my meager breakfast, I noticed that Julianus's pallet was still empty, and had clearly not been slept in. I washed as best I could, thinking longingly of an impossible bath, and dressed. We were in enemy country, so I wore my mail coat and sword belt, and put on my helmet. Then I went to the legionary headquarters, to find out the day's orders.

From the rampart of the marching camp, I could see that they were already setting up the pyres to burn the Roman bodies, and groups of captured tribesmen were digging huge pits for the British dead. There'd be no ceremony for them, and the pits would be shallow. The scavenging animals would eat well in the next few weeks, when they dug up the corpses.

As I walked up, a fellow tribune came towards me, and said, "I'm so sorry about Julianus."

At my startled look, he shook his head.

"I see you haven't heard." He shook his head sympathetically. "He had his helmet knocked off, then took a terrible blow to the head. Then some bastard tribesman speared him in the thigh as he lay there."

"Where is he?" I said. "In the hospital?" I started to turn in that direction, already almost running. His hand grabbed me before I had taken a step.

"No. the Legate wants to see you, at once. And so apparently does the Augustus."

Never in my life have I been so tempted to ignore an order. But I had been in the army too long for that. And to keep an Emperor waiting was suicidal, a fate which now no longer drew me as once it had.

I turned away to the Praetorium, at first reluctant, then quickly to get this over. When I entered, the tent was full of soldiers, with the duxes and legates of all the legions present. Constantius was seated in the center of them all, and I saluted him, even though he was talking to my legate and could not see me in the throng.

I was wrong. He looked up, and beckoned. I went forward and prostrated myself in front of him.

"Up, boy," he said. "You've earned that right twice."

I stood up, and saluted again.

"You were in the first line, Licinianus, and drove it forward," he said. "Men followed you, and that is all a leader can ask."

"Dominus," I said. "I'm in the hands of a god. I simply do what he tells me."

"So I've heard. But how is that different from anyone, except that your god is very effective at what he does?"

He pointed to the harsh-faced young man beside him. "This is my son, Constantinus. You will join his staff as a *Tribunus Vacans,* and serve him as you have me."

So I would be a member of his son's staff from now on. It was a high honor – and at least I would not be in the front line. I was glad, though Constantinus's face was not one I liked.

"You will also be awarded the Civic Crown for a second time, for having saved my life and the lives of my comrades."

What could I say? That award itself conferred senatorial rank. Now I would be spared having to run for the office of quaestor to succeed my father, who also had been a senator. Since I had no intention of going to Rome to do such a thing, that seemed like an irrelevancy. I said all I could think of to say, and it was brief: "I thank you, Dominus."

He leaned forward, smiling crookedly. In the brief time I knew him, that smile came to be what I remember most: "Now go and see your brother-in-law. He's been badly wounded, and I know you are close to him."

I saluted again, and turned, and left, heading for the valetudinarium.

I had some trouble finding Julianus, for the hospital was full of wounded from the battle. We had only lost a few hundred of our men, but many more had suffered wounds, and some would not survive. But Julianus was a high officer, and eventually I found him, attended by a grey-haired doctor who was watching as a slave rebound his wounds.

By his strong accent, the doctor was a Greek, so I switched to that language. "What are his chances?" I said. I was brusque. After the battle, I had no inclination for soft words. Julianus was one of the few people in the world I genuinely trusted; the thought that he might not survive left me bereft. And anger has often covered that feeling in me.

"He received a blow to the head, which forced a plate of bone against his brain. If the pressure's not relieved, he will die of a hemorrhage, or a stroke."

"Then why are you not doing it?"

The doctor smiled sadly. "Because trepanning is a very dangerous operation. I would have to drill a hole in the skull, and then insert a lever to force the bone up until it's flush with the skull surface again, perhaps removing it. There's no surety that this will cure him. The brain is damaged, and it will bleed when the bone is lifted. If it bleeds too much, and we cannot relieve the pressure inside the skull, he will die anyway. And even if he doesn't die... injury to the brain can have terrible effects on a man's reason or speech."

"Do you have a choice?"

He shook his head. "Not if he is to live."

"Then do it."

He lifted his eyebrows. "Sir... who are you?"

"I am Tribunus Vacans to Augustus's son Constantinus, and the brother-in-law of this man."

He nodded slowly. "Then you have the right." He looked down at his hands, and then up at me. "Tribune... I should warn you... with injuries like this, there is almost always a change in the person, even if he survives. It's very rarely a cure. At best, it's what I'd call an improvement. The result may not be what you want..."

I spoke harshly: "Better than to have to tell my sister that her husband is dead."

He spread his hands. "It shall be as you wish."

"Do it right!"

"I always do, Tribune, as well as I am able."

I turned away, and I was ashamed. I was becoming hard and unkind, and I did not like it.

I tried to turn my mind away. But all I could think of was that his brand-new helmet had not helped him at all.

+ + +

The next week the army moved north, leaving our wounded behind under a heavy guard. Our aim now was purely punitive: these people were not to attack south of the wall for a generation, and that meant fire, killing, and enslavement. I had hoped that as a staff officer, I would not be called to deal with these people myself; but Constantinus had different ideas. I think, frankly, that he enjoyed sending his men out, and hearing of what they had done. So I was sent north as the second-in-command of an ala of cataphracti, attired in the heavy armor appropriate for my new task. It was a good thing, perhaps, that I was not in charge: I had no training in this kind of warfare, and little with these weapons. But this was nevertheless my lot. As they say in the army, you learn from doing.

Our task was shocking in its simplicity: burn everything; kill all we saw, for, unlike the infantry, we had no way to take back slaves; kill all the farm animals. These people were to have nothing for the winter.

Even the seasoned soldiers did not like this. Killing human beings was one thing, but most soldiers come from rural backgrounds, and there is something in those whose families have lived off the land that revolts them about killing animals. I felt the same, and we made an unspoken agreement amongst ourselves that we would at least take back the horses, for they could follow us in a string without holding us back.

The northern tribesmen do not live in the villages we are used to, but rather in scattered crofts on land owned by their chieftains, who get a share of their crops and husbandry. But they are often clustered near the best land, and so often there were clusters of their stone houses which received our ministrations. Many of these were deserted: the tribesmen waged harsh fighting among themselves, and when war came, they knew to run for safety into the hills. We burned the empty houses and killed the cattle and sheep that we found, as we drove north, following the desperately fleeing people. We would come upon them, trying to escape to the Highlands in the north, a family here with a cow, a man on a horse there trying to shepherd his children to safety. We rode them down, and killed them all.

In later years, my son Aurelianus asked me, when he was only nine, if I had killed children like him and his sister. I shook my head. "No. Never," I said.

And that was true, in its way. But I had no choice but to lead my men against groups with children in them, and the commander of the force, a man called Postumius Albus Gallienus, of an old Roman family, watched me to see if I was weak. I already knew what happened to weak people in the Roman army, and I had no desire to experience it again. But I am very good with a bow, and it is always possible to shoot to wound, in the hope that no one will notice. Sometimes that worked. But more often it did not. One time when my arrow took a young boy in the arm, Albus smiled at me, and said, "You are usually so good with a bow, Licinianus! Are you weary today?"

And he motioned to another of his men, who rode the boy down, and killed him with a single slash of his spatha.

He was not a bad man. But he was as hard as flint.

That was how it was. And it was harsh work, even to Roman soldiers. We are not without human feeling. But we obey our orders, even though we knew too many had made their escape to the Highlands for this to be a permanent end.

It continued until that last day, the one just before we turned back.

We had ridden many miles north, just one among many such columns, leaving a trail of desolation behind us. We were north of the river Bodotria, and now the people fleeing us were desperate, for they could see the highlands ahead which offered them safety. Their vanguard might make it. The rest would not. And some then turned to fight. I admired them. To die like a slaughtered sheep is no way for anyone to go.

They died nevertheless, and finally all we were left with was one man, one of their chieftain class by his dress, and a young girl, whom I guessed to be no more than 14 or 15 years old, with hair shining red-gold in the dying sun, very like my sister's and mine. The girl was so thin I could see her bones, and her father was no better. They were starving.

We rode up, our blades still wet with the blood of their companions, bodies lying in the grass behind us. Some were still moving, but I don't think any of us had the inclination to go back to finish them off. We were all sick of this. If they lived, let them.

The man drew his sword and handed his dagger to the girl. He was talking to her, and at first, I was too far to hear what his archaic British meant. Then I could understand. "Be brave now, my sweet one, the braver you are, the easier it will be. Go at them! I'll be right behind."

And she ran at us, with him shouting, and her face determined. She was afraid… I could see that. But she was worthy of her father in bravery, if not skill. Her dagger was high; clearly, she had no understanding of how to hold a weapon. But she screamed her hatred at us nevertheless, and came on. And it was me she came at.

I felt fear then too, not because of her, but because I had no control of the Dreaming, and if it took over, I would kill her without a thought. But it never came, and as she struck at me, I turned my shield to take her blow, and with my other hand took the dagger from her hand as easily as if she were an infant. Yet she did not stop, and threw herself against my armored form, desperate to harm me before she died. And at that instant, I thought of how brave she was in her foolish determination, and I knew that I would not let her come to any harm today.

I heard her father shout, and he came at me, for he believed he knew what I intended with his little girl. He was wrong, but it made no difference. I reached down and dragged the girl across my saddle, for I knew that if I left her, he would kill her, to save her from me.

I danced my horse away from him. He screamed in anguish, and came at me again, calling his daughter's name, screaming: "No! No!"

I heard the creak of the compound bow behind me, and the whir of the arrow passing. It took him in the eye, and he stood for a while, and then fell to his knees, and then onto his face, dead before he hit the ground.

Gallienus came up to me, dropping his bow into its case.

"Well, you didn't need me, but quicker this way, I think? Better get rid of her. Unless you like them that young?"

I just looked at him, and I think my eyes showed that I would kill him if he said the wrong thing. And he, brave man though he was, my superior though he was, flinched.

"Well, do it, then."

I took a long while to answer; but when I did, the reply was simple. "No," I said.

As our eyes met, the world receded, and the girl's frenzied screaming and crying I no longer heard. I knew the dream was near.

"My sister," I said, "would hate me if I allowed it, and so would my god Litavis. We do not kill children in my family."

He had no idea what I meant, or who I was referring to. But he also knew that to fight me would be death.

"You're disobeying an order."

"Then report me to Constantinus. But this girl lives untouched, and anyone who fails to understand this, dies."

I raised my voice, and said it again, so all might hear.

He was no coward. But he knew that if he fought me, he would not live, and others would die, for the god was near.

He shrugged, and even smiled. "On your head be it."

He shouted an order, and we turned and began to ride south, to the marching camp.

The girl struggled until I was forced to bind her to my saddle, crying with desperation and despair. I spoke to her, and told her she was safe; but she did not believe me, and tried to strike at me. I don't blame her. I asked her name, but she refused to answer... I thought her father called her Veldicca. But I wasn't sure.

I had to bind her hands too, eventually, or she would have clawed my face to ribbons. She pissed on me as we rode, and she did it intentionally.

# CHAPTER 15

## Severiana: Homecoming

I waited all day for Julianus to come home. I knew that he had arrived at Isurium the previous day, and that is only twenty or so miles from Eburacum; but by the evening he had not arrived, and I went to bed disappointed. Yes, angry too, though I knew he was not yet a well man, and that his wound had been serious. No one could blame him for slowness. And I slept badly, for though it was autumn now, the weather was still warm and dry, and I could not get comfortable. I even woke the slave who slept near me at night, and told her to bring some water cooled by ice preserved from winter. I drank some of it, and splashed some on my face and coverings. But I wished, like everyone, for the cold of winter to come, or even just the chill we would have expected at this time. But the hot weather continued.

Next morning, I woke early, and after a breakfast of bread dipped in olive oil, some dates, and watered wine, I had the bath heated, and bathed when the water was hot. Normally I bathe in the evening, but I felt sweaty and dirty, and the water soothed me. Julianus had bought a masseuse for me, and I felt much better after I had been scraped clean and received her talented ministrations. She was very good at her job.

Then I waited, reading Sappho's poetry. It's a tradition in my family… my grandfather read a poem to my grandmother on their wedding night, and all of us, especially Licinianus, have loved her work. They are so beautiful, those poems… they make your heart sing. They will never die. I am so grateful to my aunt that she made me learn Aeolic Greek, so I could read them.

The sun started to set, and I gave up hope of seeing Julianus that day, and ordered dinner to be served. But then, as I was sitting down to eat, I heard the sound of horses and wheels, and ran out. He had arrived.

I do not think I have ever had a shock as terrible as when I saw him carried in. He was not the man who had left. He was emaciated, and his head, though no longer bandaged, was scarred terribly, from just above his left eye into his scalp, where no hair grew along the jagged line of the wound. Worst was his look… where before his eyes had been lively and full of laughter, now he seemed listless and exhausted. But when I grasped his hand he squeezed it, weakly.

"I'm sorry, Domina," said the optio who had brought him. "We were hoping to be here yesterday, but he was too sick to travel. Even today…"

"I can see." My eyes started to fill with tears, and I brushed them away, turning on the house slaves who were staring open-mouthed at their master. "Get him to his bed, you fools! You!" I pointed to the majordomo. "Get him some food! Milk and soup, and bread if he can swallow it! Go!"

The optio handed me a letter. "This was from the doctor, domina. It explains what happened, and what was done to help."

"Thank you."

I began to open it, then realized my manners. "Have you and your men eaten yet? Do you need something?"

He shook his head. "Thank you, but we have orders to report immediately."

I turned to Julianus's body slave. "Tell me what has been happening. Why is he in such a bad state?"

"I think the doctor's letter will tell you more than I can, domina. But after the wound, the bone was pressing on the brain, and he started having convulsions. The doctor had to drill into his skull..."

He saw my horrified face, and apologized, more than he needed to.

"Go on. I need to know."

"Well," he said uncertainly, "He got the piece up, and the seizures stopped, but the Master was in a coma for days. When he woke, he was confused and refused to eat. We had to force food down to keep him alive. He seemed not to know who he was at first, but he's been getting better and better – just very weak."

I sighed and began to open the tablet the soldier had brought. But my fingers were trembling. "Go and get something to eat. You will sleep near your Master, of course."

> *Oribasius Laertius, Medicus Vulnerarius XX Legionis Valeriae Victricis, Caeliae Vindici Severianae, a very great greeting.*
>
> *Your husband suffered a serious injury, being struck twice in the head in the Battle of Colanica. The first blow slashed his temple and the second, administered perhaps with a sword hilt, fractured his skull and drove a portion of it downwards against the front of the brain. He also had a wound in the thigh, but that was not serious. I was forced to trepan him, since he was having constant seizures, and thus I alleviated his condition. He was in a coma for some days, but then he woke up, and within a week was able to speak. I can do no more for him, but send him back to you, in the hope that you will be able to care for him better than I can. As for what will happen in the future, I cannot say. Sometimes those with wounds like this recover*

*completely. Many times they do not, or they change in their nature. I can only hope that this does not befall him. Farewell, Domina, as I hope to prosper, and hail.*

I called out. "Bring a cot and put it in the Dominus's room. I'll be sleeping there from now on."

+ + +

The next month was one of the worst in my life. I so wished that Licinianus was with me, but he was in Valentia, still with the army north of the Wall. I knew no details of what was happening there, but Licinianus's letters gave me something of an idea. They were clearing the area, killing everything they found. It was hard not to be glad that they were safeguarding us: the land around Eburacum was a horror of burned houses and destroyed towns, of skeletons of animals, and even the remains of human beings who had not yet been buried. The northern tribes had shown no mercy to our people when they broke through, and now we were showing no mercy to them. That is always how it is, and how it should be.

But I so wanted to talk to him. I've found in my life that it's hard to talk to most men: they never say enough. But Licinianus and I were different. I could tell him anything, and he me; we always understood each other. The bond of twins is real.

I could have left Julianus's care to the slaves: they would have looked after him well, for he had been a good master. But I could not do that. So I spent all my days with him, coaxing him to eat, talking to him even when he seemed not to understand me, sleeping by him in a cot, and waking when he had the terrible dreams that now seemed to be a common part of his nights. And, slowly, he got better. The first words he said were, "I lost my helmet. I lost it!" He was so agitated that he couldn't rest until I told him I'd find it.

But it seemed like this was a turning point, for he began to put on weight... and by the end of the month, he was speaking to me, getting tired very quickly, but speaking to me almost sanely. There were sudden bursts of irrational anger, but I understood; he had always been so healthy and able, and now he was not.

On the day that autumn finally came, and the air turned blessedly cold, I took him out to the garden for the first time, and we sat together, surrounded by high walls, and the sounds of the city dimly reaching us.

"I don't remember what happened to me," he said. "I was in the battle, and then suddenly I was not, and in the hospital. Weeks were gone. I'm not sure I'll ever remember... I don't think I want to know..."

101

I put my hand on his, lifted it, and kissed it. "It doesn't matter now... you're with me."

"That was all I wanted," he said. "I so hoped you were having a child..."

"No." I shook my head sadly. "But we have time. Lots of time. I've been told I can take you south to our villa to heal. You don't have to think about the army... just getting well."

I offered him some dates and olives and poured him some watered wine. He came from the south, and I knew he loved the fruits of his childhood. He ate an olive, and drank a little. "I haven't been eating much."

"But you need to. Come. Have some more."

Obediently, he ate, and I smiled at him, thinking how much like a child he was at this moment.

The knock on the door was loud, and it irritated me. I was enjoying one of the first normal times I had had with Julianus in so long. I wanted no disturbance, and I called out to the ostiarius, "Tell them to come back tomorrow!"

I didn't care if they heard my voice beyond the wall.

I heard the door open, and voices talking. Then, to my annoyance, the ostiarius approached.

"Domina," he said. "My great apologies! But it's from your brother!" He handed me a letter.

I hesitated not at all, opened it, and read it. I put it down slowly in my lap. I did not speak at first, for I was taken aback at what I had read. Then I lifted my chin, and said, "Bring her in."

"She is in the bath, Domina."

"Bring her when she is clean then."

They brought her too soon, for she was certainly not clean. She would have been pretty, had she not been dressed in such dirty and disheveled tribal clothes, so soiled and worn that they seemed like a beggar's. She was quite young, on the cusp of being a woman, yet no one would be drawn to her, for in her face was a look not just of defiance but of hatred. This was the girl my brother wanted us to look after?

The slave woman who had come with her started talking, eager to excuse herself. "Domina, we tried to make her presentable, but she won't let us wash her or change her clothes! I don't understand what she says: she has no Latin! But she claws at us if we try to clean her!"

The soldier with her said, "Domina, I can understand her. All she says is that we should kill her or send her to die up north with her father!"

"She's from the Northern tribes?" I spoke to her in British. "Why do you not let us help you?"

"Help me?" she said. "You killed my father before my eyes and took me away from my people. My father told me to die before I let you take me! And I will die, just so long as I can take one of you with me!"

I understood her, though barely. Her dialect was rude and very archaic... the language made me think of a priest reciting a ritual in a temple. But it was Julianus who shocked me, for he was now standing on his feet, swaying, and his voice filled with fury. "She's one of them," he shouted. "Kill her! They are devils!"

He tried to get to her, but his knees gave way, and he fell, clawing towards the young girl, but reaching only the mosaic floor. I saw his nails break on the tesserae, as he tried to attack her.

I had no idea what to do. It seemed my husband had suddenly lost all his senses, and even in the girl's eyes I could sense a realization that she was facing a madman. It broke through her hatred of all things Roman. In that instant, she became simply a young frightened girl, and she began to cry.

I closed my eyes, shaking, wanting to weep too, but not letting myself. When I could speak, I looked at my personal slave and said: "Take her to the bath, and bathe her. Throw these dirty clothes away, and dress her in clean ones. If she resists, have the women hold her. I will not have such a filthy creature in my home! Feed her and put her in a guest's room. My brother says she is not to be treated as a slave, and so she won't be. But guard her room! She is not to run away!"

I turned to the male slaves, my anger intense. "Pick up your master and put him in his cubicle. Can't you see he is not well?"

I stayed there as they carried Julianus away. I had been so hopeful that he would recover, become again the smiling man I knew. Now... now I was afraid. I poured a cup of unwatered wine, I drank, and let my face fall into my spread hands. And then I wept. And as I sat there sobbing, rain began to fall for the first time in months.

# CHAPTER 16
## Severiana: Helena

I had not heard from Constantius's concubine for at least a month, and I wondered if I was no longer of interest to her. This bothered me not at all, except insofar as I knew that indifference from the powerful could always be a danger. But then attention from them can be even worse. So I spent my time looking after Julianus, and as I did, I began again to have some hope that he really would get well.

But there came a time when I desperately needed to leave the house. I wanted to ride a horse! I don't think anyone who has never ridden can understand the pleasure of riding across fields with the wind of passage blowing in your face, and the exhilaration when you kick the horse into a gallop. So I decided to ride one cloudy day, though now that the drought was broken, all days were cloudy again, as we expect in the sunny land of Britannia. And, of course, this was now winter.

The sad thing is that, after the attacks of the northern tribes, and the resulting chaos, it was not very safe to be out in the countryside. The tribes have been driven back, but many of our own had lost their livelihood and become brigands. We know this kind of thing well from times past: the Bagaudae in Gallia have been a problem since my grandfather's time.

I could not go out on my own, for as a woman you are ready prey in a war-ravaged area and need an entourage to ensure your safety. So I rode out that day with five men, all old soldiers who had known Julianus. I had no woman with me, for none of our female slaves could ride. But I was not afraid. These were men I could trust. And I needed to get out! I was stifling! And sadly, it was Julianus who was stifling me, for he swayed back and forth between being the old smiling man I had known, and a dour person who would hardly talk except to mutter that he wished to be left alone.

We rode south to the Porta Praetoria and across the Abos River; I was glad to leave the road, with its rows of crucified tribesmen and brigands, and we were soon out in the countryside. It lifted my spirits to smell the grass crushed under the horses' hooves, and gallop across the frost-rimed meadows. The trees, of course, were bare, but at least I was outside.

Much of the land was fallow, but it was the fallow of desertion: many of the farmers had fled south during the attacks or taken refuge behind the walls of the city. There would be hard times for a while, until the land was brought back. The army was already bringing wagon loads of grain into the area from the south, to stave off mass starvation, but the rations would still be tight this year. By the time we turned back, I was happier and more at peace than I had been for many a day. And then, we saw riders ahead.

My men started to reach for their swords; but there was no need. These were Romans, a small party of them, and there was a woman in their midst. I guessed that they were here for the very same purpose as I, for when I came close, I saw that the woman was Helena, and the men with her imperial troops.

I would have done anything to get past this meeting, but there was no way to avoid it. I had met with Helena that one time, and it had been pleasant enough. Perhaps if we'd met under other circumstances, we could have been friends. But as it was…

So I steeled myself, and rode to meet her. As I came up, she smiled, and said: "Severiana! I've been thinking of you! How interesting that you ride too! I have been unable to get out for so long…"

"I understand." Cautiously, for raising the issue of the health of an Emperor can be seen as treasonous, I said: "It's been said that the Augustus is not well. I hope that's not true!"

She shook her head, her smile dying. She had high, round cheeks and a long nose, and they made her face seem even sadder. "It's true, my dear. The campaign was very tiring for him, and he's come back in a bad way."

"You've been together a long time," I said, not knowing what to say, and then shocked at the familiarity of my remark. But she seemed not to care.

"Yes. We have! We met in Nicomedia at the time of the Great Aurelian. We were both wearing identical silver bracelets! We knew we were destined for each other. I am very worried about him."

She turned to a man beside her, and said: "Make sure I invite this lovely young lady to visit tomorrow." She turned back to me: "In fact, let me invite you now. Come for the prandium,[15] like last time. I enjoyed your company… and to think your brother saved my husband's life!"

I knew the story, for it was common knowledge in Eburacum. Of course I had not heard it from my brother, still in the North, whose letters had said nothing about the event! Only when I got him in person could I pry loose the details he always left out!

---

[15] Midday meal.

"I've heard, but not from my brother!"

"How tedious men are in their reticence!" she said. "But do come tomorrow!"

I thanked her, as I knew I must. But I really did not want to go to the Praetorium, and perhaps meet her son and his unpleasant friend.

As she rode off, she turned and called over her shoulder: "Bring that tribal girl your brother sent you. I want to see her!"

That aside told me I was being watched.

And I realized I had said not a word to the girl in the weeks since she had arrived, all her family gone, her father dead; and I felt shame.

+ + +

The sun was almost setting when we reached our house, and I told my woman that I would have a bath; I had ordered the water to be heated every day. But as I walked past the small peristyle, I heard a voice singing, so low that I could hardly catch the sound. It was not a happy song: it was a lament, sung in her archaic British, and as I heard the words:

> *Who rocked my cradle of willow*
> *Lies now in the river clay*
> *His eyes are food for the crow*
> *And will never again see day*
> *So in the land of his foe*
> *Must I weep and stay*
> *Till one day new winds blow*
> *And the gods call me away*

I knew what this was: the eugsla... I had heard it many times throughout my childhood.

How to explain this? It's the custom of British women, when their loved ones die, to build verses in their heads, and sing laments to mourn them. They sing the songs for themselves, but they do it in groups, and it can go on intermittently for many days, weeks, even months. And that was what this girl was doing.

I walked towards her and stood on the edge of the tiny garden in the peristyle. Her voice was so low I barely heard her keening. Her head was bent, and I could see she was crying as she murmured her song. And I thought how sad this was, that she had no one to keen with her, for it is the saddest thing to sing this alone, without any woman to be with you, to weep with you, and to hold your hand. I stayed quiet, listening until I had every word. Then I walked forward, stood behind her, and started to sing with her.

"Who rocked my cradle of willow…" I sang. And her head spun around as if someone's hand had jerked it. She looked at me, her green eyes huge, and was silent for a while as I sang on. Then her voice joined mine, and I took her hand, and we sang her verses together until the light died and the slaves lit the lamps, she teaching me new ones one after the other, and I joining in when I knew them. And then, when we were done, she fell to the ground clutching my skirt and sobbed as if her very heart would leave in her next breath.

+ + +

I took her into the triclinium, where, in this house, a semi-circular stibadium[16] had replaced the three couches normally found there. I guided her to a place by my side, and ordered the evening meal to be served. The resistance that she had shown when she first arrived was gone now, and she came meekly. I poured her a cup of wine, but I saw her wince at the taste, and realized that she had never drunk it before she came here. So I beckoned the majordomo, and ordered him to find barley beer for her. I almost laughed at his expression, as he realized he was to serve this plebeian drink. "I don't know if we have any, domina!"

"Don't the slaves drink it?"

His bewildered look showed he had no idea. "Perhaps some honey-wine then."

He bowed and left, and I turned to the girl. "I'm ashamed. I don't even know your name, or what tribe you are. I know you are not of the Scotti: they do not speak our language."

She hesitated, and then said: "My name is Veldicca, daughter of a Chief of the Votadini, Brigomaglos. Your soldiers killed him."

I bowed my head. I did not think that now was the time to mention that her tribe had come across the Wall and devastated the north. "I am so sorry," I said. "I never knew my father or my mother. Both died when I was a baby."

"Oh …"

She looked up, as the disapproving majordomo brought her honey-wine. Cautiously, she sipped at it, and then, apparently approving, drank more.

"How do you speak our language?" she asked, wonderingly.

---

[16] A semi-circular couch.

"My family's native to this island. We spoke it with our nurses. It was the first language we spoke, and the language all us young ones used to each other."

"But you're a Roman…" she said, almost accusingly.

"Yes, but Romans are of many kinds. You have to realize that we're not all from our mother city."

The food began to be served, and I urged her to dip the boiled eggs in garum. She wrinkled her nose at the taste of the fish sauce, looked up, and said defiantly: "Since I am a slave now, I must do what you wish. But I do not like this."

"Then eat one with salt." I dipped one into the salt-bowl and offered it to her. "And you are not a slave. Do you think I eat with slaves like this?"

She looked lost. "What am I then?"

"My brother asked me to look after you. You know the man who brought you away when they killed your father? That man was my brother. They were going to kill you. He stopped them."

"*Why?*" she spat. "I wanted to die! I wanted to be with my father!"

I hesitated. How could I explain the strangeness of my family? "Do you know the word tungida?"

"Tungida?" She looked bewildered… then: "Oh, tungido! You mean what the gods impose on a man or woman, as their fate?"

"Yes. We have a tungida imposed on our family by Matrona and Camulus. We receive great gifts. But we cannot kill children."

"I am not a child!"

"What are you… fourteen, fifteen winters…? Your womanhood has clearly come. Your body shows it, now that you are no longer so thin."

She started to speak, then looked up at me in anger that I had asked such a question.

"But you are still very young."

She looked up, her blue eyes defiant. "Then what do you intend to do with me?"

I shook my head. "Nothing bad. We will bring you up, and then, when you are a woman, you will make your choice."

"I wanted to die with my father!"

"I know. But the gods decided otherwise. Don't you want to bring through yourself the life your father gave you?"

"Amongst my father's enemies!"

"*I* am not your enemy. *My brother* is not your enemy."

"I didn't want to live!"

"You will live, nevertheless. And to make sure you do well, we will teach you Latin, and how to read and write, and you may choose of Rome as much or as little as you wish."

I leaned forward. "Now, eat. You'll like the spiced fritters. They're fried with honey."

And for the next hour or so I tempted her with food, for I knew no better way to get her to feel at home with Romans. And even if she had never had mussels with broth before, and turned up her nose at them, her tastes would change, until she no longer felt a stranger.

I would no longer ignore her, I promised myself. I would make her happy here, even if I could not do the same for my husband.

# CHAPTER 17

## Severiana: Constantius

With an Emperor in residence, entering the Praetorium was no easy matter, even for a woman and a young girl. There was a long interval as the guards checked that I really had an invitation, and I suppose I should have been grateful that I wasn't searched for weapons: a man would have been. I believe they considered it, but there was no woman around to do the search, and for them to touch someone of my class might have meant their backs. So I was admitted, my slaves taken elsewhere to wait for my return, and Veldicca and I went into the inner rooms.

I was surprised to find not just Helena waiting for us, but Constantius as well. I was so shocked, I didn't know how to react at first, and for two wholly different reasons. First, why would he be here to greet me? I was just a provincial girl, of a good family, but still. And second: he looked terrible. My instinct told me that he would not be long for the world, for no one can look like that and be expected to live.

I began to go down on my knees, trying to pull Veldicca down with me, but he stopped us with a hoarse comment. "Your brother saved my life. Sit, and let us all talk."

His voice was a bare whisper; I had to strain to hear him.

Helena was gesturing to the slaves to serve the midday meal. It was very simple, I would guess, by the standards of an Emperor, but more than was ever served to me at that time of day: cold meat of two kinds, cheese, vegetables, fresh bread, and fruit, with wine and water, and olive oil or the garlic, herb, and cheese mixture called moretum, for dipping. There were also of course boiled eggs, which apparently Constantius loved to eat with garum, judging by how Helena coaxed him. As befitted an Emperor, there was honey cake as well, and a honey & black pepper omelet.

But he ate very little. I thought by his face that the food was making him sick; but I dared not give any indication of my suspicion. And I was so nervous that I ate very little as well, sipping instead on heavily watered wine, dipping a few fragments of bread in the oil, and eating a boiled egg with fish sauce. That was my lunch, such as it was. Veldicca ate nothing, until I urged her to eat some bread, and later a slice of the honey cake. She liked honey. I knew she wouldn't touch the watered wine.

We had finished eating when Constantinus came in, and with him was his elegant friend, Valerius Avilius Apollinaris.

To say I was unhappy was an understatement. I found Apollinaris repellent, though I did not really know why. And there was something about Constantinus that proclaimed brutishness to me. This was a pair I did not want to spend any time with. But here I was. And as I was to learn, my instincts were right.

Constantinus made no attempt to hide his interest in me. He took the chair beside me, and began to talk, at first acting as if he simply wished to congratulate me on my brother's prowess, but soon making clear that it was me he was really interested in. It was as if Veldicca wasn't there. I pulled my stola closer, for that is the sign of a married woman, but it made no difference, and he started touching my hand as he talked. I withdrew it under my clothing, and smiled as if I were happy to talk pleasantly. What else can you do with an Emperor's son?

Now Apollinaris came up, and took the chair on the other side of me. Both the men were too close, and all I wanted was to get away as they talked to me, asking so many personal questions… where my family lived, how many brothers I had, did I have any children by my husband…

"No," I said. "I am only recently married."

They looked at one another, and Constantinus laughed as Apollinaris commented: "All the more pleasure for your lovers!"

"Almost like a virgin!" said Constantinus.

And they both laughed.

I knew my face was scarlet, and I knew genuine hatred for these two men for the first time. They were enjoying tormenting a woman, I realized, as sometimes men do. They knew I was finding no pleasure in their banter. And they liked it.

It was at that moment that Helena stood up, calling on the slaves to clear the tables. She beckoned to me and smiled at her husband and son. "I hope you'll pardon us for going, but I wish to talk to this lady. Come on, Severiana, and bring the girl with you. Let's go to the garden."

As we walked, she said, conversationally, "I love my son. But when that Syrian panders to him, he can be an oaf."

"No, really, Domina, it was fine…"

"No, it wasn't. But I got you away."

I looked down at the ground. "Thank you…"

We sat on chairs under shelter, with braziers around, for it was snowing lightly, and a slave brought fruit juice. I was grateful – I'd had enough wine – and tasted it. It was peach, and cold, and delicious. I wondered where it had come from, at this season. It's strange how, even on a day that is not at all warm, cold things taste good.

Helena leaned back against her cushions, and looked at me carefully. "I've heard strange things about your family."

I felt the catch in my throat. I was afraid, though I had no idea what she was talking about.

"I don't understand, Domina."

She smiled, and in a way that made me uncomfortable. "They say that your family has unusual gifts. Your brother, for example… when he first entered the army, on a commission from the Augustus Diocletianus, his fellows – allow me to be blunt – thought very little of him. Yet now… all of a sudden, he became someone whose prowess compares to Achilles, if you'll allow me to exaggerate a little. Hardened soldiers are now afraid of him… They say he is a killer. Can you explain that to me?"

I felt my body tensing. There was nothing wrong with any of this. It had always been my family's gift. Others understood it. Other gods gave similar gifts. But I hated to hear my brother described like that.

"It's just the gift our family gods give. We're not alone in this!"

Her mouth pursed. "Yet some say this kind of gift is given by demons."

My mouth opened, and I had no idea how to respond. "Domina! These are our family gods! Not demons! They've blessed us for centuries!"

"Have they? Is that why they give the gift of killing?"

I found myself gasping at the sacrilege. The only people I had ever heard of who talked like this were Christians. And surely no Imperial would follow that cult!

"Only to one man, and that is the gift of fighting well! To a woman they give the gift of saving children!"

"Saving children… *You* have that gift?"

"I? No! I'm not claiming that. I don't know. Perhaps. My aunt has it. My brother has the gift of war, and usually his twin has the gift of life, but I've never seen any proof of that in me."

"You believe all that…"

"It's my family… We've always known this."

Then she smiled. "No matter. Tell me about your brother."

"I don't know what to say. He's someone who always loved books and poetry. I love him dearly. We are all that is left of my father and my mother. We never knew them… but we make offerings to their manes, of course…"

"I know about them. Without your father, Diocletianus would not be Emperor."

"Yes."

She smiled then, and this was not so pleasant a smile. "And I know who your mother was. Tell me… what does it feel like to be the granddaughter of the Great Aurelianus?"

I felt breathless. This was such a dangerous subject that we never talked about it to strangers. Then she leaned forward and patted me on the arm. "Don't be frightened. To have imperial blood is a dangerous thing, I know."

My mouth was dry. "We never talk about that. We just want to live our lives. In peace and quiet."

"I believe that. Neither you nor your brother seem to have the… wrong kind of ambitions." She shifted in her chair to face Veldicca. "And you, girl? Why did Severiana's brother save you?"

Veldicca's mouth was open, for she could understand not a word.

"She knows no Latin, Domina. Only her kind of British."

"You can speak it? Of course you can. You are a daughter of this land. Ask her the question."

I obeyed. And Veldicca responded. "I don't know. You were the one who told me that he saved me because I was a child!"

I translated, and Helena's eyes opened wide. "Your brother saved her because she was young?"

I thought: how am I going to explain the Celtic tungida to a woman from Asia? But I tried. She listened, and seemed oddly impressed.

"Members of your family can't just save children, they also can't kill them?"

I shook my head. "Not without endangering our fate."

"Ah," she said, and now she smiled freely. "Perhaps your family was not gifted by demons after all, then. I've always loved children. It was my regret never to have had more, or a daughter."

I bowed my head. "My husband and I wanted them… perhaps we still do, but he is so injured…"

"I hear his mind is injured. That is so sad."

I don't know why I started crying. It just came like a wave over me, and I couldn't help it. And then an astonishing thing happened. Helena got up and put her arms around me, and rocked me back and forth as I sobbed. When I had finally done, she whispered in my ear, "Being a woman is hard, for we so often have to sit and accept what is given us, no matter how terrible it is... But there is better waiting, I promise you, and a great comfort to the soul if you choose it. One day perhaps I'll talk to you about that... but not now."

I put my arms around her and sobbed some more, for it had been so long since I had felt that sense of deep sympathy from a woman.

"Let's become friends," she whispered in my ear. "Be the daughter I never had."

She laughed aloud. "And teach that girl to speak Latin! I want to know about her life!"

+ + +

I arrived home thoughtful. I had no idea what had gone on between me and Helena, or what it meant. I was not really happy for her to want to treat me like a daughter, and I wondered what her comments about my family had meant. It frightened me. There had been some menace there.

But she was right about Veldicca. I called the Majordomo and gave him orders: "From now on, no one is to speak British to her. Only Latin! If you need to tell her what the Latin word means you may do so. But that is all! Anyone who disobeys will be punished. Is that understood?"

I walked away, feeling suddenly tired. I wanted to sit outside, but it was too chilly, and the rain had started again. So I went back inside, and walked to my cubicle to lie down. And there I found Julianus, and it was the old Julianus, not the strange new one. He smiled, and I walked into his arms. I was so glad to see him back, and I thought, "This time he won't leave again!"

If only that had been true.

114

# CHAPTER 18

## Severiana: The Soul-Healer

As winter deepened, the weather became very cold, the hypocaust slaves working all day and all night to stoke the furnaces. There was an irony here: last summer had been so dry and so hot that I had had trouble sleeping. Now it was so cold that a drizzle left a slick of ice on the streets, and walking became treacherous. When snow came, it covered the city, a foot deep, and then melted into slush… which froze again within a day.

I yearned for my home in the south.

It was not just the terrible weather. It was also Julianus and my regular visits to Helena in the Basilica. In many ways I enjoyed those visits, for over the past months I had come to know her well. I became closer and closer to her. But her face was rarely happy any more, for everyone knew how sick Constantius was. No one dared say it in public, but all knew that he was dying, and it would not be long before he left this world. And that too was a frightening thought, for when an emperor died, who would succeed him, and who would oppose him? All too often it meant civil war, and we had had enough of that in the hundred years behind us.

And then there was Julianus.

I had been so hopeful that he would go back to his earlier happy self; and so he did, some of the time. But then his mood would swing, and he would fall into black rages, shouting at the slaves and even striking them. He had never done that before. We'd learned to keep Veldicca away from him in those times, for he seemed to be thrust into fury by the sight of her, and he would rise and go to her screaming in incoherent anger, calling her a murdering bitch and vowing to kill her. She hardly needed to know Latin to understand his intent, and soon she had learned the language more than enough to understand all he said.

"Why does he hate me so?" she asked me on one bad day. "What have I done?"

I shook my head. "Nothing. I don't know…" I hesitated. "But I think he knows what has happened to his mind, and blames you…"

"But I did nothing!"

I reached over, and hugged her, one of the first times I had ever done that. I was growing fond of her. I had even ordered that she be taught to read and

115

write. "I know. But it's not what you did, but what you are..." I shook my head. "My dear, I don't know what to tell you. My husband isn't well since he returned from the north. You know it, and I do too."

Julianus and I were sharing a bed again, not every night, but enough. But what had once been a pleasure was now but a task to be accomplished with stoic endurance. There were no nights when I did not fear he would lose himself in fury, or withdraw into himself, and I had a broad-shouldered slave stationed outside the door, just in case. I would have preferred to stay away from him, but his eyes were so hurt when I tried, that I just could not do it. I was caught, by the caring I once had for him, and by my own guilt at its absence.

I visited Helena the next day, and it was as miserable as a day could be. Though it was not very late in the afternoon, it was dark, and the drizzle was turning to sleet. The trees were shadows dripping icy wet on us as I was carried through the streets to the Basilica. It seemed as if all the color had been taken from the city, and everything was bleached and leaden. I huddled in my litter covered in a heavy cloak with a closed brazier at my feet and felt some pity for the slaves who carried me to my destination.

We arrived at the Basilica, and I hurried into the main entrance, eager to get away from the cold and wind. As soon as the doors had closed behind me, the warmth overwhelmed me and I breathed a sigh of pleasure, or at least of relief.

I knew the Basilica well now, and walked towards the private apartments of the lady Helena. No one hindered me, and the guards made no move to stop me: I was now well-known.

When I entered her room, she was sitting at her writing desk crying. At first, I was so taken aback I could not move. I had never seen her display such emotion, let alone sob as she was doing. I ran to her, for my heart would allow nothing less. I knelt next to her, and reached out to touch her, not without some hesitation. She was not a woman who wanted to be touched. But instead of resisting me, she leaned forward and cried into her hands, her forehead resting lightly against my shoulder. After a time, she spoke.

"The physician says that it is likely a carcinus in his lungs. And nothing can be done. One of his lungs at least would have to be removed, and that would kill him."

I sat down by her. "A carcinus? What is that?"

She shook her head. "I don't know what it is. But a growth starts in the body, and spreads, leaving dark veins... and eventually, in great pain, one dies. That is what Constantius has. The physician believes it's now in his liver.

There's no hope for him but opiates."

I knew the shock of hearing this, but I didn't understand. "The Emperor will die?"

"Yes. In a month... in six months... in a year... with the pain growing ever greater."

"There's no hope?"

"No." She began to cry again. "We've known each other so long... our rings: I told you about those I know... and now I'll be without him."

I bent my head, for I had no words.

She sat upright, breathing deeply. "No, I will not fail here. I can't save him, I can only love him as he dies, and try to urge his soul to make the right choice."

I didn't understand her. And I said so.

She shook her head. "My child... Do you think death is the end? Do you think there's no salvation to those who are dying in their body or their mind, like your husband?"

"Well, the underworld..."

She gestured dismissively with her hand, reached over, and rang a tiny bell. "I trust you enough to speak to you. And perhaps I can help your husband, even if I can't help mine."

A slave entered and bowed. "Domina."

"Bring Hilarius here."

Hilarius was an unusual man. He had the body of a soldier, and scars that seemed to prove it. He was tall and powerful, and though now he was old enough to have hair and beard of mixed grey and white, he still looked as if he could bend an iron bar. His skin was dark, as if he were from the east; but his eyes were a brilliant blue. Hilarius was not someone whom you would forget, once you had met him.

He was dressed very plainly; you might almost have thought he was a house slave, if it were not for the fact that the cloth of his tunic was of good quality and cut. He wore no rings, or, in fact, jewelry of any kind. And he bowed politely to the Lady Helena, and then to me, and asked if he could be of service.

Helena turned to me. "Hilarius is a very gifted man. He was once a soldier, and then, after he studied with Apollodorus Macrinus in Rome, he became a doctor. He's very wise in the ways both of the body and the soul. Tell him about your husband."

I had no idea how to answer at first. But then I began to speak, and the words, starting as the merest thread of a trickle, became a flood.

Hilarius listened in silence, nodding every so often, and then, at the end, reached out his hand to me, not touching me, but offering his palm for comfort. And I took his hand and cried into it, holding it against my forehead, the agony draining from me, little by little.

"Severiana... I can call you that? Will you let me talk to your husband, and see what I can do?"

I looked up at the ceiling. "What can anyone do? His wounds have destroyed him!"

"Perhaps I can do nothing. But will you let me try?"

I looked at Helena helplessly. She cocked her head to one side, and then the other. "Hilarius has done surprising things. Let him try. What harm would it do?"

I so remembered those words, later.

"What are you going to do?"

He smiled at me, and his smile was genuinely charming. "I can't do miracles. I can't heal broken bones and minds by magic. But I find that telling people about things that comfort them, about chances for salvation, these can often help. They can bring peace to a wrecked man, like your husband."

Salvation? What a strange word, I thought. What does that mean?

+ + +

He came the next day, and I offered him wine and cakes, which he refused. "Let me talk to your husband. Julianus is his name? We'll just talk."

It was a cold day, but they sat in the atrium, wrapped in warm cloaks. I had the slaves put braziers between them, for the hypocaust did not warm the floor there, but they seemed hardly to notice. And indeed they talked, if talking there can be with only one person speaking, and the other staring listlessly into the distance. Hilarius stayed for as long as an hour, which surprised me; and then he left. It was dark by that time, and I naturally offered to send a slave with him to light his way home. But he refused. "Why have a poor man go out in the sleet with me? I have no choice. But let him stay warm."

What a strange man, I thought. Why would he care about a slave? I'm not cruel to my servants, but what else are they here for but to do the tasks we give them?

He came the next day, and the next, and the one after that. And for all those days, Julianus said nothing. On the fourth day, Hilarius brought a book with him, and began reading from it to him. I didn't bother to listen, though how much I regretted later that I never had! I could hear it was in Greek, which of course Julianus understood as well as any educated person. That was all I knew. But that was when things began to change.

+ + +

A week later, Hilarius came to me, and asked if he could take Julianus away for an hour or two.

"Where are you taking him?"

"To meet with people who might help. People he might join with, to heal his soul."

"What? Who are these people?"

"Come if you wish, and see for yourself."

I was sitting at my desk, writing to my family. I leaned back in frustration. "What are you doing to my husband?"

"Doing to him? I'm trying to help him, not harm him."

"Then tell me what you're doing!"

He did something very strange then, for he knelt down on the floor, and stretched out his arms to me, his palms parallel to the floor, as if I were a goddess. I could not believe what I was seeing. He looked down and said, "I swear to you. I wish only his best. I wish only his health. I wish only his well-being. Please believe me. The lady Helena has entrusted me with him, and I will never betray her faith in me."

"Then what do you want to do?"

"To have him meet people who have been hurt as badly as he has, though perhaps not in the same way. To have him talk with them. Perhaps to break bread and drink from a cup of wine with them. And just for a little while. Come with us too, if you want, if you are afraid we'll harm him."

There was too much strangeness here, and my hand threw down the stylus as if it had a mind of its own. "Well, go then! But *I* certainly don't want to!"

+ + +

From that day on, Julianus went with him every few days, and I could not but agree that he did seem calmer, less prone to sudden rages or deep depressions. I could even often say he was more at peace. But this did not make me feel better. I had no idea where the change came from, or how. My mood was not made better by the time of the year: Samonios[17] was to begin when the sun set today, and all know that during the first three days of that month, the ways to the underworld are opened, and those who are weak in their minds can be touched by good spirits and by bad. Even the strong can sometimes be taken. And Julianus's change had been too sudden, too inexplicable. I wondered if there was magic involved, and I feared for my husband, and for our household.

The city was busy today, as the preparations for the festival began. Everyone had gotten their mistletoe from the temple of the Horned God, to remind us that, even in this dark time of winter, life still continued. They had been bound to pine branches, ready to be placed at the doors as the sun set. And in the forum stood the bonfire whose lighting from the Horned God's new-kindled need-fire would signal that Samonios was upon us.

And it was on this day, in the afternoon, that Hilarius came again, and Julianus and he prepared to leave the house.

I had had enough. I called the majordomo. "Do you know a slave who's good at not being seen?"

He began to laugh, as if at a joke, then bowed his head and made his face a model of seriousness. "I know the perfect one, Domina. He's the one who spends all his time looking after the Master's books."

I guessed why he was laughing. "Then have him follow the Master, and find out where he and Hilarius go. Find out, if he can, why they go there, and what they do there. Tell him he must *not* let himself be noticed. And tell him there will be a good addition to his *peculium*[18] if he tells me everything I want to know, and remains undiscovered."

He bowed, and I began my wait.

The slave had not yet returned when it was time to go out to get the new year's fire. As the sun began to set, while the light was still enough for us to see by, the houses began to empty, and the streets filled with people. At least one person came from each house, carrying an unlit torch, and often many, for all fires had been put out, all lamps extinguished, and they could only be rekindled from the fire that the priests of the Horned God would light. I went with them, all of us who could, dressed in the white which honors the Dead, surrounded

---

[17] A Celtic festival marking the end of the harvest season and beginning of winter or "darker half" of the year.

[18] A peculium was the sum of money a Roman slave was allowed to collect in order to buy his freedom.

by four of my slaves, two men and two women, unlit torches in their hands too. I could have stayed home, but I had never done so in all my young life, even when I was a child with my aunt and stepmother, and I had no plan to do so now, even though my heart was occupied with what I might find out when I returned home.

There was no music or laughing, for this was the festival of spirits, but the rivers of people talked and held their children's hands as they walked. There would be a feast honoring those who had gone to the underworld when they went home, and offerings at their graves tomorrow. I would honor my grandmother, as well as the mother and father I had never known, and I would cry, as I always did, that I had not been given that blessing.

We reached the forum, and we waited. No one had brought food of any kind, for no one could eat until the house fires were re-lit. But we talked. Near me were some women I had come to know in Eburacum, some when I was with Helena, and we exchanged gossip. One of them had news that made my heart jump with pleasure: "The XX Valeria Victrix is being brought south. Did you know that?"

"No," I said. "That's my brother's legion! How lovely!"

She smiled with me, and then the sun set, and silence came over the crowd.

The ceremony is not long. The priests wear headdresses with horns like the god's, and the ritual is entirely in British, or so I had always heard: the language is so archaic that few now understand it. But by its sound, it was indeed British. And then, a priest bears a burning torch from the temple where a flame has been kindled without iron, and touches it to the base of the fire. Everyone watches carefully: it's a bad omen if the fire does not ignite immediately. But this year it did. The bones of slaughtered cattle were thrown into the fire: no living creature is sacrificed at this time: it would draw the spirits who are now gathered as life departed, for the dead yearn to be alive again, and fresh blood is like water to a man dying of thirst for them.

The crowd roared with exaltation, as the priests walked sunwise around the fire, and we all followed them, to light our torches at the flames as we finished our circuit. And then we walked home, the torches carried high. When we reached my home, we walked around it sunwise once more, and then entered, to light the lamps and the kitchen fire and the hypocaust from the torches we brought. The mistletoe and branches were placed at the entrances; and Samonios was upon us. For each of the next three nights we would eat a meal in honor of the dead.

I saw Julianus before I saw my spy. I heard him enter, and I hurried to the entrance to see him come in.

"Welcome home, Julianus. You didn't come to the Samonios fire with me."

I saw what I thought was a look of distaste on his face. I had no idea how to interpret that. "You came last year…"

His face was inscrutable. "Things change, Severiana. I won't be coming from now on."

I stared at him. "What's happened?"

He stared back, then shook his head, and walked away to his cubicle.

"Will you come for the Night-Meal? You know I need to honor my parents."

He turned furiously. "No! This is a feast for demons!"

"What?" I said incredulously, suddenly angry. That word again, like Helena. "What? A feast to honor my father and mother a feast for demons? My *mother and father*?"

"Yes!" he said, and flung himself away.

When I could control myself, I called for the majordomo. "Where is that slave? Is he back?"

"He is, domina. Let me get him."

When the slave came in, he was clearly terrified, and he fell to his knees in front of me.

"Tell me," I said. "Where did the Master go?"

"Domina, I am afraid to tell you!"

My heart sank. "Tell me."

The majordomo spoke, comfortingly. "Tell the Lady. You have nothing to fear, if you tell the truth."

The man was terrified. "Domina! The Master went to a house in the poorest part of the city. I asked the people around who went there, and a woman whispered that it was where Christians went for their rituals. Another man heard me and could see I was shocked, for they drink blood and eat human flesh. He laughed at me. 'We do nothing bad. You want to see what we do? Come with me. You'll be safe.' I couldn't understand why he wasn't afraid. But he laughed when I asked. 'We're protected by the Emperor himself,' he said. 'The Lady Helena is one of us.' I didn't want to go in, I was afraid. But if I was to find out about the Master for you, I had to. So I let him take me in.

"I saw them, and the Master, enter with others. There was a ritual, and they were blessed and called *catechumeni*. The Master too! I've never heard the word before, but the man told me that it meant they were now learning to be

Christians, but not yet blessed by the water that takes away their sins. I didn't see any water. But that's what they told me!"

I said nothing. I knew only that I was sick to my heart, and furious too. This was how Helena believed she was helping me, by making my husband a member of a criminal sect?

"Add 200 denarii to this man's peculium."

This was very generous, but I didn't wait to accept the slave's gratitude. I felt too angry and betrayed.

I needed to talk to Licinianus. I thanked the gods that he was coming back.

# CHAPTER 19

## Licinianus: Reunion

I arrived on the outskirts of Eburacum, on a cold winter's day, with sleet falling heavily and flakes of snow beginning in the air. It was late winter, and I was in some ways happy, and in others not. I was not unhappy with being seconded away from my legion to the staff of the Emperor's son: more and more the army was shifting away from legions to more flexible formations, but I had made some friends. I was certainly glad to be away from the fighting, and especially glad to be away from the unrelenting and merciless punitive attacks we were launching. But I had come to find a certain joy in battle which, once, I would have seen as inconceivable. And for that change in me I was by no means happy, even while I craved it, and understood its source: what one does well, one comes to like. I wished I had known my father, for it was said he had felt the same conflict in his time, and, as I sheltered under my icy, sodden cloak, I vowed I would make a sacrifice to his manes when I returned to Oak River.

I was leading a much-depleted cohort back to Eburacum, one which had lost most of its men in an ill-judged raid up north and needed now to be reconstituted. We were all exhausted. There was no hurry, but a cup of heated wine and some food would do us all good right now. But where would we find a place outside a military barracks that could serve 130 men? I decided sadly that, good idea though it was, we would have to finish our march unrefreshed.

I was wrong. As we passed by an inn, a man ran out, shouting and calling to us. I hesitated, but then called a halt, wondering what he wanted, feeling the icy sleet running down my face. I was irritated. I wanted to finish this journey as soon as possible.

"Tribune!" He called. "Tribune!"

"What?" I said harshly. "What are you holding me up for?"

"Tribune! Do your men want food? To rest? To drink?"

"What?"

He raised his hands. "Sir! I am the organizer of the Collegium Pistorum in Eburacum. And this is our day of feast! But none have come! The weather...!"

I started laughing. "And what am I to do about that? Drag them from their beds?"

"Sir... the feast is prepared! Someone must eat it. I will be ruined if it's not paid for! If your men eat it, will the army pay for it?"

I shook my head, trying to understand… then I laughed more. I had no idea if the army would pay for it. But I thought that either the army would pay for it, or it would not, and either way, we would enjoy it. "Right wheel!" I called. "Into the Inn!"

I was still laughing as we entered the hall where the food was served. It was a wonderful meal: the collegia never stinted themselves. And the men had earned it, for they had suffered greatly.

We slept all together in the hall, and none complained at the hard floor, for we had been campaigning too long to feel anything but pleasure at just being warm again. And in the morning, after eating the remnants of the meal, and leaving a letter with the Collegium Master swearing that the army owed him for what we had eaten, we formed up and marched on. It took us only one hour to reach the barracks. We had been closer than we realized, and that made me feel a little guilty. But not for long.

I went to the bath, and felt wonderful to be clean again. Then I dressed in my warmest clothing – the sleet was now snow driven by a harsh wind – and told the Adiutor[19] that I could be found at my sister's house. I had missed her so much that I had no intention of waiting to see her.

I was frozen by the time I reached it, and the ostiarius failed to recognize me. After yelling at him and shivering for some minutes outside, my sister came to the door, and we fell into each other's arms.

The wind had risen to a downright howl by the time we sat down to dinner, and it was obvious I would be staying the night. I had no objection. We talked and laughed, and she gave me all the news from the Villa. Aurelia Paulina was being pursued by an older gentleman, to her annoyance… The drought had done damage to the crops, which had ripened too soon, and the yield had been bad… The grass had not grown well, and we had been forced to sell off cattle and horses. But the vines, though the harvest was small, had survived, and the grapes had turned into raisins from the heat. So we had been able to make a sweet wine from them which should sell well. It was not all bad, then.

The most interesting was the news from Numerianus, who was enamored of a girl he had met near the Villa. She gave me the letter to read:

> *I have been thinking about you and Licinianus up in the North.*
> *It has been very cold here, and my guess is that it's even colder there,*
> *so stay warm. Life is very boring at the Villa, and I have been spending*

---

[19] Loosely, Adjutant.

*most of my time in Londinium, where my work is. But recently I have been home a lot of the time. A new family has taken Senovarius's old villa, a man from the east with a daughter, who is very pretty. Her father is from Egypt, so the family is more Greek than Roman. The girl especially is very pleasant, but of course she is not suitable for a match, which, naturally, I am not considering. She has dark hair and nice eyes.*

We started laughing. We knew our brother, and why he was suddenly spending more time at the Villa. It was this girl, we knew.

"Looks like he's falling for her!" I said.

"It does! But he's too young yet! Our stepmother will soon put a stop to that!"

We laughed again, and drank to it.

How wonderful a conversation with someone you love feels! And this, my sister, was a person as close to me as a lover… except that our love was of the soul, not the body. But now our conversation turned to things more serious, for I put down my cup, I rose, and I walked to kneel beside her side of the couch. Then I took her hands in mine, and kissed the scars on her arm. "Thank you," I said.

"You know, then," she whispered. We often never needed to speak to know.

"Yes. Julianus told me. You saved me."

"I wanted you to live, and come back to me…"

"And I did."

"Was it a good thing I did?"

"Yes. I believe so. It gave me back my respect for myself. I had lost it. I felt worthless. I don't enjoy war… but it's so good to do something well, to feel the respect of others, and to know that I have something my father had!"

She started crying. "I have so worried that I did wrong!"

I took her in my arms, and the tears rose in my eyes too. We both knew that the gifts our family gods gave were not free. They had a price. So, we held each other close, and only when I heard a slight noise behind me did I move, with the speed of someone who had spent months in places where death was around every tree. I spun with my hand going to my dagger… which was not there. Before I had even thought, my hand had reached for a knife on the table. And I turned, with the blade ready.

But what faced me was no enemy. Instead it was a young girl with red hair bound up in curls around her face, in the mode that was then fashionable. She was wearing a pale tunic embroidered with yellow flowers, tight enough to show a budding figure, reaching down to her feet in their red dyed sandals. It was clear to me that this was no slave, but a well-bred woman, and I turned questioningly to my sister. And she started laughing, though her face was still wet with tears.

"You don't remember her?" she said. "You should! You sent her to me!"

Enlightenment struck. "This is the girl?" I said. "I can't believe it! She looks like a young Roman lady!"

What told me that she now knew enough Latin to understand me was that her face changed from surprise to anger.

"I am not Roman lady!" she said in accented Latin, and her voice was indignant. "The daughter of a chief of the Votadini I am, and I *never* be a Roman, which I hate!"

Her language was not entirely grammatical; but it was clear she was versed enough to understand, and to speak in our language.

I bowed towards her, and apologized. "It was just the surprise. Forgive me. When I last saw you, you were not as you now are."

She looked so resentful that now I started laughing. I was caught both ways. If I implied she had looked terrible when I last saw her, I was doomed; and if I implied she looked Roman now, I felt she might do me violence. I conceded the point, and suggested she join us on the stibadium, and have some wine and food.

"I have eat," she said stiffly, but Severiana coaxed her down, and poured her a cup of watered wine.

"She used not to like it," said Severiana. "But I suppose you get used to anything."

"Beer better," said Veldicca. I wondered if it was true. I felt she would have said it anyway. "But wine sweet," she added.

I was amazed to look at her, though. When I had last seen her, she had been thin almost to the point of starvation, and dressed in ragged clothes, her hair and body covered in the filth of her desperate flight and her father's. What a difference now… she was still a young girl on the cusp of womanhood, but you could see now she was well on the way, and unless I mistook things, she would be beautiful very soon. She almost was now.

She saw me looking at her critically and blushed, her chin lifting against me. I smiled. "Was I wrong to bring you here?" I spoke in British, but she replied in her struggling, accented Latin: "I not know. I am dead if you left me, and I think I like living again. Your sister … very kind to me. But…" she stumbled, "it very hard to live among my father's enemies."

I reached out and touched her hand. "We are not your enemies, here in this house," I said, speaking again in British, to make sure she understood. "We will treat you instead as if you are our own bone and blood."

I turned towards Severiana and whispered: "It's amazing how fast she's learned Latin. This is just in a few months!"

"She's a very smart girl," Severiana said. "Never forgets a word. She'll speak without an accent in a year."

When Veldicca had left, I could not help myself. "She is so pretty!"

Severiana gave me a sidelong look, and I hastily turned to more serious matters. "Everyone knows that Constantius is ill," she whispered, not wanting the slaves to hear such treasonous words. "And Helena has told me he's dying."

I shook my head. "What will happen then? No one knows. Will the emperor Galerius intervene and make sure that Severus becomes Emperor in the West?"

She leaned closer. "I think that Constantinus intends to try to seize power. I don't know it for sure… but I have met him often enough not to believe that he will simply hand over the purple to Severus because Galerius orders him to."

"Not when Galerius all but imprisoned him. But the soldiers will have to support him…"

"Yes. You would know better than I about that!"

I hesitated and drank some wine to give myself time to think. "The soldiers like and respect Constantius. They don't know a lot about Constantinus, though he led one arm of the invasion into Caledonia with credit. But they might well support him for his father's sake. If they do…"

"I don't like him, Licinianus. I don't like Constantinus at all! Or his friend Valerius Apollinaris!" She twisted her lips in distaste.

I had never heard that name before. But from the way she said it, I knew I needed to remember it.

"Civil war again," said Severiana bitterly. "I am so sick of it! We have been so spoiled under Diocletianus! Look at our father! Hardly a day in his life when he was not fighting a war during the Time of Troubles, against one pretender there, for another here! He spent so little time with our mother… and we know how much they missed one another. Aunt Flavilla and Aurelia Paulina both believe he died from plague because he had no will to live after he lost her. That's the price you'll now pay for your gift… and your life… eternal war."

She brushed away the tears from her eyes. "But you're alive! My dear brother is alive when I thought he had died! And I don't think you would be, without your gift..."

She hesitated. Then: "But there is worse to tell you, about Julianus..."

"I think I know. The doctor spoke to me. His mind was damaged by his wound."

She nodded, and then shook her head. "Yes... and no. His mind is damaged. And... though I had such high hopes, he doesn't seem to be getting any better. He has sudden spells of furious anger, he has spells of calmness, and – worst of all – he is sometimes the old Julianus! But that never lasts, and at times I fear for my life, Licinianus! I fear he might kill me!"

"Severiana, my soul, you can't live like this. If he hurt you... You must divorce him."

"I can't leave him. Sometimes I'm the only one who can calm him. And he is so lost, Licinianus! So lost! He knows what's happened to him. He just can't control it!"

"You need to divorce him, Severiana. He could hurt you... he has family who could take him..."

"No." And her voice was final. "I have two slaves who watch him night and day. They won't let him hurt me."

I had to accept it. And it was true, for if the Master or Mistress of a house is murdered, every slave in the house is tortured to death for their negligence. I cannot imagine a stronger incentive for them to ensure Severiana lived.

"But there's something perhaps worse," she said. "He's become a Christian!"

I was resting on my left elbow on the couch, facing her, and I almost fell backwards. We were talking of one of our own committing a capital crime here. And angering our gods! She told me all she knew.

"I can't believe Constantius's wife is one of them!"

"She is. And Constantius is sheltering them. Licinianus, they walk openly here in Eburacum! The Praeses leaves them alone, provided they do not insult the gods in public, ordered I suppose by Constantius; and they have a temple or gathering place or whatever they call it, known to everyone, where you can go if you wish. They make no attempt to hide it! I have no idea what we should do! Yet the Emperor Diocletianus has ordered that they recant or die!"

"Except that he has retired," I said. "Galerius rules in the East, and Constantius in the West. Diocletianus lives his life by the sea now, tending his cabbages in Illyria. Everyone knows he's not well. He won't try and return to power."

She closed her eyes. "The edict still stands, even if Constantius doesn't enforce it. Perhaps it's all to the good," she said. "I have no taste for seeing people executed, even if they follow such a vile god-denying religion."

I had no words at first. Then I said: "If the news got out about his Christianity, it could ruin our family! I think there's only one option if you won't divorce him... Take Julianus home. Take him south, to the Oak Villa, far away from this place. Where an Emperor lives, no one is safe, and they can change in the blink of an eye. Julianus may be secure now; but what will happen when Constantius dies, and perhaps Constantinus takes power? Will he listen to his mother, as his father has? Will he protect Christians? Will Severus or Galerius take over? No one can know. Everyone knows Julianus is no longer fit to serve in the Army. Leave this place... and do it soon!"

And she nodded.

If only she had.

# CHAPTER 20

## Licinianus: Conspiracy

I had been supposed to go north to Isurium to deal with the supplies the Augustus was stockpiling there, but the high winds and torrential rain, turned now into sleet and heavy snow and ice as the temperature fell, made the roads and fords impassable. So I was able to take two weeks off from my duties. By the time that was over, they had changed their minds, and told me I was to stay. I even received permission to stay at my sister's house. It was no wonder. Everyone was hunkering down in barracks and the Abos had broken its banks and flooded the lower levels of Eburacum. Fortunately, we lived nowhere near those: they were mainly inhabited by "Brittunculi" as many in the army contemptuously called them.

I'm one of those strange people who love storms. There is something wonderfully tumultuous about wind-driven rain and lightning and sheets of water pouring down... and snow is so beautiful... provided of course you are in a warm and snug place. A leaking leather tent or a chilly barracks, as I had discovered in my army life, was not the place to be. But my sister's house was very comfortable, with warm floors, a well-provisioned larder, and a decent library. Only Julianus was unhappy: he wanted to go and visit his Christian friends, and all of us were happy he could not, for they lived in the part of the town which had been flooded.

The rest of us played games... dice, ludus latrunculorum, and Duodecim Scripta, whose puns and jokes made us all laugh– except of course Veldicca, whose Latin was still not good enough. But she was determined, and soon became a decent player. She had the knack. For all except dice, we had to play each other one at a time, of course, since only two can play those games; and Julianus, once a good player, seemed no longer to be able to keep count in his head of the pieces, and abandoned the games in a fury that made us all stand back.

The games we played, though, were nothing. It was Veldicca I could not keep my eyes away from.

She was dressed as an upper-class Roman girl, her hair pulled up and arranged in curls around her forehead, and that day wore a green linen tunic, which reached to her ankles. It hung in soft folds to her high-belted waist, and more folds formed the sleeves. I thought it was charming, and wondered how a girl could be so pretty without doing anything at all. When she moved, I loved to watch her. The tendrils of her hair would come loose and tickle her neck, and she would flip them away impatiently with her long, elegant fingers. I thought how graceful she was. I tried not to be too obvious, but I would see Severiana giving me sidelong glances. She knew me too well.

And it did worry me. You must understand, I had never been struck by a woman before. I was not a virgin; but all I had experienced before was the affection that slave women provide. I had enjoyed the experiences very much, but it was purely physical: they cannot refuse you, so there is no closeness. Now, I was starting to fear I was falling in love. And, though she was not a slave, she was without question a most unsuitable choice for a wife, though at fifteen or so she was of a marriageable age. There were men who would simply have compelled her: she could not, after all, offer resistance to me, and I would suffer no consequences. But I realized how bitterly ashamed I would be if I did that. I had offered her safety and a place as a loving family-member. I would keep that promise, even if it killed me. And at times it seemed as if that was a real possibility.

I tried to act more distant, but I could not. Everything she did fascinated me, even her rapidly growing expertise in Latin. She insisted I correct her when she got something wrong, and she never needed to be told twice. She even asked me to help her with her reading. But the thought of sitting by her and doing this with her inches away was more than I could stand. I instead rented the slave a neighbor had bought to teach his son. I was astonished and delighted when I found out she had gotten the slave to teach her the Greek alphabet too. I would have loved to read Sappho with her; but of course, she had no Greek. So I read some poems to her, translating into British as I went. That did not go well: she wanted to sit close by me so I could point out the words I was reading, for she wanted to know more of the language. That was too much for me.

It made me think of my father, who had not wanted to live when my mother died bearing me and my sister. For the first time, I understood how a man can feel like that.

I was so disturbed that I almost wished for the weather to improve, so that I could go away to my post in Isurium. Except I really did not…

I worried also about my sister. She was so down in her spirits. There was scarcely a need to ask why: Julianus was like a madman sometimes, and I remember having to protect Veldicca from him when one of his moods overcame him, and his hatred of the Northerners made him turn on her. I genuinely believe he would have killed her in one of those times, if I or a burly slave had not been there to stop him.

The strange thing happened one day when I went out one day to report to the Praesidium, though it was bitter outside: an occasional visit was the price of my being allowed to stay off-barracks with my sister. I spent very little time there: my commanding officer was as eager as I was to get out of the cold draughts and the icy floors. Marble and mosaic floors look very pretty, but they are remarkably cold if there's no hypocaust under them!

As I was leaving, eager to get home, a man came up to me. I didn't recognize him, though there was something vaguely familiar about him, but by his cloak and boots and manner, he was obviously a soldier. His Latin was educated: this was not a common man.

"Licinianus," he said, as if he knew me.

I nodded, but warily. I knew no reason why he would want to talk to me.

He handed me a folded piece of papyrus. It was closed with my stepmother Aurelia Paulina's seal. Its content was brief:

*"Talk to this man."*

He raised his eyebrows, and I nodded.

"I know a caupona that has good wine, and even good things to eat. But best of all, it's warm."

He took me down an alley two streets from the praesidium, and came to a closed door. He opened it, and a wave of heat struck us, and cooking smells that were more than savory. The counter was impressive: there were eight dolia set into it, all filled with wines and food. The heated floor showed that this was not a run-of-the-mill place, and the prices on the walls reinforced that feeling. The poor would not be eating here.

"In Italia the cauponas are open to the street," the man commented affably. "We'd freeze our balls off if they did that here." He reached out a hand. "You don't remember me?"

I shook my head. "I don't think so."

"Think back. I brought a letter to you from the senior Augustus, and we rode back to Londinium together."

Suddenly I remembered. "I know! What was your name?"

"Milo."

"Yes, Milo! Nothing else?"

"It's enough. We have a delicate subject to talk about."

133

I took his hand, but reluctantly.

"I still don't know why you want to talk to me. Unless you have another letter to give me."

"No. Let me get you a drink instead."

He came back from the counter with a jug of hot wine, two cups, and a bowl of chick peas fried crisp in olive oil. He poured for us both.

I sipped my wine, my eyes widening in surprise. It was very good.

"Even the Praeses[20] comes here sometimes," he said, seeing my expression. "Best wine in Eburacum."

I was in no mood for small-talk. "Tell me what you want from me."

"You've heard of the Amici Carausii, I believe."

I leaned back. "Once I'd have said I've never heard of them. But I've seen those words come up too often recently. And clearly my family – or at least my stepmother – is somehow involved with them."

"Your family has been for years. Let me tell you about us."

He hesitated, as if wondering where to begin. Then: "We started as a group of supporters of the Emperor Carausius. Do you remember he called himself the Emperor of the North? That tells you his ambitions. Some say he wanted to be a joint Augustus with Diocletianus, but he really didn't. He had a narrower goal."

"Which was?"

"An independent Britannia. Not any longer part of the Empire. He held on to Gaul only as a precaution."

"Until he lost it," I said. And he nodded.

I leaned back. This was long past and done, but it still shocked me. To try to break away from the Empire... that was treason of the highest kind.

"Why did he want this? What good would that do?"

"What good? Think over the last hundred years, until at least Diocletianus became Emperor. One civil war after another! What did we have but constant civil war after Severus Alexander was murdered? Five Emperors in one year! Even in your lifetime, young as you are, you've seen five emperors come, and some of them go. Another cup?"

I nodded. I felt bemused.

"Look at your family. Aren't you a descendant of the divine Aurelianus?"

---

[20] Provincial governor.

"Yes. I and my sister."

"Of course, your sister too. And your stepmother... daughter of Emperor Carus, sister of Emperor Carinus, *damnationis memoriae*? Your family is in the thick of it all."

I took some more wine. "No, we are not in the thick of it. We just want to live peacefully. And what is this to me? At least since Diocletianus took power we've had peace."

"For how long? What happens when he dies? He's sick, you know, hardly able to work his cabbages in Aspalatum. His days are few. Have some chickpeas."

"Again, I don't understand what this has to do with me."

"Tell me... what happens here in Britannia each time a new pretender decides to make a bid for the throne? Doesn't matter if he's from the province or not, for the effects are the same. What happens?"

I shrugged. "Whoever's in charge takes the troops stationed here to go fight in the civil war."

"And do they come back?"

"Mostly, no."

"Which means that each time the number of troops here gets fewer. And Britannia becomes more and more defenseless. Once we had one of the largest concentrations of troops in the Empire. Now? How much longer do you think we have before all the barbarians realize this, and join to destroy us?"

"They just tried. And we punished them badly."

He laughed. "We made them hesitate for a while. In twenty years, they'll try again, and will the Empire care enough by then to help?"

I shook my head. He was right. I didn't know if it would. We seemed to be getting more isolated by the day.

He ate some more chickpeas. "So here's the question. Should we here in Britannia wait for our doom, or should we do something that will stop it?"

I suddenly knew what he meant. "You want to recreate Carausius's Empire of the North?"

He nodded. "We do. The Empire is failing. We need to look after our own. And in this case, that's Britannia. And what do you think Constantinus will do when his father dies, and the civil war starts?"

He smiled. "And you are right next to Constantinus."

What could I possibly say to that?

"I don't like Constantinus," I said. "And I agree that we'd be better off if we

135

were separate from the civil wars in the rest of the Empire. But his father is a good Emperor, and has done well by me."

"As I said… what happens when he dies? Do you loyally serve his unpleasant son too, as he drains this land of its soldiers to make himself Emperor of all? And when the Saxons and White Shields seize their chance and burn your lands and take your women?"

He leaned forward. "Carausius has a living son… and your family saved him…" he said. His eye cocked, as if amused. "Remember Artorius?"

+ + +

I walked back to my sister's house deep in thought. Milo had made no offers, but his aim was clear. He wanted me to join the Amici, and he wanted me to be part of their conspiracy.

I shivered at the thought of what this could do to my family. I had refused, of course, but even the thought sent fear through me. Those who attacked an Emperor rarely died well, and nor did their close relatives. I was not about to join this conspiracy, though clearly my stepmother already had. That, too, frightened me. We could all die horrible deaths even if I did nothing. My sister, my aunt, my stepmother, my brother… all of us… I was not sure if it was even possible for us to evade this plot now.

I reached my sister's house, and banged loudly for the ostiarius to let me in. As I walked in, I heard the noise: loud shouting, the screams of my sister and Veldicca, and the grunts of men struggling. I began to run.

I reached the peristyle, and saw a knot of men struggling in the bitter cold.

At first I couldn't figure out what was happening, and then realized that at the heart of the group was Julianus, and he was wielding a pugio, and struggling to get free of two slaves who were holding him. To one side were Severiana, and Veldicca. There was blood on her cloak.

I raced to the group of men, and the three of us manhandled Julianus to the floor.

"Bind him," I shouted, dragging the dagger from his hand. "He's not sane!"

"She's a demon," he was panting as he fought, "a demon from the North! She must be killed or she will give us over to evil!"

I helped the slaves drag him to a cubicula, where we tied him to the bed, locking the door.

"What happened?" I asked. Veldicca and my sister were now in the tablinum, with the doors closed against the cold. Severiana's maid was binding up Veldicca's arm.

"How is she?" I asked. I could not see the wound, and I was anxious.

"It's a small cut, Dominus," said the slave woman. "I've washed it with wine and put honey on it. It will keep the wound sweet."

I looked at my sister. "What happened?"

She was crying. "He suddenly took after Veldicca. There was no warning. He stabbed at her. If the slaves hadn't been there, I don't know what would have happened."

I went over to Veldicca. It was so strange how anxious I felt about her. "Are you alright?"

There were tears in her eyes too. "I'm fine… hardly hurt. I'm just so sad that he sees me as so evil." She burst into tears, and before I could think of the consequences, I took her in my arms, cradled her head, and without thinking I found myself kissing her shining hair. I stopped immediately I realized what I was doing. But Severiana had already seen me.

I turned to my sister. "This ends it. You must divorce him. It's no longer safe. And you must go home."

I went over to Severiana. "You *must* do this! It's not safe here for you!"

# CHAPTER 21
## Severiana: Shame

I don't know why I took so long to make my plans to leave Eburacum. I've always tended to put things off, I suppose, and I was hesitant to tell Helena that I was leaving. I justified all this by the complexity of the arrangements I had to make, and I wanted to stay until Licinianus had to leave. But eventually, he was called away to Isurium, and was to be gone for months.

Yet still it was two weeks more before I was ready, because I could not make up my mind about Julianus. I knew I should divorce him, and send him back to his family for care. But I hardly knew them, and the memory of the wonderful man he used to be stopped me. In the end I knew I could not bear to abandon him, and I decided to take him with me, no matter the danger.

But something else caused the real damage, the damage that changed my life, and the lives of so many others. I often think that tiny things decide your destiny, even though you see them as nothing at the time. In this case it was something almost absurd: on the day I had decided to visit Helena and tell her I was leaving, I could not find the amber necklace I wanted to wear with my pale yellow stola. If I look back now, of course, it's clear that the huge fuss I made had little to do with the necklace. I simply didn't want to go. But nevertheless, it was hours later when the necklace was found, with the slave girls in tears and myself unjustifiably angered with them long before then, and instead of the visit occurring in early afternoon, it was late when I set off, and the sun was about to set, for it was winter, and the days were short.

That mislaid necklace changed my life. No… It's true to say that, but not enough: it changed many people's lives. It changed the world.

It was cold, and a wind blew, but the day was not miserable, for the sky was clear, and no rain or snow was falling, nor was there mist. The streets were almost empty, for most were at home keeping warm, and the intentionally staggered slap-slap-slap of my litter-bearers' boots on the cold stones of the roadway was all I heard as we headed for the Basilica.

There were black alder trees that grew around the Principia, old trees, dark grey and fissured, their branches bare of leaves in winter. I remembered the little doll I had had as a young girl, its wood white when it was carved, but slowly turning to red, as alder always does. I have it still. The roads leading to the building were like gorges which channeled the wind, and all that they touched was chilled.

The sun was setting, but the building was not dark, for light shone from it everywhere. It was as if it was to be a shining symbol of what was not, outside in the winter landscape. Even the sentries were outlined in flaring torches, against the paleness of the building's limestone blocks. It frightened me, as this was not normal; but I went forward, and the soldiers let me through, for they knew me.

As I entered, I could hear the sound of male voices talking loudly and of music, all coming from one side of the building. I had been here often enough to know where Helena's apartments were, and I thankfully headed in the opposite direction to the sounds. I was sorry now that I'd come, and I intended to make my farewell and apologies, and leave quickly.

I waited as I was announced, and then her personal slave, an older woman she had known from childhood, ushered me in. The wind was rising outside, and Helena was standing looking out the window as the sun set. Her face was not just somber, but tinged with anger, and I quickly learned why.

"My husband is so sick he cannot rise from his bed... and my Constantinus's friends have given him a feast!"

This was not the greeting I had expected.

"What do I do, Severiana? If I could, I would send his friends to the place where the demons hold sway... but my husband says he must be allowed to be a young man, with a young man's foolishnesses! But they will ruin him! If he is to succeed his father, do we want another Nero? Another *Caligula*?"

She could hardly control her anger, but I could see that even she felt that she had gone too far, for her eyes were wary, as if wondering if I was safe to be sharing such a confidence. You do not talk of an Emperor's death lightly. And though she was clearly referring to Hades, she had not used that word, which confirmed everything I already knew and feared.

She brushed herself as if from an offensive insect, walked away from the window, and sat down. "This is an odd time for you to come, Severiana. I'm glad to see you. But is there a reason?"

"Yes, Domina," I said. "I'm going home, to my family, and I wanted to wish you well."

"Going home? You mean to your childhood home? Why? I was hoping you'd stay here until..."

She stopped. But I knew what she meant.

"Julianus is not in good health, and I fear that he never again may be. I think he would be better in my home. It's a very peaceful place, in beautiful, peaceful country. And we have the best horses in our pastures. He always loved riding. Perhaps he will again."

"You could wait until Spring… the roads are terrible at this time."

I bent my head and spoke to the floor, quietly. "I wish to go home."

I heard silence. Then: "Hilarius. That is the reason, isn't it?"

I didn't want to answer. I wanted to deny it. And indeed, it was not all the answer. There was more to it than that. I could not stop myself, as I felt my anger rise. But I kept control of myself.

"He's not well. He's not sane. And I think he never will be again. But he has become a Christian, even though he's not capable of making that decision by his own free will."

"Of course he was! He was called," she whispered, as if imparting a secret.

"What? Called by whom?"

"By God, and his divine son."

She believed this?

"And my gods, Domina? They don't matter?"

Her face was so intense. "They matter. But they are demons! Only God and Christ are real gods! Only *they* call us to what is good!"

I leaned back, horrified. Our gods, who had given so much to our family, were demons? Litavis, who had promised me the gift of life for children? Cicoluis, who had given my brother the gift of war, and so saved him from death in the north?

I was shaking, with a mixture of horror and anger. To say this to me was blasphemy, and denied all I believed in, all that our family believed in.

I stood up. "I think I should leave, Domina. I wished merely to bid you farewell."

She grasped my arm, and held me back. "You need to listen!"

A wave of raucous noise came from the feast in the other wing of the Praetoria, as if to mock her comment.

"The Christ is here to save us! To grant us peace! To bring us to salvation!"

"Thank you, Domina, but I must go."

She stood straight, and said: "Severiana, I have grown to be very fond of you. And from what I have heard and seen of your brother, he is a good man too. But you don't realize how your family gods are bringing you to damnation. They are false, they belong to the underworld, and they will take you to their home, in the dark. The Christ can save you. Let him do so!"

140

"Save us from what? What do you mean?"

"Save you from sin!"

"Sin?" I didn't even really know what she meant by that word, for she used the Greek *hamartia*. "My brother and I? My aunt? My stepmother?" I knew my voice was shaking, for I was filled with anger. "What are we guilty of that we need to be saved from it? What have we done to earn damnation? Not believing in your dead god?"

Now she was no longer calm. "Dead? No! He died as a man but he is eternal! And I am trying to bring you to him to save you and yours!"

I was furious. She made as nothing what my family had lived for, supported, loved, treasured. "No! I hold true to my gods! I respect you, Lady Helena, but your Christ is not for me! And he never will be!"

I turned, the tears streaming from my eyes, and ran and ran, with her calling out to me, her voice fading yet going shriller with anger as I left her behind.

I was so upset that I didn't realize where I was going, until suddenly I turned a corner, and was in a corridor leading to a room filled with men and noise. For a moment I had no idea where I was; and then I realized that I was about to enter the area where the men were carousing. My breath caught in fear, and I began to turn, and run in the opposite direction. But a hard male hand caught me, and spun me around, and I saw it was Valerius Avilius Apollinaris.

There is no one I would have rather less have seen, but I could not escape. And now he was calling: "Constantinus! Look who has come to join us! The lady Severiana!"

He was drunk. Everyone here was drunk, including Constantinus, and now they were clustered around me. And they were looking at me in a way that every woman knows... the look of men beholding their prey. I knew I had to get out of here as quickly as I could, for I was in dreadful danger. These were all powerful men, men used to taking what they wanted, knowing there would be no consequences. I tried with my best weapon: "I am looking for the Lady Helena. She asked me to come!"

A lie, but the best I could do, and it did make them pause. But not for long. I could see that his mother's name had made Constantinus angry.

"Oh, yes, your mother's young friend!" I knew the voice. It belonged to Apollinaris. "Of course! No need to hurry to her! Stay with us and drink a cup of wine. Let's go into this room here, away from the noise!"

I struggled to go the other way, but Apollinaris grabbed me, and then I was surrounded, and they turned me as easily as a shepherd does a sheep in a pasture, and forced me in, acting as if they were doing so solicitously. But when three strong young men cluster around a woman, she moves whether she wants to or not.

There's no use acting as if I was anything other than terrified, and angry too, for I could not help thinking that they would not actually do what I feared to a woman of my status. I was no slave girl, or a prostitute. "No," I said. "No, I don't want to be here!" I tried to run, and they held me, and they laughed. I was their plaything, and they would not let it go.

I started screaming. But no one came.

+ + +

I have nothing more I wish to say about what then happened. I remember every single detail, though I wish I could forget it all. Sometimes at night I have nightmares about it. But I remember it. I remember that the last one tried, and then, looked around as if in terror. "We shouldn't!" he said. And they all backed away then, and on their faces was a sickened realization that they had done something that could well destroy them, if Helena or the Emperor heard.

I heard one of the men's voices, and I was surprised to hear not bravado in his voice, but a kind of chastened fear. He was swearing: "Madness, madness! Apollinaris! What have you made us do!"

I heard their voices arguing, as if from a distance. "You know who she is," the man was shouting. "We've made her family our enemy!"

"They wouldn't dare. Constantinus is an emperor's son!"

"Get her litter! Get her home! Do you think your mother isn't already being told?"

They wrapped my torn clothing around me, someone threw a man's cloak over me, and they picked me up, carrying me like a sack to the litter. I was crying, but not loudly, not screaming, filled only with a hopelessness from which there was no escape. I could never recover from this, once it was known. And if Julianus left me, I would never have another husband, if I should ever come to want such a thing, such a repulsive thing.

As I left, through my agony, I saw a man looking at me as if sympathetic, and on the walls of the Praesidium the scribble: "*Expectate veni.*" It made no sense to me, though I later remembered the coins Carausius had given me and my brother. And I cared nothing. I wanted to die.

I bathed immediately once I was home, sobbing still, hoping somehow to wash myself even inside from what they had done.

Useless.

There was no sleep for me that night. I was not even tired. I had reached that point where you are beyond it, beyond all emotion too, and you almost think that you are able to put it aside, except that when you try, something pulls you up short, warning you that there is something vile lurking, waiting to get you if you do.

There is something about what they did to me that makes a woman feel worthless. We spend our lives being appreciated because, perhaps, we are charming, or pretty, or amusing, attractive to men and an object of envy to other women, or, if we're lucky, loved and protected by our family. And we enjoy these things largely because we know that what we have, we can bestow on men or not, as we wish. We are powerful in our femaleness.

That was gone now. Whatever I was, whatever I had, could be taken by force.

The dawn came, and I watched the light grow, yellow because of the lowering clouds and the spitting hail. A slave-girl came to bring me my morning fare; I waved it to a table, left it untouched, and lay unmoving. I had bathed before I went to bed, but the bruises on my wrists and ankles and body were clear. I had long stopped crying. There was no need any more, and my eyes were drained.

Midmorning came, and with it, Helena.

She came right into my room, and I made no effort to rise. After what her son had done to me, she no longer merited that respect. So, instead of welcoming her, I stared at her, and waited for her voice. She surprised me, for she knelt by my bed, and began to cry, her head bowed into the blankets.

"I cannot say... I cannot express... the horror that I feel at what my son and his friends have done to you. There is no recompense possible... only my humiliation for my family, and my deepest anguish at what they did to you. I tell you truly; I love my son, but I will never forgive him for what he did. He will pay for it to the end of my days."

I could hardly speak; but I managed. "Your son? And his friends? Do you love them too?"

She reached down into her breast and drew forth three documents.

"This is a document of iniuria. All those involved in what happened last night have signed it, and it has been affirmed by three separate notaries. This gives their lives into your hands. If you choose to use it, you can beggar them, seize their property, all given to your family."

"And where do I go to get my honor back? Is there a court for that?"

She bent her head, weeping until her face ran. "No."

I read the signatures. "I notice one remarkable absence, my lady Helena."

Her eyes were steady on me. "He will be the next emperor."

"So he goes free."

"Not quite," she said.

She handed me an imperial note-of-hand. It was signed by the Emperor Constantius, and was for 50,000 aurei.

If I had not been so isolated from my emotions, I would have been furious. Instead, I said: "A gigantic sum. Do you think my family needs money? And that this recompenses me?"

She stood up. "No. Nothing can recompense you. But I can do no more."

"Not even an apology from him."

She stared long at me, and I knew the answer. He was to be emperor.

And then she handed me the third document. I read it through my tears. It was a diploma giving me the right to use the imperial mansios[21] to travel in Britannia. She wanted me gone.

Then she kissed me on my hand, as if I were her superior, and left.

I lay there for long hours, and in the evening Veldicca came, as I was crying again, as new tears had found themselves. She came to sit with me, and asked what had happened. Then I realized that I was bursting with emotions, of anger and shame and rage and anguish. I needed to talk to someone, but I could not tell my brother. I could not! It was so shameful! All I had was this young girl whom womanhood had not even touched. What would be the use?

But I told her anyway. And she told me about revenge as her tribesmen would do it. And its harshness and cruelty made me regret that I was not a member of the Northern tribes.

Yes, I would leave. But I would have my revenge if Fate gave me that chance. I would have my revenge!

---

[21] An inn and horse-changing station on a road maintained by the Imperial Government for those on official business. A document called a diploma gave the right to use them.

# CHAPTER 22

## Severiana: A Dangerous Road

I have no idea how I managed to function in the next few days, let alone organize the movement of the entire household from Eburacum to the South. I was lucky to have such efficient household servants; they did all the work, while I hid in my room and tried not to fall into anger, despair, tears... and most of all shame. I tried to act calmly with the slaves, to hide my humiliation; but in the end I found myself falling into fury at the slightest thing, or bursting into tears. So in the end I just hid.

I was lucky: Julianus seemed oddly eager to go south, into the new province of Maxima Caesariensis, where his uncle-in-law was Praeses.

The journey was miserable, for there was constant snow, or, failing that, a partial melting which turned the roads into places impossible for the animals drawing our carpenta, or the plaustra behind carrying our household goods and slaves, to find their feet. The fact that the weather was warming into Spring made it worse, for roads that melt into mud and then refreeze do not make for good travel. It would take us weeks to do the journey at this rate; in summer we could have done it in 10 days. I could not bear it. I used the Diploma Helena had given me, but I would almost rather have died in the chilled fields. I could only look forward to an endless succession of miserable mansios, the truculent imperial overseers running them, the disgusting fare. I suppose I was lucky. I had too many slaves with me and was clearly too high in status for them to display their rudeness too openly. But on the very first night I wished I were one of those who would set their slaves on to beat the insolent. Unfortunately, I am not, and at that time I felt not just uninclined, but unworthy. I was nothing anymore.

And Julianus? It was like he simply wasn't there. The furious rages were gone, but so was he. He was just a smiling man who seemed unconnected with anything except when he prayed to his new Christian god, as he did every day, for hours. I could not stand it, and moved to the second of our carpenta, where Veldicca and the maids were. He hardly even noticed, I think. His god had him fast.

+ + +

Not far from Eburacum, we were attacked.

145

None of us were expecting it. The northern marauders had been cleared from this region, and things had gone back to a relatively peaceful state. Here there was nothing like the widespread ravages of the Bagaudae in Gallia which had driven my grandfather to Britannia. Of course, there was the occasional robber, but against them I had hired three old soldiers who had received their honestae missiones, and were thus headed home to a deserved retirement. For them it was a good deal, especially in winter: they were paid for a journey they had to make anyway, with food and lodging along the road included. Along with the six slaves with me, three of whom were men, I felt safe enough. I would have felt even safer if Catigernus had been with me; but he was far to the south at the villa.

Yet I was not safe.

The first hint that there might be something wrong was that a group of mounted men rode up as we were leaving the mansio. Mounted men are nothing strange; many merchants prefer to move their goods on pack mules, which are much faster than carts. But these men had no mules, and they were all armed… well-armed. They had the look of imperial cavalry, but that worried me, for their shields lacked the signa of such troops. What men go about armed like soldiers and yet carry no sign of their ala with them? I began to feel fear, and I could see Veldicca did too.

The man who seemed to be their leader walked up to me, and spoke in an accented Latin that was clearly Dalmatian. That did not relieve my feelings; now I was certain he was a soldier.

He bowed, and did not seem at all unfriendly. "You're going south too I see. What's your destination?"

I felt my chin go up. "And may I ask why you wish to know?"

He moved his head from side to side. My accent had given me away. "No reason, Domina," showing that he knew my status. "It's not usual to find women traveling this early in the year."

"Ah," he said. "And would you be the wife of the Clarissimus Julianus? I understand he is going south with his wife."

"That is none of your business."

He nodded. "You must pardon me. I am sometimes too talkative for my own good."

And then he bowed again, and turned on his heel.

Now we were worried, and I told the head soldier of my concern. Not that we could do much against a detachment of soldiers – there were at least twenty of them – but I ordered that the slaves be armed with staves: little good that would do them against swords. And we asked one of the ex-soldiers to scout the road ahead of us, just in case.

I knew the futility of all this. If the riders meant harm against us, they would sweep us from the road like chaff. But I would not turn round. What was the purpose anyway? I felt as if I deserved whatever happened to me

We saw the riders disappear in front of us, and round the bend heading down the road to Petuaria. We followed, for we had no choice: this was the road that led to the ferry across the Abos, and from there on to Lindum.

As we settled into our carpentum, Veldicca turned to me, and said: "Where did they spend the night? It was almost as they were waiting for us." And she was clearly frightened.

It began quite peaceably, in late afternoon. We heard the sound of bridles and hooves approaching from behind us, and turned to see. That was not strange in and of itself. It may have been winter, but there were always some who had to journey all year round. But Veldicca was so alert after this morning that she jumped up to open the window and look back along the road.

"Riders!" she said.

"The same ones?"

"No! These are different! They're wearing birri![22]"

A horseman wearing that very hooded cloak came up to the side of the carpentum, and shouted at us: "The Domina Severiana?"

He didn't need an answer. He saw me. "This is them, boys! Take 'em!"

And his sword was out. I heard the choking scream of our driver as he took the blow, and saw him fall to the side as we moved on, the mules slowing down now that the reins were loose. I could hear the sounds of fighting all around us, as my few soldiers tried to fight back against a force three times our size. There was screaming as men fought one another, and died. And then the door opened, and the rider I had just seen was at it, grinning. "Now, ladies, it's your turn!"

I knew what that meant, and the thought of that happening again made me ill. Veldicca reached down, and threw the brazier we had glowing at our feet into his face.

He shouted in pain and anger and came at us; but then another rider came from in front of us, and the flat of his sword struck down at the man's hooded head. There was more screaming, more fighting, and then the noise died down,

---

[22] Hooded British cloaks.

leaving only the groans of the wounded. I felt so frightened I could barely move, but I needed to know what was happening, for things made no sense. I got down from the carpentum.

There were bodies everywhere. Two of my male slaves were dead, and two of the soldiers I had hired. But most of the men on the ground wore cloaks like the man whom I had just seen stricken down. The living ones… those were almost all men from the band I had seen this morning. They had saved us, and I had no idea why.

Their leader rode his horse up to me, and bowed as he had that morning. "Lady Severiana… I am glad to have been of service. I think these men were trying to kill you."

I felt the breath tighten in my throat, and I was shaking my head as if to deny the truth. "Who are you? And why would they want to kill me?"

"My name doesn't matter, though you may call me Milo," he said. "You only need to know that we are all Amici Carausii, and we owe your family a great debt, for you saved Carausius's son. But now let's answer your question for you." He turned to his men. "Build a fire. Just a small one will do."

He pointed at the man whom he had clubbed to the ground. "Fortunately for us, he's still alive. Unfortunately for him."

"Get inside the carpentum, my ladies, where it is warmer. It will be a little while before you can go on. We need ask some questions of this man."

"I'll stay here," I said. I felt a little steel come back into me.

He simply nodded, and we waited as one of my slave women refilled the brazier with fresh charcoal for our carpentum, rekindling it from the fire his men were making.

"There," Milo said. "That's hot enough." He beckoned the men who held the hooded rider. "Now," he said, "tell us who told you to kill this lady."

The hooded man looked terrified. "We were just going to rob them! That's all."

"You're a liar," said Milo. "I don't think this illustrious lady likes liars."

He laughed, and pointed at one of his men, who came up, carrying a burning brand. Two others held the hooded man, and a third dragged down his breeches.

"Sure you don't want to talk? No?"

"I can't! I'll die!"

"That's going to happen anyway." He nodded at the man with the brand, and the hooded man began to scream.

"More?"

"Please, please!"

"Yes, more, I see."

The screams of torment came again.

"I'll tell, I'll tell! It was Valerius Apollinaris, the Caesar's friend!"

"And did the Caesar know this?"

"Yes! He was there when we were told!"

"And you were to kill all?"

"Yes!"

"Ah," said Milo. He turned to me. "Do you know why the Caesar wanted you dead?"

"Yes," I said bitterly. "But how did *you* know this might happen?"

He smiled wryly. "Let me just say that a man in very high places knows what Constantinus is like, and is very sorry about what happened to you. Perhaps one day soon you'll meet him."

"But now," he said, "we must get you on your way. You have lost a few people and some of my men will take their place."

He turned to his men and made a quick gesture across his throat. I heard the choking and gurgling as the hooded man's throat was cut. All his men were already dead.

"We'll come with you the rest of the way," said Milo. "I don't believe they'll try again, but to be sure we'll stay with you."

He swung himself onto his horse. "In any case, I have business with your family."

+ + +

The day came when we finally crested the ridge, and there was the Oak Villa, the fields bare and frost-dusted, the vines rows of twisted naked stick-men, but smoke still rising from the chimneys of the kitchen and the bathhouse. We pulled into the space beside the barn my grandfather had built, and made our presence known.

The next few hours were agonizing. My aunt and stepmother welcomed me as we drove up, and I would once have been so comforted by their warmth, and their hugs and tears of welcome, muffled though they were by their thick winter clothing. They brought me in, gave me cups of mulled wine, and set the slaves heating the bathwater. But there was a horrible, horrible thing that happened then. I didn't want to enter the bath... I felt as if someone like me could not merit going into the hot water, though I yearned for it: it was water for cleansing, and I could never be cleansed. So I held back, until my aunt and stepmother made me tell what had happened. Their horror and anger almost broke me: Aunt Flavilla's face twisted in fury, my stepmother's rigid as granite.

"We will not let this pass," she hissed. And Flavilla nodded, and nodded again. "We will deal with this when your brother comes home. Oh, yes, we will deal with this! And to try to kill you, just to remove his crime from sight! Oh yes, our family will deal with this! And our friends!"

Just telling them made me feel better, and they coaxed me into the bath, and came in with me. I felt warm again for the first time in weeks.

# CHAPTER 23

## Licinianus: His god had him fast

It was late in the spring, and I was freed from my duties organizing the movement against the North in Isurium. The Votadini needed a finishing blow, and they were going to get it.

Those who have never served think that army-life is all battles and marching. But the main work of officers is not training the men: that the centurions handle more than competently. It's organizing the vast amount of stores an army needs if it is to march, the huge number of animals, not just horses for riding, but draft beasts, the wagons that will carry all this material, the men who will drive them. The work is relentless, and exhausting, but if badly done, a campaign will fail. And all this was being staged at Isurium. While I was there, I had learned that my sister had gone south to the Villa; and I was wondering if I should follow her, or just send a letter to my aunt and stepmother asking for news, for I had heard nothing from her.

Then the worst news came, all by itself. As I came from the Praetorium, a man sidled up to me, and I could see the mark of a helmet on his head: he was a soldier. But this was not Milo, as it had been before. He gave me a small piece of papyrus. Its contents were brief:

> "Your sister was attacked on her way home. Some did not want her to live, and we know why. But we protected her. Go to your home to see what happened, and talk to your stepmother about us.
> Amici Carausii.
> Destroy this."

I didn't hesitate. I asked for leave, and went south.

The weather was, as it had been all winter, miserable, but now in Spring it was unceasing rain and drizzle rather than cold that was the problem. I rode south with my slave Lugobelenos, accompanying a small group of cavalry heading to Londinium. The roads were not as dangerous as they had been, for the brigands who take advantage of bad times had mostly been cleared away by imperial troops, or run for cover for fear of the crosses that awaited them if they persisted. But every so often we'd pass by a desiccated, frozen body nailed up by the road, a sign of one who had not run fast enough. Those who are crucified in winter here in the north are lucky: they die quickly from the cold, and that's an easier death.

Twins like us cannot be separated long; it nags at us, for we are two halves of a single soul, and I was in a fever from the message I had received. It said she was alive; but had she been harmed?

I reached Londinium in the evening with a chilly drizzle to accompany me, and went to the Governor's Palace in hope of a bed. But meeting my uncle Aetius was not easy now that he was Praeses of the Province. The guards greeted me with suspicion, even though I was a Tribune, and implied that I should come back next day and line up with the rest of the supplicants for the Governor's favor. The family owned a house in Londinium, but I doubted I could stay there, for it was unlikely to be staffed in winter. So I was about to give up and see if I could find an inn, when an older centurion appeared and squinted at me in the torchlight.

"You said you were the Governor's nephew?"

I nodded, too weary now to care whether he believed me. He beckoned me in, and I gratefully entered the warmth of the entrance hall. He sat me down, and I actually fell asleep, only to be woken by Aetius shaking my shoulder.

"Ha," he said. "I thought you were in Eburacum!"

There is nothing like a hot bath after a long ride, and I experienced the pleasures of the imperial bureaucrat at the hands of a talented masseur who used perfumed oil, and enjoyed more than one cup of hot, honeyed wine as I was dressed in fresh, clean clothes for the first time in days.

As I said to Aetius at dinner that night, "I smell like I spent the day in a lupanar!"

His shoulders shook. "I assure you, my dear Licinianus, that 'brothel' is a rather good description of a governor's palace. Everyone is trying to sell themselves to the highest bidder, and it's my job to stop them."

"Are you successful?"

"Only partially. I've learned to accept that though one can produce good, the perfect is beyond the ability of all but gods."

He helped himself to another hardboiled egg, dribbled some garum onto it, and continued. "This is a difficult position to be in. The Vicarius of the whole Diocese is here, of course, so in some ways I have less independence than the other governors. But Eutropius is not the interfering kind, and he spends more of his time dealing – gingerly, I might add – with the imperials in Eburacum. My biggest problem is these damned Christians!"

I wanted to tell him about my contact with the Amici. But I hesitated, even though he was family: he owed loyalty to the Emperor, and I rather doubted the Amici felt the same. So I merely sipped my wine, and tasted some of the sausage, smoked in Lucanian style. "How is that?"

He spread his hands wide. "You know that the Emperor Diocletianus has banned the religion. In theory that means death by burning or the beasts for following their rites if you don't recant, and certainly if you spurn the Emperor. But none of the governors in Britannia enforce the edict, unless they have no choice. Constantius has made his wishes clear on that. But these Christians seem to yearn for death! So, every so often one of them will commit a sacrilege which we can't ignore, and... there you are. Another death sentence, which we have to reluctantly carry out! I've reached out to the leaders of these people, and begged them to keep control of their members... all to no good. Every couple of months, another martyr appears. And then we have the courts! If you're a Christian you can't petition them, since you won't swear by the gods, which means you're subject to judicial torture if you want to testify. I've had to silently rescue nobles from that outrage more than once."

"Are there many Christians?" I said. "I've never met any, unless you count a slave girl my sister once caught."

"No, very few. But they cause most of my problems! They just won't keep quiet!" He leaned forward. "But I don't think that has anything to do with what brought you south. You're going to the Villa?"

"Yes."

"And it's Severiana that brought you, I think."

"Yes. I've heard nothing from her for months. Do you know what's happened? I'm very worried."

Aetius shook his head. "That is the strange thing. Your aunt and stepmother will say nothing about what's happening. She came home, and the old Severiana was gone, it seems. Something happened in Eburacum, Licinianus... but it's so bad that everyone is keeping their mouth shut. Not even my wife will tell me."

+ + +

Aetius sent five cavalrymen to accompany me to the Villa. In early spring the Saxons never raided, but there were some runaway slaves who were believed to be about, and though the roads were as bad as you could expect at this season, we reached Oak Villa by sunset after an early start. I was soaked, but I was so worried after what I had heard, that I hardly noticed it. Lugobelenos too was sodden, and complaining in a low voice as he liked to do, in his amusing way. And the cavalrymen were talking about the pleasure that only dry warmth could bring, and eyeing me, wondering if I had a welcoming family.

It was Numerianus who saw us first, and he called out, to be joined by men of the estate armed with swords and shields. I was glad to see this: all Britannia had been beset by brigands this past year, and it was good to see my family prepared. I rode forward, shouting; and he recognized me, and laughed loud, running to meet me. I leaned down, and held him in my embrace as my horse skittered and pawed at the ground. We insulted one another, as males who care for one another do, and I dismounted. He led me inside, but not before I had made sure that the cavalrymen and Lugobelenos had been taken care of. They would have a good meal, wine, and a warm bed tonight.

"A bath?" Numerianus said.

"I should think so! I need to get rid of this mud, not to mention the smell of horse!"

"I'll join you in the bathhouse. But let me tell the women you're here! It is so good to see you! They'll be so happy!"

It was at the tip of my tongue to ask about Severiana, but now was not the time. Someone in the Villa was singing, a sad song in a high sweet voice, and it seemed to me it was in British, not Latin. I couldn't be sure. But I was sure that no slave sang like that.

+ + +

"She never eats with us anymore," said Aunt Flavilla. "Never. Always in her cubicle, always alone. She has lost so much weight! She is so frail now! I fear for her, I fear so much. I know what happened. But she still won't talk to me!"

"Happened?" I was horrified. "What happened? Tell me!"

"No. She must tell you."

I shook my head in frustration. "And Julianus?"

She shook her head. "I don't understand him. It's like he lives in a place many miles away from us. He seems to care nothing for anyone, even his wife. But he prays to that Christian god of his all the time!"

"He's mad?"

"Is there any other way to describe it?"

"Will she see me tomorrow?"

"I don't know. But speak to Veldicca first. She's the only one she talks to."

I raised my head quickly. "Veldicca?"

She laughed. "Men are supposed to be oblivious. And they are! You sent her to Severiana! The British girl, remember?"

"I know who she is," I said. "I could not ever forget her."

And for that comment, I received an odd look from my aunt.

"Come," she said, still keeping her weighing look. "Let's eat."

+ + +

I woke early from second sleep next morning, and found everyone still in bed, apart from the slaves who were stoking the hypocaust and beginning work in the kitchen. They had oiled olives there, which delighted me; I had missed them in the north. I took a bowl of them with some cheese, fresh bread and watered wine to the winter dining room; and there I came upon Severiana, my sister, all alone.

I can hardly describe my feelings when I saw her. She was so thin! I hardly recognized her, and I ran to her to take her in my arms. She tried to avoid me, which horrified me. This was my dear twin, my other half! I could not let her shun me like that, and I hugged her reluctant body to me.

I spoke to her, begging her to tell me what had happened to her, and her green eyes, as green as mine, turned away, as if they had cried too much already.

Then she spoke, in a slow, measured way, the vibrancy I knew as hers so recently utterly gone. "I'm glad to see you, my brother."

"Glad to see me? That's all? That's it?"

She began to cry, and she ran away. I tried to follow her, and then I realized that she was in agony, and I could only make it worse.

That was our first meeting, after months.

I looked for Veldicca.

Each time I saw her, she had changed. She was still very young, but now her Latin had improved a great deal, she spoke with only a slight accent, and she hardly made a mistake. And she was becoming more and more pretty. I will be frank: my breath caught when I saw her, and I remembered how sweet her hair smelled when I hugged her after Julianus's attack. I chose to speak to her in British, anyway, for I had the idea that I would learn more in the language of her childhood.

"I know what happened to her," she said. "And I can only say that it was the worst for a woman that you can imagine."

I kept still, for I could imagine the worst, and the thought of that happening to my sister made me know fury. I felt the god rising in me. *I wanted to kill.*

There was suddenly noise from the other side of the villa, and I heard my aunt's voices rising. I went to the audience room, and found my stepmother and aunt there, and Severiana too, which surprised me. I had thought nothing brought her out. But then I disentangled the distraught speech, and realized

155

what had done this. Julianus had been becoming more and more erratic, and now he had gone to Londinium. And his body-slave said that he had gone there to "witness".

No one knew what that meant. But all were sure it didn't bode well.

"Did he use the word 'testis'?" asked Aurelia Paulina.

"No, Domina. He used another word."

"Was it 'martys'?"

"It may have been, Domina."

She shook her head. She was so wealthy that she received regular letters from her factors and agents, describing what was going on with her properties in different provinces, and with the empire. If anyone knew what this meant, it would be her. It took her a while to speak, and when she did, her eyes were warily on Severiana, as if she was afraid what result her words would have on her.

"I understand these Christians very little," she said, and her words were so measured. "I hesitate to speak of them as if I knew what they do. But they have a – I don't know what to call it – 'a rite'? They demonstrate their faith by exposing themselves to judicial punishment by doing something sacrilegious. They call this being a 'witness'. And they always use the Greek word 'martys' for that." She added, as if in explanation: "This is an Eastern religion, so Greek is their common tongue."

Severiana spoke for the first time, and I heard in her voice for the first time a little of the old fire. "Where will he have gone to do this?"

"There's only one place," I said. "Londinium, where the Praeses is."

"Aetius!" said Flavilla. "He's going to make his own uncle kill him!" She turned to me. "Licinianus... Numerianus... You have to follow him and stop him! This is suicide! Get Catigernus!"

I turned to obey, and then stopped. "When did he leave?"

Aunt Flavilla shook her head. "Sometime yesterday. No one missed him... he keeps so to himself..."

I hoped we would be in time. But I doubted it.

+ + +

We were saddling the horses when a man rode up. I took no notice of him at first, but then he greeted me. At first I didn't recognize him; but then suddenly I did.

"Milo!" I said. surprised.

"Yes. A long way from Eburacum. But here I am."

My stepmother came forward. "He brought Severiana home after she was attacked on the road. He's been staying with us…"

Why? I wanted to ask.

I shouted angrily. "I know about the attack. But who was it? Who attacked her? Tell me!"

"Later!" said my stepmother. "When you get back from Londinium. That's more important now!"

She explained to Milo, and he sighed. "I've just come from Londinium," he said tiredly. "Back I will go with you. But can I have a fresh horse?"

We rode hard, the four of us, and as we reached the unpaved road to Noviomagus, we saw a lone rider behind us, racing to catch up. We reined in, and we realized who it was: Severiana. We didn't argue with her: she had the right, frail as she now was, and we waited for her to catch up. I said nothing to her, but I stayed at her side, afraid that she would fall; and a few miles later she swayed in her saddle and I caught her just in time. I scooped her up in my arms, and settled her in the saddle in front of me; and she let herself go limp against me as Catigernus grabbed the bridle of her horse. I kissed the top of her head, and I felt tears rise in my eyes, and anger in my heart.

This was insanity. She was too weak. But we kept on. We reached Londinium in the evening, with pauses when we walked the horses, and though they were tired by the time we got there, they were not wind-broken. We crossed the bridge across the Tamesis, and turned east to our town house. Aurelia Paulina had told us that, although it was not fully staffed, there were slaves enough there to at least provide a meal and a bed. So there we found rest, and there I put my sister to bed, to watch her fall asleep. I stayed by her all night, and when she woke, I had watered wine, and bread to soak in milk warmed on a brazier waiting for her, and little bits of tender cooked meat I had cut up, and I coaxed her to eat and drink as I fed her little by little. I think she had not eaten in a long while. And then she smiled, took my hand and placed it against her cheek, and fell asleep again. And I fell asleep next to her, leaning against the wall, my hand held fast.

+ + +

In the morning, the hard part came. Londinium is hardly Rome, but it is the biggest city in Britannia: there are tens of thousands of people there, and finding one man is no easy task. We knew why he was there, or thought we did; and that meant that there were only a few occasions that would suit him. So I went to the Governor's Palace once more, and this time the guards knew me. I learned very quickly why Julianus had chosen this time to come to Londinium. Tomorrow there would be sacrifices to all the gods of the area, including the Imperial Divi, to laud the advent of Spring. All the prominent people of the city would be there.

"Diocletianus ordered that all prominent people should make sacrifices to the gods," said Aetius. "But all the governors just look the other way if someone of note doesn't appear. Christians are small in number, but they have some important people among them. You know Constantius's feelings on this."

I nodded. "I don't think Julianus intends to sacrifice. But I am very sure he'll be there."

Aetius shook his head. "If he speaks up… if he performs sacrilege…"

"I know. So we must find him before he can. Can you help?"

He shrugged. "He's my nephew." He called out, and a slave appeared. "Get the Tribune of the city guard."

We waited until he came. "Severiana…" I said.

"I've heard."

"She's in such a bad way. You said you didn't know what happened to her?"

He shook his head. "I don't. Nothing. But something bad. And something connected to Constantius's family."

"His family…" I echoed, softly.

"I don't know more. Rumors. And money was paid to her by the Emperor. A huge amount of money. That Flavilla told me. That's all I know."

There was silence between us. "Money? Money?" I had been fearing the worst. Now I was sure of it.

He put his hand on my arm hastily. "Shhh. Nothing is safe here."

The tribune appeared, and saluted Aetius.

"Send out every man you can. Focus on the Christians. We must find a man before tomorrow. He is not to be harmed. These are his details…"

We sat there together in silence. Neither of us knew what to say about this terrible thing that was happening to our family.

"Has this anything to do with Severiana?" he said at last, as he refilled our cups.

"I don't believe so. I just don't understand this at all!"

A slave appeared, and bowed. "Dominus, a lady has appeared at the gate. She says she is your niece."

"*My* niece? Severiana?"

"I believe that is her name, dominus."

"Get her in here!"

She looked better and stronger today than yesterday, and her hair was brushed and pinned onto her head. I wondered who in our house, deprived as it was of slaves, had that skill, and had found clean clothes for her as well. But my heart lifted to see her. She was still as thin as a wraith, but in her eyes was a spark that told me she was coming back to us. I went to her, and put my arms around her, and this time she hugged me back.

"You need me," she said. "Or you won't understand."

She accepted a cup of watered wine, sipped, and then said. "You need to know this. After Julianus recovered from his wound, he was nothing like what he had been. Well, perhaps sometimes. But most of the time, no. Moody. Often angry. I had a slave sleep near me because I was afraid of him!" There were tears in her eyes. "And then the Lady Helena sent a Christian priest to talk to him..." She looked up. "Licinianus, Aetius... she is a Christian! I can't believe it, but she is! And she turned him. He was unhappy before, but he became a fanatic! He wouldn't even come near me anymore. Women, he said, were paths to the devil, because we make men lust for us!"

Aetius and I looked at each other. It was so alien to everything we had grown up with, especially in our family.

"What do they want then?" I asked. "That men and women never find joy in each other?"

She put her head in her hands. "I don't know. I don't know what they want. But it seems so... different from anything I was taught to want. I don't understand these people, and what they did to my poor husband!" Her shoulders shook. "He was such a kind man... and then after the battle..."

I so wanted to ask her more, for I was sure this was not the whole reason for her distress. But now was not the time.

Aetius said: "The penalty for sacrilege at the Imperial Ceremonies is being sent to the beasts. We *must* find him."

I said the unthinkable. "Or, if we can't, we must make sure..." I looked at him, and he nodded.

"Yes. We must make sure of that." He got up. "I'll give the orders." He started to leave. "Stay here tonight, both of you. It will make things simpler. I'll send a message to your fellows to come here."

The guards did not find Julianus, so they brought in the head of the Christian community that evening, as we were eating dinner. They called him an "overseer", I believe, though they used the Greek word *episkopos* for it.

He was not an old man, no more than forty or forty-five, his skin sallow, as if he came from the East. His accent in Latin seemed to show that too, as he bowed and gave his obeisance to the governor, and nodded to the rest of us at the table, for we were not reclining that evening.

He clearly knew why he was here, and spoke after he was called to. "I don't know where he is, governor. I'm not sure I would tell you if I did."

Aetius is not a proud or ungenerous man, but the sheer insolence of this utterance shocked him, and the guard beside the man struck him a blow to his face that sent him to his knees. "Be respectful, you Christian filth!"

The man slowly got up to his feet, and wiped the blood from his mouth. "I mean no disrespect, Governor. You have been a fair ruler to everyone, including us. But there are higher loyalties. My religion is greater to me than anything, and I would see it as a great evil if I stopped a fellow from witnessing to his faith."

"By killing himself?" asked Aetius incredulously.

"He believes, as I do, that sacrifice in this world will give him great rewards in the afterlife. Death is not the end to us."

"What is the end, then?" I asked.

"Witnessing for the Christ, and thus finding everlasting salvation."

"The Christ? Your crucified god?"

He nodded. "Yes. And his Father, the one god."

Aetius spoke up. "Do you understand that we mean no harm to this man? He's my nephew! We wish only to save him from a horrible death!"

The man shook his head. "You wish to save him from martyrdom, and thus eternal joy with God. Can you be sure that you are not depriving him of the greatest gift he could have?" He bowed his head. "I swear to you that I don't know where he is. That is the truth. But I wish him well, and I pray for his eternal life. I wish I were as brave."

+ + +

The next morning was one of the loveliest days we had had in a long while after weeks of rain. It was even warm, and there were just a few wisps of cloud in the blue sky. For the first time in a long while a cloak was superfluous. The sun gave us all the comfort we needed.

The soldiers were still scouring the city, but without result, and by the time the sun had risen high, the citizens of Londinium were gathering before the Governor's Palace. Sacrifices like this are times of feasting: the gods are given the life-force and the viscera, but the rest of the meat goes to those who gave the animals. Since in this case the governor was providing most of them, the population would eat meat today, more than they normally could afford in a month or more. So the mood was happy, itinerant sellers were out, trying to interest people in their wares, and huge braziers and spits had been placed to grill the meat as it came from the altars. Among the Greeks, I know, the sacrificing priests are also cooks; but that custom has never caught on with Romans. Amphorae of wine had been set out, with others containing clean water to mix it with, and there were musicians playing, and actors miming. When the sacrifices were over, dancing and laughing would begin, and there was to be a play in the city theatre. Gladiators were seen as inauspicious on a day like this, so there would be no fights in the amphitheater.

The sacrifices were due to begin at the fifth hour of the day, which at this time of the year would be before noon. That was only an hour or so from now.

We stood on the steps of the palace. "This is not good," said Catigernus. "What can we see from here?"

"We need to get into the crowd," said Numerianus. "He must be here somewhere, unless he's abandoned his plan."

"So, we split up," I said. "Each of us in a different direction. And if we find him, we call as loudly as we can for the guards. He may have lost his senses, but he's a strong man."

"What if we can't stop him?" said Catigernus.

I shook my head. "Being sent to the beasts is a horrible death."

No more was needed.

We moved off, and, soon we were lost to each other in the crowd. Only Milo and I were together.

I wandered through the thousands of people... the mothers with their children, the men with their families, the beggars with their piteous calls. A small girl tried to pick my pocket, and I smacked her hard, but left her alone, for she was young. A woman in a meretrix's toga offered to take me and Milo to a lupanar, with both girls and boys available for our delectation, or to take advantage of her own charms, if I wished; but that has never been my taste, and especially not that day. I did buy some sweet fried cheese balls in honey from a seller with a huge tray of them hanging from his neck, for I was oddly hungry; but that was all.

Behind me, the ceremonies in honor of the Augusti and their Caesars were beginning, and the prominent citizens were lining up to perform their sacrifices to the Imperial manes. I heard the priests and priestesses chanting, the horns and flutes blowing, Aetius's voice calling the people to the sacrifices. They were beginning, and after a while I could hear the calls of the sacrificers to the gods, and sense the copper-iron smell of blood shed on the ground, and spilling on the altars as the animals were sacrificed. The scent of roasting meat came perhaps a quarter hour later, as the animals were butchered and began to roast. I began to feel desperate, for I'd seen nothing of Julianus. I decided that, if Julianus were here, he would be in front, waiting his chance to act, and we forced my way through the crowd until we were near the altars.

There was nothing there that I could see but the prominent men of the city lining up to fulfill their obligation. And then, as a man walked up to sacrifice to the manes of the deified emperors, Milo grabbed my arm. "Is that him?"

We began to run, shouldering shocked people aside, men who turned in anger to feel themselves pushed aside. I leapt over a child, boy or girl, I never remembered. A man in a butcher's apron turned to me, his fists raised, and I smashed them aside, and left him lying on the flagstones bleeding. The god was in me.

In front of Julianus was a tall, thin, grey-haired man, dressed in fine clothes, with the gold ring of the senatorial class on his hand, along with their red shoes. His slaves led a cow to be sacrificed, a sign to all the world of his wealth. He moved forward as the priest of the Deified Emperors called for the next sacrifice. The priest took the halter of the beast, and he and the slave led it to the altar so that the blood would flow over it. He raised the knife.

I tried to force my way through the last few lines of people, Milo helping to push people aside, but I was not in time. And I heard Julianus say the words that condemned him, and take the actions which could not be forgiven. He threw himself forward, his voice calling loudly: "The demons are here! These are not gods! Human beings can never be gods! Emperors are not gods! Demons show themselves through these false images!"

And he threw himself against the altar heaving until it fell over, huge and heavy as it was. He spat on it. "Only the Christ and his father are real! Abandon those false gods, these demons!"

He still stood there, living. But he was in all ways that mattered dead. And tomorrow, or the next day, or the one after that, he would be eaten alive by the beasts. What he had done was too public, too unforgivable. He had defamed the manes of the Emperors of Rome, shamed the Augusti.

I saw Aetius looking at me, and perhaps I saw what I wanted to see; but I thought I saw tears. He had liked the Julianus who had once existed. And he made a slight stabbing gesture with his hand, and it was as if he were imploring me. I knew what to do, and I was still in the Dream; so I could do it.

There was no hurry now, and I walked through the people, who parted now before me, shocked at what they had seen. Julianus stood there, in front of the toppled opera, and his face was radiant, as if he had seen the Sun-God himself... except, of course, he had no belief in him. He was proud, happy, ecstatic. He had witnessed, as his fellows called it.

We walked up to him, and Milo took him by the upper arms, holding him helpless, as the god took me. Tears were in my eyes, for I loved this man, or what he had once been. And then, I took his hand and forced it down to the pugio in my military belt, and shouted, "No, no Julianus!" And I grasped the dagger, with his hand clasped around it, and stabbed upwards below his ribs, as I had been taught. Two inches is all that is needed. He took six, and started to fall, his heart bursting. And the god fell from me too, and I was alone, and weeping. Julianus's eyes were on me, and his other hand reached out towards me as if to touch my cheek. And then Milo let him go, and he fell.

# CHAPTER 24

## Licinianus: Vengeance

We took his body home the next day in a plaustrum Aetius had lent us, but with mules yoked instead of oxen. Severiana had collapsed, and was not dealing well with the world; so she rode in a carruca. There was no way we could return as fast as we had come, and the weather had turned rainy again, so we took two days to get home.

I had talked to Aetius before we left, and he had asked me about Julianus's death.

"He committed suicide?"

"He got my dagger, and stabbed himself to death. I didn't have time to stop him."

He looked at me for a long while. "That is what we will tell everyone then. I'll just say thank you. You have more steel than me."

"Not I," I said, and he took me in an embrace.

"Tell your stepmother I'll be home for the funeral next week."

We put Severiana to bed when we arrived, and I, my brother and my aunt and stepmother sat down to talk over dinner. To say we were somber is an understatement. Julianus had been a problem; now he had become a tragedy. And no one yet knew what to do about Severiana.

"I'll talk to her tomorrow. Now..." I took a jar of wine from a slave's hand, picked up my cup, and left for my cubicle. And there, with unwatered wine, I drank myself to sleep.

I woke up at dawn with a raging thirst, and lifted the jug of water to drink from it. Then, in the corner of my eye, I detected a flicker of movement, and, the dangers of life on the frontier having taught me well, my hand flashed over to where my dagger was, and grasped it.

Her voice was very soft, but I knew it so well, as if I myself had produced it. "It's just me."

I was still, saying nothing.

Her voice continued. "When I saw you kill Julianus, I realized that I had been cruel. I can't keep my misery and shame from you without hurting those I love best. So I came to you this morning. I waited for the sun to rise, because I wanted to do this in the light."

"I didn't kill Julianus..."

"There's no need to lie. You did. I know why you did it. To save him from the beasts."

I drank more from the water-jug.

"Now, I'm going to tell you what happened to make me as I now am. I want you to listen, and be silent as I do. This is what happened…"

And then she told me. "Two of them raped me," she said. "The third … they urged him to. But he wouldn't. But he did hold me down."

I have never known fury like this. I wanted to kill. I wanted to see these men's bellies slashed open. I wanted vengeance. This was my sister, my twin. And they had done this to her. Death? How could that be enough for those who had done this to her. My lovely, kind, sweet sister?

"You know who these men were?"

"Yes," she whispered. "Helena made them write to me abasing themselves for what they had done."

I have no idea how I managed to reply calmly. I so wanted to kill. "And I would guess all of them are high in Constantius's court."

"Yes." She lifted her chin. "One was Constantinus himself."

My fists balled, and I wanted to howl so loudly in fury and frustration that I would surely wake the household. I had to wait minutes before I could speak calmly again.

"You know our name," I said, "the name of our family."

"Yes."

"Say it to me."

"Vindex."

"And what does that mean?"

Her face was so open, so bereft. "It means avenger."

"This was an *iniuria* committed against you, and thus against our whole family. Because all of us are harmed, I could claim vengeance myself, as eldest male of the familia. But instead, I give you the choice. Do you want to turn away from this, or do you want vengeance?"

She bent her head, and began to cry. I waited. It took a long while before she could speak. "Will you take vengeance if I ask for it?"

"Yes. I will."

Her head bent again. And then she rose and her fists were balled in front of her and she shouted. "Then take it! I want vengeance! None should do this and escape!"

I bowed and kissed her hand.

"Then that is what we will do. You have the document listing these men? Bring it. We'll all go to the Temple. But let me talk to the others first."

"Will they agree? I'm afraid…"

"If they won't, then you and I will do it alone." I took her shoulders in my hands, almost shaking her. "We're not victims! Our family never has been, and never will be! We descend from the Great Aurelianus! And you are not a weak person to do nothing in the face of such an injury. You are strong! We are strong! Do you remember what we once read? *Adesse tamen deos iustae vindictae*,[23] Severiana," I said quoting Tacitus. "And we'll take as much of it as we can."

"On Constantinus?"

"Even on him, if we can."

"There is one thing more."

She paused.

"I am pregnant."

Then I did howl. The shame on our family was complete.

+ + +

On the evening of the next day, after the sun set, we gathered in the temple where my father and my mother lay, I, my sister, Numerianus and my stepmother and my aunt. Only the family could be there, in the cella with the priest and priestess, but Catigernus had joined us, though he had to stand outside, viewing the ceremony through the door.

We asked the god and goddess for ultio, for vengeance, and begged for their approval, for without it we could not go on. Six black cocks were sacrificed to the twin gods, one for each of the men, and one each for their death, for what we were calling for belonged to the night, not the day. Then we offered flowers, for this would be the end of this path, when all was done, and all was healed. Then we awaited the decision.

It came, and the priestess chanted from the altar, for vengeance is always given by the female side.

*"What you wish you may be given. But all that you ask has consequences. So be careful what you take. Let less suffice you. Read the names."*

We read them:

"Valerius Avilius Apollinaris."

---

[23] The gods are on the side of righteous vengeance.

*"Vindicta is given; His death and destruction is given as your choice."*

"Aufidius Candidus Rufinus"

*"Vindicta is given; His death and destruction is given as your choice."*

"Flavius Valerius Aurelius Constantinus"

*"Vindicta is given; his death and destruction is given as your choice, if you wish to change the world. Is that what you wish?"*

I had no idea what that meant. And I did not care.

"Yes!" I said.

*"Then it is granted to you, and all the good and evil that will follow."*

I felt fear then, for there was in me a deep foreboding. But we withdrew somberly, for we were determined, and we knew we had what we had asked for.

Later that night, my stepmother came up to me. "If we are to fulfill this burden, we need help, for Constantinus will surely be Augustus when his father dies. And there are men who want to see Britannia ruling itself. You have already met people who are from the Amici Carausii. They have long been bonded with our family, and it's time they knew you better. One of them is already here."

I knew it had to be Milo.

# CHAPTER 25

## Severiana: The funeral

I wondered how many women have taken two such tremendous blows as I just had, in such a short period of time? But when I caught myself in such thoughts, I felt shame at my weakness. I am a Vindex. Yes, we can be harmed, we can be brutalized, but we do not give in. And we do not sit idly feeling sorry for ourselves: we take vengeance. That I was determined to do... not to give in, but to overcome those who had done this to us, to make them pay!

And yet, in all this, there was an uncomfortable sense of relief. Julianus, my dear sweet, kind husband, had not died just a few days ago. He had died in battle in Valentia, months back. So now all I could remember was the Julianus that had existed before his wound. And I hated the Christians. I *hated* them!

That was why I decided that my husband must be buried the old way... burned on a pyre as his ancestors were, with all the rites that his ancestors had hewn to. He would not be buried, as the new custom was, for that was how Christians also dealt with their dead. Only my mother and father had not been sent on their way to the twilight land on a path lit by fire, for they needed to lie forever together in the temple.

All the family gathered the night that Julianus's body came home. He had been laid on the earth, as was customary, and called by name... and then he had been brought in to lie on a bier in the atrium, his body washed and anointed, dressed in his toga, and a coin placed in his mouth. I saw the single stab wound, I knew that he could never have done that to himself, and I leaned over and took Licinianus's hand tightly in my own to show I loved him still. A branch of pine had been placed on his breast, as was the custom in Britannia, for the pine is green all year round. But pine boughs are also the sign that a house is polluted by death. There he was left. We set up incense burners around the body, for we could not burn him until seven days had passed. It was winter, so he could have no flowers.

I cried daily, for myself, for my shame, for the young, energetic man Julianus had been when we first met him. I remembered how he had saved my whole family. There was really nothing to do but cry. Rage does not serve revenge.

Then, on the second day of his lying, there came something to jolt me from the fog I was living in.

The man who awakened me was unprepossessing: dressed plainly, but not poorly. And he came in a small two-wheeled covered carruca, large enough for a pair of passengers only, with two slaves riding behind. None but the wealthy traveled in such things, and then only for short distances. That told me they were from nearby, or relatively nearby, and that they were not poor.

The man bowed, hesitated, and then spoke. "I do not wish to intrude on your bereavement. My name is Audacianus Pollion Crescentius, and I am your neighbor. I've bought the villa Senovarius used to own."

He spoke with an accent that implied his native language was Greek, and from Egypt too.

Claudia Paulina had walked up now, and joined me with Aetius and my aunt. Licinianus and Veldicca also came up: the two were now spending a great deal of time together, I had noticed. My aunt spoke first: "Then we should welcome you as neighbors." She went on. "It is kind of you to make your presence known to us. Sadly, we cannot bring you into the villa, since it is polluted by death. So may we offer you some refreshments here in the vestibulum?"

"Thank you," Crescentius said. "But I'm afraid I have another purpose in coming here."

We all sat down outside the entrance, and soon a slave brought wine, water and small cakes. The day was a little chilly, and all of us huddled in our clothes. I doubted he would stay long. I hugged my cloak around me: my pregnancy was starting to show, and I would rather have been anywhere else than with strangers. I had entered a time of resignation, and I no longer spent hours in tears. But I knew my face was pinched and white, for my maid kept on urging me to color my cheeks, and in the mirror, I saw someone very different from what I remembered from before.

"It is tragic that your husband died as he did," said Crescentius. "But I see that you have a child to look forward to in the future to remember him by."

Everyone froze into rigidity. I felt the blood drain from my face, and fury strike like a spear. I half rose, and then I felt the steel of my stepmother's fingers gripping my arm, pulling me down again. I saw the bruises her fingers left when I undressed that night to go to bed: she must have held me very tightly indeed.

"Thank you for your kind comment," she said, entirely the Emperor's daughter, and Crescentius's mouth gaped a little at the ice in her voice, utterly unaware of what he had done.

"Now, neighbor," she went on. "May I ask why are you here, if not to greet us?"

169

I had managed to control myself, and could see his discomfort.

"Domina," he said, as if he were a slave, "It is a delicate matter."

He paused, and all of us waited.

"You know, I'm sure, that the Clarissimus Asclepiodotus Julianus had become a Christian."

"We are aware of that shame."

He shifted in his seat. "We do not believe it is a shame, domina. Indeed, we believe he died a martyr."

There was that Greek word again, I thought: a Christian who commits suicide for his faith.

Claudia Paulina raised her eyebrows. "You are Christians?"

"We are, domina."

"That is illegal. How do you know we will not report you?"

"That is not how I judge you."

"Do you know who this is?" And she pointed to Aetius. "Do you recognize him?"

Crescentius shook his head, bemused.

"This is Aetius, Praeses of this province. And you admit to being a Christian in front of him?"

I saw sudden fear in Crescentius's face. His mouth opened, and then closed. He had some steel in him.

"I believe what my god calls me to, my Lady. May I talk, dominus?"

He was addressing Aetius.

"We believe that death in the faith brings eternal life. And that is what we wish to discuss."

"Go on," said Licinianus. "Let us hear."

A wind had begun to blow, and suddenly there was a flurry of old dead leaves flying around us, the remains of last summer.

I know my brother. His voice was quiet, in a way that only he had. I knew how very dangerous that was.

Crescentius ran his palm across his mouth as if he was nervous. "It is reported that you intend his funeral to be the old way, by burning. We ask that you do it the new way, by burial."

Flavilla started forward in her chair, clearly angry now. "What? What right do you have to ask anything? We are his family! Who are you to even talk of this?"

I felt that Crescentius, while he might not be a brave man, was a determined one.

"I beg you to forgive me this. But I must ask. The Clarissimus was a Christian. And to us, the body must be preserved so that it may rise again on the day when God judges all. To burn him risks his hope of eternal life!"

I saw Licinianus stand up, and I had never seen him like this. If a person can shake with rage without moving, he managed to do it. Tanned though his face was, you could see it had deepened in color: the callus around his brow where his helmet had for so long shaded him from the sun showed it most. I heard Veldicca call his name softly.

But none of that mattered to me, for I was on my feet. I never even realized that I had moved, and was about to strike Crescentius in the face with my clenched fist. Veldicca caught my hand just in time to halt the blow, but she could not stop what I screamed at him. I was crying at the same time: "You dare come here and ask for this? You evil people! He is dead because of you! If he had never met you he would have never tried to commit sacrilege! He would be with us now, if it weren't for your vile cult!"

Looking back, it seemed utterly fitting that a drizzle had begun to fall. Crescentius had recoiled, and his face showed his fright. He knew that one word from my uncle would mean his death. How I hated him!

"Get off our land," Licinianus said. "Get off it, and never come back! If you do, I will kill you."

He said it so calmly, his anger now contained. But he meant every word of it.

When he had left, we all stood there, simply looking at one another. None of us knew what to say. This had been the most appalling intrusion on our family. What kind of people would do this?

But part of me was glad. I had been dragged out of the nightmare I was in by this insult. And that was good.

I looked at Numerianus, then, and saw that his face was white and anguished. And I suddenly remembered the letter he had sent to me in Eburacum before all this horror had come upon us, and how Licinianus and I had laughed at his clear interest in a new girl… whose father owned Senovarius's old villa.

+ + +

The night of the funeral finally came, and we prepared ourselves. Death is something that turns everything upside down: the women walk with their hair uncovered and loose, and the men cover their heads. The ancient words calling all to the funeral were uttered: *"Ollus Quiris lētō datus. Exsequiās, quibus est commodum, ire iam tempus est. Ollus ex aedibus effertur.[24]* " In the old days, the days of my grandfather, there would have been praeficae, women who would wail and scream at the death, clawing at their breasts… but not any longer. But the nenia was still sung, for that was how the gods were summoned to take this man to the underworld.

It was drizzling when Licinianus gave the oration, yet it was a good one, and we were all grateful for that. Julianus had been a lovely man before his mind was destroyed by a northern sword. And I cried bitterly, remembering the person I had come to love, and now had lost. I felt such anger that I had been shamed by others, and therefore that he had been. But that I would deal with when the time came.

We sacrificed a bull at his pyre, for he deserved it; and then the pyre was lit by Licinianus as the eldest surviving male of the family, being careful to make sure that he did not see the flames catch: that could make a soul stay, and such spirits are not good to have near a house. We ate the funeral feast, and then all were separately purified from the death. The pyre would burn through the night, consuming the body. Nothing remained now but to return to the villa to offer the lares a sacrifice of purification.

Julianus was gone. It was over.

But it was not. In the morning we heard excited voices talking in hasty British: "The pyre! Someone has defiled it!"

We ran down in our sleeping clothes to the atrium, where the slaves were.

"What is going on?" said my brother.

"Dominus! Someone has defiled the pyre and taken the Clarissimus's bones! None are there! All are gone!"

We all looked at each other, unable to believe it.

"Who? Who would do this?"

It was my stepmother's voice that I heard answering, though she was behind me and I could not see her.

"Only one kind of person would do this. Christians."

"But why?" I screamed. "Why would they want my dead husband's bones?"

"He was a martyr to them. They wanted his relics."

I felt the disgust rise in me, and I felt sick fury at the thought of how Julianus's poor remnants would be used by these creatures.

---

[24] This citizen has been surrendered to death. For those who find it convenient, it is now time to attend the funeral. He is being brought from his house.

# CHAPTER 26

## Severiana: Amici Carausii

Slaves are useful, but they are everywhere, and nothing can be kept secret from them. There was no language we could use: they all knew Latin, most knew British, and one or two even knew Greek. There was no place safe from their eyes and ears in the Villa. In the end, we went riding, and took no slaves with us. That alone was cause for their curiosity, but it could not be helped. We were about to talk high treason.

I remember that day very well, for it was then that the thing was decided, the decision that changed the world. So I'll list all who were there. My aunt Flavilla was, but not her husband: he was a good man, but could not be trusted with this, for he was a Praeses, and his loyalty might well lie elsewhere. My stepmother Claudia Aurelia was there. My brother was there, of course, for on him would depend so much. Catigernus was there; he had once been our slave, but that was a long time ago, and our loyalty to him was as powerful as his was to us. And then there was Milo. That was all: six people coming together to plan the fall of an emperor.

Numerianus was not there. He was gone to Londinium, in profound misery at the way that his mother had forbidden him to see Crescentius's daughter. Not that it mattered; she had told him that she would not marry any but a Christian. We felt he was better not involved in this, for we were unsure of where his heart lay.

In reality, of course, there were more of us, if you but counted what was growing in my belly. Sometimes I felt as if everyone was looking at me, seeing it; but of course, it was showing only to the observant. I was into my third month now, and even my morning sickness was gone. But in another month it would be obvious to all, and everyone would believe it was Julianus's child I bore. I hated it. And the night before I had told my stepmother that, as clearly as I could.

She had leaned forward and said: "Severiana... you don't know who the father is! It could be Julianus! You just don't *know*. How can you reject a child who has done nothing to earn your dislike, and may be from your husband?"

"It is not Julianus's!" I said. "We should expose him when he's born!"

These were just words spoken in anger; but my stepmother took them seriously. And now she was angry. "Expose a child who could be your husband's? Expose the grandchild of your parents, whoever the father is? Like they expose a slave's whom people do not wish to rear? That is *not* you, to talk like that! You should be ashamed of yourself! It would also curse our family! The Vindex do not kill children! And don't tell me you haven't thought to get rid of it already! I was told you were asking for rue and hellebore!"

"It failed!" I spat.

"Yes! I made sure of that! I'll talk no more until you stop speaking such vileness!"

"What? You did that?"

I was so angry I could barely speak. But the truth was that I had not drunk the potion. I could not. "Thank Cicoluis that my brother will take revenge for what happened!"

And then I was silent too, for I was indeed ashamed.

We rode to a hill overlooking a stream perhaps two miles from our villa, and dismounted, sitting on the grass in a circle.

"Today is more your decision than ours," said Milo. "The Friends will do what we will do, whatever you decide."

"Constantius is still emperor," said my stepmother.

"But not for long," I said. "He's dying. Helena told me."

Milo nodded. "And then Constantinus will become emperor, and again he will drain Britannia of its army to fight for those rights the other Augusti will refuse to give him. But we will do what we will do."

I was annoyed. "Who are you 'Friends' to decide? Where does *that* right come from?"

"Wait," said Aurelia Paulina to me, looking around at the others, then back at me. "Let me explain."

A look passed between her and Milo, and she nodded, as if to say yes. "I'm going to tell a long story, so bear with me, I beg you."

"Think back to when you were a little girl, and the Emperor Carausius came to our villa by the Oak River. You remember?"

I nodded.

"You were very young... and I don't think you ever knew what an...*impression*... he made on us. He seemed like a salvation."

She leaned forward. "We called him *Restitutor Britanniae*, the Restorer of Britain, and *Genius Britanniae*, the Spirit of Britain. Most important of all, we said: *Expectate veni*... 'Come, expected one.' Why did we do this?"

"I remember that," I said, suddenly struck by the memory of a day far in the past. "He gave me a coin with that on it! I still have it!"

"Yes, he did. But let me ask you. Did you ever wonder why Carausius came to our villa? He didn't come just to visit. He came to see me. He had heard that there was a plot to kill him, and all his family. He came to warn me."

She smiled wryly to herself, as if remembering the past. "I should say that we knew each other well. Yes, we were lovers... In another time, we might have married. There was a glow to the man that no woman with feelings could fail to be drawn to."

She reached out both hands, one to me, and one to Licinianus. "I want you to know... I never stopped loving your father. He was always – is still always – the first man in my life. But Carausius too was a lovely man. You must forgive me."

I wanted to speak, to tell her that no one would blame her, for my father was so long dead. But she put her finger to her lips, and I subsided.

"To be subject to constant plots and conspiracies is part of being an Emperor. He knew that. All of us here know Britannia, all of us love this place. I came here for my beloved, your father. But it's home to me now, and what I saw before I left Rome made me feel such contempt for what it has become. Carausius too had come to love this island. He was afraid of what would happen to Britannia if he were murdered.

"Both of us agreed that the Empire was dying, though it seemed an almost impossible thought. Carausius and I talked long about that. Diocletian had staved off the end, after the never-ending chaos that preceded him, but what did we have now? His solution to the threats from outside was to divide the Empire into pieces, each ruled by Caesars and Augusti... But was this not a recipe for constant conflict? How can this not lead to civil war again and again between Emperors, as each tries to become the only one? Year by year, more of our soldiers had been marched off into the empire to fight in wars that decided nothing permanently. And, meanwhile, here in Britannia, we had constant raids by the Saxons, by the Picti, by the Scotti, by their kin the White Shields from Hibernia. We were being bled dry. Eventually, we'll be overwhelmed. And the empire, as it fails, won't protect us. We're on the edge of Oceanus here. They just won't care.

"Carausius told me his fears, and his plan for the future. He was no longer going to contest any lands outside of Britannia. His defeat in Gallia had convinced him that there was no gain to be had there and in Hispania. He was going to withdraw all his forces from the continent, and bring them here. Then he would proclaim an independent Britannia.

"But he was afraid for his son as much as anything, and he came to me to ask me to shelter him if the worst happened. If Carausius was killed, he knew, Artorius would be as much at risk as his father was. He did not know who the plotters were – one of his weaknesses was that he trusted people too much. He trusted Allectus."

She repeated, as if in wonder. "He trusted *Allectus*..." She shook her head bitterly. "Well, what is in the past cannot be changed. But I agreed, and that was why I went to Londinium. I took Licinianus and Severiana with me, as a treat, and because I had made plans for the boy's safety, and intended to come back with him. I never expected the conspirators to move so fast."

I saw that there were tears in her eyes. "It was my burden to see him die. But I made a promise to myself: I would make sure that his vision of a separate Britannia would live on, as long as I could sustain it. I am," she said, and smiled, "a very rich and well-connected woman."

At first, I did not understand what she was saying. She so rarely said anything bluntly, and this was one such time. Then I realized what she was saying. "You? *You* built the Amici Carausii?"

"I did. It made sense to me. You see, at heart I'm a merchant, a trader. And how do traders work? Do we send huge sums on dangerous journeys? No. We form associations. We send letters, and someone who owes us, pays the money to those we tell them to. Their debt is cancelled, and so it goes. We work the same way. Everything we do is done behind the scenes.

"Do you see that we are now in exactly the place Carausius feared we would be? Once Constantinus is acclaimed Augustus in Britannia and Gaul, war is inevitable. Galerius hates him. What will Maximianus do? Or his son?"

"And that," said Milo, "Is why Constantinus must be killed. To save this land."

"Killed," I said, and the words shocked me, even though I had prayed our Twin Gods for vengeance on him. "So, nothing whatsoever to do with what happened to me, then," I said.

He shook his head. "No, I'm afraid not. But you are the means, both to our goal and your vengeance. Without you, nothing will happen. In five months... six months... you will have a child. Is there a better way to gain access to the Lady Helena and her son? Is that not the perfect revenge... to reach him because of the crime he committed against you?"

176

I saw my brother looking at me, and I knew the pity he felt for me, to be placed in this position. My mouth curled. "Do you think this disturbs me? My family will have its revenge. And if to do that I must betray Helena's trust in me, that I will do."

"If there is any trust left when you return to Eburacum," said Flavilla. "And if you can convince her that what you bear is Constantinus's."

She paused. "And for that matter…why are you so sure it's his?"

"I don't know. But I am."

But I did know. I had had a dream, and Cicoluis had come to me. She spoke no words, but it was if I heard her say them: "Your deepest fears are true. But if you kill it, I must abandon you."

And the next day, when the draft was brought to me, I had poured it away. The irony was that my aunt had already made sure it contained nothing that would harm the infant.

"I will go to Eburacum if you wish. But what do you expect me to do there? Poison him?"

Milo's face was utterly still. "If necessary."

I felt a chill in me again. I have never seen myself as a poisoner. It is a dishonorable way to kill. "This is just half a plan. If Constantinus is killed, someone must succeed him. Who could that possibly be?"

"You have already met him," Aurelia Paulina said. "Carausius's son still lives. He is still alive, though living under the name Aurelius Paludius. And as he told us, he is Carausius's son."

I couldn't help smiling a little. The name he had taken to hide under meant "marshy", and the Menapians lived in the marshes near the mouth of the Rhine.

"You cannot just produce him and expect the army to accept him," said my brother.

"No," said Milo. "There will have to be a mutiny. That will have to be prepared for. And it will have to be one that cannot be ignored."

"Have you contacted Galerius?" asked my stepmother.

I looked at her in shock. Galerius? The senior Emperor? Ah, I thought. Who hates Constantinus more?

"A week or so ago."

"With suitable lies, I presume."

Milo smiled. "We can hardly tell him we intended to break from the Empire. But we did tell him we would be his loyal subjects."

Aurelia Paulina laughed. "No Emperor believes assurances like that. Let's hope his hatred overcomes his caution."

"But will Carausius's son do it?" I asked, returning to the main question. I had noticed that in my pregnancy sometimes torpor overtook my mind. "It's his death if he fails."

"That we must find out," said Milo. "He's in Corinium, a notary for the governor of Britannia Prima. And he has been one of the Amici for a long time. He knows what we are sworn to do. We need to go there, and talk with him." He became silent. "But Galerius is crucial. If he supports us, Constantinus will fall. There are powerful forces of troops who are more loyal to him than Constantinus."

# CHAPTER 27

## Licinianus: In the North

Spring is a wonderful season, when the weather is right. And after the drought of last year, we had exactly that. Everything was now green; everything was now lush; we savored the smell of grass and growing things. I was back at my post in Eburacum, and I smiled at Constantinus and his friends as if I knew nothing of what they had done to my sister.

I had never realized that I had a talent for dissembling. I learned I did. Inside, however, I reveled in my hatred for them. To harm my sister was to harm my own soul, and my family, too. They would pay, and so I smiled at them, at Constantinus, and Valerius Avilius Apollinaris, Aufidius Candidus Rufinus, and even their friends. I even spoke with the Lady Helena, and it was obvious what her goal was. She wanted to know if I knew, and thus if I was to be trusted.

We were eating oysters, brought in barrels from the south, as we talked, I remember, and her voice was so cautious. "Severiana is in good health," she said. "Oh yes," I replied. "She was a little depressed, about what I don't know." I smiled. "Young women often seem overtaken by moods, I'm afraid. But she's much better now. Smiling, and talking about her coming child."

I hate spite, but I felt it then. I saw her eyes widen, and she took a brief indrawn breath.

"Her child?"

"Yes. She's pregnant. Julianus will have an heir, it seems, despite his sad death."

"She's pregnant..." Her voice was almost a whisper.

"Yes. Very unexpected." My mouth curled a little, as if in a tiny laugh. "We all thought Julianus was..."

I left my sentence unfinished. Both of us understood.

"It seems not then."

"Yes," I said. But in my head, I was hearing Severiana's voice: "I know whose it is, and it's not Julianus's!"

I went on. "How is the Augustus? And his son?"

I was shaking with rage as I walked out, but she never saw that.

+ + +

There was a great deal to do. There were meetings I had to attend, as the

179

Amici prepared for our coup. I was surprised at how many soldiers belonged to the organization, far more than I thought; but, perhaps unsurprisingly, they were often amongst the older, more experienced soldiers who had known Carausius themselves. I was even more surprised to find how many soldiers were in Galerius's pay.

More to the point, at this time, the whole army was preparing for the drive north under Constantius's leadership, to deal, finally, with the British beyond the Wall.

But then, as we were to move north, everything fell into confusion.

I emphasize: it was not a surprise. We all knew that Constantius had been sick, and there had been no word that he had recovered. He had not even been seen, except when carried in a litter. But when he called an assembly, and we all stood in our ranks, waiting for him to speak, we knew that things were about to change.

We assembled in the fields outside Eburacum: the army was far too large for the square inside the city. But it was a fine day, and birds sang, even though thousands of men were gathered. But that was because we were so quiet. I have never seen so many men so quiet. We feared what was to come, though we guessed, and we knew nothing of what this would mean in the end.

I've often read in the works of past scholars how generals give speeches to their armies, and it seems they believe everyone hears all that a general says. But there are thousands and thousands of men gathered, and only a few of those in the front can hear everything. So there are men with very loud voices stationed throughout the ranks whose job is to repeat what is said so that all can understand. But do they? As the general speaks, pieces get lost, words get changed; and at the end we often hardly know what the general actually said.

But today there was little doubt, for the words were very simple, and were repeated again and again by the callers.

"My days are short," said Constantius from his litter, and all I could hear was the thread of his voice in the distance with no words clear. And then it was repeated, and came to me like an echo from afar, one echo following another.

"And I will be with the shades soon. So, I ask you to give my son Constantinus the loyalty you have given me. As you love me, I ask that of you. And I pray you to be as loyal to him as you have been to me."

And that was all he said. And, those brief words were the last we heard from him, for he was dead by morning.

The next day, Constantinus was acclaimed by the assembled army, not just as Caesar, but as Imperator too. This did not please everyone; there was a lot of murmuring, even a few calls of disagreement. We all knew it meant war against Galerius... and the gods knew who else. Roman soldiers do not like fighting their brethren, no matter how often it has happened in the past. It is daunting to recognize the face of someone trying to kill you.

But I had other business. *Always start with the least one,* they say. So, I chose Aufidius Candidus Rufinus.

Things were not settled in the North, and we knew that if we wanted peace for the next generation, we would have to wreak final havoc on the tribes beyond the Wall. We had re-garrisoned the Antonine Wall, so the lowland tribes were caught between that and the Aelian wall. And beyond, of course, were the tribes of the highlands, eager as always to kill Romans, or anyone else for that matter. All needed to be dealt with. And in the chaos of preparing to march north, I made friends with Rufinus.

This was not easy. He was wary of me. No... he was afraid of me. He didn't know if I knew, and I made sure that he never had any inkling that I did. I was friendly. I talked about the war I had experienced to those who were eager for such stories. And I talked about poetry to those who enjoyed it, and Rufinus was one. It was as if the old Licinianus was still there; and of course, he was, in a way. But the new one was here too... the hidden one... the one who wanted revenge... the one who wanted death for those who had shamed his sister. I discovered a liking for Sappho in him, and my family has always felt a special place for her. So, we matched verses, and then I gritted my teeth and made jokes about unwilling girls, and how to convince them. And he started to smile at what I said, and even laugh.

We started exercising together, and I taught him what I knew about fighting, for he had not been well-trained. I had no fear of what he learned from me. I knew what I now was. And I remember a day when we lay panting together from our bout on cool grass, the sweat dripping from our bodies, and the smell of crushed clover in our nostrils, as we laughed together and talked about how much we wished we were in the soft pleasant south, where we could drink good wine and eat delicious food and meet lovely girls. And so we became closer and closer.

We all went hunting one day, when we were waiting for the order to march. I am not a great hunter: some just like to kill animals, but I am not such a person. I don't mind hunting for the food I eat. That is the way life is. This day we went looking for deer, and I do love venison.

There were four of us: myself, Rufinus, and two others. But suddenly one dropped out, and Valerius Avilius Apollinaris joined us. I wanted to kill him the moment I saw him. I saw him as Constantinus's evil daemon. But I smiled of course, and took his arm, and tried to enjoy the day as well as one can with two men you intend to kill.

It had poured during the night, but the sun was shining now, and the rain had only stopped a few minutes before. On the leaves were shining drops of water, and in our nostrils was the strangely enticing smell of leaves decaying in water. There were a few wisps of mist in the early morning, but white clouds were rising above the hills, and we all knew the day would be hot once the sun burned off the mist. And so we set out early, with one slave holding the leash of the sighthound who would run the deer down for us.

We rode up over the hills, the grass on them so green and lush that the hooves were almost silent. The drought of last year was well past now. I think none of us really cared if we saw a deer; the day itself was enough. We were happy, insofar as we could be, even I; and we passed a flask of unwatered wine between us, enjoying the mood.

We sat down and ate bread dipped in the wine, along with hard cheese and green olives, laughing about the delay in our moving north as we spat out the seeds. All of them were young men, and all wanted the thrill of a fight. I wondered how many had ever experienced that sensation, and whether they would enjoy it as much as they thought, no matter how exhilarating it could be.

"Wait," said Apollinaris suddenly. "Look, on that hillside!"

We saw it... a red deer, with antlers high. And then he began to run, up the hill.

"Let the hound loose," said Apollinaris. "Get him!"

We jumped into our saddles, reaching for our bows. And then we were in full pursuit.

The deer was much fleeter of foot than we were, and if it had just been us against him, he would have won. But the sighthound is a different matter. They are bred to be fast.

We labored up the hill, seeing the deer and the hound disappear over its top, long before we reached it. But when we crested it, we saw a sight that was not what we had expected.

The deer was indeed running, with the hound following him. But behind them was a wolfpack, twelve strong, running hard to take down their prey, and probably our hound too.

None deal lightly with a wolfpack, even Roman soldiers. Being attacked from half a dozen directions at once is enough to loosen one's bladder, as soldiers crudely say, for the wolves will dash in, slash with their teeth, and retreat, again and again, until even the most fearless man has his calves in ribbons, and, if mounted, his horse can no longer stay on its feet for its torn tendons.

I knew the wolves would turn on us soon, leaving some of the pack to pursue the deer, for they are animals of great cunning. So I reached for an arrow in my quiver, and thanked the gods that I had been trained to shoot as a cataphractus, from horseback, and at the gallop.

As I had thought, five of the wolves came for us.

Apollinaris was in front. Somehow, he always was, for he was that kind of man. But that was his undoing, for a huge brindled wolf came at him, dodged behind as he tried to slash at it, and threw himself up, to take his horse in the haunch, his teeth spraying blood from the flesh as they struck. You can't get a wolf with a sword unless you are very lucky: they are too fast. You need a bow.

I saw him fall as the horse's rear collapsed, hurtling over the head of his mount, and I waited, my arrow ready in case any of the wolves came at me. I saw the big wolf come at him, and take his arm in its mouth, and he screamed at the pain. I hesitated. Was this the way to see him die?

And then I laughed. No. Let him know this pain for a while. Apollinaris would die with my blade in his belly, slowly. So, after a while, but only after a while, I loosed the arrow, and saw the wolf bound yelping into the air as it struck; and then it fell back, the arrow fixed in his heart, and he was dead.

I could see that none of the others knew how to shoot from horseback, and I loosed another arrow. It struck a second wolf, but did not kill him, and the rest of his pack, knowing the odds, began to run from us, and he limped with them. I've often wondered: how are wolves so smart? They are like well-trained soldiers. When they cannot win, they run, to fight another day.

We lost the deer, and our sighthound too. But we managed to shoot a rabbit, and that was our sparse dinner that night. We were not miserable. We had dried meat, and stale bread, and we had wine. We laughed, and joked, and I knew I had done my job. Only Apollinaris spent an unpleasant night.

I smiled.

+ + +

But then the time came, and the order with it: we were to march north. Rufinus was placed in my legion, I found, so we met often. "I'm to be in your vexillation, Licinianus!" he said.

He saw me as a friend. I did not like that feeling.

I embraced him. "We'll fight together!" I said. "Stay by me, and we'll protect one another!"

The aim of this attack was to finish off the northerners. Constantius had mauled the Western tribes: they were now too bloodied to fight. But the eastern tribes, and especially the Votadini, had lost only their westernmost clans, and it was our intent to make sure they would not be a danger for a long time.

We were soon north of the Aelian wall, and Constantinus was there with his staff, of which I was one. I knew this land a little now, and I spoke British, as none other in the staff did, so I was put in charge of the exploratores or scouts, and oversaw their movements, for many were of the land. I did not ride with them at first. But then, I was not intended to. I was just the Roman officer who received their reports, and made judgments as to what should be done with that information, before I reported it with my recommendations to the legates, and to Constantinus.

But then I began to hear ominous things, that Saxon ships had been seen on the eastern coast of Valentia, and even on the coast north of the Antonine Wall, where the Picts and wild tribes were. And they were not raiding: they were being met by the tribesmen, and talks were taking place.

I spoke to an explorator, and since we spoke in his language, his tongue ran free. I was never one to keep separate from my scouts anyway, so we drank barley beer together in my quarters.

"I swear," he said, "There are Saxons in Curia. I didn't see them; but I spoke to more than one from there, and all talked of the strangeness of them being there. The Saxons have been raiding all of the eastern coast of Britannia for decades, not caring who was there. They've been killing Romans and Brits... anyone they found. And now they're all of a sudden talking and playing nice to the Votadini and the Taexali and Venicones and northern Damnonii? I even heard that chiefs of the Novantae and Selgovae were also in Curia, though I doubt very much! They were too hurt at Colanica. But chiefs of the Vacomagi were there! Picts! Nah. Something's happening. They're planning something, and who is the greatest enemy of them all? Us! Rome!"

There is a place for vengeance, but this was not the time for it. I was suddenly focused on the danger to the Empire, and though I hated Constantinus, this was greater than him, for a concerted attack on Britannia by the Saxons, the tribesmen and the Picts would be a disaster for the whole province, for my family, and for all I loved. He and his friends could wait. I wanted to send out scouts, but the legates were skeptical of the reports, and I couldn't blame them. The Saxons allying themselves with the tribesmen, whom they had so often raided, as they raided us to the south? Who could believe that?

But I wondered. I went to the Emperor's council next day, and waited for my chance. It came as we were finishing, and the Emperor asked if there were any other matters to discuss. I stood up.

"Dominus," I said. "I have an issue I wish to raise, one that concerns me greatly."

There was a kind of wariness in Constantinus's eyes. Surely he didn't expect me to bring up his attack on my sister here?

Then, after a pause, "Speak," he said.

"I've received worrisome news…" And I explained what I'd heard about the conspiracy.

I had expected indifference, but instead there was a hubbub, as legates and high officers began to talk over one another.

One stood up, and Constantinus quieted the others so we could hear him. "Are we to believe, Dominus, that the Saxons and the northern tribes are to join together? The Saxons have tormented them as much as they have us. And they have had no fleet to protect them."

Everyone nodded, agreeing, but Constantinus turned to me, and asked what I thought.

"Master," I said, "I can only report what our scouts are saying. A number of them have close relations with the Votadini, and some have even been in Curia, their capital. They say that the Saxons are coming in their ships, but to talk, not to raid. I can't say anything more than that. But these are men who seem to be telling the truth."

A legate stood up. "I was in Curia only a month back, discussing peace with the Votadini, and I saw no Saxons."

I did not say the obvious: that he was there as a Roman emissary, and if Saxons had been there, he would not have been allowed to see them.

Constantinus's face was still, and thoughtful. I hated him. But he was no fool.

I have often wondered why, if Constantinus was wary of my enmity, that he did not simply have me killed, as he had tried to kill my sister. He was not the kind of man to show quarter to potential enemies even if the threat was small, for he was a merciless, cruel man. I can only think that it was his superstition that saved me. He knew that I had preserved his father's life when he had almost been killed in that ambush, and to us Romans that puts a burden on a son, even if it is one all too often discarded. And then there was his mother, who was, in her own way, a good woman, and she had guilt for what had been done. But now he spoke to me, and perhaps he saw in what he was suggesting a solution to his dilemma.

"You believe this, Tribune?"

I bowed. "I am inclined to, Master. At the least we should send men out to find what the truth is."

"Spies, you mean."

"Yes, Master."

He always had big, almost bulging eyes, and now they were fixed on me. "You speak British, I understand."

"Yes, Master. I spoke it from childhood. I cannot pass as one of these northerners, for they speak a strange dialect. But I can understand them."

"Then you would not mind going north to Curia to find out if there is any truth in these claims."

I am no more cowardly than most men; but I knew the odds of surviving such a trip were not good. He was sending me to die.

I bowed. "If that is your order, Dominus."

"It is."

Before I left, I passed a message on to the Amici telling what had happened, for I was not at all sure I would be coming back.

# CHAPTER 28

## Licinianus: Curia

I spent the next day planning our journey. We could not be a large group; three at most, I thought, so we would seem like an isolated group going north to Curia. One would be myself; another would be Lugobelenos, my slave.

Many don't trust slaves, and for good reason. They are there because they have no choice, and owe no real loyalty to their master. That is why all slaves are tortured if their master is murdered, for how can you be sure of any of them or believe their testimony outside of torment? But there are some who show great loyalty and perseverance in their duties, and Lugobelenos was one such. I trusted him not to betray me, he spoke British as well as I did, and, being a member of the Brigantes, his dialect was much closer to that of the Votadini than mine.

I asked him to his face: "Will you hold trust to me, Lugobelenos? You'll be among your own people, north of the wall."

He bowed his head. "My own people, Dominus? I'm from the Brigantes, and we and the Votadini have fought for many years, long before the Romans came. They aren't my people. We were always enemies."

He paused. "You've always been kind and generous to me. I would lose my honor if I betrayed you." And then his voice acquired a slight bitterness. "And even a slave has honor, to be preserved."

I looked long at him. "How old are you?"

"I'm twenty-eight, Dominus."

"No. You are thirty. Do you understand?"

He shook his head, clearly bewildered.

"The law doesn't allow me to free a slave under thirty. So, you are now thirty. Remember that when you're asked."

I raised my voice and called the orderly outside. "Tell the legion's notary I need him to write a document of manumission for this man."

We waited as the manumission was drawn up, and then some hours before we could see the Legate. No manumission can be legal without a magistrate, and in a legion the Legate stands in that role. Then it was done, and we left for my quarters.

Lugobelenos's blue eyes were wide, as they had been when he was turned and pushed away in the ceremony of freedom.

"We're going into great danger, Lugobelenos," I said, "and I would prefer that only free men go with me, and go willingly. You've served me well. You've earned it. Welcome to my family, Licinianus Vindex Lugobelenos. Now you have a choice, the choice of a free man. Go with me, or not, as you decide."

He stood up. "I'll go with you."

"You'll have to play the role of a slave…"

He laughed, with joy: "But I won't be one!"

+ + +

We got clothes from the exploratores, clothes that would mark us as traders… faded blue check for me, ragged red check for Lugobelenos, a hunting spear and daggers for both of us and a British sword for me as well. Even swords as old as this one were expensive, so we could not all carry them; that would make us suspicious. Certainly, Lugobelenos could not carry one.

We were to be jewelry sellers: jet and slate from the south, carved shells, carved walrus tusk that came across the Rhenus from the Suebian Sea. These sold well, we were told, and we spent days practicing how to be hucksters, and how to drive the price up, for that would be expected of us.

But there was Aufidius Candidus Rufinus too, to consider. I wanted him with me, though I did not need him. I dared not ask Constantinus for his service, for that might raise his suspicions; but the Legate could send him with me, as his commanding officer. I intended to do my duty; but that did not mean that the task of revenging my sister was to be abandoned.

The Legate was a good man, accomplished at his job and a good administrator, but certainly not a subtle one. He had risen from the ranks, and it showed, for he had a crudeness to him that the well-born usually lacked; but he did not have the prickliness that so often shows in men who had come from nothing to high office. He was Menapian, as Carausius had been, so of Belgic origin, which meant half German and half Celt; but of this he never spoke, for any suggestion of a relation to that pretender to the purple would have been unwise. We spoke in a mixture of Latin and Celtic when we were together, for that made him feel at home, and me closer to him. His British was small, but I had learned enough Gaulish from my aunt so we could understand each other well enough, for the language is close to his. The German words he used I never fully understood, but I could figure some of them out.

"I'd like another Roman to go with me, Legate. I'm going with my slave – my ex-slave – and you know that one can never fully trust someone who's spent his life in servitude."

I felt so guilty as I said that. I trusted Lugobelenos more than I trusted any Roman but my family. But dishonesty was what the time called for.

He nodded. "I understand. But who? No one else speaks British as you do. Except among the exploratores?"

I shook my head. "Dangerous. They have so much contact with these people. Some are members of northern tribes. Trusting them? I don't know. It's why I'm not taking any of them."

I stopped as if I were thinking. "I wonder..."

He raised his eyebrows.

"Well, sir... One thing occurs to me. Do we have any officers with fair hair... who are fair enough to seem as if they are northern?"

"Ah. I see. But none can speak the language."

"No need, perhaps. But... a thought? Deaf-mutes are seen as touched by the gods, I know. You think that might work?"

"Mmm," he said. "True. But I think we only have two fair-haired officers... Aegidius and Rufinus?"

"Yes... Aegidius I've hardly spoken to, and his hair's just brown. But I know Rufinus. Could he be seconded?"

"You think he could do it?"

"That's my guess. Yes. He'd be perfect."

"If you think it'll work, I'll give him his orders, then."

+ + +

The last time I slipped north was a time of terror for me, and I had almost died. But things were different now. Both walls now had garrisons, so escape would be possible both to the north and the south. But in between was a lawless land where lived the Votadini, who were no friends of ours, and kept in check by fear of our army, through which our forces moved only in strength. Small groups of Romans were prey to the tribesmen, and we had already had reports of killings, not to mention heads thrown over our ramparts in the night. But now I had the gift that my father had had, and fear never overcame me as it once had, and even then, was more like an echo of voices in the distance. Except when I dreamed...

The gift worried me; this was not what I had been born to. It was just my divine burden... my tungida.

We left in the early morning, while it was still dark, just after *concubia nocte*, first sleep. None of us went back to bed as we would normally have done, and it was pitch dark of course, for there was no moon. The gate swung slowly open, the guards silent as they had been told, and we rode straight north, leading two mules with our stock and packs on their backs.

As we left, I remembered again the time before this when I had gone north, and felt a shiver cross my soul. But I also remembered the silent voice of the god speaking to me, and the gift he had given me. But I said nothing out loud. None of us did. We needed to be quiet, for though traders passed through the Wall all the time, this was not the place where they were normally allowed, for it went right through the middle of the army. We needed to get as far from the Wall as possible before sunrise came upon us.

We rode hard. And as the sunrise started to color the sky to the east, we had reached as far from the Wall as we could, and slowed down, for to be seen as hurrying might draw suspicion. We rested the animals by a stream, and ate a breakfast of barley bread, hard cheese and weak native ale. I was sweating, and the drink was refreshing. It was good to be free of the sour posca which we, due to a shortage of wine, had been drinking in the camp.

Then irony came upon us, for as we sat there, a Roman patrol rode over the incline behind us, and came towards us. We made no attempt to run, for it would have been useless, but I saw Rufinus about to open his mouth to shout. I hissed out the side of my mouth, "No Latin! We're British!" and prayed that no one would fail me.

"But they're Romans!" he said.

"They mustn't know who we are! Say nothing!"

The optio in charge of the patrol was a stocky, bearded man who spoke with a strong Hispanian accent as he called his men to halt. And it was clear what he thought of the "Brittunculi" in front of him. Contempt is so often a useful means for soldiers to keep their control.

"Who you? Why you here, in this place?" he said, not leaving his saddle. His British was terrible, accented so strongly I could hardly understand him. I shook my head, and turned helplessly to my fellows. Then I started to speak in broken farm-worker Latin, in the way that we as naughty children had spoken when we wished to irritate our aunt and stepmother. I can still do it quite well, all these decades later.

"We trade. We sell jewelry. We buy in the south, trade it up north. We just trade. Back and forth, sir, back and forth."

"Hmm," He said. "Check their packs."

"What can we hide there?" I said, protesting weakly.

"Shut up, little Briton!"

His men dismounted, and began to pull the packs off our mounts. There was no attempt to do it neatly. They pulled everything open, tearing the cloth that held the bundles together, leaving our jewelry scattered on the ground.

Of course, they found nothing. They hadn't expected to. One or two of them stole some of the jewelry for their women back in camp, and made no attempt to hide it. Then their leader spat on the ground, and they rode off.

"Well," I said to Rufinus. "There you see why Romans are not appreciated as much as they could be."

I saw Lugobelenos look at me sidelong. But he was still too newly freed to say anything. "Let's get things back together."

But we had hardly begun when we heard horses again, and I wondered why the Roman patrol was returning. But it wasn't. It was a group of Britons, riding on their painted horses, and certainly no Romans at all. I prepared to die.

The leader was a red-haired man with bright blue eyes; and I realized he had no intention of killing us.

"I see," he said smiling, "that you are not favorites of the Romans."

"They stole from us," I said, with as much resentment in my voice as I could level.

"I saw. Where are you going?"

"To Curia. We trade jewelry."

"There'll be many women eager to buy your wares. Traders are rare these days."

"The war?"

"Yes. And you're brave to come up here now."

I looked down. "I have a family, and if I don't trade, they don't eat. And I've heard prices are high now because of scarcity. This is my chance."

He looked at us speculatively. "We're going to Curia. We're all Votadini here. You're from the south, I can tell. But I saw how the Romans treated you. You can ride with us if you wish."

He saw my hesitation. "We're not robbers. You have my promise." He reached down his hand, offering it to me. "My name is Trahayarnos mappos Vortipori, a chief of the Votadini. Will you take my hand in friendship?"

I reached up. "I am Ariogaisos mappos Glūnomāri. I am honored."

Luck is a strange thing. If I had thought of how useful having a Roman patrol harass us would be, I would have organized it myself.

+ + +

Curia slowly lifted above the horizon as we rode north, and by the time we were close, I was impressed. It was not the biggest oppidum I had ever seen, but it would have been hard to take, even for Romans. The land to the east fell off sharply in what was almost a rock cliff, edged by a timber palisade. Trying to scale that would have been suicide for an attacking army. The slope to the west was much gentler, but it was guarded by a deep ditch, surmounted by a rough stone slab wall with wooden ramparts on top. To enter, we had to curve over to the southwest where the main gate was, and there the stone walls bulged out to left and right, forming between them a road just wide enough for a native wagon, so that anyone attempting to enter could be attacked on both sides from the wall-tops before even reaching the entrance-way.

There were guards at the gate, but when they saw Trahayarnos, they waved and stood aside, welcoming us. I turned to him and thanked him for escorting us here. "It was a pleasure to be with you, my lord. Thank you for being so kind as to escort us."

He smiled. "There was nothing to it." He pointed to the left, and I saw there was a small area there, below a second rampart that enclosed the higher oppidum. Every other area was packed with roundhouses. "Traders set up in that place, so pitch your tent there. The women will find you, I promise!" He laughed, then added, his face much stiller, and very serious. "Don't try to go up to the higher town. There's a lot of hatred for the Romans since they attacked, and even though you're not one, you're from their land. Someone will claim you're a spy, and no one will be able to save you."

It had been late in the afternoon when we entered the oppidum, and so we contented ourselves with setting up our tent and building a fire, all almost in silence. Only two other traders were camped there, but they were so close that everyone could hear each other. Since Rufinus could not speak British, we had to resort to low-spoken Latin. But everyone knew we came from below the Wall, so that in itself was not suspicious. We cooked our evening meal of porridge and dried meat, and tried to act as if we were at peace. "We need to spend tomorrow selling our goods," I whispered. "Nothing else."

"What will we gain from doing nothing?" said Rufinus. "We are here on a mission."

"We aren't here to get killed before we find out what's happening," said Lugobelenos.

Rufinus looked at him, astonished. He knew he had just recently been freed, and he still had difficulty treating him as an equal. And Lugobelenos was showing a part of himself that I had never seen when he was a slave. I grinned, though I certainly did not feel amusement.

"He's right," I said. "Tomorrow, we sell jewelry. That's all. But we keep our eyes open, and see if we can find a chance to find out more."

+ + +

As dawn came, and the smoke of a thousand cooking fires rose across the hill, we set up, and waited for those who wanted to buy our wares. We stood up, and shouted what we had to sell, again and again, and we did not have to wait long. I had the feeling that women had been waiting for just such as we, as they came very soon, along with some young men, looking for gifts for their sweethearts.

If our purpose had been to make money, we would have had no problem at all. There had been no traders selling jewelry here for over a year or more because of the fighting, and women want pretty things to flaunt on their bodies, even in a time of war. Our suppliers had found choice things for us to sell, almost all seized from smugglers: necklaces of iridescent shell, rings of precious gold and electrum and silver, enameled brooches, emerald and garnet bracelets, hair ornaments of many-colored stones. We had lines of women waiting to see our wares, and even sometimes fighting to buy an object. Like good traders, we quickly organized auctions for the choicest items. One beautiful carnelian necklace almost caused a riot, and the granulated gold pieces sold out in an hour. It was, in its way, oddly enjoyable, and I found myself almost excited as our stock went down. I had never been a trader before, after all. The problem was that if this went on, we'd sell out so soon, and we'd have no reason to stay. But then I realized that no trader would go back empty-handed, so I ceased worrying.

I was doing everything I could to talk to the women as I worked, and some were more than willing to have a conversation. Some seemed eager, in fact. I tried to ask questions that would make sense for a trader such as I. And I found something very interesting as I spoke to a young woman who bought a granulated gold ring.

"Do you know of anyone selling amber?" I asked, as I had a number of others. "I'll take second-hand pieces as well, even broken pieces. I can remake them, and they sell well in the south. I'll give good prices."

She was a girl of around sixteen, with fair hair and blue eyes, and she smiled prettily, before saying hesitantly. "Well, I know someone who's sold some, and he still has more. He might want to sell it. I'll tell him."

193

She waved as she left, and I turned to Lugobelenos, an edge of excitement in me.

"Amber, sir?" he asked, speaking low. "Why?"

"Know where it comes from, Lugobelenos? The shores of the Mare Suebicum. And where do the Saxons live? To the south of that same sea."

He nodded, understanding.

"The usual Amber Road is down the Rhenus from the north into the Empire. How would it get here unless it was brought straight across the sea from the Saxon land?"

+ + +

The next day was a tense one, as I waited to see if my bait would be taken. By nightfall no one had come, and our supply of jewelry was low. I began to ask around to see if there were people who had goods I could buy to trade to the south.

There lay the problem. The north produced very little that was not bulky and yet would sell in the south, and it was important that I seem like a genuine trader. I could buy fleeces and hides, and also dried fish; but the return on these would be small considering the work it would take to transport them. This was a poor land, and the best I could do was some silver ingots, tribal jewelry, and some copper, and not much of those, which came from the northern islands, or so I was told. The lead they extracted the silver from was too heavy.

There was an irony here: I was collecting goods which would take many pack animals to return south of the Wall, yet I cared nothing about them. Such is the nature of subterfuge. So there I was, duly collecting goods I would much rather have left behind, when he appeared.

At first, I hardly noticed him, for he stood behind me silently. But then he suddenly started speaking, and in Latin, not British. That shocked me. But he surely would know a trader from south of the wall would know some of that language. It was very bad Latin, but I could understand it. I responded in the somewhat better but very rustic British Latin I had learned in my childhood until my tutor beat it out of me.

"I help you, sir?" I said.

His accent was clearly German. I'd heard it from auxiliaries many a time. I tried to speak in British, but he shook his head. "I not know that language. But hear you want amber. I have."

He was a stocky man of middling height, wearing the close-fitting breeches and long shirt that most Germans wore. He carried a sword and seax, which was interesting itself. We had been told not to wear our arms. Outsiders, we had been warned, were not allowed to. Odd.

"You show me," I said.

He shook his head. "You come to high town tonight. Then I show you. I must not have someone see me."

"Why?"

"No matter. You want amber you come. I sell. Bring silver. Bring gold!"

I had been warned. I knew the possible penalty of going up there. But I also knew that if I was to find out what we had come for, the answer lay in the high town. And I was almost certain this man was a Saxon.

"Where?" I said.

"In high town, big tower, there." He pointed. "In front, door. Behind, where no door. When moon sets! No tell anyone! Or we all die!"

I could see why. Trading that particular merchandise while on a mission to conspire with the British to attack us would not be seen as a wise move. Where, after all, would the tribes in Valentia get amber from the Suevian Sea?

+ + +

That evening, we cooked our meal – barley porridge and dried meat again, as I remember – and sat in a huddle, discussing what we should do. There was some disagreement. As you would expect, Lugobelenos said little. But Rufinus was a different matter.

"We've found that a Saxon is selling amber," he whispered. "That proves all we need to prove. We can return, and tell the Emperor that!"

"What does it prove? That one Saxon is here? That doesn't prove a conspiracy! It proves just that one is selling amber. We need more."

"And how do we get that?" he said, almost angry.

"I don't know. But we need to go to this meeting, and see what we can find out."

He shook his head, and I could see he was frightened. I wondered if he had been frightened when he helped his master rape my sister? But I said nothing of that. "We're here to find out for sure what is going on. We can't do that if we sit here."

I dug a stick into the fire. "You'll stay here tonight. You can't speak British. So remain here."

He was not a coward, and I saw his chin go up, as if to protest. But he was also not a fool, and he knew the logic of what I said.

"If we don't return, try to get away, and tell the command what we've learned," I said. "You can't do anything else. Don't try."

There was something going on in the upper town, for we could hear the noise, and the music, and there were bonfires lit in the open. It made us hesitate, but perhaps this was to our advantage: we could much more easily be lost in a crowd, rather than in near-empty alleys. So just before the moon set, we set off anyway, dressed in clothes that would look as northern as we could find.

The entrance to the upper town was not guarded in any useful sense. There was a single man sitting there, by a meager fire, and he had about as much interest in those passing through as a drunk would. Since by the smell he seemed to be drinking heather ale, I would guess that was precisely accurate. In any case, what was he guarding against?

We went past and were met by a different scene than in the lower town. Here was where the chieftains and their families lived, and it was not filled with the smoke and crush that the lower town was. There was much more empty space, and the round huts were far bigger, often with lean-tos outside where servants and slaves clearly lived. But tonight, it was loud, and we could hear drums and bagpipes.

We walked as confidently as we could. To be furtive would be suicidal, here where we had been told not to come. So we had to look as if we belonged. I kept back. My British was so clearly of the south, whereas Lugobelenos's was more northern, and might, at a pinch, pass muster, if no one listened too hard.

It was well after sunset, and the music was coming from ahead. When we climbed a little more, we saw that there was a large roundhouse near the top of the hill, and from its entrance we could see torch and firelight pouring, and the raucous noise that men who have drunk too much mead and beer make. In front it was thronged with people, with a man singing and men and women dancing around the fire. We moved on up, closer and closer to the roundhouse, for we could see the stone tower beyond it, and that was our goal.

Three drunk men came past, laughing and pointedly forcing us to the side. My hand was near my knife, which was all I had dared carry. But I wished I had a sword.

We were near enough now to peer into the roundhouse, and I could see that at the opposite end, beyond the fire that was lit in the center, Votadini with rich clothes were seated, drinking and talking and laughing. That was no surprise. What was strange was the six men sitting beside them, for they were certainly not Votadini, or Picts for that matter. Their clothes were of a kind I had not seen except on the crucified bodies of Saxon pirates, and their jewelry... they wore no torcs, but German neck ornaments and arm-rings they certainly wore. One I could see had a huge hand's-breadth pendant of Jupiter, whom they call, I believe, Woden. They were Saxons. There was no doubt of that.

I wanted to go closer, so I eased forward, knowing that over the firelight they would have a hard time seeing out of the door into the darkness. It was not good that I did, for I heard a rough voice shouting at me: "You there! What are you doing skulking here?"

I felt sudden panic. Then my instincts took over, and I stumbled onto the earth, and started laughing, bending over as if I was having difficulty staying upright.

I heard Lugobelenos calling out, his voice badly slurred: "He's drunk too much mead! And so have I!" He laughed hysterically.

A man came forward suspiciously, his clothes showing that he was no ordinary Votadini, for his tunic was finely embroidered, and a gold-touched sword hung at his waist.

Would he believe us? I waited to see, and my hand slipped closer to my dagger, wondering if I could survive in this press if I had to stab him. But then he spoke. "Get away from here. This is the chieftain's home, and certainly no place for drunks like you!"

And he turned away.

I was not prepared to do more... To what purpose? There were clearly men guarding this place, and I could not get closer. So I moved on, past the roundhouse, and then we were at the tower. We walked around it from its entrance, and then peered into the darkness, our eyes still blinded by the fire's glare. But there was no one there waiting for us, and we sat down on a stone, to wait.

"We can't stay here long," whispered Lugobelenos.

"No. But we can stay here for a while. Lie back, as if we're drunk, and sleeping it off."

"That might work... but not for long..."

We waited. At least an hour passed... or so it seemed to us, whose nerves were as tight as a harp's strings. Lugobelenos was more patient than I was, for I was just about to say that our trip had been useless when I heard the sound of footsteps on stone. We both tensed, and my hand was again on my dagger. Then I saw a body loom up around the tower, and it seemed to me it was the stocky shape of the Saxon we had spoken to.

He came up to us, and threw a bag down on the ground, before joining it. "Amber!" he whispered. "Look!"

He had a small hooded lamp with him, already lit, and I saw that it was Roman, in terracotta with a penis molded into the top for luck. He opened the bag, and, shielding the light so it shone closely, he opened the bag.

I saw amber, and not just small fragments, but big chunks, shining gold and red in the weak lamplight. I was no merchant, but even I could see that there was a fortune here. Any trader's mouth would have salivated over it. I dug in, pulling up piece after piece and looking through it towards the thin beam the lantern threw, as if I knew what I was doing. Then I looked up:

"Ten aurei for all!"

He recoiled in contempt, and the bargaining began.

Lugobelenos was a better bargainer than I was, and he had no hesitation in joining in. I knew the price I had proposed was a low one, and gradually it rose. Finally, we reached a price: twenty-one aurei for the bag. It was a fortune, almost half a pound of gold, and I knew from the smile of the Saxon that he thought I had been taken. But I cared nothing for that. I was after other things. I started to count out the aurei, and I did it slowly.

"How come you here," I said in bad Latin. "This amber from the Amber Sea?"

"Yes!" he said eagerly. "From the best shores! I am one of the Juti, and live there by the sea."

"What are you doing here? It's a long way away from your home."

We had brought a flask of wine with us, and I poured him a cup. He drank it happily. "Roman wine! Good!"

"Why you here?" I asked again, pouring him a second cup.

This was a happy man, but not a foolish one. He looked at me a little suspiciously. "Why you ask?"

"I never see amber like this in the North." I added anxiously: "You not cheat me? This real Amber Sea? How it get here?"

He became calmer, even smiled. "Real! You make lots of money. I come here with three chiefs from Saxonland, Angleland, Juteland! In good ships, all now on the river Tueda. You go there, you see! And die!"

He took another cup of wine, and leaned forward. "You go south, far south! Soon! Otherwise... you die!" And he started laughing. "You soon die!" he said again, and lost himself in his quiet laughter.

"Why will I die?" I said, incredulously.

His laughter overcame him. "You stay one month more, then you see!"

+ + +

By the time we left, the music and noise were beginning to die down a little. It was getting very late, and even drunken Celts eventually feel the call of their bladders and their beds. I had stayed as long as possible, pouring wine down the Jute's throat, but we only had two flasks, and he just drank them and laughed. But I came away convinced: there was a conspiracy between the Northern British and the Saxons. I would get nothing more. But I had enough. Now we would leave.

I believe in Fortuna, which is why I had made an offering to her before we left. Perhaps it should have been bigger, because sometimes you run out of luck. This is what happened today.

We were just leaving the upper town, when some figures came through the dark, heading for the gate we had just left. I kept my head down, but one of the men looked at me curiously, and I knew he recognized me. He was one of Trahayarnos's men. But I had hope: he said nothing. I could only pray that he would say nothing to his master either.

But now we hurried, and reached our tent in the marketplace as fast as we could. I told Rufinus what we had found out, and that we had to leave as soon as the gates opened at dawn. The next few hours were spent hurriedly loading the horses and mules with the trading goods we had bought with our profits. I would have been delighted to leave everything behind and race south to the Wall; but I could think of nothing that would raise suspicions than a trader abandoning his wares. They would be much of his year's income. And then we waited for the sun's light to set us free.

It came, and I could hear the creaking as the timber gates were slowly pushed open. They were huge and heavy, and I wanted to run forward and help the gatekeepers who were taking so much time to open them. But then at last we could ride forward, and we were through the gates. We headed south.

We rode as the sun rose on our left hand, and I started to relax as we left Curia behind. When it was finally hidden by the swell of the green earth, I started to breathe easier. But we were a long way from safety... two days at least if we pushed the animals to their limit without killing them, three if we didn't. We had no choice: two days it must be. This land was too dangerous for us, and the memory of Trahayarnos's man was haunting me. I could not shake the feeling that he would have told his master. And if he did? What would he tell him? That he had seen us coming from the upper city, where we had been warned not to go?

I could not but help laughing wryly to myself, for I remembered running for the wall when I had almost died, and when my near-death had transformed me into what I now was. I was not eager to repeat that experience.

But nightfall came, and half the distance was done, though our animals were lathered. We camped, but I would allow no fires. Instead, I looked to the north for them, and wondered if our pursuers, if we had them, would be foolish enough to light fires.

We huddled, and we considered our options. Rufinus and Lugobelenos were both wary. There is that heightened alertness that comes on you when you feel you're being followed, and I think all of us had it. So that night, late, Rufinus and I crept out into the dark, going north to see what we would find. I left Lugobelenos behind, ordering him to race for the Wall if we never came back.

It was a quiet night, with almost no wind but a gentle breeze shaking the grass tops. We kept low, so that we would not show against the night sky, for the moon was quite high, and when we crested the hill that gave only the slope that led north for so many miles, we stopped, and peered through the dark.

All we could see were two pricks of light, one to the far west, and one to the far east. They were nowhere on the line that a pursuer would take if they were following us, so we guessed they were simply the fires of the roundhouses crofters lived in. Once we were below the ridgeline, we could walk upright again, and we headed away from Curia.

There comes a time, when you search long, that your mind starts to tell you that the task is hopeless. What you fear is not in fact there, it tells you, and a sense of relief starts to come over you. But sometimes that sense of relief is false; and then you feel the sinking in your stomach that lets you know that ahead lie things you would prefer not happen.

That feeling came to me that night, for suddenly we heard in the distance the sounds that horses make as they stamp their feet and blow through their lips, and then as we crept closer there came the sound of men speaking low. And there was no fire. That was the real sign. *There was no fire.*

I could not make out the words, but there were a number of men there, perhaps five or six; and from the cadence of their speech it was clearly British, and northern, for their voices dip and rise at the end of their sentences, as if every utterance was a question of great import. And it was clear they were following us, for otherwise they would have made a fire. My heart sank, for I thought they were twice our number, or close enough to that to make no difference.

We crept back to Lugobelenos and the horses, and when we reached them, I had made up my mind.

"We can't go south," I said. "If we go south, we'll be caught and die."

I heard Rufinus protest: "But Trimontium has been reoccupied. It's no more than ten or twelve miles away!"

"We'll never make it. They'll catch up with us in an hour tomorrow morning. We need to hide our tracks, and the only way to do that is to get into the water. The Tueda river is to the east, and I'd guess this stream leads to it." I laughed. "It had better. Into the stream and stay with it. We can turn south later."

As we worked in the darkness, I knew on what shaky ground I stood. But we could not strike out for the nearest Roman outpost. And when you have no choice, your one option is perfection. I prayed, dropping a coin to the ground as an offering, wishing I had even a pigeon to offer, and the time to do it.

"The stream leads northeast," said Rufinus. "We'll be almost backtracking!"

"Yes," I said. "If we wish to live. We leave the mules. Then northeast we go!"

I said, to comfort them: "You think they'll believe we've headed back? Into the stream, and we follow it north as far as we can so they can't see our hoof-prints, while they go south! And then we'll turn back, and reach the Wall!"

# CHAPTER 29

## Severiana: Five Temples

I rode furiously along the Oak River, the path along the bank wide enough for one horse, and no more, so that Veldicca and the two slaves accompanying me had to follow in single file. I rode up the bank into the hills above the villa, riding until the horse was in a sweat. I was crying, as I so often was at that time of my life, for riding always made me remember that Julianus had taught me how. I missed him; and yet my soul had been more than eased when he died. And that just made the tears well up more, for it made me feel almost as if I had deserved what had happened to me.

It was a beautiful summer, yet I can only call my life at this time a desolation. Autumn was approaching, and I hated the thought. Not for the usual reasons people have to hate Winter; I had always rather liked the coziness of the time after the slaves stoked the furnace and warmth crept into the floors and walls: it felt safe against the icy winds and rain. But this year I dreaded the coming of the cold for in autumn I would bear the vileness that had been violently forced into my body.

I had not wanted to ride out that day; I simply wanted to sit in a dark room and stare at the walls. I had mostly gotten past what had happened to me, if indulging in deep depression is that. But every so often fury and humiliation would come to me, and they are such an odd mix of emotions. The first calls for strength, so that you can vent your anger on the one you hate. But humiliation lessens you, and makes you weak and incapable. I vacillated between these two states, angry one day, and helpless the next.

But Aunt Flavilla would have none of this. She had been stern as only she could be, a shocking sternness that rarely ever came from her. I protested that Roman ladies should not ride horses; she had laughed in my face, for she knew I had never taken any notice of that stricture before, and ordered my maid Servilla to get me dressed. Then she leaned close, and whispered: "Veldicca has no problem with riding: she's not a Roman lady. And think. If you ride very, very hard you may lose the baby."

I was utterly shocked, as she intended, and I knew it was just to take me out of myself. That was not what my kind aunt would ever say, and certainly not about a child, even unborn, for she loved them.

It worked, and I did ride, and hard, though not for the reason she had mentioned.

I came back late, as the sun was about to set, and looked down from the hill at our villa

The garden that my grandmother had planted and loved so much had come into its own this year, and there were so many flowers blooming that the beds were bright even as the sun's light faded. She had planted well, and as one plant's blooms withered and faded, another flowered, so there was always color. But that caught my eyes less than two figures, hidden in the trees above the villa, little in the distance. At first I could not see who they were; and then a flash of green caught my eye. Numerianus had been dressed in a tunic of that color at lunch. He was not alone: he was talking to someone who was surely a woman, for she was much slighter than him, and her clothes were bright and reached to her ankles.

I had no desire to meet anyone, and I was not alone in that, for Numerianus, hearing my horse's hooves, looked around as if scared, and tried to pull the woman he was talking to further back into the trees, as if to hide. But I started the horse down to the path leading through the woods towards them anyway, for I wanted to go home, and this was the way.

When I got close enough, I could see the girl was not wearing a stola, so she was unmarried; but at that moment a slave came for my horse, and I jumped down. Numerianus was looking desperate, as if the last thing he wanted was for me to stop.

The girl was young, no more than fifteen or sixteen, I guessed, but now that I was close, Numerianus was clearly not happy. She was of average height, with dark hair and brown eyes that set off the green amber earrings in her lobes, and the simple matching necklace. Her jewels were tasteful and expensive, and her tunic was of silk. This was not a poor girl, and perhaps even of good family. I greeted her in correct Latin, for this was a formal occasion, as Numerianus introduced us, with such patent reluctance that my brows met.

"This is Audaciana Pollion Verena. My sister, Severiana."

The name at first just seemed odd in almost every way, and somehow familiar. I could not help showing my surprise. She spoke, then, in Greek-accented Latin: "My family is from Egypt, Lady Severiana. Many of us are descended from the great Alexander's men."

Or they *say* they are, I thought, thinking she was a little sallow for that.

She smiled, and tried harder: "Numerianus has told me that your family was Gallic, who came to a new land. So we have something in common."

"Her father is a merchant in the eastern trade," said Numerianus eagerly, as if he wanted to help her. "They've bought the villa that Senovarius used to own."

Then it struck me. I remembered. "Audaciana Pollion?" I said, and if my voice was suddenly cold, there was good reason. "The daughter of the man who came to ask us not to cremate my husband? And a Christian, like him?"

Her cheeks went scarlet, and it seemed as if she could hardly speak. "Yes," she whispered.

Numerianus's face turned pale and I felt such fury that I almost struck her. "How dare you come here! And how dare you let her, Numerianus!"

I turned and did strike him, before I had even thought. The fury and sadness I had been keeping in me welled out, and I struck him again.

"These people are Christians! Are you mad? You are with a girl whose father stole my husband's bones?"

The girl was weeping, and trying to speak. "It was not us! Others did that, my father tried to stop them—"

I swept by her, forcing her out of my way, leaving her already turning to my brother, and I heard her futilely calling to my brother as she sobbed.

My head ached now, and I ran back to the Villa, and shouted for my stepmother. When she came, I told her what I had seen, and went to my cubicle, though I was still trembling with rage.

Veldicca came and stroked my head and massaged my neck, singing a lullaby to me in her strange British. It comforted me, and I don't remember how I fell asleep, so angry was I. But the villa was dark when I woke, and I heard the sound of my stepmother and my aunt's furiously raised voices. Numerianus was trying to reply, but the anger of the two women overmatched him, and I heard them talking about "that girl", the contempt clear in their voices. I was glad to be woken, even to the sound of that argument, for my dream had been terrible.

+ + +

The days passed, and the time came for the Summer Festival. Every year we went to Vagniacis and, with all the people of the country around, we sacrificed there to Epona, thanking her for the coming fruits of the harvest. Of course, we never called it that: to us it was just Quinque Templa, the five temples, or Pempe Dewoi[25] in British, for the five gods were the main reason anyone ever

---

[25] Five gods.

went there. But it was often just called "Templa."

When I was a child I loved the Summer Festival, for everyone was there, traders set up booths to sell their wares from, and there was dancing and singing and music and even, sometimes, a band of traveling actors. For a little girl who lived in a villa far from a town, it was very exciting.

That was the past, of course. This summer I had no desire to go anywhere, for I was becoming heavier as my belly swelled, and my spirits were sinking with it.

I got up to go to the privy, as I did so often these days, and went down the stairs to encounter my aunt, stepmother and Numerianus, blocking the way. They were clearly having a disagreement.

"We always go to Quinque Templa for the Summer Festival!"

It was Aurelia Paulina.

Numerianus looked shifty, I thought. But really, I just needed to get by them and relieve myself.

"I promised Verena I would not."

Aunt Flavilla spoke, in a voice so icy anyone who knew her well understood what was coming. "You promised *what*? You promised this Christian girl you would not go to one of our most *sacred ceremonies*?"

"Could you let me through please," I said. "I really need—"

They were intent on each other, and hardly heard me.

My stepmother was looking at her son angrily. She was his mother, and she knew him well. He began to speak, but she put her hand on his arm, and he stopped in mid-sentence.

"How dare you choose her over your family!" Her voice was peremptory. She was furious, and that was never good. She was fearsome when angry.

Numerianus looked suddenly panicked, and stammered at her, trying, I think, to invent an excuse.

"And how dare you even speak to a member of a family who so disgraced Julianus's death rites!"

My brother recoiled from his mother as if he had seen a snake, and she turned her back on him in fury. I managed to slip between her and Numerianus, and make my grateful way to the privy.

+ + +

The next few days were tense in the house, with no one speaking to anyone else except in brief asides. It was bad enough that Verena's family was Greek and Egyptian, not to mention that her father was a merchant. We were

Senatorial class – *viri clarissimi* – after all. But to be a follower of the hateful, illegal *superstitio* which had stolen my husband's bones was beyond bearing. Numerianus had gone from wanting an unsuitable girl to courting someone he could never marry without terrible effect. All of us had reasons to hate the Christians. Flavilla, kind as she was, would never forget what had happened after her mother's death, or forgive the Christians for what she still saw as rank disrespect. I hated them for how they had turned Julianus's poor, mad mind. And my stepmother could never forget the shameful dishonor they had brought to Julianus's funeral, and the grave-robbing that followed.

And what about our gods? How could they ever forgive a member of our family turning away from them to such a creature?

Numerianus had killed all the good feeling in the house.

I remembered sadly how full of love and comfort it had once been, and I tried to console myself that at least it could not get worse.

I was wrong.

We set out for Quinque Templa in the mid-morning three days later, traveling in a carpentum, with our offerings in an essedum behind, and the slaves in a raeda behind that. We were a little cramped, for with me, my aunt and stepmother, Veldicca – not to mention a morose Numerianus – there were five in a carriage that comfortably held only four. But it was only half a day's travel. The trip was uneventful, and we arrived at Templa in the afternoon.

We always stayed two nights so we could have a full day there, and we rented the same house every time. There were people who made money doing that, for there were many festivals at different times of the year at Templa, according to which god was being worshiped.

At another time I would have enjoyed the visit, for the little town was all I remembered, and there was a festive air about the place. I was forced to leave our rental – my aunt and stepmother were determined that I would not be left alone – and we all went for breakfast to the viewing platforms overlooking the place, with the slaves carrying folding chairs and food and wine.

The town was built at the source of a river which led down to the Tamesis, and from here we could see over it all. Below us were two shrines and the sacred oak dedicated to the God of Lightning, Ambisagros, and we went down after we had eaten to leave an offering to him, for our villa was called after his tree. Once this had been a place of druids, and terrible things had happened here, with men burned and children killed; but we Romans do not like human sacrifice, and we had exterminated them all, and a good thing too.

Then we went to the sacred pool, where we washed in its waters, asking for a blessing on our lives. Finally, we went into the town to go to the temple of the Goddess Epona, built next to a tall statue to Belenos, the God of the Sky, riding a horse. This was fitting: Epona is not just the goddess of what is fertile, but horses are her special love and care.

I can only say that we were later deeply grateful that we had come early, for we were able to go to Epona's temple and pray and make our offerings without waiting in line. It would have been a terrible omen if what was to come had happened before that. But it did not; and we were leaving when it happened.

There was a huge relief of Epona in front of her temple, showing her seated on a throne with a horse on either side of her. On her lap was a large basket of corn and fruit. The carving was some of the finest I had seen, and the colors of her clothes and hair were perfect. The horses were roans, for they were horses sacred to her, and their flanks seemed almost entirely real. We stood outside the cella in the ambulatory, and offered each gift in turn. When the time came for the sacrifice, we moved to the enclosure and the animals we had brought were offered. I prayed to the goddess for peace. I had lacked it for so long, and she was the Lady of Increase. She knew my predicament.

We were moving away to allow others to offer, and we saw a group of dark-gowned men enter. They were a strange sight: they led no animals or slaves, yet they moved with purpose. And then they started running, pulling hammers and axes out from under their robes, heading for the Temple. They were shouting and, at first, I could understand nothing. Then I realized it was broken Greek, and they were shouting about something called the God of armies and the Christus, calling on them to destroy the demon in the temple.

They were Christians. There was nothing else that made sense.

I thought for a moment that they were going to attack us, but the Temple was their goal, and as they reached it, I saw them attack the relief of Epona. I heard the axes and the hammers smash into the stone, and saw fragments fall from it. One blow smashed Epona's face into a ruin. Two of them ran into the temple, and I heard shouts and screams.

"Smash the demon!" I heard. "Drive her out in Christ's name!"

Our beautiful temple! I will never forget the horror and anger of it, the sacrilege. Some things are so terrible that they can rip aside the most terrible misery, and all of us, I know, were afraid that the goddess's inevitable retribution would fall on us, too. My aunt, my stepmother and I, our slaves, all stood there as if frozen, hearing the noise of hammer blows and screaming from inside the temple.

But the noise had carried, and men were running into the temple enclosure to see what was happening. That was when Aurelia Paulina shouted to the slaves: "Go! Go into the Temple! Help the priests! Stop them!"

None of the women dared to follow, but the men brought out the priestess, carrying her as they wept, for she was dead, her skull smashed by a hammer.

When the gathering crowd saw this, a low moan began, and then a growl that grew and grew. They broke like a wave over the Christians.

Only one of the Christians was killed as they caught them. The rest were taken to the open land outside Epona's temple. But then someone came shouting that the priestess was dead, and a howl of grief and anger rose. I heard the call in British: "Burn them! Burn them!"

It is an old way of killing the sacrilegious among the Celts, and I have never seen it happen before. Yet I have much of the Celt in me too…

I never knew people could scream as those Christians screamed, for their death was as slow as the crowd could make it, using small fires of well-dried wood so they would not smoke and smother the men, who were tied to green wood withies above them. Burning can be quick; but it doesn't have to be. Everyone knows that Christians believe that burning means that their bodies can never be reborn. That's why they bury their dead. So when they were finally done, the remnants were stamped into the ground, and the ashes and fragments of bone were thrown into the midden heap outside the town.

We stayed and watched and listened, for if we had not, we would not have shown devotion to the goddess, and we too might have suffered retribution from her.

The townsmen should have called to the governor for justice. But the horror of the sacrilege meant that it needed to be wiped away at once. And the governor would understand, and thus do nothing. I knew my uncle.

I saw tears in Numerianus's eyes, I thought, but it was not for the suffering men. No one could feel for them, after what they had done. It was the loss of his hopes that he was mourning, for he knew how this would harden our hearts yet more against any Christian, and his love especially.

# CHAPTER 30

## Licinianus: Saxon ships

We had lost them. We had never seen our pursuers, but only heard them receding in the distance, as they saw we had entered the stream and went south to find where we had come out. We instead crept northeast as the sun rose, staying in the stream until it became too rocky to lead the horses without danger.

It took us a full day and a half to reach the Tueda river for the trackways were poor and muddy, and we were very cautious; and then we followed it, staying away from the river itself, for every few miles along it there was a settlement. We traveled mostly at night, but then, at dawn on the second day, we crested a hill and saw the coast, the sea shimmering more grey than blue beyond a white-edged brown shore. The sun shone weakly through the dull sky, as if fearful of touching the land, and we felt chilled by the northern breeze, sharp and cold off the water. Summer here was not what we were used to in the south.

I blew a kiss to the Sun, for I did not want my thoughts to give the god offence, and we waited for darkness to come before we descended, lying all the while in a defile on the ridge. I thought of my sister, and yearned for her, for I was fearful that she would never recover from what had been done to her. The rage rose in me, but I overcame it; and when the moon was high, I called the others to their feet, and we went down the slope, far enough down that we could see details on the coast, but not so far that we could be seen easily from below.

I had no idea how close we were to the Wall there, but I knew we would find it to the south, somewhere along the coast; so that was the way we went. We hoped to reach Arbeia, on the far eastern edge of the wall, in two to three days, even if we traveled only at night, fearful to be seen. We turned south, traveling carefully, and thus slowly.

But on the second morning, as the sun was rising, we saw a large group of Votadini, and they were heading north along the coast, as if to Curia. This was not just a raiding band; it was a small army, and they were smart enough to have scouts ranging along their route, and on their flanks. If we rode south, we could not avoid them. We had to turn inland, and go west again. But then, in the distance ahead, we saw another group of tribesmen, also heading north. We could not take the chance that they would believe our story: we were nowhere near a path that traders took, for this only the road to Curia for those who lived in the far east of the land, and there was nothing to trade in that region.

It was Lugobelenos who put it succinctly: "We're fucked," he said. And I could not help but laugh, though one's death is no laughing matter, and these people tortured Romans until they died; no clean death lay ahead for us.

We got off our horses to make it harder for them to see us, and led the mounts into a hollow.

"We can't go south," said Rufinus, stating the obvious. "And we can't go west."

We sat there thinking. And then Lugobelenos spoke. "Where are these bands going?"

I handed out some stale bread and cheese, and we chewed thoughtfully.

"There's only one place that makes sense," I said. "They're gathering at Curia."

"For an attack on us," said Lugobelenos, and I looked up and smiled to see my freed slave see himself as a Roman. For that is what he was now.

I nodded. "Nothing else makes sense. And that means…"

"That they will turn away from the coast, at some point… and head for the oppidum we just left."

"And then we can head south again," said Rufinus.

"Exactly. All we need to do is just stay out of sight, and travel north ahead of them, until they turn west."

"And if we are wrong, or if they see us," I said, and smiled. "Then we die."

And we all laughed, as if at a joke.

+ + +

The next two days were torture, of a particularly excruciating kind. We stayed in the hills, hiding in the heather, as the tribesmen moved below us. When there was cover, we moved during the day. When there was not, we moved at night. Always we moved north, away from the Wall, with the tribesmen behind us. We had no choice. We hardly slept, for we were always afraid we'd be discovered, and the ache of exhaustion overcame us.

And then we reached a river, and the bands turned west. They could only be heading for Curia, and we lay watching as they disappeared into the setting sun, deeply thankful. Then we crept up the rise, turned towards the sea, and prepared to go south again. There below us, we saw the prickling lights of fires at the mouth of the river.

The estuary was wide and sheltered by a huge sandbank. On the south was a small cluster of round-houses, no more than ten or twelve. But that was not the thing that made our breath catch. Even in the dying light we could see the sun-reddened shadows of three long ships drawn up on the brown sand shore. Britons don't build such ships. But Saxons do.

"Well," said Lugobelenos, "I think we have found our proof. As if we needed it."

I sat down on the grass, and put my head in my hands. I had no idea what to do; I was too tired. If we went south, would we encounter more bands of tribesmen, heading north to gather at Curia? There was an attack planned. The tribesmen were gathering.

"We're all so exhausted," I said, "that the only thing we can do is sleep. We need it. And tomorrow, we'll go south, and hope we don't meet more Votadini…"

We dug holes for our hips, lay down as the sun set over the land, and wrapped ourselves in our cloaks, afraid of what might happen as we slept. Yet I doubt any of us were still awake as the sun fully set.

+ + +

I woke at sunrise, and the others stirred groggily too: I had slept through the night. We were no longer so exhausted that we could not think; but we were all wondering what to do. We needed to go south, and that was what we prepared to do. But there was something tickling at my mind. We were so close to the Saxon ships. There didn't seem to be many crew… But of course, there would be some. What if we managed to burn them… even one of them? Wasn't it our duty to do something about them?

I gathered the others, and we talked. "We're here to find out as much as we can. But these ships may have more men than we like in them."

"Do they know enough to recognize us as being from below the Wall?" said Rufinus. "As Romans?"

Lugobelenos shook his head. "I don't know. My people certainly would. But these Saxons?"

We made our decision, and in the end decided that the risk was too great. We prepared to move south.

But we had not traveled for more than a few minutes when Lugobelenos swore, and pointed south. "Look. Another group coming north."

I joined him in the expletive, adding a few more of my own.

This was a small group, no more than five or six. But they were enough to stop us, enough to remember us. And since we had backtracked so much, Curia was again very close...

"Do we try to avoid them?" said Rufinus, and it was clear he was afraid. But then, so were we all.

"Won't work. They've seen us. And I think this might be luck for us... Their clothes..."

"Ah," said Lugobelenos. "Yes. Their clothes."

"They're more than we are," said Rufinus.

"Only two more. And we're Romans. If we're quick enough... We attack them, and we kill them all. No survivors... or we die!"

We sat our horses, and waited on the shore, as if we were simple traders going to Curia, looking for new clients. We smiled as they came up to us, and waved our arms at them.

"We have jewels to trade," we called. "Do you want them? Good prices!"

The chieftain in front, a young man with a golden beard, called back, laughing: "No jewels for us! We have no women with us!"

"Going north for the gathering?" Lugobelenos called in his northern British. "Kill the Romans?"

And the young chieftain laughed. "Yes! Then south to the wall, to kill them all!"

I moved up close, holding out something in my hand. It was nothing but a piece of empty cloth. "Look at this amber," I said, "Is there a girl who wouldn't love it? Or... are you already married?"

"Not yet!" he said, laughing, and died as I jerked my sword from its scabbard, and with one stroke struck him in his throat. His mouth widened as the blood spurted from him in a huge stream, and then he fell. The others were striking, and I saw Rufinus fell one tribesman with a blow to his unprotected chest. Lugobelenos's right arm swung in a wide arc, and another fell from his horse, his neck cut through by his axe head. And two were left.

They spurred their horses, trying to escape; but I drove my sword into the side of one of the horses, and it fell, the breath leaving the animal in a terrible dying cry. I leaned over, and struck hard at the rider's head, feeling the skull split under my blade. And Lugobelenos reached down, leaning low from his horse, and gathered the spear that was still held loosely in the hand of the man dying as he slid off his horse, and he hurled it, taking the last fleeing man in the back.

The god's killing madness had hardly taken me, it was all so quick. And it was over now.

We started stripping the men of their clothes, washing off the blood as best we could in the cold water of a stream that flowed here to the sea. There was an inlet nearby, and we carried the bodies to it, covering them with rocks and seaweed. But they'd be easy to see, if anyone looked even a little. There was nothing we could do about that. We had to move fast.

Lugobelenos spoke up then, and I knew how right I had been to free him.

"Sir…" he said, "Sir! An hour to the north of us are the Saxon ships. We're going there anyway! What if British tribesmen burned even one of them?"

I saw the fear on Rufinus's face at the idea of going into harm's way again. The problem was, of course, that it was quite likely we'd die too. And then a thought came into my mind, as if from another entity: how had we come to be here? We were heading south… It was almost as if we had been driven here, and only a god could have done that. And that decided me. Things like this do not happen by chance.

I nodded slowly. "Yes," I said. "I think the gods have just told us that we should turn and go north! Let's see how much damage we can do to those ships, and make the Saxons think it's the British who did it. The gods know the Brittunculi hate the Saxons enough to do it themselves! And if we're going to die, let's do it well!"

+ + +

It is a good thing that fresh blood comes out so easily in cold water, but the clothes are not pleasant to wear afterwards, and I found myself freezing as the sun set. The North, even in summer, is rarely warm, and it can get cold very quickly. I would have loved to wrap myself in a heavy, dry cloak and slept; but that is not the lot of a Roman soldier, even if an officer.

We crept closer, and it was late in the Second Watch – if there had been Watches here – that we arrived close to the hamlet and its roundhouses, and the three ships on the beach.

This was no rich place, where people stayed up late with candles or torches, and almost everyone was asleep. We could smell the wood smoke, and the intense reek of the seaweed these people put into their bread, and the drying fish they lived on. We heard a dog or two; but that was all. The dogs were the biggest problem. They would bark when they heard us, and I had no taste for killing them. Animals, unlike human beings, are beloved of the gods in their innocence, which is why we give them as sacrifices.

At the ships a single fire burned on the beach. It was quite a large fire, and around it sat three men. They were Saxon, judging by their clothes, and I hoped this was all the guard there was. But I was sure that there were men sleeping in the ships. Their lords would not have taken all of the rowers as guards to Curia.

The brown sand of the river estuary looked almost pale in the darkness: there was only a sliver of a moon tonight, and the bright points of the stars were almost all the light there was. We were, in that, lucky.

We lay on the dunes, considering all this, whispering to one another.

"The dogs," Lugobelenos whispered. "They'll start barking when we move down."

"They will," I said. "We need to deal with them somehow."

Lugobelenos spoke, slowly, as if considering his words carefully. "Perhaps the way is not to stop them barking," he said, "but to make them bark too much."

I controlled my laughter. I liked the idea a great deal. "Oh, very good! I like that. How would you do it?"

Lugobelenos was smiling. I knew that, even though I could not see his face clearly. "I have a sling…"

Four times we did it. Lugobelenos would sling a stone at one of the dogs, and it would yelp and bark if he hit it, and all the other dogs would bark too. People came out of the huts, and the Saxons hefted their weapons, and searched the shore. And then they would go back, disgruntled with the uselessness of their alarm.

And then again we did it, and out they came… And again they found nothing. And then again… and then again… and this time no one came out to look.

Then we moved.

The dogs barked again, and no sound or movement, but for a man loudly cursing the dogs. The Saxons stayed where they were, drinking from what seemed, to our straining eyes, to be a leather skin.

My mind was whirling, trying to think of a plan. For the guards to see three men suddenly walk from the dark at this hour? Even if they ignored the dogs, did this make any sense? Not to me.

There was a sudden rush of voices, and we all threw ourselves down in the darkness of the brown beach, hoping we were not seen. We could hear the sound of their barbaric language, as they talked back and forth. A man was rising from one of the ships, and saying something incomprehensible to the men around the fire.

"I think they're bringing on a new guard," whispered Lugobelenos, for he saw that the man from the ship was sitting down by the fire, and one of the other men was returning to the ship.

"How many men are on the ships?" I asked uselessly. We didn't know, and on that knowledge so much depended. "Can you swim, Rufinus?"

He looked helplessly at me.

"Well, I can," I said.

I slipped into the water, far from the beached ships, controlling my involuntary shivering with difficulty. I cursed my stepmother, who had insisted I learn. "Do you want to drown if your boat sinks?" she had said to me. "Into the water!"

Mercy was not strong in her.

I wore only a belt with a dagger. If only this place was not so cold!

I swam out into the sea, using a stroke that disturbed the water the least. If I were in another place, I would have been taken by the phosphorescent edge of the waves as they moved towards me, and the horizon where, even now, a line of light seemed to flicker in pale beauty. But I was here for other reasons.

When I was far enough out not to be easily seen, I turned north towards the ships.

I reached the stern of the nearest one, and hung on to the steering oar, panting, but quietly. Then I moved forward and, as silently as I could, slowly levered myself up and over the side. My wet naked body made little noise as I found firm footing on the planks. Then I waited, utterly still, listening. At first, I heard nothing. Then there was a sudden loud snore, that died away, and then rose again. It came from forward, and I stepped slowly towards it. I prayed I would not trip and alert the Saxons.

There were two of them, sleeping on the deck, both sound asleep. As I leaned over them, I could smell that they had gone to their hard bed drunk. I drew my dagger.

When the Dream comes on me, everything recedes. I become inhuman, and the first man died without even knowing it, with my blade through the left eye into his brain, and my hand over his mouth in case he cried out. But nothing came from him, and the man next to him hardly stirred at that slight indrawn breath. My dagger took him under his lowest left rib, angled up into his heart. His death gasp was almost inaudible. I slipped over the side and on to the next ship. I guessed there were two men there too, but I was wrong: there was no one there. On the last ship, things were more difficult: there someone was awake. I guessed it was the man who had gotten up from the fire. And I had to wait for my chance, for I was sure there was another man as well.

That was when Lugobelenos staggered up to the fire.

He was singing off-key in his Northern British, and unless I was mistaken, it was a song about a lost love whom the water nymphs had taken. He fell down more than once, and the Saxons at first rose in fear, reaching for their weapons; but when they saw what they confronted, they began to laugh, and shout, and if they were not taunting him, I was no judge of men.

There was a shout from the ship I had not yet been to, and a man jumped off the prow, and walked towards the fire, shouting: "Hwá is sé wer? Bídaþ. Kómu ðǽr tó sehanni."

I could understand nothing, but I was sure he was the man in charge. His manner was unmistakable.

He jumped off the ship, and began to walk towards the fire. I seized my chance, and heaved myself up over the side of the ship, hoping the last man would not see me. But he did. "Hwá ertu?" he shouted, and reached for his sword.

He had no mail on, nor a sword or a helmet. But he wore a padded tunic, enough to stop all but the most serious of blows. I walked towards him, my hands up as if in supplication. But he was having none of it, and he stabbed straight at my chest. That told me he was no novice. A novice swings his blade, and that is all too easy to evade.

"No, no," I said. I wanted to lie that I was no enemy, but I lacked the words. He stabbed, and I felt the god shrug in me. I dropped to the deck, and in one motion my hand took my dagger from my belt, and slashed across the back of his knee as he tried to cut down at me. I heard him shout in pain, and he staggered back. His tendons were cut now, he could not support himself on that leg, and he stumbled. I was fully in the Dream now, and I whirled, slashing at his wrist. The sword fell, into my hand's reaching grasp, and I felt the god in that victory. It was as if the sword moved all by itself, and now it was reversed and stabbing at his stomach. I knew in my dream that to get through the padded cloth I would need all my force, and I used it. It was like a knife sliding into a fat pig's belly, and he screamed as his stomach was pierced. He fell backwards, and the sword swung up and around, and took out his throat.

We had made so much noise, that I was sure that the Saxons on the shore would have noticed. But they had not. The tide was coming in, the waves were growing, and the wind was rising; there was a great deal of water noise, and, I would surmise, the sounds of the men on the shore shouting uselessly at Lugobelenos.

I stripped the clothes off one of the dead Saxons, and put them on, in part to cover my shivering body, but in part to hide who I was. There was blood on them; but why would there not be?

I jumped off the ship, still carrying the sword I had taken and walked towards the fire. I was still in the Dream, and I cared nothing if I was noticed or not. We were three, they were four, but I cared nothing for that.

One Saxon sitting on the other side of the fire saw me, but my clothes made him believe that I was one of them, and he turned his attention back to Lugobelenos. I smiled, and drove my sword into the back of one of the men who was mocking my freedman. He screamed, and fell, and then Lugobelenos transformed from a drunk into a warrior, and the axe that hung from his belt came up, and struck. He was brave, but he was not accurate, for he had been a slave too long. The man fell, crying out in agony at the blow, which had split his shoulder in half. But Lugobelenos had good instincts: he ignored the man at his feet, and struck at a second Saxon, who threw himself back so hard that he tripped. Lugobelenos chopped, and the axe buried itself in the Saxon's stomach. Now there were two left, and Rufinus had come from the darkness and was attacking one. A rapist he might have been; but a coward he was not. And I was left facing the man who had jumped off the ship.

He shouted at me, but I would never know what he said. And then he attacked. He was no untried fighter: he knew how to kill, and he thought he could kill me.

Neither of us had a shield, but both of us had swords. That was how we would decide this.

I have noticed that, when I am in the Dream, I never strike first. It is as if something needs to know how the other will fight before it begins its work. And his first blow was a work of art. He lunged at my throat, but as he did the sword flashed downwards and struck at the side of my knee.

If I had been anyone else, it would have worked, and I would have known my death that night. But instead, I whirled around, and his blade missed my knee by a finger; and as I came back at him, I struck, and I saw a line of red appear in the skin of his neck. It was a tiny wound, but it warned him that this would be no easy fight. We circled one another, and then he struck again. I dropped to my knees, a small part of me sad that it was almost over, and drove my sword up at his stomach. It penetrated no more than two inches, but he knew he was going to die as he started to bleed. I saw panic on his face at the pain of the wound; belly wounds rarely heal. And he threw himself at me, determined not to die alone. But he did.

I looked around. All the Saxons were dead, Lugobelenos was standing leaning on his axe; but where was Rufinus? Then I saw he was down, clutching at his shoulder. I looked at the wound, pulling his tunic wide to see it.

"Not very bad," I said. "You'd survive it."

His eyes widened suddenly, bewildered by what I'd said.

"Of course, I will!"

"No," I said. "A pity. I'm no lover of killing. I just do it well, as a gift from my family gods."

"I don't understand you!"

"Why, Rufinus," I said, "Do you remember my sister and the way you helped Constantinus and his friend rape her?"

His eyes were so wide. "Oh no! Not that! I had no choice! I thought you didn't know!"

"Indeed," I said, "I do know. All of my family know. And all of you are going to die. *All* of you. Do you think my family would forget? Look at our name… We are not called Vindex for nothing."

Lugobelenos and I carried coals to the three vessels, and spread them in the hulls pulling the sails over them. The flames began to rise, and we watched, briefly, for we feared discovery, just enough to make sure that the ships were well alight.

I left Rufinus on the shore in his Votadini clothes for the dawn to discover with its light, his lifeblood still oozing from his cut throat. We had arranged him artfully with a Saxon, as if they had killed each other in the battle. He was serving a purpose, at least, and that is what few men do in their deaths: if we were lucky, the Saxons would blame the Votadini for the death of their men. Rufinus was not a bad man; but blood revenge once begun cannot be abandoned. The gods, having once given vengeance, never withdraw it; rather it will be turned on those who asked for it if their gift is wasted. But I could not but feel pain in my soul at what I had done. No, pain is not the right word. But I didn't know what that feeling was, and so I had no word for it.

As we ran, hearing the distant shouts of men as they saw the flames, I knew. I felt shame.

He was the first. The others would be easier, for they were worse men.

# CHAPTER 31

## Licinianus: Against the Tribes

It had taken no more than a month for the wildfire to break out in the north. At first, we heard only whispers of it, but now we knew that the Saxon and British alliance was in fragments. The Saxons, discarding all attempts to remain hidden, had accused the Votadini of betraying their trust by burning their ships; and they had sent the only boat they had left, a tiny sailing skiff, to their homeland begging for a ship to take them home. They had retreated to a small village on the coast, only a little south from where they had beached their ships. The Votadini were gathering against them, because the Saxons, in their usual fashion, had killed all the fisherfolk who lived there, and stolen and burned everything they could reach. They were never generous in battle, or thoughtful of the consequences. They liked to kill.

The Roman army moved north now, along the eastern coast, towards Curia, and though Constantinus never spoke to me, I could see his intent. The northern tribes were in disarray and conflict; the Saxons were sure that the tribes had attacked them, and the Saxons had attacked them in retaliation. We made a marching camp not too far south of the fishing village where we had burned the ships, and waited for what fortune would bring.

Fortune brought a beautiful, sunny day, with a cool breeze. It also brought four Saxon ships from the east, and they were full of men. We sat our horses on the rise near the village, and watched the Saxons beach, and attack the Votadini to save their compatriots. I could not but admit that Constantinus had made a brilliant decision: to march north, even though no one had yet attacked us, even though there was truce between us, was treacherous, but right. They had been planning to spill our blood, and leave Britannia desolate. They deserved treachery.

The battle swirled, back and forth. The Saxons knew they could not win against the hundreds of British; their aim was simply to get their friends off the shore. But the British were not having it. And that was when we attacked.

It did not matter whom we killed. The Votadini, the Epidii, the Novantae, Damnonii, the Picti, the Saxons... all were our enemies. They might be fighting one another, but our aim was to kill as many of them as we could. We needed to see so many die that it would be fifty years before they would dare attack again. And this was the perfect time.

We attacked with cavalry, as is not our Roman habit, for we prefer an infantry charge. But only the impact of heavily armored horsemen would do here, and the land was flat. Our missile troops on either flank were already shooting at the men ahead, but it seemed almost as if no one there noticed the whirring arrows and singing slingstones as they killed them from behind.

The fighting was so loud near the coast that very few of those there even knew we had come until they felt the pain of our lances in their backs, the impact of the maces on their helmets, and the shock of plumbata as we hurled them into the formation. I felt the Dream that is the mark of my family take me. I was in the Battle-Joy our family god gives as a gift, and I rode to kill. The fact that I was fighting for an army Constantinus led mattered nothing. And as we struck, the standard bearers let the Dragons free and they began their shrieking as air entered the trumpets in their snarling mouth and their painted cloth tails snapped in the wind.

I lowered my contus and drove the point into the back of a tall Celt. He shouted in agony as it took him in the spine, and the chain which held the spear to the horse jerked tight, and drove it through his mail, pulling him around and sideways as the horse wrenched it free of his back. The point came free and I rode at the next man, who was starting to turn as the screams and furor behind him caught his attention. The lance took him in his open mouth, for I knew I would get it free from his throat, and be able to strike again. The men at the rear were now turning to face our onslaught, and my lance took a third man in the chest. I let the horse ride it on through him; and when it came free, I dropped it and let the lance fall to hang on its chains by the horse's side. Its time was over. I drew my spatha, for most of the tribesmen had little armor, and swung it hard to split a man's skull as he ran from me. The sound of the barritus rose and fell around me, and I roared it with the others, my mind knowing only the joy of battle.

Often, I can remember very little of battles: it is literally a dream for me. But sometimes things stand out, and on this day that happened to me, for I met someone I knew: Trahayarnos.

There is a sad thing about the Dream… It never matters who is there, their sex, their age; if they fight me, I will kill them. I have no control over it, I have no restraint. It only shies away from children.

I look back on it now with sadness. He was a good man. He helped us, and if he tried to kill us later when he knew that we were spies, that was just what his loyalty demanded. I had no desire to attack him, but he placed himself in my path, and struck at me.

My shield rose, and the blow glanced away, for my arm knew which way to go all by itself. I leaned low and struck upwards at his belly, and he leaned away to make the blow slide sideways. He saw my face. "You fight too well, trader!" and he laughed. I laughed too, but there was no humor in me. This man would die. I feinted at his thigh, and he pulled his horse away, rearing; and I struck with all my force at his side. I felt the mail break, and the blade bite into flesh. He flinched and cried out, but it was not deep. He struck backhanded at me, and I bent low in the saddle and the blade hissed over my head. He struggled to turn the horse, and I let him until his sword-arm was raised to strike; and then I leaned in and drove the sword-point into his belly. The blade did not penetrate, but the breath was driven from him. And I switched my blade into my other hand to avoid his shield, and swung at his neck. I felt it bite, and blood spurted from the side of his neck. He leaned down, his mouth wide and bloody; and I thrust again and took out his throat.

He leaned forward and then fell sideways, as if tired; and my horse's hooves smashed his face into the grass, turning it red with blood and white with splinters of broken bone.

I rode on, to kill more.

+ + +

We crucified every Saxon we found alive, and then moved on to Curia. We burned it, and killed everyone who did not run, man woman and child. Constantinus was not after slaves to sell as his father had been: he wanted to wreak havoc, to destroy the tribe, and those who had gathered to support them. But that is hard to do, once they know their cause is lost. They run. They hide. We found a whole family in a river, under the water and breathing through reeds to stay hidden. None were let to live, after the women were raped. I have no taste for that, after what happened to my sister, but made no attempt to try and stop them. It would have been futile. This is how war is, and the soldiers are only controllable as long as you do not ask too much from them, or try to take from them their due.

We fanned out into small detachments, driving north of the Wall of Antoninus, and did worse than Constantius had done so recently, for we left nothing living. And then, finally, we left that blackened land and its swarming carrion crows, and went south. Looking at that desolation, I could only believe it would be two generations at least before they would think to attack us again. Valentia was ours again. For a time.

In late summer, almost autumn, we marched south, heading for winter quarters at Eburacum. All of us were sure that Constantinus was not long for Britannia. Gaul, and Spain were also his, by agreement with Galerius, the senior Emperor. But how long could that last? Galerius hated Constantinus with a hatred that surpassed Cicero's for Catilina, and Constantinus had no warmer feelings in return. He would leave soon, and be gone from us.

# CHAPTER 32

## Severiana: Travail

As the days passed, and the birth approached, I found myself entering into a period of greater and greater torpor. All through my pregnancy I had swung from misery to anger and back again. But I was active, for a pregnant woman, even to the extent of regularly horse-riding, which no woman in my condition is supposed to do, or so the slaves whispered in hushed tones. Perhaps I wanted to lose the baby, they muttered to each other, and perhaps they were even right.

Most of all I was angry at my own female body. The rape had been bad enough; the pregnancy was betrayal compounded. Why had my body not refused to accept the vileness of the seed that had been forced into me? Why was this burden imposed on women, to bear children even for evil men who deserved to leave nothing of themselves behind?

Who can answer questions like that? They are part of the way life is, and in life no justice is to be found.

But on this particular day I was suddenly free of my lethargy, and I wanted to be out in the air. The weather was warm and the sun was out; there were only a few clouds. It was early in the morning, and the birds were sounding their distinctive voices all around. It was a good day to be out.

I left the villa without telling anyone, without even waiting to eat a crust of bread. I walked up the hill to the temple: I always found it gave peace to me when I thought of the mother and father whom I had never known, but who lay there, under the floor. As I reached the door, I felt another cramp in my belly. But that did not disturb me. In the last day or so, I had often felt cramps.

I prayed a little, asking for better things from our gods, and, though they had more than once granted us our prayers, I expected nothing this time. Then I continued up the hill into the forest, enjoying the smell that leaves in water always bring.

I was perhaps fifteen minutes into the forest when I came to a clearing; and there, sitting on a log, was Numerianus. Inside, I groaned, for did not want company today. But I groaned also because he was intolerable to be around these days, so morose had he become. The sacrilege at Five Temples had only made his Aurelia Paulina turn on him with a fury wilder than I had ever seen from my measured stepmother, telling him with brutal finality that he was never

223

to meet the "Christian girl" again, on pain of being cast off. With any other parent, one could believe that her love for her son would eventually overcome her resolve; but not my stepmother. Her nature had always been like steel in that regard: what she said, she did. So, depression was Numerianus's lot these days.

"Oh merda," I muttered under my breath in an unladylike manner, and greeted him, trying to act as if I was glad to see him.

I sat down beside him, because I could think of no way to avoid it. But I was going to make it quick, if I could.

I saw how sad his face looked and suddenly felt sorry for him. "Not feeling good, Numerianus?"

He shook his head. "No. And there's nothing I can do."

"You've kept away from the girl?"

"I have no choice. Even her father says I am to have nothing to do with her. He will never let her marry someone who is not a Christian."

"Well, you can't do that. Think of our family."

"We worship demons, he said."

I gasped. "What? How dare he? Our gods? Who have given us so much?"

And at that point I doubled over, for I was struck by two pains at once... a brutal cramp in my stomach and an equally bad one in my lower back. I cried out. I couldn't help it.

Numerianus, even in his misery, noticed. "Are you all right?"

I stood up, trying to relieve the pressure; but it did no good. The pain remained. I looked down at my skirt. There was a pink stain on it.

"Oh, Numerianus... I think I am starting. Help me! I need to get back to the villa!"

Leaning on Numerianus, I began to walk back towards our home, and I was fine for a while. But we were walking so slowly that it was not long before I had another contraction, and would have fallen to my knees had Numerianus not held me up.

He looked panicked. Then he came to a decision. "Sit here." He leaned me against a tree. "I'm going to get men to carry you. Stay here! I'll be back as soon as I can!"

I felt terror. What if no one came? Would I die here? Licinianus would so miss me, he would never forgive me for not taking better care of myself! Why was this happening so quickly?

I tried to control myself, breathing deeply to stop myself sobbing. For a long while everything was fine, and I wondered if I could walk down the path by myself... then the pain hit again. "So this," I thought, "is what it's like to have a child. I don't think I like it..."

I put my head in my hands, and when I looked up, Numerianus was coming through the bushes with slaves and a board to carry me on, and behind them, my stepmother too.

I hardly remember being taken back to the villa. I know I lay in my bed feeling the squeezing in my belly come and go. The midwife, a woman who normally dealt with births among the slaves and tenants, assured me it would be a long time before the actual labor began, since this was my first birth; but she was wrong. My water broke only a few hours later.

+ + +

I remember the unutterable relief as the baby finally came. To me the travail seemed long, though in fact it was not. I simply knew that at last I could rest, that at last the pain would stop.

The gods may have given me a quick birth, but they did not refrain from their own kind of humor, as I would soon learn. I heard my stepmother saying, "There it is, the head is out... the rest will come easily." And I felt the motion of the body squeezing from me.

"It's over, Severiana. A boy! Soon you'll be able to sleep."

Then I heard the midwife. "Domina..." I could sense her hands feeling me, and her voice sounded strange. "Domina, I think there's another one."

"Oh, please no..." It was my voice, but I could not remember speaking.

How could there be? The intense desire to push had gone from me, and minutes passed without more of it... Then it came again.

"Will it be a second boy perhaps?" The midwife seemed hopeful.

"No," I shouted. "It will be a girl! It is always a boy and a girl in our family!"

I screamed, and the second one started to come.

"It's a girl," said my stepmother, and I began to cry.

"Of course it is," said Flavilla. "Of course it is." She understood why I was sobbing at the betrayal I felt. Our twin gods had bestowed their gift on the product of my rape.

# CHAPTER 33

## Licinianus: Deva

It took us almost three days to get to Deva from Eburacum, riding horses all the way. None of us dared to wear any clothes that marked us as military, nor did we use a diploma to avail ourselves of the mansios or their horse changes along the route for the same reason.

My mind was in a fever. I had received a message that my sister had been brought to bed, and given birth to twins, a boy and a girl. I was appalled. Such twins mean something special in our family, and I could not understand why our gods had done this to us. It was as if they were determined to force us to derive some meaning from this assault on our honor, even as they gave us the vengeance we had asked, for this sign was unequivocal: the children were to become as much part of our family as I and my sister were.

I remembered that the Emperor Marcus Aurelius had likened life more to being a wrestler than a dancer. I often felt that way, and especially I felt that way now. I would have to wrestle with this fact, and try somehow to comprehend it, and live with it. I needed to be with my sister, to talk with her, so that we could understand this together; but I could not. To Deva I must go.

The reason was simple. We might be able to get the forces at Eburacum to rouse themselves. They were unsettled, they were angry, for they had fought a hard war, and done it well, and as yet they had not been paid. But the chances of our success depended so much on us not being the only force to revolt, not because we needed the men, but because we needed to be seen as representing all the soldiers in Britannia. If we could get the XX Valeria Victrix to join us, together we would seem exactly that.

We entered at the eastern gate, and made our way towards the inn we were to stay at. I had not been to Deva before, but Milo had, so he knew where to go. It surprised me to realize that the city was bigger than Eburacum. I had never thought of it as being such a size.

"Who are we going to talk to? The Legate?"

Milo laughed. "Someone much more powerful. A man called Ulpius Silvanus Firmus… Primus Pilus Iterum."

If you have not served in the army, you cannot know the power of Primi Pili. In theory they are below the Legate and the tribunes, but it's a brave tribune who would ignore their advice. Even I, a senior Tribunus Laticlavius, treated such with great respect. And a Primus Pilus Iterum could only be the Prefect of the Camp, for that meant that he had risen to the peak of his profession, and then been in addition been appointed as second-in-command of the legion.

"The Legate doesn't matter?"

"Not this Legate. He collects carved jewels, hunts pretty young boys, and dreams of going back to Rome as soon as he can."

"Ah," I said. "I've heard about commanders like that."

"If the Prefect turns us down, we can forget about this legion. But he was a soldier of Carausius, so we have hope. Never an Amicus, though."

It had begun to drizzle, which in Britannia we hardly notice, but the way was easy to find. As it always is in legion-built cities, everything is a right angle. We found our hospitium, and received our room as our horses were rubbed down and stabled. Since it was almost sundown, we went to sleep.

Milo snored.

+ + +

We waited a full day before we acted. Milo, in a teasing mood, would not tell me why, but I soon learned: Artorius came in the night.

I admit that I did not recognize him at first, for the boy I had seen all those years ago was now a man. But the resemblance to the Carausius I remembered from all those years ago was strong, when I thought about it: the same curly red-brown hair, the same square face, even the same stocky build. He did not look happy.

We talked over cups of wine, sitting in the inner courtyard of the hospitium. He came right out and told us why he looked so morose.

"You want me to become emperor... but I have no desire for power! Whatever my father was, I have no ambition there! That was his desire, but it's never been mine. When I think of him, I think only that he died because of his choices! I want to live a peaceful life!"

"Aren't you involved with the Amici Carausii?"

"Yes, but just because of my father!"

"So, tell me," said Milo, "Does it feel good to deny your father as you are forced to? And though *you* may have no ambitions, but what would happen if Constantinus found out who you are? Don't you think he might get rid of you just to be safe? Do you think he'll let you live a peaceful life?"

Artorius shook his head. "Why would they bother me? I'm not involved in anything that could be dangerous to the Emperor."

"Then perhaps you should read this. It's a copy of a letter sent to the

227

Emperor Constantinus by the head of the Agentes in Rebus[26] in Eburacum. As you can see by the date, it's recent. Don't ask me how I got it."

> *Following my conversation with your illustriousness about the secret organization of the Amici Carausii, we have discovered that it is much larger than we had guessed, and that its members are everywhere, even in the administration of the British provinces, and in the armies that obey your gloriousness's commands. We have found no clear evidence of a plot in Britannia, but, based as it is on admiration of an illegal ruler, the very presence of such a secret organization must be seen as dangerous. We would thus suggest that your illustriousness consider acting against them. In particular, we have discovered that the son of the usurper Carausius is still alive, and, we believe, living in Corinium. While we have no evidence that he is involved in anything dangerous to your serenity, he is nevertheless a threat that cannot be ignored. We would like thus to have your eternity's permission to proceed as we discussed last time we met, to find this man and remove him before he can be used by the Amici Carausii against your majesty. It will not be difficult to do this. We already have some indication of who and where he is.*

I could see Artorius's face pale. He knew that this was his death sentence, either soon or late; and no man can face that with calm.

Artorius dropped the tablet onto the table. It fell hard. I pushed his wine-cup towards him, and he drank deep.

"This is real?" he said, without looking up.

"It's real."

"This is not the life I want!"

Milo reached over and held his shoulder tight. "So often we have no choice about the life we lead. You cannot escape the power of an Emperor when the Emperor comes after you."

"I could run!"

"You could try. But the Agentes are everywhere, and their fortune depends on finding those who do not want to be found."

We all sat silent in the courtyard. I felt such pity for Artorius. Both Milo and I lived lives of danger and violence. Artorius was just a notary whose life was one of pens and tablets and lists. From this to becoming part of a conspiracy

---

[26] Literally "Those Active in Matters." These were the secret police of later Rome.

to remove the emperor was a leap indeed.

"You have a room here," I said. "Go to it and think what is best for you to do."

Artorius said: "I just don't know…" Then he nodded, no longer looking at us, and stood up.

"Remember," said Milo at his retreating back. "There is someone who wants to meet you this evening."

+ + +

It was summer, and the sun sets late in Britannia in that season; so it was still light when we set out on our trip. Tonight we would meet the Prefect of the Legion, and we would see how he responded to our plan. I admit that I was not optimistic. He was a man at the end of a long and successful career. Why should he become involved in such a risky endeavor? Death was the only reward that failure would grant us, and that is not an encouraging thought.

I was struck by the legionaries at the Principia. This may have been a force nominally headed by an incompetent Legate, but clearly someone kept a tight rein on his men: they were in immaculate dress, and their discipline was manifest. They made us wait politely before they led us to where the Prefect was waiting, sitting in a small room at a table with a slave just then laying it sparsely with bread, wine, water and olives. There was to be no fancy welcome here.

He motioned us to sit and examined us. There was something very impressive about the man, and his unfashionable grey beard seemed to indicate that he held to older values. Some men have a character and strength that show very clearly when you meet them: this was such a man. I did not think anyone would cross him with impunity.

He indicated that we should help ourselves from the table, and we did. I had the feeling that no one dared not to. I poured myself a small amount of wine and a great deal of water.

He started at Artorius. "I don't need, I think, to ask which one of you is Carausius's son."

"Am I that much like him?" asked Artorius. "I can hardly remember his face now."

"You are very like him. And I knew him well. I was with him right until the end when that bastard murdered him. I was on the steps of the Basilica when it happened. I had to run for my life. I was too close to him for Allectus to have let me live."

"I was there too," I said.

"You? How old were you?"

"Very young. My stepmother took us to see the sight."

"And you saw more than you had expected," he said wryly, his mouth twisting just a little.

"I had actually met him at our villa a day or so before. He came to visit on his way to Londinium."

"Ah… then I know who you are. You are a Vindex. Your stepmother and Carausius were close."

"Yes, Prefect."

"That leaves you," he said, pointing at Milo. "You are the man who asked for this meeting. You are an Amicus Carausii. A dangerous thing to be. Constantinus, if he knows about your people – and I'm sure he does, for his father did – would not like such a secret organization. The Frumentarii – no, they're called Agentes in Rebus now, I believe – have always been busy creatures. I have one on my staff now, who thinks I don't know about him."

And he laughed a little.

"Enough. Time for you to speak, and at length. Begin."

When Milo had finished, Firmus said nothing; but he leaned back in his chair and grunted in the back of his throat. I had no idea how to take that.

He leaned forward, resting his chin on his folded hands. Finally, he spoke. "You realize, of course, that you've given your lives over to me. All I would have to do is call the guards, and send you to Constantinus. It would not be pleasant for you. So, tell me: why do you think to trust me?"

I had no answer. But Milo did. "You have very close friends. Some of them are members of the Amici. And they have told us, in confidence, how you feel about Britannia and what lies ahead. They believe you are as unhappy as we are at the constant drain of soldiers to wars between pretenders to the Imperial throne. That is one reason."

I heard Firmus say a contemptuous word under his breath, and at first, I could not understand it. Then I realized: it was British.

"That is all?" Firmus said.

I don't know why I spoke up then: it was pure intuition, I think. Instead of the Latin we had been using, I spoke in British. "Perhaps it's also because of the fact that you were born to this land. Perhaps your wife was also. And your children."

And then he answered in British too, and his tone was ironic. His accent was very like my own. I doubt he was born very far from my home.

"Very clever. Yes, I'm British... one of the few to rise to this position. And I intend to stay in this land when I leave the army, with my British children. And that matters to me. Tell me why *you* want to do this."

Neither of the other two understood us. Their bemused faces told me that. That was no surprise. Milo was from Dalmatia; and Artorius had been brought up in a city, where most speak only Latin.

I told him, leaving out none of the shameful facts, none of what Constantinus had done to my family. He understood.

"Yes," he said in Latin. "That is the best of reasons."

The silence was long. We all waited. We had said all we could.

"I will say this. Like you, I think the end of the Empire is approaching. The last century proved that. And though I have faith in Diocletianus, he is a sick man, and the vegetables he tends so carefully now will not help to keep him alive longer. I have no faith in those who will follow him. And Constantinus will take every man he can from Britannia when he moves against Galerius. This legion will be no exception. So... I am inclined towards your cause. But tell me... what will make the army at Eburacum rise against him?"

"There is only one answer to that," said Milo. "The men's pay."

"And?"

"The coin will have to be brought up from the mints. There is nowhere near enough in Eburacum."

Firmus nodded. "So you intend to make sure it never arrives. You believe you can do that?"

"I believe so. There are a great many of us."

"That is a good answer, since I know of nothing else that would so certainly rouse the men. And you have given me a good excuse, for my men also have not been paid."

He stood up. It was clearly our time to go. "I will not move until I hear you have succeeded, for I'm not minded to commit suicide. Understand me clearly: until I hear, I will not move."

Milo nodded. "You will hear."

"And my men get paid too!"

+ + +

We rode south early the next morning, all three of us: myself, Milo, and the despairing Artorius. We had a meeting with my stepmother and my sister, though Artorius did not yet know that, for our task with him was not yet finished. He was riding in his carruca a little ahead of us, while we were on

231

horseback. I leaned over to Milo, and, in as low a voice as I could, asked him the question that I had been wanting to ask for the last day.

"How did you get that letter?"

"You mean the letter to Constantinus about Artorius?"

"Yes!"

"Oh, I wrote it at the hospitium a day or so ago. I thought we'd need it."

"*You* wrote it…"

"Yes."

# CHAPTER 34

## Severiana: Villa on the Hill

And then my stepmother had dragged me away from Oak Villa? For what? To view a villa she thought I should buy with the money I had gotten from Helena? But she was implacable.

"Constantinus has already tried to kill you once," said Aurelia Paulina calmly, as if talking to a child. "He clearly believes you are pregnant by him, and is afraid of the consequences of having an heir he cannot control flying in the wind, a member of a family that must hate him. Why should he not try to kill you again? I doubt that the knowledge that he has two children rather than one, and a boy among them, will make him stop. Quite the opposite."

"And why should buying a villa make him stop?" I protested.

"It will give you a refuge, if you need it, for we will make sure no one knows you own it. Trust me. When you arrive at the villa, you will find a nice surprise waiting there. It is very beautifully situated."

We went west to Corinium. We had some old soldiers with us, as well of course as the slaves. I was not in a good mood. I had only had the babies six weeks before, yet my stepmother felt that it was important that I go on this long journey... And the babies, of course, had to go with us, for I had not yet dried. I nursed them, because that was the best way to relieve my aching breasts; but for all the rest of the time I left them in the care of Pulcheria, his nurse. I already had a wetnurse to feed them when I didn't want to, was too angry, or just too tired. I was so often tired, since the birth.

I thought we would rest in Corinium (which, strangely, the natives apparently call Cironium), but instead we passed by the city and turned northwest. Then we headed for our final destination: a villa[27] about fifteen or twenty miles towards the road to Glevum and Deva.

It was less than a day's journey to the villa we had come to see, but it had been raining for days, and we had had to leave the paved road very soon after our departure. What we had entered on was at best a road-wide length of mire, and the pace of our carriage, slow on the driest days, was snail-like.

My stepmother was reading her accounts and letters in the way she often

---

[27] Great Witcombe

now did, tilting her head back, for, as she got closer to old age, what she read got further away. She finished dictating her letter to her secretary, and, looking up at me, saw how tired I was.

"Perhaps you could lean back and try to sleep for a little, my dear? We'll be there soon. And then we'll put you to bed."

I don't remember arriving at the villa, I was so tired. I vaguely sensed being lifted by two slaves and carried inside; I remember being set into a deliciously soft bed, and my clothes being removed by a pair of women, and my body being bathed with wet cloths and then dried; and I slept.

I woke soon after dawn, and for the first time since the birth I felt refreshed and full of energy. It was as if something had happened inside me, and I was no longer exhausted, in my body and in my mind, as I had been ever since the birth. I seemed to hear a woman's voice saying, "That is enough. No more of this. Time to be strong again. Time to act."

I sat up, and looked around me.

I was in a pleasant cubicle, with wall paintings showing scenes of the Nile, with flowers and animals. It made me remember the paintings that my grandfather had had painted for my mother in our own villa, and it made me happy. I had not come close to happiness in a long time.

I was in someone else's house, and I had no idea how to act, for we had come here, not as friends visiting, but as strangers and prospective buyers being given lodging. So I called tentatively, not really expecting a response. But one came immediately, and a slave woman entered as if by magic, with a tray of wine, water, olive oil, olives, bread and cheese. She had clearly been waiting. But I ate nothing: I just didn't want to eat then. I wanted to move!

Her head bowed, she said, "Would you like a bath, domina? The water is heated."

How long was it since I had had a bath? I had lacked the energy, and my women had bathed me from ewers instead.

"Yes!" I said, "I would love a bath!"

The bath here was lovely, and you could reach it without going outside, just as at home. I lay in luxury as a slave-woman rubbed oil on my body, and scraped it off with a strigil. Then she fitted thick-soled bath-sandals on my feet so I could go into the tepidarium. There were soft couches there, and the steam rose around me, until my body ran with sweat. Then I went into the caldarium, had my sandals removed, and stepped into the deliciously hot water. I lay in it so long, luxuriating and wrinkling in the heat, that the slave-woman called anxiously to me, asking if I were all right. I was… and when I threw myself into the cold water of the frigidarium, it was as if all my hesitations had gone from me in the shock of the chill.

I lay there as they perfumed me with rose and arranged my hair, dressing me in my own fine clothes, clothes I had not worn for months. I had not even been aware that Aurelia Paulina had had them packed. Then I went outside for the first time, and stood on the terrace overlooking the villa and the rise and fall of the land in the distance.

I don't think I have seen a more lovely place. It was on a hillside, and the house was built on three levels… or was it four? The skies had cleared, and the views of the hills in the distance were delightful, some green with pines and wet winter pasture, some pale yellow with the stalks left by the harvest of the summer grain. It stretched far away into the distance. I adore our own dear Oak Villa… but this was much bigger, and in such a lovely spot, even covered as parts of it were now with a pale morning mist. Can you say you have fallen in love at a glance? I suppose so; for that is what I did.

Aurelia Paulina was suddenly at my elbow, and I was glad for that, for I wanted to know more about this place as we walked among the buildings.

Aurelia Paulina said: "It's well situated: only 13 miles to Corinium. And look at this view! This is the perfect place for you."

"Why is he selling this lovely place?"

"His two sons have died, the daughters are gone to their husbands … and the last one near is the wife of an official living in Londinium. The owner is ill and wants to die with his family and his grandchildren."

"So, he has no one to leave it to. That's sad. How much does he want?"

My stepmother told me, and I gasped. "That much?"

She shrugged. "Forty centuria of land, everything is in perfect condition, and it comes with 120 or so slaves to work it. There are also industries on the property that provide a good revenue. It's a very good price."

"I love it," I said.

I had never really wanted to own such a place as this, but with the money I now had, I could afford this… easily. I wondered…

Aurelia Paulina looked at me, suddenly alert. "I haven't heard words from you that show any feeling for a very long while."

The breeze was blowing strands of my hair into my eyes, and tears started in my eyes, not from sadness anymore, but because I felt at last free of my nightmare. I could only manage a few words: "Yes, I know." And I flicked my head to clear the hair away.

My stepmother turned suddenly. "This is the owner, Cassianus Egnatius Silvanus," she said.

I had not heard him come, and I bowed my head in respect to the gentleman. He was quite old, it seemed to me… but then at that young age, everyone much older than me seemed quite old. But I think he really was. He was white-haired where he still had hair, his skin was mottled as old skin often is, and he walked with difficulty.

"I'm pleased to meet you, sir," I said, bowing politely.

He smiled, and suddenly I liked him, for he had a very pleasant smile.

"I'm so surprised you want to sell this lovely place! I never would!"

"Sometimes, my dear," he said, "you just get too old. It's very large you know, and a lot of work. And it's filled with memories of my children and wife, all now gone."

I felt sad at those words, but I did not reply, for I had no idea how to do so. To cover my confusion, I gestured at my stepmother. "You two know each other, I gather?"

He laughed. "Oh, we know each other very well!"

I looked at Aurelia, not understanding.

She shrugged her shoulders, amused. "I've known this gentleman for a long time. I sell on his products… wool, wheat… And tiles too! Very high-quality tiles, I might add. That's why it's a good buy."

The old man coughed, amused. "We have good clay here."

Aurelia Paulina nodded her head as if confirming something, and sadly; but she said nothing more on this subject. Instead she said: "Well, unless I'm mistaken, the persons we came to meet just arrived." And she pointed down the hill to where some slaves were gathering around a carruca and two horsemen. The three men began walking up the steps that led to where we were.

And that was when I shrieked in a most unladylike manner, for one of them was my dear brother, walking along with Milo! I started running to Licinianus, and he swept me up in his arms, holding me tight. I hugged him until I no longer could, waving at Milo. He was laughing at me.

"I hope you like your surprise!" said my stepmother.

"You are a witch to tease me like this! I didn't want to come, Licinianus! She never told me you'd be here!"

"You needed this," said Aurelia Paulina. "You've had a very hard time."

"You look so much better, my soul!" Licinianus said. "So much better than when I last saw you!"

"I am. I really am. You know about the twins…"

"Yes. And we must talk about that, and what it means. But for now, let me introduce you to Marcus Aurelius Mausaeus Artorius, the person who saved you in Londinium when you were young. You must remember."

Artorius was wearing the kind of staid, unbright but expensive clothing that government officials tend to favor, and the brimless hat which was called the Pannonian pileus, trimmed in red and gold. He was a pleasant-looking man, I thought.

I bowed my head to him. "I am very glad to see you again."

He smiled back, and it was a lovely smile, but a strained one, I thought. He was not happy to be here.

"You have indeed changed!" I said, saying the obvious. But I could not think of anything more original in that moment.

"Well, I remember you well, Severiana, so well! I remember how brave you were when we were trying to escape in Londinium!"

But I was thinking only of how rude I was being. "I can't remember being brave. I was too terrified!"

Impulsively, I started to reach out my hand to touch him; and then my body cringed, and I drew back at the thought of being close to his strange male body. I was so grateful that I had not felt that way with my brother!

I saw Artorius looking at me, a little hurt, for he had seen my sudden recoil. But there was nothing I could do now, and instead I tried to smile and laugh, as if I cared nothing about anything of consequence. Aurelia Paulina, with her usual acuity, turned the conversation to one side.

"Artorius comes to us from Corinium, where he works for the new praeses of Flavia Caesariensis."

"Via Deva," said Milo.

"Things went well?" asked my stepmother.

"As well as anyone could expect," said Milo. "He agreed, with conditions."

She nodded. "We'll talk later."

"I've so often thought of you!" I lied to Artorius. "Tell me how you've been!"

I had the distinct impression he saw right through me, and his mouth smiled only a little, and wryly. "I'd say I've been very lucky. Through your aunt and stepmother, I was put with a family I could call my own, after my father and my family were all murdered. I'd call that lucky… wouldn't you?"

"Fortuna has indeed smiled on you," I said. "I am very glad."

I hate meaningless words, said just because of the place and time, but that's what one needs to do, sometimes.

Silvanus had raised his hand, and slaves were suddenly bringing chairs for us to sit on, and a table, where they began to places dishes for us to eat on.

"I thought," he said, "that we would eat our lunch here, since the weather has cleared. It's very pretty, isn't it, to sit here and look down at the estate? I often eat here in summer. Of course, it's a little chilly today, but we'll have braziers brought. I hope you don't mind?"

The slaves were setting bowls of Samian ware on the table, one of large black olives, the other of green. They looked luscious.

"Spanish," he said. "Some of the best eating olives, I think."

There was a bowl of olive oil put down, and another of epityrum; I could almost taste the mint and fennel and olive paste from where I sat. But that was not all: there was a cheesy and garlicky moretum as well. Of course, there was garum, for the hard eggs to be dipped into. What is a meal without it? They laid down baskets of bread so fresh it still steamed, and I wanted to grab a loaf, tear off a piece of it and dip it at once. But I controlled myself. And well I did, for there was more: a dish of small deep-fried fish to be eaten whole – I never knew what they were, but they were delicious – and honey-sweetened cheese globuli and fruit for dessert.

It was a sumptuous lunch, and I wondered how I would be able to handle the cena to come that evening, which is always a much larger meal. I remembered the advice of my stepmother and aunt, often said in unison: "Always eat sparingly, even when the food is delightful. You don't want to get fat." I had always laughed at that, for my Aunt Flavilla ate like a millstone, as they say, and never put on weight.

Silvanus smiled at me, and said, as if he knew what I was thinking: "I know you ate no breakfast, so here you are. We'll have a light dinner, if that seems good to you, so eat well."

The wine was good, but not up to the standard of the rest of the meal. But as the small-talk faded, and we relaxed in our chairs to enjoy the view, the serious talk began.

My stepmother began it. "Severiana, I ask your permission to tell these people what happened to you in Eburacum. If we are to do what we need to do, they must know."

I felt a sudden rush of anger. I wanted to rise and turn on my stepmother and shout at her. How dared she tell others of the shame that had been mine? I wanted to throw my wine in her face. But Aurelia Paulina reached out her hand, and gripped my arm tight. "They must hear! They must understand why our family needs our revenge! Then you can say and do all you like to me."

My hands were trembling, but I took a sip of my wine, and sat back as if at ease, saying one word: "Tell."

I tried to close my ears to what was said then. Even mention of Constantinus's name made me want to take the cup I held and smash it as I remembered him thrusting drunkenly on top of me. But the gods are merciless. They will let us shut out the sight of something, but not its sound.

I saw the shocked faces of Silvanus and Artorius. To do what Constantinus had done to a woman of my rank was unforgivable. There was not a family who would not seek vengeance.

"You see what they have done to us," said Aurelia Paulina. "Is this the man who should be Emperor?"

Artorius slowly shook his head. "Such a man... to do that to a married woman! He will be like Nero, or Caligula... or Heliogabalus!"

Silvanus spoke up, speaking directly to Artorius: "Everyone here is a member of the Amici Carausii, and our aim is simple. We want to bring to fruition what Carausius tried to do: to break our island free of the empire, to stop the drain of our men and wealth to the Empire, to husband our forces so that they can protect us."

I knew all this, yet I cringed. This was still outright treason, and the penalties for it were horrible. At best, death. At worst, death by torture, for that person and even perhaps all his family.

"I know why you brought me here," said Artorius. "I learned that from your brother and Milo in Deva. But I ask myself: how can you possibly hope that this can succeed? My father died thirteen years ago! Even his murderer died ten years ago. Who is left to remember him?"

"More than you could imagine," said Milo. "Most of the soldiers now in Britannia were once Carausius's men. I and my men are of those. Asklepiodotus brought in some others, but most have left. Constantius also brought in some, and a fair number of those were Galerius's men, and do not love Constantius's line... and now perhaps the Legion at Deva..."

"They all supported Constantinus..." Artorius said.

"Of course. Who else was there?"

I poured myself more wine, and my hand was shaking.

He pointed at Artorius. "You are Carausius's son. His natural one. But still his son."

Aurelia Paulina spoke. "Have you thought how similar these times are to when Carausius ruled? As it was then, we have a ruler who controls Britannia and Gaul. He may even control Hispania, if he can, but I doubt it: Carausius never could. Constantinus is in the North, preparing for a campaign against the Franks, but that is just an excuse. He will never return, for he will want all the Empire, and Galerius will never allow it. There'll be civil war again, our troops will be gone, and we'll be yet weaker."

"This is why," said Milo, speaking for the first time since the lunch had begun, "this is the last chance we have. We won't have another, I believe."

"You want to make me emperor?" Artorius said, shaking his head.

"Yes. But only of Britannia," said my stepmother. "We have people here who have good reason to want revenge on Constantinus. It's very clear that my daughter believes the children she has just borne are Constantinus's. And she wants revenge."

"The question you should perhaps think of asking yourself," said Milo, "Would your father want his dream of a free Britannia to succeed, even after his death? I think he would."

That struck home to Artorius. I could see it clearly, and I thought how much he must think of his father.

He shook his head. "I don't see how this can be done. How would anyone get near enough to Constantinus to kill him?"

"My stepdaughter is the path... if you want it. Indeed, if she and the children are to live, it's essential she go to the court."

"What?" said Artorius. "Why?"

"Because Constantinus has already tried to kill her once, before he even knew she was pregnant. He failed because of our friend here." She gestured at Milo. "But he won't just give up. The only thing that will stop him is if Severiana gets Helena to accept that the babies are her grandchildren."

Artorius was looking as if he wanted to say something. Then he shook his head. "He is not a good man."

"No. Far from it. As we said: do we want such a person as Emperor?"

I looked at my stepmother's face, so smooth and unmarred despite her age, and then at Artorius trying to make the decision.

"When I was told of the plan in Deva," said Artorius, "I said I would have to think on it. And I have! And even though it will mean my death if I refuse, I still don't know what to do!" he said.

I saw my stepmother look up sharply at that.

"I showed him the letter to Constantinus from the Agentes in Rebus, asking for permission to kill him," said Milo.

My stepmother nodded. But her face twitched, I thought.

"We may have Galerius on our side," said Milo.

"Galerius? The senior Emperor? Why!"

"Read this. We sent him a message, and this is how he answered." He passed over a scrap of papyrus.

Artorius read it, and sat there stunned, I think.

"Can I see it?" said my stepmother. She read it and passed it to me.

It was very brief, and to someone who did not know the subject, quite opaque.

> *Some have disturbed me for many months. It would be a pleasure if the disturbance were gone, and anyone who achieves this would earn his just reward.*

We were all silent, trying to interpret exactly what this meant. Its basic meaning was obvious: Galerius wanted us to kill Constantinus, and would reward us if we did. But it was from an Emperor, and few Emperors keep their promises.

I turned to look at the lovely slope below us, needing to rest my eyes from the tension between us. And as I did, the strangest thing happened: a raven came down, and perched on the table in front of Artorius. I have never seen a raven do what it did, for it sat there looking at him. And then it picked up some bread, and held it in its mouth, bending over, as if offering it to him.

As it sat there, looking at him, I knew he was being asked to decide. And he reached out his hand.

It dropped the piece of bread into it, and flew off. And he dipped the bread into the olive oil, and ate it. The die was cast.

I heard the inhaled breaths of the people watching this. They knew what this said: no omen could be clearer. That it was a raven that had come brought home to all how much death lay ahead of us, for ravens come to feed after a battle.

He looked at us. "It seems the gods give me no choice. I accept. I want vindication for my father's murder, and I do not want to die. It seems I have the choice of dying by Constantinus's hand soon, or dying by it later, and that is not a choice worth making. Now show me how we do this."

+ + +

On the day we left, Silvanus gave us his farewell, and his wishes for the success of our endeavor as we sacrificed two cocks to Mars Ultor and Ultio, the gods of vengeance. Silvanus read the words of Seneca, who cautioned that effective ultio required self-control or moderation. We all promised to remember that admonition; but I was not sure we would be able to follow it.

Then as, we turned away, my stepmother and I for the east, Milo and my brother for the North, an impulse came over me, and I knew it was the right one. "Will you sell it to me?" I said to Silvanus.

I have no idea why I said that so impulsively. It was just that I needed something to lift my soul, and this place, with its slopes and far hills seemed all I could wish for.

"What?" said Silvanus.

"I want to buy your estate. I will pay your price, with no haggling."

I heard my stepmother laugh. "She has the money, Silvanus, and I think she is serious."

"I am indeed," I said. I remembered the huge sum I had been given to pay for my shame, and I began to feel angry at that thought. I shook it off.

I let my lips curve, a little. "If I know my mother Aurelia Paulina, she's already chosen a factor for me if I buy it!"

I looked down on the hills and paddocks and forests. "No, nothing will change what has happened. But perhaps," I said, and I was pensive, "this place will give me some solace." I paused. "If I live."

# CHAPTER 35

## Severiana: At Eburacum

Crossing the Abos to Eburacum at nightfall, we saw flames. The entire city was not on fire, but there was a whole section burning; and there was enough noise so that, even at this distance, I could hear the faint shouts of the people trying to control the blaze. Veldicca cried out, wondering what was going on. She was so used to speaking Latin now that that was the language she used.

We went forward to the Porta Praetoria gate, and the guards saw us, and waved us back. "You can't go through here," one called. "The Vigiles are trying to pull down buildings to stop the spread. Go to another gate!"

"What's happening?" Catigernus shouted.

"Soldiers! They set fires. They want their pay," the guards shouted back. "And so do we!"

I had told the others I would go back to Eburacum. But I had also said that if Catigernus didn't come with me, I would not go near that vile place.

He had lived on the estate with his family ever since my father had freed him, acting as overseer. He had done this so loyally, and very well. But that was not why I wanted him. I wanted him because he was the kind of man who was very good when things turned very bad. His hair was grey now, and his face lined; but he was still powerful and sure. I loved him, as one can only love a man you've known all your life, and who has never failed you or your family. I needed someone like him to do what I was going to do, and to comfort me, when my brother was so far away.

"Come away," he said, beckoning to me and the driver of the carriage behind that carried my things, and the slaves that came behind. "If the soldiers are out, this is not safe!"

Had someone been alert, he would have noticed how many brawny male slaves there were in a single woman's entourage, how many armed men, and how few women. But no one was that alert, especially when soldiers are rioting. It was just a fearful woman traveling.

Sometimes being a woman is useful, for no one expects ill from us. A fearful woman is more useful still: we are weak and ineffectual, until we are not.

We made our way around the wall, and after a while tried the Porta Principalis to the east. There we could enter. The fire was to our left now, and seemed to be dying out, as the vigiles contained it and the soldiers' officers retook control. We made our way to the house Julianus had bought, and which was now mine. One of our slaves had to scale the wall to open the gate to the courtyard, and it was like entering a tomb. There was no one there. No one had been there since I left, 14 months before, and the flagstones were littered with leaves and the debris of my anguished departure.

I said nothing, but Catigernus did, as he ordered the slaves to clear the place and open the house. It was still summer, so we did not need a heated floor, but we still needed light and cover as the sun set, and the beds inside the house were damp and covered in dust.

"I'm sorry, my Lady," said Catigernus. "We can light a brazier or two, but you'll have to use the coverings and provisions we brought until we can get everything washed and more food bought in the market tomorrow. I assure you; we'll get everything comfortable tomorrow."

I reached out and hugged him. "That doesn't matter. And since when am I your lady, my dear friend? Talk to me as you always have."

"Only in private, Severianilla!" he whispered, smiling. "In private."

They brought the babies to me, and I suckled them as they prepared food. I still hated it. I couldn't help it. Other women would have called them sweet babies, and I would have too, in another place and at another time. But now I just yearned to see them passed over to their wetnurse. Soon I would no longer have this distasteful task for my own. I hoped I would dry up so I could no longer give them much milk.

Then we all went to sleep, I on my old bed in my old cubicle, wrapped in my traveling cloak, for the bedclothes were gone to be washed. But I slept well. Like a baby, in fact.

+ + +

Morning… when I woke the house was already bustling, as slaves cleaned out the rooms, washed what could be salvaged, dusted the furniture, and left to shop for food. I woke reluctantly, but the noise was too much for me to continue sleeping. My maidservant, Servilla, brought me some wine, fresh bread, apples and olives, and I realized how late it was: she and the other slaves must have been up for an hour or more by now. The boxes of clothes and belongings were being unpacked as soon as the presses were clean, and there was so much activity that I wanted to join them, for I have never liked being idle. But Catigernus came up to me, and led me into the peristyle, which had already been swept. A slave brought a small table, and set our food on it, and jugs of wine and of water with cups for us.

"We are here. And now we need to plan," said Catigernus. He was always serious, and I saw that he knew my disquiet, for he smiled at me, as if to comfort me. I took a deep breath. As always, we spoke in British, for we had been careful to bring only slaves from other parts of the Empire who did not know our language. We did not want to be overheard.

It was a fine day for Britannia. As always here in Eburacum, the sky was almost never entirely blue; but the air was clear, and the clouds were soft and wispy, rather than dark and sharp-edged as so often. Birds were calling. You could see nothing of them, for the walls were too high here; but there were small trees around the building, far enough away to be hidden by the peaked roof tiles. I had dimly heard the dawn chorus, though I had fallen back asleep immediately. But now I could hear the shrill scraping of swifts, and the chirruping of robins, and the high squee of a blackbird. I poured wine, watered it, and washed some bread down with it. The time had come to plan, as Catigernus spoke.

"The first thing is that we must make sure that the Lady Helena learns of your return. And quickly. The attempt to kill you shows that is imperative. We also need to have a good reason for the return, and I can only think of one."

"Constantinus's children."

"Yes. You know that to the imperial family suspicion is their first instinct. A girl who was raped coming back with the children the rape bore? What? So... tell me why?"

"They are the Emperor's children."

"How do you know that?"

"I feel it in me!" I cried out, angry despite myself. "I know it!"

"That's a wronged woman's answer," said Catigernus. "Now give me one his mother will believe. She is very wary: she spent too much time with Constantius, keeping him alive. Do you know how many attempts were made to assassinate him?"

I shook my head.

"Five. And everyone thinks Galerius was responsible for most of them. This is now a very careful family."

I sat in thought for a long while. Then I clapped my hands. A slave appeared, and I switched to the rough sermo vulgaris that such men knew.

"Tell the wetnurse to bring the boy here. And go to my room and tell my maid to bring the picture I brought in my personal box."

The baby was brought in, and he was quiet, for he had just been fed and wanted to sleep. My maid came in a short while later, and handed the portrait to me. It was wrapped in cloth, and I unwrapped it.

"You recognize this, I'm sure," I said. "When he became Emperor a few months back, many copies of this were sent around to be placed in public buildings. Look at it." I put it on the table.

"Now bring the boy," I said to the nurse curtly, and she brought it forward.

We all looked at the over-big, slightly bulging eyes of Constantinus's portrait, the brutally hard features, and then at the baby.

"There is a resemblance," he said cautiously. "The eyes... but he is very young... his features could become more like Constantinus's later... the framework is there..." He paused. "He's not even six months old." "You just can't tell this young... his eyes are blue! Constantinus's eyes are green."

I laughed. "Once I knew very little about infants. Now I know more. Many babies' eyes are blue this young. They change before they are past a year old. But look how long his index finger is. Just like Constantinus."

He nodded, and then said: "He's still too young. But perhaps that's all we need... the suggestion."

"If it's there," I said, "Helena will see it. I am sure this is his son." I felt the rage rise in me. I choked it back. "And she will feel it too."

Catigernus poured another cup of watered wine for me, then one for himself. "We must somehow get this to Helena..."

I laughed. "How little you know women. And how little you know mothers... and Helena. We will clean this place, buy what is needed, and wait. We need do nothing more. Helena will find us. You think there won't be people heading to the palace this very day to tell her we've returned? We'll hear from her. And very soon."

I realized with a shock of pleasure that now, suddenly, I was no longer the pawn in this game. Catigernus would follow my lead in this. And I looked forward to the future. For the first time in many months, I looked forward to it very much.

It took all that day and the next to wash everything, clean the courtyard and rooms of dust and debris and mice's nests, and restart the furnace so we could bathe. I took my first bath that evening with Veldicca, and noticed how lovely she was becoming, now that she had lost the awkwardness of puberty, and her figure had rounded out. We had been almost eleven days on the road, for traveling in a carpentum from south of Londinium, nothing happens quickly.

I envied her, that she had never been violated as I had been. But I stifled my spitefulness, for she was a sweet girl. It felt like luxury to be in the hot water, our skin softening, our fingers wrinkling, and the sweet pleasure of being clean overcoming us. Finally, reluctantly, we vacated the bathhouse so that Catigernus could have his bath, too.

We all sat to dinner together that evening, a simple meal of river fish, fresh bread, a cheese tart, and fruit, washed down with honeyed wine. We had been talking– about what I can't remember–but it was light-hearted for once, or as light-hearted as I knew how to be in those days. And then, in the distance, we heard the knock at the door.

I raised my eyebrows at the others, and Veldicca looked at me anxiously. She was now quite used to Roman ways, but still she showed the anxiety of her past foreignness when she failed to understand what was happening. But the rest of us knew what this knock very likely heralded, and we waited to see.

A slave entered, bowed and handed me a letter. No word came from him. We could all see the imperial seal. It's not a small thing to be easily missed, and its purple wax rested on fine papyrus.

I put the letter down, and took up again the piece of apple I had been eating. I saw the others looking at me, and Catigernus started to laugh.

"You intend to torture us, I see!"

I began to laugh too, though only a little. I have no idea why... but I felt a thrill that this was at last going to begin. From now on, none of us would know what the future held. I liked this feeling... the beginning of my revenge.

I broke the seal. I read it, put it down, and nodded. If they had been less in control of their emotions, they would have sighed.

+ + +

We met in the Basilica. I had first thought this a strange choice, but it really made eminent sense: to meet in the residence of the palace would immediately raise the interest of all. Women, on the other hand, often went to the Basilica, for inside on each wall were the more elegant shops, and outside were the shopfronts of those who had not managed to buy or beg one of the coveted places inside.

Eburacum was not Londinium, but it was a major city in Britannia, and there was little that could be imported that was not on sale there. The outer market was packed with ragged Caledonian slaves, jammed together in pens by the army factors: most would be shipped south across the water to the southern Empire, for few wanted to use slaves so near their homeland: it's just too tempting for them to flee.

But I was not looking for slaves today, but rather one woman. That did not mean I had not come with a list of things to buy: we needed black and green olives, olive oil, honey, wheat and garum, and I had six strong slaves to carry them home on hurdles. I bought an amphora of oil as I waited, and two modii each of brined black and green olives. I was looking for garum and honey when I felt a tug on my sleeve, and saw my maid pointing at a corridor where a slave in imperial livery was beckoning.

"Go ask what she wants," I said, though I knew. But I wanted the delay to get my thoughts together.

"A Lady, Domina," the girl whispered when she came back. "She wishes to speak with you…"

I swept my pretty silk stola up onto my arm, lifted my decorated hem off the floor, and walked towards the alcove. I was dressed for the occasion. And every single nummus I had spent on those lavish clothes had come from Helena and Constantius.

I walked into the alcove, past the slave whose task was clearly to keep others out. I turned the corner, and there was a small room, and in it Helena was waiting. Her face was angry.

She wasted no time. "Why are you here? We gave you a huge sum in compensation. Why come back here? To get more?"

I looked down at her; I was taller than she, but not by much. "I come," I said, "from an old Gallic family. We have been of senatorial rank for many years, have been here for a generation. Do you think, my lady, that I would come asking for money?"

Her eyes took my eyes, at first defiantly, then, as if reality had overcome her anger, they softened. "Then why?" she asked.

"Have you seen my children? The children who were forced upon me by *your* son?"

"Of course not! Wait… *children?*"

"I had twins, my lady. A son and a daughter. Twins run in my family."

I could see she was shocked. "Twins… I had not heard…"

She shook herself. "You claim they're my son's?"

I shook my head. "I claim nothing. I say come to my house, and look, and see for yourself. If you believe they are not your son's children, I will leave. But I know they are, and so will you. So come… and look…"

And I turned on my heel, and took steps to leave. But I turned as I reached the corner, and spoke over my shoulder. "And when you see my children, then you'll see why I came back."

+ + +

I've found from my own life that how long a woman takes to get her nerve up to action is a measure of her indecision. And it took Helena three and a half days before she came. She came, not in the morning, as if she had made her decision early and in a wakeful mind, but in the evening, when the summer sun was about to set, as if she had fought with herself all day, and failed in the battle. The robins and nightingales were beginning to sing again, as they had in the early morning, and the sedge warblers were joining them. That was the time she appeared at our western door, with the setting sun behind her silk stola, a yellow red shadow glowing through the fabric, and a maidservant at each shoulder.

I should have been frightened, for all she would have had to do was tell her guards to kill us, and expose the babies, and that would have been the end. But I had come to learn a little about her, in the time we had almost been friends, and I knew that she would not bring herself to kill babies who might be Constantius's grandchildren, or indeed, any child. Now came the crucial time, for if she did not see her son in my children, I had no idea what she would do. But it would probably not be pleasant, for we had become a danger to her and her family; and Helena, though a kind woman, was not of a family kind to its enemies.

I would never have normally waited for her at the door, leaving that to the ostiarius. But today I heard her come, and stood at the door as it opened, waiting to greet her. I have no idea why I did so, except that there still remained in me some respect for her, whatever her son had done. I wished we were still friends; but that we never could be again.

We said not a word as we met, but I bowed to her, as befitted the concubine of an Emperor and the mother of an Emperor. Her face was set like iron, and her lips were thin; she looked at me, and nodded. She did not look human, I thought, but I understood why. She was afraid of what she would find out.

"May I offer you some wine and refreshment, and perhaps…"

She cut me off short. "No. I want one thing only: to see the children. That is *all*."

I called for a slave, and told him to have the nurse bring the children to the summer triclinium. The table had been set there for the dinner to come, and the lamps lit; but there was no one there yet. We waited, in absolute silence. I could hear the nightingales, dimly, through the door that opened on the atrium.

249

There was the pad of the nurse's footsteps on the mosaic, and then she was there, holding the two bundles, one in each of her arms. I motioned her forward to Helena.

The slave's face was panicked, and she looked back and forth to me, to Helena, and to the door, as if seeking a way out.

Helena lost her temper. "Show me, girl!"

The girl began to cry, and I feared she might drop the babies in her fright; I walked over, and took them from her. I went to Helena, and offered them to her. She recoiled at first as if they were monsters, and then she took them from me, with such obvious reluctance. She looked long down into their faces, and then did something I would never have expected: she exhaled audibly, bent down, pressed her nose against their skin, one after the other, inhaling deeply. There was a very long pause. Then she looked up.

"They are my son's."

She stood up, and walked out of the room. I heard the front door close, and she was gone.

I am not sure which one of us felt worse: she for deciding this, or I, for having my conviction confirmed. I put my head down into my palms, for I now was shivering and crying as the slave girl had been, but where she had responded to her terror, I was overwhelmed by my anguish. And my rage. Oh, yes. That too.

# CHAPTER 36

## Severiana: Pseudolus

Time passed, and I was accepted again in the Praetorium, if acceptance was what I endured there. Helena was almost desperate to keep contact with my children, and I knew why: Constantinus had no others, he was to be away at war, and many who are young and healthy die anyway. But my presence was a deep humiliation to her, for she had never come to accept what her son had done to produce these children. It violated everything she believed in, and as I learned about her strange religion, I understood more and more why. The Christians saw sexual joining as licit only for procreation. Lust was, in their minds, a stain, and rape can be nothing but lust. So, these children had been born from what they called "hamartia", a Greek word – as so many of their words are – which indicates that you yourself have failed, and have not been driven to it by their god. I suppose that the nearest meaning in Latin is *peccatum*, though that does not mean the same thing. But I knew how violently she was repelled by *hamartia*. I learned later that these strange people even form communities of men and women – always separate from each other – who live in desolate areas far from places where they might meet others, and berate themselves constantly for the temptations that their "vile" bodies coax them towards.

I never understood how desire could be evil, even after what had happened to me, for desire and decency are not forever and finally divided from one another, and nor are evil and desire the same. There was something that revolted me about that belief, and it made me despise the Christians more.

There was also the fact that her son had tried to have me killed, and would have unknowingly killed the children too. I believe she knew this, how I don't know. She had her own network of spies. But I noticed that when I went out, I was always followed, and by people who almost certainly belonged to the imperial household. I thought, at first, that I was being followed in case I was a threat; but then I realized that in fact they were there to make sure there were no more attempts on my life, for they acted more like guards than watchers.

If she wanted to see the twins, she had to accept me. And she did, as much as she could. I knew that when she and Constantinus left, she would take her grandchildren with her, and leave me behind, whether I wished it or not. I would not care about that, of course, for I could not touch my son or daughter without revulsion. But she knew nothing of that, and thought that I had a normal mother's love for them. She had no idea that I was using them, and certainly not that I was deeply ashamed of doing so. For whatever I felt about them, I was indeed stricken by my feelings. Not even a child of rape deserve to be so despised, for a baby, whatever its origin, is innocent of guilt.

I knew I was not trusted one bit in the Praetorium. Whenever I was there, there was always someone discreetly shadowing me, and this time I was certainly being spied upon, I knew. I understood that. Such great harm had been done me… how could they be sure I was not there to do equal harm back? But until they had proof, they simply watched. And I gave them no reason to do more.

When I was in the Praetorium, I smiled. When I went home, I cried. And in the dark of the night, I lay consumed with hatred, and woke exhausted.

Hatred is tiring.

After one of those bad nights, I discovered by chance that Numerianus had arrived in Eburacum.

I received no message from him. It was simply that it was a pleasant day, though a little cool, and I felt that I really had to change my mood, for I was so low that I could barely stand my thoughts. Then, as I was listlessly eating bread dipped in olive oil with some dried grapes, I remembered that the day before, as I was returning from the Praetorium, I had seen a sign painted on a wall advertising that a play by Plautus was to performed in the city theater. This caught me in two ways. I had read some of his plays when I was a girl, and they were amusing. But I had also been struck by how very old-fashioned the language was. I rather doubted that many would understand dialog written at the time we were fighting the Carthaginians. Yet it piqued my interest. I wondered what they would do, and still keep the play funny. And it was late in the year. I doubted there would be any more plays until next year.

Poor Catigernus! He far preferred the amphitheater, for he enjoyed the fights, but he knew I could not go alone. So, he and three husky slaves walked beside my litter as I and Veldicca were carried to the theater.

The theater was surprisingly full, though I should have known that it would be: here in the North, entertainment was not as common as in Corinium or Londinium in the South. As my slaves manhandled the crowd to get me into the Senatorial seats in front, I heard murmurs as people complained that women should sit in their own high tier, and not in such an honorable place. I laughed to myself at that. My family was of Senatorial class, and I was the daughter of a

Senator. Let them argue, if they dared, with Catigernus and his three brawny henchmen.

We had brought cushions and snacks, and I sent a slave to buy crisp-fried chickpeas for us all, as well. A crier was walking around the edge of the Orchestra, loudly calling the name of the play to be performed, and exhorting us to stretch our legs and empty our bladders, for:

*Plautina longa fabula in scaenam venit!*

Indeed. The play was a long one. But I knew it well. It was the Pseudolus.

There was a blare of music from the orchestra, as loud as the few musicians could make it. And the play began.

I could now see what they had done. The lines were almost the same, as far as I could remember them, but the language was modern spoken Latin, and not educated Latin at that. And every so often, when someone cried out with surprise or lamentation, instead of using Latin, they used the grossest of British expressions, some of them utterly obscene. Everyone laughed at those, and I too, I must admit.

The play is a simple one: the son of a rich man has fallen in love with a prostitute, who is about to be sold off. Somehow, he must find the money to buy her himself, but he knows his rich father will never give him the cash. So, the slave, Pseudolus, must find a way to trick it out of the father, despite his contempt for the lack of education that the execrable handwriting of the young woman exhibits.

I must admit that I was enjoying the play, sipping wine as I listened to the interplay of music and words and curses. The troupe was good at their work. Act one ended with the clever, devious slave managing to get his master to bet him that he could get the money to buy the prostitute despite the obstacles. And I leaned back, laughing, to wait for the next act, and looked to my right, and up.

And there he was standing, two tiers higher.

I cannot describe the shock I felt. I had not thought of Numerianus since I had met him in the woods as my pains began. No. That's not true... the three of us were all close, though not as close as I and Licinianus. I had thought of Numerianus sometimes, and worried about his dashed hopes. But I had been so involved in my own emotions that I had almost forgotten about how he might feel, what he might need from me, and my twin. And as things were, with my fears about how the Imperial Family might treat me and my children, it was a shock to see my half-brother in Eburacum.

I looked at him astonished, and was about to call to a slave to go to him and call him to me, when I was shocked again, for sitting next to him was Verena, and she was wearing the stola of a married woman under her palla.

I felt the tenseness that comes from shock and anger, for I knew in a rush what this must mean. I swallowed the rest of my cup of wine in a gulp, my fingers trembling, and called a slave to me. My words were terse. I pointed at my brother: "Bring that man to me."

This is not how you should talk about a free man to a slave, still less your brother, but I was too upset to care.

I saw the slave reach Numerianus, and point back to where I was sitting. My brother looked down at me, and I swear that I could see his face whiten at the realization that I was there. He seemed so disconcerted that I would have laughed had I not been so angry. Then he seemed to steel himself, and began making his way towards me.

He had hardly reached me before he spoke. "What are you doing in Eburacum?" he said, as if he were accusing me.

"What am *I* doing? What are *you* doing here? I gather you didn't know I was here!"

"No…" Then, "they said you were at your new villa with Catigernus! This place, of all?"

"Yes. I am. And what is *she* doing here?" I jerked my head at Verena, who was looking anxiously down at us.

I'd seen Numerianus look shifty more than once as a child, and here it was again. He even licked his lips. Then: "She's my wife now."

"So I'd guessed. And how did that happen?"

"I did nothing wrong! I love her!"

"She's a Christian!"

"Yes! And what does that matter? I love her."

"What nonsense! Are you someone in a Greek romance to marry for love? Surely you know that her kind came with her father to try to take Julianus's bones away to one of their charnel houses! And yet still you married her?"

"Her father says he had no part of that—"

"Do you think that matters? I just got a letter from your mother," I lied, to get him to tell more. "When I read it will I find out more about this?"

He was growing a beard, I noticed suddenly. They were still common among older men, but the new fashion was starting to go back to being clean-shaven again. Then I remembered that every Christian I had ever seen was bearded, and a cold vice took my stomach.

"You've become a Christian..." I whispered, and I was not sure he heard me. So I said it again, almost shouting it.

He flinched, literally, his body recoiling.

"That's how you got her to marry you! You betrayed our family, our twin gods! If they desert us, it'll be your fault!"

I tried to take control of myself, but there were tears of anger in my eyes. "Don't you remember the gifts they've given us? And you've abandoned them?"

I stood up, and hit him with all my force, leaving a red imprint on his face. I didn't care if I never saw him again.

I left the theater, Catigernus and Veldicca keeping a cautious distance behind me. They knew what my temper could be like, and I was in a fury I had not felt in a long while.

I had never liked the Christians, but after Julianus's death, I despised them. I hated them. They had taken that sad, wounded man and made him into one of their death-seeking cult. And to try to take his poor remains to venerate? How could I *not* hate them? My poor, sick husband would have been sent to the beasts for sacrilege if my brother had not intervened. He had never told me he was the one who stabbed him to death, but he was my twin, and I knew it. It was the only kind thing he could do, the only way to save him, who had once been such a dear friend.

It seemed like the journey home never happened, so furious was I. One minute I was at the theater, the next I was at home, balling my fists around my skirts as I walked into the house. A slave came out to welcome me, but suddenly, seeing my face, gaped and slid to one side to efface himself. It was good he did: I would have struck him too if he had gotten in my way. I walked straight past the old-fashioned impluvium and into the tablinum. Behind me I heard Catigernus calling for wine to be brought there, and I think he was wise to do so. I sat down as it was brought in, now trembling with the tension that the anger had built in me, and saw him pour a cup for me. He did not water it.

He handed it to me.

"Drink this. I think it will help. And when you feel calmer, you can read this letter."

"What?" I said. "A letter?"

"Yes. From the Lady Aurelia Paulina."

He must have thought I was mad, for all of a sudden, I started laughing. He couldn't know that I had lied to Numerianus about exactly this, and to see that it was indeed here was too much for me. The anger began to fade.

I drank on the wine as I opened the letter. It was, of course, written on expensive parchment. My stepmother Aurelia, an Emperor's daughter, would use nothing else. She was old-fashioned enough to use the old cursive letters most of the time, sometimes mixed in with the new, so some of this was hard to read. It reminded me of the play I had just seen part of, where Pseudolus comments to his Master about the letter his uneducated love had sent him, *"In my opinion, these letters are seeking children for themselves: one mounts the other."*

I would have laughed at any other time. Instead, I struggled on.

> *Severiana Cariana Aurelia Paulina Galeriae Vindici Flavillae, plurimam suae salutem dicit.*
>
> *I must tell you the terrible news about your brother Numerianus. I am ashamed to call him my son, for he has broken with the family in a way that is unforgivable, both to our family gods, and to you, given what they did to your husband. You remember that girl Verena, whom you met during the terrible time of your husband's funeral. That on its own would have made me object to his marrying her not to mention that her family is not of the Clarissimi. But when I realized that she would only marry him if he too took on the beliefs of her vile superstitio, I made clear to him that I would not countenance the marriage, and if he pursued it, he would no longer be welcome here.*
>
> *I returned from buying your new villa, believing that he had accepted that to desert the gods of our family could only bring disaster, but I was wrong. In the days that followed he was making his plans, arranging with his woman and her father to be married. And why not? They could expect him to inherit my wealth, and as such he would be a choice prize for a family of their station! He will not now, that I promise, for I will never forgive him! He came home with his new wife wearing a brand new stola and begged my forgiveness and acceptance. I refused! But I am still his mother, and he the son of your father, whom I loved so dearly. I have arranged for him to have a stipend sufficient for him to live decently with his Christian wife, but I told him to leave, for I would not have her or him there as long as*

*either were Christians. I do not know where he has gone, and I do not
care. I have made no effort to find out.*

*I have arranged for copious sacrifices and offerings to our gods, in
the hope that they will not visit his sacrilege on the rest of us, who
remain loyal to their beneficence. You and Licinianus must do the
same when you return.*

*Be well, daughter, as I hope to prosper, and hail.*

I sighed as I finished. My stepmother was the daughter of an Emperor, and
in many ways showed it in this letter. She was never unkind, but she had steel
in her: she would keep her promise, I thought, even against her own son.

And I wanted her to do that. I would never forgive these people. I was done
with them.

+ + +

But as the next day proved, I was not done with them, for Numerianus, he
who had so betrayed us, appeared at my door asking to see me.

At first, I was furious that he would dare to come to me. But then, I
remembered that he was still my brother, the young boy I had played with and
built silly canals with, and I told them to let him in.

He had always had a kind of confidence before, but today it was nowhere
visible: he looked drawn and unhappy. Indeed, it had vanished around the time
when he realized that his family would never countenance a marriage to a
Christian. If he had been a woman he would have been crying, I think. But
Roman men do not cry.

"Did you think," I said cruelly, "that I would welcome you?"

"No," he said. "No one in the family will. Even Aunt Flavilla isn't answering
my letters."

I knew he mentioned her because she was such a kind person, quite unlike
the sheathed steel of his mother. If my aunt rejected him, all was lost.

I relented a little. "Sit down," I said. But I did not offer him any
refreshments.

He leaned his elbows on the table, and put his head in his hands. "Have you
never been in love, Severiana, so in love that nothing else matters?"

I felt shocked, as I realized that the answer was that I never had been. I had
cared deeply for Julianus, but love? That was more than I could claim. I avoided
the question.

"That is not the issue. The issue is our gods, and the tungida we live under!
You know that! Our family has been through such difficult times, and we have

always somehow won through, because of the gifts they give us! I and Licinianus lived only because when our mother died, Aunt Flavilla had the gift to save us from dying with her! Don't you see that we are all terrified that you will make them desert us?" I paused. "I cannot *believe* you did this! You *know* our gods are real! You've known it since you were a child! You've had so much proof! How can you believe in this dead Christian god you have chosen to follow?"

It took him a long time to reply. But when he did, his voice was firm. "I don't."

That terse comment rocked me.

"What? You mean you lied to this woman? You loved her enough to *lie* to her?"

"Yes."

I took a breath of relief. There was hope still.

"Then all is not yet lost. Will you sacrifice to our gods with me?"

I saw the fear on his face. "If she finds out she will leave me!"

"If she finds out you are lying to her, she will leave you. Well, I won't tell her. But I will tell the family if you sacrifice with me. And that will go far to stopping them from turning their backs on you!"

His face looked panicked! "If I do that, and she ever finds out... they hate our gods! They call them demons!"

"Let them."

I stood up. "I'm leaving now, to make the sacrifice. If you don't come, it will be a ceremony of mourning for a brother I will lose forever. If you refuse, I will never receive you again."

He bowed his head. "I can't bear to lose the family!"

"Then you must risk losing your wife, loved or no." I said, "Sacrifice, and we will forgive you... but only after a time! You will have to earn our forgiveness!"

# CHAPTER 37

## Licinianus: Return to Eburacum

The preparations for the campaign against the Franks were done, and it was late in autumn. Most of the army had already marched south, and had settled into camp at Eburacum. Everyone in the army had been eager to return, though there was grumbling, for it was so long since they'd been paid. But we'd all had enough of war for the time being, and the lures of a city with brothels and wine-shops were very tempting, if they could but get the coin to pay for them. And I so wanted to see my sister... I was sure I could get leave to go south to see her.

I wondered a little about Veldicca too, which surprised me. I certainly had not flirted with her, or made any attempt to do so, for she was so young, and, though she was much over the marriageable age of twelve, I am not someone who finds the very young attractive. But I had been amazed when I last saw her how quickly she was growing up. I always pulled back into myself when that thought came, for the idea of being attracted to a northern barbarian woman was not a pleasant one. They are savages.

I had been ordered to take one of the last detachments south, and now, back in Eburacum, I saw to the settling of my men in their barracks, giving them the obligatory warnings about wine, thieves and whores. They would ignore them, of course, but it was the custom, and we smiled at one another, knowing the uselessness of it. But one shouted that since they hadn't been paid in 9 months, how were they supposed to pay for whores? I could only shrug, and assure them that Constantinus had promised the money would be theirs once they got to Eburacum.

But I knew there would be trouble if nothing was forthcoming.

Then I went to the Praetorium to talk to my commander Flaccus, and get permission to travel south to visit my family.

He was very busy, and saw me as an annoyance. I knew he saw me as a spoiled upper-class officer who was too often away. I had, after all, received leave just a month or two before, and now I wanted it again? But he called for a slave to come and write the order, for officers of my rank were hard to refuse. I was leaving the building with it in my hand when I was hailed by someone: "Licinianus! Back from the north, I see!"

I turned and saw who had called to me. It was Apollinaris. And my fist balled. *You next, you piece of filth!* But I smiled, and called back to him in as friendly a voice as I could muster.

"Hail to you, Valerius Avilius Apollinaris! How have things been with you? Well, I hope?"

"Well enough!" he shouted. He came up to me. "I wanted so much to be with the army up north! I'm told the fighting was hard but fine."

You cowardly little shit, I thought. You fight? You'd soil your loincloth.

"We did well. But we're all glad to be in Winter Quarters. Five months is enough in the field."

"Are you staying in Eburacum? We must arrange a dinner!"

"I'd be happy to!" I lied. "But I'm going south to visit my sister and my family."

He laughed loudly. "You don't have to go south for that! Your sister's in Eburacum, and your little brother too! He's become a Christian, stupid boy, and the Lady Helena dotes on him for it!"

I stood there, shocked at that news. When I came out of my stupor, he was gone.

I saw that someone had scrawled *"Expectate venite atque stipendium"*[28] in crude letters and belabored Latin on the wall, and clearly the last words were a reference to the missing pay. But the first part of phrase was very familiar. Carausius's coins had had that legend. The Amici, it seemed, were being busy.

+ + +

We sat around the table in the tablinum without speaking. Then, in hushed tones: "I'm afraid. We've never had a member of our family desert our gods. What will happen?"

"I don't know, Severiana. Aurelia Paulina has done everything she could."

She shook her head. "This comes so soon after that dreadful attack on the temple at Pempe Dewoi. Christians again! And then stealing Julianus's bones! They are vile!"

Her face changed. I didn't think she would ever forgive them for what had happened to Julianus. Not only had they killed him, but in her mind, they had made her prey to Constantinus, for Julianus was never there to protect her anymore. I didn't see what a man so damaged could have done for her; but I saw no point in saying so. And I could understand. As far back as our grandmother's death it seemed that at every terrible time in our lives, Christians

---

[28] Come expected one and the pay too.

had been involved. But I didn't want to hate them. I just thought them dangerous, for if they ever grew too large and powerful, they would not let others be. Look at what they do to our holy places when they get the chance!

"He sacrificed to our gods you say? He asked for their forgiveness?"

"Yes. And they have always been kind. They will know what foolishness love can bring upon mortals."

"Perhaps. But I worry... I can't imagine his marriage lasting: what happens when his wife finds out he is not really a Christian?"

I looked up, and Catigernus was walking in. I stood up, crying out in pleasure. I'd had no idea he was here in the north.

"Welcome, Catigernus!" I called out. "I'm so glad to see you, old friend!"

We embraced, and Severiana poured out some wine for him.

"There are slaves who speak British here, I'm sure..."

"No, there are none. We made sure of that."

"Still, let us speak very low. Tell me why you are for this plan."

He leaned close to me, and his voice was very low. "Do you know how I became a slave, before your father freed me?"

I shook my head, bewildered. I'd never even thought of it. He had been a slave. He had been freed. As children we had called him uncle, as if he were our father's brother. He had taught us how to use a bow and hunt. He was as much a part of our family as Aurelia Paulina, our stepmother, or Flavilla, the aunt of our blood.

"Let me tell you," he said. "I was not born a slave. My father was from Britannia, and my mother too, and I grew up here. But in the time when Postumus took over the west of the empire, and formed his Gallic Empire, my father was called with his cavalry from Britannia to Gallia when Laelianus revolted against him. Britannia was drained of men, and all protested that the province would be left helpless. But Postumus cared more about Gallia than he ever did about Britannia, and it was only by a miracle that the tribes here did not seize their chance.

"Very few of those British troops ever reached home again. My father never did. When Postumus was murdered, Victorinus purged all those who were his closest supporters in Gallia, and one was my father. My mother killed herself. I was sold as a slave."

"I never knew any of this," said Severiana, and placed her hand on his. "You are part of our *familia* now..."

He smiled. "I know. I have your family's name now."

She laughed. "That was not what I meant, and you know it!"

It lifted our moods a little, and I poured wine for us all, and watered it. We lifted our cups to each other, and drank.

But there was something I needed to say to her, and there was no better time, for it needed no discussion. "I must tell you... Rufinus: I killed him. He's dead."

I heard her breath catch, and she stood and came to my side, putting her arms around me.

"How did you kill him?"

I hesitated. Then: "I cut his throat."

She kissed me on my forehead. "I thank you, my brother. And I thank our gods. There are just two left now."

But all conversation then had to cease, for in walked Veldicca, and I was amazed. She was so lovely.

# CHAPTER 38

## Licinianus: Veldicca

It was the time of the month when we made offerings to the Lares. The figures we had here in Eburacum were copies of the ones we had at the Villa on Oak River, of course, two of them, dancing in their niche. But we were a special family, with special gods, and so with them were images of our twin household gods, male and female, who gave us our family's gifts. At home we went to the Temple where my father and mother were buried; here we offered to them at the same altar as the Lares. We called them the Di Penates; but in our household, they were much more. When we went home, we would make a sacrifice of expiation that we did not have a separate place to offer to them here, for they give us great things. And these days, we were asking them greater things still.

I had covered my head, as a man must in such times, and offered them incense and wine, and I was whispering the ancient words one always did. I had learned them as a child, as my grandmother had taught them to me, for with my father and grandfather both dead, she had had to take over this duty. I treated the words with reverence, as they deserved, though I hardly understood them, they were so archaic. But I had been given a worthwhile life because of these gods, and so must honor them as we always had. If there is one single mistake, one must start all over again; and for that I had no inclination. I had things on my mind.

I struggled with the last part, for it was in Gaulish, the language of my ancestors, and British is my tongue. But they are close enough, and I arose and pushed the cover from my head, relieved that I had done all well.

I turned, and Veldicca was standing there, watching me.

She was wearing two tunics, as girls often did, a long one and a shorter one, so that the two colors showed and contrasted. The longer one was russet, and the shorter one a blue: the combination was charming. She wore tiny aquamarine earrings, and her sandals matched her russet tunic. Her hair was relatively simple: the hair was braided around her head in the way that was fashionable in those days. It was parted at the back, I saw later. But now I saw only the braids.

It looked glorious, and I could only think that my sister was sparing no expense to make her at home: she looked like a girl of high family.

"You look lovely!" I said in British. "I would have hardly recognized you!"

"You can speak in Latin," she said, and her cheeks reddened just a little. "I know it well now."

"If you want me to. But you know my family use British to each other. It's what we grew up with. And you are part of our family now."

I made my mind up, and threw my mantle onto a chair. "Will you walk with me?"

"Where are we going to walk to?" she asked, her expression bemused and wary.

"The market perhaps? I was thinking I might buy my sister a little gift, now that I'm home."

She hesitated. "I can't go alone with you."

"Then call up a slave woman. Severiana won't mind."

Again, she hesitated, but then seemed to make up her mind. She called for a mantle and her maid; and in a little while, we set out.

"Those earrings are very pretty," I said by way of beginning, looking at her earrings. "But you're not thinking of going somewhere by sea, are you?"

She looked at me, startled.

I felt silly, all of a sudden. "I was trying to make a stupid joke," I explained. "Romans believe aquamarine gives safety on the sea."

"Oh," she said. "I didn't know."

"Forgive me. I don't know how to talk to you."

"What?"

She looked at me as if I were from another world. "You? That's *me*! I don't know how to talk to *you*!"

I started laughing. "If neither one of us know how to talk, we're doomed to silence!"

We had slipped back into our respective dialects of British, now. That was always to be our language when we were alone, just as it was with my sister. We both started laughing.

We turned the corner, heading for the Basilica, where the best shops were, and I grasped her arm to stop her for a little. "But there is one thing... your father... have you forgiven me? Or at least put it aside? I can't stand the thought of you hating me..."

At first, I thought she was not going to answer. But then she said: "You didn't kill him yourself. It was one of your men."

"Yes. But you know I would have had to, if he had not."

"I know that too. But I know enough about you and your family that you would have done so with reluctance. You are not a killer."

I could have laughed if the situation had not been so tense, for that was exactly what people called me.

She saw the expression on my face and laid her hand on my arm. "That's not the same. That is the gods' tungida on you. You have no choice, and therefore no blame." She hesitated. "The thing my father most wanted was that I not be shamed or enslaved. This is not the way he would have thought that could come about, but it's the way it happened. You and your sister have treated me as if I were your own blood. He would have been pleased at that. And sometimes I dream that he knows, and is pleased." She paused. "He had no one but me, you see."

"I didn't know that. But I hope he knows. I very much hope so."

We walked on, chatting about small things, and the people we saw as we walked. There was a lot to talk about. Eburacum is the greatest city in the North, and accessible by river from the sea, so a great deal of trade passes through. There were many whose home was clearly faraway, if we judged by their dress. Once there would also have been many from north of the wall, but the war had stopped that. But others had taken their place. There were even a few from Hibernia, though as a soldier I looked darkly on the people we call White Shields. They are savage in war, and lack any mercy: villages they attack are left without a living creature. They even sacrifice men and women to their gods.

We were approaching the Basilica now, and we heard shouting and the sounds of a crowd. As we turned the corner, we saw why. There is a big parade ground there, and it was filled with men in kilts, and nothing more, if you discount their sandals. The noise was very loud, for perhaps fifty men were running madly on the ground, head-butting one another, smashing others in the face, and screaming as they did. Many were bleeding and men were being tackled and thrown to the ground, and I saw from the look of horror on Veldicca's face that she thought we had come upon a riot. Involuntarily, her hand grasped my arm, and tried to hold me back. "They have gone mad!" she said.

Then I saw the ball, and started to laugh. She looked at me as if I were insane.

"It's not a riot, Veldicca! They are playing harpastum!"

"What?"

"It's a ball game. There are two teams, and each team has to try to get the ball over a line on the other team's side."

"This is a game? They're killing one another!"

"Well, I agree, the game is very rough, and there are few rules. But people rarely die, though a broken bone is not uncommon."

The crowd suddenly roared, as a goal was scored, though one lone voice called out angrily "Out of bounds! Out of bounds!"

Everyone ignored him.

"Licinianus!"

I heard my name called, and turned to see Flaccus, standing watching the game. He came over.

"I thought you went south! I signed your leave!"

"No, sir, I found I didn't have to. My family is visiting Eburacum, or most of them."

"Well, don't think you're going to escape duties, now that I know you're here!"

"Who's doing battle here?"

"The First cohorts of the Sixth and Twentieth. Grudge match."

"It looks like it. Who's your money on?"

"The Sixth. But only a quarter aureus. Or am I supposed to call it a solidus now?"

I laughed. Indeed, the name of the gold coin had changed, and everyone was confused. He waved as we left, carefully walking around the heaving mass of men. "You'll be hearing from me!" he shouted at our backs. I groaned, and Veldicca started laughing, even if she did hide her mouth with her palm.

We had no real purpose in going to the Basilica, but I discovered quickly that Veldicca, like my sister, loved browsing around the shops and examining their wares. The last shipments before winter made the roads difficult were in, so the stalls were quite well stocked. We spent a long time at the fabric merchants, and Veldicca exclaimed at the beautiful silks that were displayed. I offered to buy one she particularly liked.

"I could never take these from you," she said wistfully. "Your sister would ask who they came from, and though I'm not a slave, I might as well be, since I have nothing that your family hasn't given me."

"Veldicca," I said, shocked. "Haven't we tried to do our best for you?"

"Of course! Your sister has been – well, like a sister to me. If not a mother! But I think: what is my life going to be? Who will marry me? I'm penniless, and it doesn't matter that my father was a chief of the Votadini, and I am not sure how many of my family are still alive. I have no brothers and sisters to help. So I have no dowry, and I will always be a barbarian to you."

I grasped her shoulders. "No. Not to me. Never to me."

"Oh," she said. "Don't you call us Brittunculi in your army?"

It shocked me to hear that contemptuous term used by her. Yes, soldiers did use that word to refer to the Britons north of the Wall, and sometimes even to those south of it. But my men had learned that I was of this land, and that they needed to be careful of what they said, for fear of my staff across their face.

"I would never call you that. You are my..." and I hesitated. I was about to say "sister", but then I suddenly realized that the last thing I wanted her to be was that. "My friend." I finished lamely. "Please let me buy you some of that silk," I ended, helplessly.

"No. Where would I ever be able to wear it?"

And she turned away in the direction of the house, followed by her slave-woman chaperone.

"Wait," I said, and darted back to the stalls. She looked puzzled, but stopped as I did my business with the stall-owner.

When we reached Severiana's house, I pressed a small cloth-wrapped package into Veldicca's hand.

"What is this?"

"Open it."

She drew the cloth back, and laid bare the small, round pendant I had bought for her. It was very simple: just a rough round of green amber, shot through with yellow light, enclosed by a gold circlet, on a gold chain. It reminded me of her eyes.

"You may not be able to wear silk without arousing my sister's interest. But you can wear this."

I did not mention that anyone who had an eye would be able to tell how much such a thing must have cost. I just walked away. But I knew the odds that Severiana would fail to guess where it must have come from were not high.

I didn't care.

+ + +

The next morning my fears were realized. A soldier came to the door of my sister's house, and, requesting to see me, saluted and told me stiffly that Flaccus wanted to see me, at once. I took a deep breath, and headed for the Praetorium, wondering what unpleasant duty he had in store for me.

I found him in his office, surrounded by secretaries, one writing at his dictation, others copying documents. Something was going on. He looked up at me, and spread his hands helplessly.

"As you see," he said.

"Is something happening, sir? Has there been an attack?"

"Worse than that. A deputation from the legions and auxiliaries begging for their wages to be paid."

"Ah," I said. "Well, sir, even their annonae have not been fully paid. You can understand…"

"The message has been very clearly understood. The storehouses have been opened up, and the annonae will be fully paid this coming week. But you know that if coins are not in their hands very soon, they will not ask so respectfully next time. You can't buy a whore's time with corn. Armies have been known to bring down even emperors when unhappy. Or unpaid."

"Do we have enough in the storehouses?"

"For this ration, yes, though we'll have to denude the province for the next one. But that doesn't matter. The soldiers want money. And it is not just here! There are disturbing reports from Deva."

"Valeria Victrix? Surprising."

"Not really. The legions feel less proud than they used to, and neither Constantius or Constantinus have made any effort to hide their preference for cavalry."

I waited for more. I thought how ironic it was that here he was talking of exactly the issue we had just discussed in my sister's house

"So," he said. "We need to get the army paid. That means the mints down south."

"There's one at Londinium isn't there?"

"There is. But the amount needed is huge. So, we'll need to collect what Londinium has, and then get the rest at Verulamium."

"You want me to go and get the coin?"

"No, you're spared that. A detachment from the Londinium garrison will escort it to Lindum. You will escort it from there to Petuaria and then Eburacum." He laughed. "I want you to choose the most trustworthy men. Obviously, we need cavalry, and your cataphracti are good with a bow and mace as well. Twenty-five men. Be careful in your choice. They will be escorting so much wealth that it would tempt anyone. They're going to have to empty the mints to pay the army, and the amount will be vast. We can't afford to lose it."

I felt my ears prick, but I merely let myself scratch my chin. Inside I laughed. Probity is not what soldiers are chosen for. Most are blackguards who would rob their own mother if they were sure they could get away with it. "How many men again?"

"Twenty-five."

"Mmm," I said, thoughtfully. "That's a lot. Not sure I can find that many troopers I'd trust."

"If you know of others outside your ala, you can choose them. Ask other commanders to suggest names. You know there are high odds that news like this will get out, and the prize is a very big one. So, we need enough men to make sure that thieves avoid the temptation for fear of a broken head. And hurry! The money will be at Lindum in six days. That means you must be ready the day after tomorrow."

# CHAPTER 39

## Licinianus: Night Meeting

I told the others as soon as I returned home again, and we marveled at our luck. The sheer size of the detachment was startling: Constantinus clearly felt that it was vitally important that the troops' pay arrived safely. Twenty-five loyal men defending it would have meant something close to a pitched battle if we had tried to take it.

We did not meet at my sister's house, for fear the arrival of others would cause the slaves to talk. So I and Milo made our way instead to a small house well away from where we lived.

The room where we met was lit only with a few feebly burning oil lamps, and in it were three men. Milo recognized one of them, and walked to him. "Artorius! You are in Eburacum! It's good to see you here!"

He smiled at him wryly. "I am. Though when I see you, things usually become fraught for me. So I'm not so sure I'm glad to see you!"

He offered his hand to me. "Be well, Licinianus!"

"As with you!"

A man stepped forward. "I wonder if you remember me?" he said to me. He grinned. "You should but probably don't."

I shook my head, bewildered. "I'm sorry..."

"Do you remember a doctor in Coria who asked you whether you were a friend of Carausius?"

I still could not remember his name.

He took my forearm, and said: "Let me reintroduce myself. I am Vegetius Flavius Poenicus, a surgeon in the legions. Now do you remember?"

I threw my head back. "Ahhh... I do... now. You were my doctor in Coria!"

I looked at the third man. "You I've never met... I'm sure."

"But perhaps you've seen me... from afar... probably. I am Lucius Castus Macer, Praeses of Britannia Secunda."

I felt my breath catch. This was the province in which we now stood. The Amici Carausii's branches reached higher than I had thought.

The Praeses spoke. "I think all of us want this meeting to be done quickly. We must have no one talking about our absences. So you've been ordered to detail 25 men to guard the shipment from Lindum?"

"That's correct. But I have no idea whom we can trust."

"We can help there. But we need more information. When is the shipment going to be made? Do you know that yet?"

"All I know is that the shipment will be at Lindum in six days. That is when I am to meet it."

"That means," said the Praeses, "they must have left some time ago. The men are as restless as I've ever seen them. You've heard about Deva?"

We nodded. "They're close to mutiny there, I hear," I said.

He nodded. "Very close. They *would* have mutinied, if they did not have the Prefect they do have. He's managed to keep them under control, but only barely. Someone has been busy." He smiled. We all knew who those were: the Amici.

He mused a little. "We need to choose the spot where we make our move, and it must be a place that we can escape with the carts without being noticed too much. Vegetius Flavius, can you use your contacts to do that?"

"I can."

The Praeses smiled at Licinianus. "He was not always a surgeon, you know. Once he was an explorator…"

"And a frumentarius[29] too," said Vegetius. "It was not a job I enjoyed, and as I had trained to be a surgeon, I went back to my old calling. But this task I will like very much indeed."

"And meanwhile," said the Praeses, "the Amici will be constantly reminding everyone in the army how good it was when Carausius was Emperor in Britannia. If only he had had a son… It's working in Deva."

We laughed at the joke.

He turned to go, then stopped. "By the way…" he said, "I probably have no need to say this to you, for you are not a fool. I believe your brother is in Eburacum. He is dangerous. His wife's family is Christian and so reputed to be close to Helena, and he himself may now be a Christian. I have reason to believe that is what Constantinus's mother also is, and that Constantinus is sympathetic to that *superstitio*, though they will admit that in public to no one. Your brother must obviously learn nothing of this."

I touched his elbow as he was turning to go. "Do I have you to thank for saving my sister's life when she left Eburacum?"

"You have Milo to thank for that. But yes… I was the one who warned him."

---

[29] Originally, someone who provided troops with supplies. But at this time, a member of the imperial secret intelligence service.

I said nothing, but I bent and touched his hand to my forehead.

As we were about to leave a niggling thought finally rose uppermost in my mind. I voiced it: "One thing puzzles me. Why am *I* being chosen for this task? There is something very strange about that. Constantinus doesn't trust me. He fears I may know too much about what happened to my sister, and thus that I'm unreliable. Why would he choose me for something so important? And it must have been him. This is too important a task."

"Hmm…" said the Praeses, frowning hard now. "You have a point. That is very puzzling. I think we need to make more inquiries before we make any moves. I will arrange that."

# CHAPTER 40

## Licinianus: Change of Plan

I've seen this in battles. Before it starts, you feel yourself tensing, getting ready for the challenge. What you experience is not so much fear, as an anticipation, a question in your mind as to how you'll act. In three days, I would ride out with my 25 men, and it would begin. In the time left, all I could do was to try to distract myself.

It was not as if there was nothing to distract myself with. Veldicca was on my mind all too often; and I could not forget that my brother was in Eburacum. He had come only once, to see my sister. I had seen nothing of him. And why would I, when he knew we were still unsure of him? To betray the Twin Gods is to betray all of us, and though he had shown he had not abandoned belief in them, he knew my sister's bitter dislike of the sect he had married into. And to do this for a woman? Would I join such a group just to win Veldicca?

It was at that instant that I realized, with a sudden shock, that such an outlandish thought had come into my mind. People of our rank married others of the same rank, and love was rarely part of the arrangement. Veldicca had nothing but what we had given her, and she was what all my friends would call a contemptible northern savage, a "Brittuncula". I could imagine few who were less suitable.

Yet the thought had come to my mind, and now that it was there, it clearly had no intention of going elsewhere. I could only remember her shining red-gold hair and her green eyes, and her neck, so long and slender. And her white skin... I loved that she had no freckles, as so many red-heads do...

I shook myself to banish that thought, and found something much less pleasant rising in my mind: my brother. Severiana was still so angry with him that she refused to discuss him; and I was very close to feeling the same. I felt such fury at what he had done, endangering everything our family was, abandoning us for this Egyptian girl. For love? Why would you do that? And then I thought again of Veldicca.

In the end I could not contain myself. I had to go and have it out with him.

It was a momentous decision, done just to mollify my emotions; but what effects it was to have!

Yet first I had to find out where he was living.

Eburacum is a substantial place, but it is not Londinium, and newcomers

273

are remarked upon. I also knew that Numerianus had married a rich woman, so I did not have to search the slums, and after a day I found them. If I'd thought about it, I'd have found them sooner. All I would have had to do is ask myself why my brother had come here, to where Helena and her son now were. Sometimes I feel I'm just thick-headed.

My brother was, it seems, now part of the Imperial household, serving as a *notarius argentarius*. This was no small thing, and was belied by its humble name. A notary could rise very high, especially one who dealt with the finances of the state. It didn't surprise me that he had a such a position. Like his mother, Numerianus had a head for figures. We used to tease him about his name because of that, in those far off days when we still could, still would. I didn't see anything like that happening today.

The entrance to the house, when I came to it, was between two shops, one selling leather goods, and the other a silversmith. I noted one thing that rocked me: a scribbled text on the wall that said:

*mⲥⳙoⲅⲥⱴmⲥⱶⱷⱷⲓoⲥⱷⱷmⱷ*

"We were better with Carausius."

I had been seeing scribbles like that all over. The Amici were being busy.

I knocked on the door, and waited. A pleasant-looking older man opened the door, and looked at me enquiringly.

"My name is Galerius Vindex Licinianus, and I wish to speak to your master."

The ostiarius's eyes widened, for he recognized the name, and knew I must be family.

"Sir, my Master is not at home. He is at the Basilica, dealing with the affairs of the Emperor."

"And your Mistress? Is she at home?"

"Yes, dominus. Do you wish to see her?"

I nodded. I had no idea if she would want to talk to me. Her last encounter with the family had not been pleasant. But at least I was important enough to be let through the passage leading to the atrium, rather than to be left out to wait on the doorstep.

I waited there, taking stock of the house. It was much bigger than the entrance would have implied, of an old-fashioned plan: an atrium with an impluvium, and a tablinum on the far side, with a large and elegant peristyle on the other side, which I could distantly see surrounded a piscina bordered by beds of boxwood hedges and flowers.

I heard the sound of sandals moving quickly on the stone floor, and from the far side of the peristyle I saw a woman hurrying towards me. I had never met her, but I remembered my sister talking of the "dark Egyptian" that Numerianus had fallen victim to. As she came close, I could see that she was dark in eye and hair, but that her skin was only a little sallow. She was too well-dressed to be a slave, and I thought she was very pretty, in a quiet way. I could see why Numerianus had fallen for her.

She spoke to me in a voice that was high and clearly flustered. I could tell she had grown up in the east: her Latin was of a character that told me she was more used to speaking Greek, and it was the old-fashioned kind that is taught in schools.

"Sir!" She said, sounding a little breathless. "You are my husband's brother?"

I nodded.

"Welcome, then! We knew only that your sister was in the city, but not you!"

Color rose into her cheeks and I could almost hear the unspoken words *"…and we certainly did not expect any of you to come to see us…"*

I decided to be gentle. "We're a very close family, as perhaps Numerianus has told you. I wanted to make sure that I came here to see my brother before I was too long in Eburacum."

"Come," she said, still flustered. "Come into the peristyle and let me offer you some wine. Numerianus should be here very soon, and I know he'll want to see you."

*"I don't know about that,"* I thought as I followed her.

She had clearly been sitting reading, for there was a codex lying on a table open, and a cup half-filled with something. I sat down opposite her, and waited until a slave brought wine, water and little cakes for us. She gestured to me to help myself, and I poured half a cup of wine, topping it up with water.

I took a sip, and said: "We were surprised when we heard you had been married. Numerianus did not tell us of his plans."

Her mouth worked as she tried to find an answer. "His mother knew. We told her."

"After, I gather, the deed was done." I said, smiling, but not in amusement. Her color heightened.

I said nothing, waiting for her to say more.

She took a deep breath, and then said firmly. "I think you know that I and my family are Christians. Numerianus and I were bereft. He knew I could not marry a pagan."

"I noticed," I said, gesturing towards the empty shrine to the lares and penates with its bare, newly whitewashed walls.

She blushed, then said firmly. "I know your family traditions. And I fully understand that to you Numerianus has deserted them. But I hope you'll come to see that we Christians are not evil, not aiming at the destruction of your beliefs."

"Well, it's hard to believe that, since the fact remains that you shun us, your religion is illegal, and your fellows attack our temples. Why should you do that if you say we are free to hold to our beliefs?"

For a moment I thought she would not reply. But she was made of sterner stuff than that. She lifted her chin.

"We believe they are demons sent to draw you to evil. They are trying to save you from them."

My lip curled. "But yet you wish me to believe that you are content to leave my family to our evil demons? Not to try to save us from them?"

I saw her face tense. She knew that was not so. I went on.

"Has Numerianus told you of the gifts our 'demons' have given our family?"

"He told me."

"And you think nothing of them?"

She was silent a very longtime. Then: "Gifts can be given by many supernatural beings. They are not always good gifts."

"So there are no good gifts given by them?"

"Only God and his Son can do that."

"So how do you know that the gifts my family has been given don't come from them?"

I don't think anyone had ever asked her that question before.

"God does not appear as an idol!"

I looked at her long. I could see the look of a fanatic in her, for her color was growing yet redder, and it was clear she was close to anger. Such questions were—what was the word they used—'sinful'?

I had no use for an argument with her. So I desisted, and asked instead when my brother could be expected home.

"Now," she said, stiffly. "He always comes at this time, to spend the time before dinner with me."

I decided to stay awhile, and see if Numerianus would appear. The next half hour was a very uncomfortable one, but I kept the conversation going, talking about her flowers, which she clearly loved, and what she had done to the house. I learnt her name, which was Verena. I made only one misstep, when I mentioned my love for Sappho's poetry. She clearly knew about it – she was well-read – for her lips pursed as she said, "I've never read any of her poetry. I've never wanted to. She was a sinful woman!"

There was that word again. I thought how strange it was that a cult could take what I believed to be a rather nice, intelligent girl like her, and make her into someone who had a distaste for beauty just because of who wrote it. But that was what you'd expect from a *superstitio*.

I was just about to leave in exasperation when my brother came home.

Mercifully, once Verena had greeted her husband, she withdrew hastily, leaving us alone.

There are few things so uncomfortable as when you meet someone you were once close to, after you've been separated by a disagreement. In the past, if you are men, you met each other with banter and friendly insults. No more, for the insults may be taken as real. So both of you are tentative.

I could see Numerianus was flustered. Indeed, his first words were, "I didn't know you would be here."

"You surely must have expected me to be in Eburacum sometime. I'm an officer in Constantinus's army."

He nodded. "Yes, yes I know." Then: "Say your piece."

"You think I have one?"

"You and Severiana are twins. I know how that is in my family."

I made sure that Verena was well gone, and saw her back disappearing down a corridor. I lowered my voice.

"You know I would not be here if you had not made sure the family knows you are not totally lost to us. Yet still you live with a woman who calls our gods demons!"

He drew back. "I know! I know!"

"So how could you do this to us? Tell me how you intend to resolve this? Have you been... initiated into their faith?"

He looked shocked. "No! That is for later! I am just a catechumen... under instruction. For three years."

"I see these Christians are choosy about who joins them, to take such a time. But how will they – and your wife – respond when they learn you have lied to them, and have not abandoned our gods?"

He shook his head despairingly. "I don't know! But I know I can never abandon them!"

I did not pursue how he intended to contrive this with a Christian wife, for I had not come here to argue. But I admit that I was angry. "But they may abandon us, because of you!"

"Don't say it! That would devastate me, so much!" He grasped my arm and looked into my eyes intently. "I'm still the same person, still your brother! I love you and Severiana, and always will! I just loved Verena too much to give her up!"

I shook my head. I had never experienced love like that. But then... I suddenly wondered if that was still true.

"I doubt Severiana will ever truly forgive you. You know how she's felt about Christians since Julianus's funeral." I sighed. "The family can't forget this or ignore it. I just have no idea how this will work out. For that matter, why are you here in Eburacum?"

"When Verena and I were married, Mother was so angry that I knew I couldn't stay at the villa. Aunt Flavilla was kinder, but even she said we should leave, that my presence might pollute it for the Twin Gods..." his mouth twisted in what seemed to me genuine distress "...and to see if separation might soften Mother's heart. Verena's father has had many contacts with the Lady Helena, and she kindly said that I would have a notary's position in the Emperor's establishment."

"No surprise. They're both Christians, I believe. What is your position?"

"I'm in the fiscal office."

"Ha! From what I hear, that's in a fine mess, since there's no money to pay anyone!"

He nodded. "But that will change. A shipment of coins should be here soon."

"It had better be! The soldiers are on the edge of mutiny! I've been asked to provide 25 soldiers to guard the shipment!"

His eyes widened. "What? You're going off in that column? Licinianus, please be careful! It's all a fraud! You're just going to be a decoy!"

I could see that he knew he had already said too much. But I would not let it pass. "What do you mean?"

He put his head in his hands. "I've said too much already."

"Maybe. But if I'm in danger, you must tell me!"

He lifted his head. "They've found out that the shipment is to be attacked. So they've sent a train to Lindum to act as if it has the money, so it will be attacked instead! The actual detachment left at night three weeks ago, and will be coming back by a different route!"

"What?" I said, struggling to keep my voice steady.

"They did! There's been information laid that some don't like Constantinus, and they plan to attack the convoy and steal the money. The actual money will come back with the column sent by a longer route, but a much safer one, disguised as a supply column. They left weeks ago! Licinianus: be careful! They don't care what happens to the second column, so don't lose your life trying to protect sacks of grain! Don't go and get killed for nothing!"

I think my jaw was hanging open. "Nice!" I said. "They don't care if we're attacked?"

"No," said Numerianus, shaking his head. And I could see he was ashamed. "I think they'd like it if you were attacked. It would show their ruse worked, for the money should be almost reaching Eburacum by then."

I wanted to ask more, but I was afraid of making him suspicious. His loyalty might not lie with us anymore.

That made me sad.

I felt his hand on my shoulder, holding me back, heard his voice whisper from behind me: "Tell her... please tell her to remember that I sacrificed as she told me! Tell her I'm not lost!"

+ + +

I walked home in a fever. All our plans to remove Constantinus had been for nothing. My suspicions were confirmed. I had been chosen by Constantinus as a useful victim. I felt fury at him. And someone in our group was either a spy or had too loose a tongue.

I had no idea whether we could fix this now. Our carefully chosen amici would be sent off on a useless errand while the actual shipment came by another route. All I could do was hurry home, and make sure the news reached the others.

I pushed the ostiarius aside as he let me in, and saw a slave walking to the kitchen.

"My sister and Catigernus! And Milo! Where are they?"

"Ipsa is away, Domine, but Dominus Catigernus is in the Peristyle."

I walked quickly. I wanted to run, but I had alerted the slave enough without adding to his astonishment. Catigernus was seated by the pool as Milo wrote a letter.

When I had told my tale, and he had gotten me to sit down by him, he stroked his beard and thought long.

"Ha," he sighed. "I suppose we can rely on what your brother said?"

"You know him as well as I do. He has no guile. We used to tease him unmercifully when we were children, because he always believed us."

Milo had dropped his pen. "Then we must change our plans," he said. "You say they left weeks ago?"

"Yes."

"But you don't know how many. But we can find out. Someone will have noticed them going. Fourteen days for the journey down. One day in Londinium, a half a day in Verulamium if the money is ready for them. Then fourteen days back, using carts with mules."

"They could do it thirteen each way if they change mules often."

"Yes. I think we can do this. But we'll have to find out their route back, and when they left! We must move quickly! They could be almost here!"

"Numerianus said they were coming back by a different route."

"Exactly. Also, there's no bridge at Petuaria. I thought it was strange when you said you'd have to come back through there. They'd have to take the carts over by ferry, one by one, since they'll be so heavy. It would take forever. So, my guess is that they'll turn off well short of Eburacum. There's a road that heads towards a town... I can't remember what it's called. But it ends up at Eburacum. We must ask the Praeses if he might have heard anything about this."

"What about the men? We've chosen them carefully! We need them."

"Yes. But who knows who they are but us? You'll detail twenty-five others, and send them off under someone else's command. You'll have to make an excuse for why you can't go."

He got up. "And let us pray that we are not being misled again."

I sat down at the table, and ordered a slave to bring wine and water. There was nothing more I could do.

After I had drunk two cups of lightly watered wine, I felt better. I had done everything I could, and now all we could do is wait. My thoughts turned to Numerianus.

I was glad I had made contact with him, and it had been lucky that I had. But I could not be as sanguine as he about the family. We have always been bonded together by our Twin Gods; this was in our blood and bone, and as much a part of us as our kin. Numerianus might have felt that he could remain loyal to them and yet be a Christian; but I did not believe his wife or his new religion would tolerate that. He would either be divorced from us, or from his new wife, and I could only feel very sad about that, for, as I remembered our childhood and the "engineering" projects all three of us had undertaken, I knew that I still loved him.

How much he had given up for a woman!

As if called forth by magic, I heard a girl's voice, and looked up to see Veldicca standing over me, smiling. I was so preoccupied that I had not heard her approach.

"May I sit with you?" she said smiling. "I am tired of being alone in this house with no one to talk to! See, I have my tablet here. I could practice my Greek with you!"

I have never had so much pleasure, before or since, in seeing Greek verbs so prettily mispronounced, and in correcting them to the scent of a girl's hair. That scent made every muscle tense. I wanted to take her in my arms. I wanted to lose myself in her.

But I still had good self-control.

# CHAPTER 41

## Severiana: Waiting

I hated the next few days. Licinianus delegated twenty-five cataphracti for their useless task, telling his commander that he was ill in his stomach. That was nothing strange in a military camp: diarrhea is rife. As he put it, he'd chosen those who, in camp, were the most likely to cause trouble, while the reliable soldiers went on the real task. But with the help of the Praeses and the doctor we'd found out when the supply train had left, and guessed where the returning supply train must plan to turn off: the road about nine or ten miles outside Lindum led off towards a mean place called Segolocum, and it was on a road that curved round to come to Eburacum from the west, rather than the east, as the main road did. If our guesses about timing or route were wrong, everything would be lost. But they would certainly not be on the route their decoy was taking, and any other route would add days to the journey. We did not think they would take such a chance.

No one but a tiny inner circle had been told about the change in plan, and it was planned so that the chosen men would leave individually, and meet up where the Verbeia river intersected the road outside Calcaria. There they would wait, and we could but hope that we had not been misled. Everyone knew to keep their mouths shut, for clearly someone had told Constantinus that the gold shipment was to be attacked. Even the soldiers had no idea what they were about to be called upon to do. Licinianus would leave to join his men, just as – we hoped – the wagon train with the money was approaching Eburacum. And then they would wait, perhaps for one or two days, to see if we had guessed right.

I was frightened. Any failure or betrayal would mean the death of all of our family.

I had other things to worry about, however. I had noticed how much time Veldicca and Licinianus now spent with each other. I had no real idea how my brother was with women, for he had left before I saw him deal much with us. But I could see how he was in this case. If he was not in love with her, he was fast approaching it.

They had breakfast together, and, worse, I saw each waiting to eat until the other appeared. I saw their faces as they met, and the reddening hue of Veldicca's face when they did. They went out together on shopping trips, and no man does that for a woman unless he is captivated by her, for normal men hate shopping. They rode together along the banks of the Abos to the north of the city. I had been surprised to discover that she could ride, even though I myself could; but I was unusual. Then I remembered that she had been brought up as a barbarian in the North, and it did not seem so strange. He read to her, and was even trying to teach her Greek, so that she could love the poetry that he did. She had a knack for languages, and so she learned more than I would have thought; but explaining Sappho to a tribeswoman seemed like a lost cause. Clearly, though, neither he nor she cared. And in the evening, they talked intimately, and there were private jokes and smiles between them at dinner.

I worried about Licinianus, for I did not see how there could be any hope that he could marry her. And I worried for Veldicca, for we had become friends, and if he did not marry her after her love was captured, her heart would be broken. Yet I could see how much she had changed since Licinianus brought her to me. She was a woman now, who spoke educated Latin with no accent at all; she had learnt to read, and seemed to enjoy doing so, and her manner was that of a well-brought-up Roman girl. And despite her startling red-gold hair and brilliant green eyes, she was remarkably beautiful. What young man would not fall in love with her?

I feared for the future. I didn't want to approach my brother: he was about to go into danger, and I feared I would distract him. So, I went to Veldicca instead.

As if to confirm my feelings about her, she was trying to memorize a Greek paradigm when I found her in the garden. It seemed amazing to me that this girl had been a northern barbarian just a few years ago. But I was also sad to think that she was only trying to learn Greek because my brother loved its poetry.

I sat down beside her, and asked, before I had considered the question, "How old are you, Veldicca?"

She was clearly surprised. "I'm not sure. I think I'm either sixteen or seventeen. If I were with my own people, I would be able to ask the old women, but here..." she shrugged.

"You're still very young. Are you happy with us?"

I could tell that she was being made wary by these odd questions, and she looked at me directly. She was a very astute girl.

"Perhaps," she said, "You'll tell me why you're asking these questions."

I made a gesture of resignation with my hand. "I am worried. And it is your friendship with my brother that worries me."

Her face reddened very slightly, and she looked down at the hands folded in her lap.

"Your brother is a good man. He brought me here when he should have killed me. And he made sure that my life was honorable. My father was so sure that was impossible that he wanted me to die. And it would have been so, if it were not for Licinianus."

I nodded. "But I see you together. You are more than friends."

"Yes," she whispered. "Oh, yes. I am… but I don't know how he feels about me… I think he likes me…"

"He does, and more than that, I can tell you. But I don't want to see you hurt."

"You mean, that I am not worthy to be his wife? Only perhaps his concubine?"

"No. I know my brother. He would never do that. But he comes from a very old family, of Senatorial rank. If he marries, he must marry a girl who brings wealth and standing to the family. At least, that is what we were taught."

Her chin lifted. "I am the daughter of a high chief of the Votadini! I'm not a peasant! Am I not worthy?"

I shook my head. "No, that's not what I mean. I know you well, and you *are* worthy. But will my family agree? You have no standing in the Roman world, and no dowry."

Her shoulders slumped. "So, I am to accept my place, and withdraw?"

"No. That is my brother's decision. I know him well enough to know that he would take you as a wife despite all that, if that was his desire. But will it be?"

She began to cry. "Oh, I don't know. I think I love him. And I think he may love me. But we have never even kissed!"

I got up, and took her in my arms. "I too love you, Veldicca. But…."

We both knew what I was not saying, so we held each other, and wept together. I was glad that my brother had brought this sweet girl into my life, for I felt so alone. And I needed someone. I so needed someone. But I could not see how this would work.

# CHAPTER 42

## Licinianus: The Bridge

I and Catigernus had ridden out immediately when we woke up from First Sleep, for it was still dark then, and we wanted none to notice us. We brought our weapons and armor wrapped in cloth on bundles on the withers of the horses, so that we should not seem preparing for war, and both of us wore the hooded British birri[30] to hide our faces. Milo did not go with us. He had work to do.

I did not even say goodbye to my sister, or to Veldicca, and, absurdly, it worried me to think I might die without seeing either one again.

We went to one particular city gate, where they were expecting us, and opened it up for us, acting as if we were invisible; and then we were in the countryside, taking the road until it forked towards Calcaria. After a day's ride, we reached the Derventio riverbank opposite Lagentium, and there we stopped, where Vegetius awaited us. He led us a little way to a clearing in the woods. There we camped, though in late Autumn it was quite cold, for we dared not enter any inhabited place. Over the next few hours, the others of our little force joined us. We were forty-five strong. Which was the largest force we had been able to put together. We had no idea how many we were to face.

I stood with Vegetius, talking. He had had some intelligence that a mule-train was traveling north on Ermine Street, and had passed through Lindum Colonia three days ago. It was clearly not just a merchant train: it had cavalry protecting it, and it was also heavily laden. His informant said it was moving slowly, though drawn by mules, which meant the loads were heavy. He estimated that it was a day or a day and a half away, but we could not be sure. So much was guesswork. Was this the train we wanted? How fast could it get here, if indeed it turned off on the road to Calcaria?

My head ached from the possibilities. I didn't want to think of what would happen if we failed here.

"How many soldiers were there with this wagon train?" I asked.

Vegetius shook his head. "I'm not sure. At least fifty."

"It must be the right one. Fifty men for mule wagons carrying grain or

---

[30] A hooded, waterproof cloak.

military supplies?"

"It seems unlikely. We must wait and see."

"Did you find out who betrayed us?"

"Yes. If such you can call it. One of the Praeses's slaves heard too much, and boasted to his girlfriend that Constantinus was doomed. She too was talkative, and passed it on. But both she and her lover have disappeared. Very strange."

I raised my eyebrows, and he slid his index finger across his throat. "We had too much to lose."

"But clearly Constantinus took precautions," I said. "We shall see if he foresaw this."

I hesitated, and then added. "I'm worried. I think we should not treat this in a simple way."

"What do you mean?"

"I mean," I said, "that we are not going to wait here for the wagon train to come to us. I am going to send a few men along the road to see if there are any surprises for us. You follow on behind us, but slowly."

"You are in charge of this."

"You know my tungida."

"Yes. Though I am no Celt, I understand. In this you rule."

"We'll sleep tonight, and tomorrow we send them out."

"And you will go with them?"

"Yes," I said, nodding slowly.

"If you must, but don't be seen. Your face is much better known than anyone else's here."

+ + +

It rained hard the next day, but still we rode south. The British cloaks helped: made from untreated wool, they shed water well. But, better than that, the hoods hid our faces, and none thought anything strange in that, given the unpleasant weather. We stayed that night in an inn next to a mansio: we had no diploma, so the mansio was out of reach, but these wayside inns will take anyone who can stand the fleas and lice, and can pay. This was cleaner than most, and gave us a mutton stew with barley bread that was quite tasty, even if the drink was so watery that I wondered if any wine at all was in it. The two scouts who were with me chose barley beer instead, and I think they were wise to do so. The inn was still better than the outdoors. At dawn, we rode on.

On the second day, we traveled until the sun was low in the sky, and I wondered if we would have to spend the night in the woods. At least the rain had stopped, and the sun had begun to show itself, if weakly. Then, in the distance, I heard the sound of hooves.

We had passed a number of other travelers heading north: laden mules, an ox wagon or two, and many riders, grouping together for safety. But this sounded noisier. It was not just one wagon, or even two; it was many. I gestured to those with me, pulled my hood over my face, and rode forward along the side of the road. The moment I saw the head of the wagon train, I knew this was what we were searching for, and that was because at its head rode Apollinaris.

His eyes were not on me; he was talking to the man beside him. And as I rode past him, I mused on how devious Constantinus had been.

We rode on, three Brittunculi keeping our heads down, not wishing to attract the attention of the soldiers who guarded the wagons.

There were thirty of them, the mules pulling hard against their weight, and two soldiers on either side of each wagon. Sixty guards. That was not good, though not impossible. At the rear were four more cavalrymen. Sixty-four.

We rode past the wagon-train, and when they were behind us, I whispered to Catigernus. "They outnumber us."

"Yes. But we will have surprise on our side."

We rode on, for perhaps five minutes, and then, all of a sudden, we looked ahead. If one can say that my heart dropped through my boots, then that was what it did. There were at least another forty cavalry following behind.

"This is a trap," I said to Catigernus.

"Indeed it is. Oh, indeed it is."

"The last group is riding far enough behind so it can't be seen. But the call of a horn..."

"And they will come galloping up, and destroy whoever is attacking."

We pulled off the road, far enough away so that we could not be seen by travelers.

We dismounted, and sat down on a fallen log.

"We have a chance against sixty men. Most of our riders are cataphracti. But against almost a hundred men?"

We had some dried meat and posca with us, and we ate a little, perhaps just to keep our spirits up.

I put my head in my hands. It hurt. "I remember, Catigernus, how as a young boy all I wanted to do was read the great writers of the past, and write about them. I even dreamed of writing a history of Britannia. And yet here I am."

"You are very different from that boy. But I remember him well."

"You've been in so many bad places for the sake of my family."

He laughed, that wonderful low humming laugh of his. I loved this man.

"Our only hope," I said at length, "Is to separate the rear-guard from the rest. Then we stand a chance."

"But how to do that?"

"There's only one place to do that, and I think you know as well as I do where that is." I stood up. "We must ride through the night. We need to get back to the others, and in enough time to do what we need to do."

+ + +

We had ridden hard, and reached our companions on the morning of the third day. We had almost no sleep, but the going had been hard, for the rain had begun again. The river by Lagentium was almost overtaking its banks, and we rode over the bridge looking down at the swirling waters, filled with the debris of branches and wood. The Derventio, when it rained hard, apparently flooded easily. And that was good. A dry period with low water would destroy our last hope.

We slept for a few hours, for we were exhausted, but woke in the afternoon. Vegetius had already had men go down the bank to see the state of the bridge.

"The timbers are worn, and a little rotten," he said. "It dates from the time of Trajanus, according to the plaque. So it's quite old. But they built well, and there are two platforms of concrete that the main span rests on."

"The best way to destroy a bridge like this is to burn the timbers. But in this rain, they are too soaked. We'll have to use axes."

"But not so as to bring the bridge down before the mule wagons are across. It's going to be difficult, Licinianus. And where do we get axes?"

"Raid the houses on this side of the bridge. There are smallholdings here, and some will have axes. Leave Lagentium alone. We don't want them alerted. And no one... *no one* ... is to cross the bridge traveling south from tomorrow. What we're doing will be too obvious. If they try to insist, make clear that we will kill them if they do."

+ + +

The timbers holding up the bridge were huge and thick, clearly designed to last for a long time: the Roman legionary engineer who had built it was good at his job. I felt almost regretful that I was undoing his work, but that was how it had to be.

The river was so flooded that we had to use ropes to stop the men being swept away, and getting a good swing with the axes was difficult, since the water was too deep to stand in, so we had to use the narrow ledge of the concrete slabs that supported the balks. But that still meant that the water was up to our chests, and fighting the flooding water at the same time was exhausting. Finally, though, the task was completed. The balks were hacked through, and all that kept the bridge up were logs we had placed to stop the superstructure collapsing. We attached camouflaged ropes to these so they could be pulled from the bank. But we all stood there and shook our heads at the precariousness of our work.

Catigernus shook his head. "If we get much more rain and the water rises and brings debris down..." He had no need to say more.

"I just hope this will support the wagons as they cross," said Vegetius dubiously. "They'll be as heavy as a parricide's conscience."

I laughed. "Heavier!"

I shrugged. "Well, we can do no more. Either it works or it does not. But I can't think of anything else we could try. We just don't have enough men to take them all on. I just hope it's not raining when they come, or our bows will be useless. And then we're really in trouble."

+ + +

There came a time when I was almost sure that the mule train would never appear, that they had changed their minds and turned around; and then we saw the head of the column appear from the heavily wooded bank on the other side.

"Now we'll see how our handiwork will stand up," said Catigernus. He, like I, was armored as a cataphractus, and I hoped he would be able to handle the weight of the armor. But I knew he was a good bowman, and excellent with a spear as well, and I did not want the man I loved so much to die without protection. We were in the woods, far enough to see, but off our horses and kneeling so we could not be seen.

I swear that I could barely breathe as I saw the first mule-cart reach the bridge... and then another... and another. I heard Vegetius murmur a prayer to Mithras, and I echoed it, but to Cicoluis and Litavis. They passed by, one by one.

And then the last one was on the bridge, and I saw it shake as if it were about to fall... but the wagon made it over.

It was at that point that the bridge collapsed.

I swear by all the gods that we had done nothing. The ropes we had attached to the timbers we never pulled, and the last four troopers were still on the far bank. But I heard that huge groan, as if a giant were protesting, and the bridge collapsed before our eyes into the river.

"Mount up," I shouted. "Mount up!"

And then we were riding out of the woods at the mule-train, and there were drivers and soldiers turning to stare wide-eyed at the ruin behind them, and then, horrified, looking back to stare at us as we came for them. They were blowing horns to call up the rearguard, but it would do no good. The river would ensure that. They had even lost their four rear outriders.

I heard the thrum of bows and my own was in my hands, and an arrow on the string. I saw a centurion turn to look at me, and I loosed. It took him in the face, and he swayed and slowly fell over backwards. The sudden realization that these were ordinary cavalrymen, not cataphracti, struck. They had no bows!

"Pull back! Use your bows!" I shouted. "Just your bows! Kill them with arrows!"

I was heard, and I saw the men obey. The air was suddenly full of the sound of bows flexing and arrows thrumming, as our riders reined in and started raining arrows on the cavalrymen. It was good that I gave the order when I did, for the battle-madness was overtaking me, and nothing now mattered but killing.

I saw man after man fall from their horses: mail will slow the arrow from a compound bow but not stop it; only steel will do that. And all you need is an inch or two in the right place. I could see their hopelessness grow, and then their resolve. If they were to die, they would do so like soldiers. And they abandoned the mule train and came at us, shouting like demons. Men fell to our bows, but many made it through, their lances pointed to strike. Then they were slashing at us, too close for anything but sword and mace.

I rode forward. With nothing in my mind but the death of those we fought. I could not get up a full gallop – there were too many bushes in my path – but my contus took the first man in front of me in the throat, and drove through him, lifting him off his horse. I dropped the lance and drew my spatha. I felt the impact of a sword from my left as it glanced off the armor plating on my shoulder: it hurt, but that mattered nothing, as I turned and half-handed my sword and drove it with both hands into the gap where his mail ended at his shoulder. I saw blood gout as I sliced through an artery, and joy filled me, as I spun towards the right to block a blow aimed at my face.

There was fury in that fight, for on our side we knew that only death awaited us if we failed, and on their side terror at what Constantinus would do if they lost the train. Two men came at me at once, trying to take me down between them, but the Dream was on me, and I swayed to left and right as they swung, and slashed at the thigh of one, leaving bone gleaming whitely in the blood. As he screamed in agony, the other man swung at me, and his blade skittered across the plates of my shoulder. I turned my head quickly, bending my head to the side, so that the edge, instead of slicing unto my neck, was deflected by the ridge of my helmet. I felt the sharpness of a cut, but I ignored it, and drove my sword into his mailed stomach to wind him, and as he bent over, smashed the metal-bound edge of my shield into the back of his neck. I heard bone break, and he fell away from me. I felt a sharp pain in my arm, and saw a man in the final act of throwing a javelin at me. I used my knees to turn the horse to attack him, and I heard him scream as he tried to turn away. I drove my spatha into his neck and he fell without a further sound.

The battle noise was dying around me, as the cavalrymen tried to run away, or beg for quarter. None was given. But many of the wagon drivers had not even tried to fight: they had simply run. We killed as many as we could find, but some would survive, and the news would get out.

The Dream was dying from me, as the battle faded, and I realized I had not seen Apollinaris. I walked my horse slowly through the dead, looking down for him.

The road was not silent, for there was the groaning of men and, worse, the agonized sound of injured horses. Catigernus rode up to me, and jerked with his head to the other side of the road. "Over there."

"Is he dead?" I asked.

"No."

We rode through the wagon train and I saw him. He was sitting against a tree, his sword still in his hand. He was bleeding heavily from his right arm, and blood was running down it to the ground.

"Tie that off," I said. "He's not going to die that way."

He smiled at me. He had always had a charming smile.

"Am I to live, after all, Licinianus?"

I dismounted and stood over him. "Do you think I don't know what you did to my sister?"

"Ahhh," he said, nodding. "I remember the Lady Helena and the Emperor saying you could not know, and fail to show it. The Emperor wanted you killed anyway, but Helena is weaker than him."

"You forget my family's name is Vindex. We bide our time."

He nodded again.

"And there is nothing closer than twins."

"You are bleeding," he said.

"Small wounds."

"So now what?"

"So now you die, shamefully."

I took out my dagger. "I am not a cruel man. But you brought shame on my family, and misery to my sister. Before the gods, only your degradation can wash that away." I turned to my men. "Hold him."

He was wearing the breeches all cavalrymen wore, reaching down just below his knees.

"Cut them away," I ordered.

"Hold him."

I have never heard someone scream as he did as he was castrated. It gave joy to my heart.

We hanged him naked from a tree, and watched him for long minutes choking to his death, for that is the proper death for criminals when they cannot be crucified. He kicked for a long time; and only when he stopped did I knock an arrow to my bow, and loose the shot into his heart to make sure he was dead, for I did not want to touch him. Then we cut him down, and two men carried his body deep into the forest where they covered him over in a shallow grave. If we were lucky, he would never be found. The smell of his rotting body would bring all the scavengers for miles, and they would dig him up and scatter his limbs. If his body was gone, there was a good chance that Constantinus would think he had had a hand in the theft. And that was to our advantage. He was the kind of man who might indeed do such a thing, for he had no honor.

I cursed my weakness in giving him such an easy death, but we had no time for more. Behind us came the wagons, driven now by thirty soldiers, their horses tethered behind. I had made sure to check the contents, for Constantinus was not beyond tricking us, even at the cost of so many dead. But the coin was there, in sacks and all of it real to the bottom. We had the payroll. Under my breath I promised an ox and a ewe to Cicoluis and Litavis, for I had no doubt as to why the bridge had failed at exactly the right time.

I have ever since remembered the saying that if you want a god's help, you have to prepare the way first.

# CHAPTER 43

## Severiana: Tumult

Licinianus had come home, but he told me almost nothing of the details. I understood why: torture can move anyone to tell what they know, and none can resist it. It's better that I know very little, for that way I can tell exactly that. But I knew enough. I know that another one of the three who degraded our family and me is dead, and in a way shameful enough that the stain is much wiped from us. I know that the Amici, led by my brother, had taken Constantinus's desperately needed pay chests, and I exulted at the anger and despair he must be feeling. And I knew that Licinianus had returned safe and well, even though he, like every officer in the city, had been called back to his men.

Normally I visit the Basilica at least once a week, for the Lady Helena loves her grandchildren. She wants to hold them, play with them, and even dress them in clothes she buys for them. One day, I've always thought, she'll tell me to go, and never come back, leaving them behind, and I have no idea how I'll feel if that happens. I spend little time with them, and to think of them as my children sends a burst of rage through me. Yet, as they get older, I find it harder and harder to hate them as I once so easily did. As they grow, he's becoming a chubby, happy boy, and she a sweet little girl. I hear the slave-women playing with them and their gurgles of laughter. One time I heard the glad sounds coming from the nursery, and I was so angry at the feelings it roused that I had the nurses beaten. But then I was overwhelmed by remorse, and made as much of amends as a mistress can to slaves she has wronged. But the worst was to hear them trying to ensure their silence whenever I was anywhere near, and I knew that no child should be without joy in their life. I told them that I would be angry if they hushed them anymore.

I am convinced they thought I was completely mad, and I think they may have been right. It's hard to hate a very young child, no matter how he arrived in this world. You might as well hate a kitten because he is of a color you dislike.

So, I had not been allowed near the Basilica for more than a week, and that told me that things were bad there.

I hardly needed that hint. The streets were full of talk about the soldiers and their anger at receiving nothing but the short rations of their annonae. No coin, even the debased nummi that they were now paid in... no whores, no wine, no little presents for their women. Men care about such things, though women often think otherwise. As yet there was no mutiny, but everywhere there were scribbled things on the walls about Carausius, and others asking where his son was. Groups of soldiers wandered the streets, and they were truculent at best. Any sensible woman stayed home.

The soldiers had been promised their wages three days ago... and they had not arrived. How many emperors had been killed by their mutinying troops? I could think of at least five in the last hundred years or so, going back to Elagabalus and Alexander Severus. If fact, when I thought about it, I realized I had underestimated things greatly, for I was hard put to remember a single Emperor who had not died violently, most of them killed by their men. My stepmother's own father and brother were two such. Indeed, so was my own grandfather, Aurelianus. We all knew that it would take but one little thing to set all this afire. But no one knew what that was to be.

Rumors often spread from the Praesidium and Basilica to the rest of the population, for there are so many slaves in both places that it is very hard to keep a secret. And one story had indeed come to our ears, and that was that Constantinus was in a rage so violent that none dared go near him. That was no surprise; he was known for that, and for his brutality when he was angry. And my guess was that he had sent men to find the wagons when they failed to appear, and they had found the dead rotting on the ground, but not the money. And there would have been survivors, at least among the wagon drivers. There were even rumors that they were being tortured because he did not believe they were innocent. I believed that. Constantinus was a vindictive man.

And I suppose I am a vindictive woman: I was glorying in the death of his closest friend, and in his fear. I prayed to our Twin Gods, and thanked them with a small offering. We would give them a much greater one when we could, later, for they were keeping their promises to us.

I was surprised, then, when suddenly there was a thunderous knock on the door, and, when the ostiarius opened it, there was an imperial guardsman announcing that the Lady Helena wished entry.

I don't think anyone could have been more frightened than I. I feared for my brother. I feared for myself. I feared for my family. I feared for Veldicca. We were all in danger, for who knew what mutinous soldiers would do to anyone they encountered? Yet I went to the door myself, and Helena entered;

and as she did, my terror slackened, for I realized that if this heralded the arrest and death of myself and my brother, they would not have sent her of all people.

When she entered, she was more than agitated. Her hands were not steady. She spoke without any hesitation, however. "I need your help, and this is the only place I could think of to stay. And I wanted to be by my grandchildren, if things become bad."

"What is it?"

"The army is close to mutiny. They are demanding their pay, and are shouting at my son."

"What?"

And then I realized. I could hear the shouting, dimly in the distance. It had a regular cadence to it, and then I heard the rumbling, as if from drums.

"They are beating their swords against their shields. And this time it's not in acclamation."

"Can't your son pay them?"

"With what? Don't you realize? Don't you know? I would have thought the story would be all over the city by now. The wagons bringing the payroll were stolen. Apollinaris is gone, and with him all the money!"

"Was it him?"

"No one knows. But his body was not found. Constantinus thinks it might have been him. Or the agents of the other Augusti. All had good reason. We simply don't know. But *who* did it matters less than the effects. My son wanted me to leave the Basilica. He believes it will be attacked, if this mutiny goes on."

"Aren't there loyal troops nearby?"

"None. No one who has not been paid is loyal. The nearest troops we can trust are far to the south, around Londinium."

I had no idea what to say. I could not refuse her: Helena was a good person, and I could not blame her for her loyalty to her son.

"Do you wish a room to rest in?"

"No," she whispered. "But I do want to see my grandchildren. They may soon be all I have left."

I nodded, and was turning to order a slave to get refreshments and her grandchildren for her. I heard Helena's voice, speaking low.

"If only Constantius had not died. He was loved. But my son is too hard a man for the men to like." She looked at me. "I shudder to say that to you of all people. It is very difficult for me to know that you, whom my son so wronged, is the only one I can trust in this city."

I turned to Catigernus, who had come into the room. "I've armed every man whom we can be sure of," he said. "When soldiers mutiny, no one is safe, still least women. With Licinianus's men, we have twenty-five armed, and most were once soldiers."

# CHAPTER 44

## Licinianus: Mutiny

We were all together standing on the dais before the Praesidium with Flaccus. He was not the only commander: all of them were there, trying to decide what to do. In front of us, the Praefectus Praetorio, Flavius Anicius, wearing a Pannonian cap[31], was trying vainly to calm them.

He waved desperately for silence, and they calmed down enough to let him speak.

"We all know that you were promised your pay. But it has been stolen by robbers! It is them you should be angry at! And the emperor himself has promised that you will be paid soon, and a donative on top of it!"

That caught their attention. "How much?" someone shouted.

"That the Emperor will decide…"

He got no further. A murmur began, which turned into a roar, and a stone flew at him, hitting the straight side of his cap hard enough that he had to wildly catch at it to stop it being swept off his head.

"Should have worn a helmet," someone said behind me, and everyone laughed nervously.

The noise from below was deafening now: the angry cries of the men, the sound of drawn swords beating shields, the cursing at us. And every commander was afraid to do a thing, for soldiers who had reached this stage of mutiny are as unpredictable as lightning.

"Does anyone else want try to calm them?" said Flaccus wryly over the tumult.

"Unless you have wagons of coin, I don't think that will help."

The voice came from the mass of men standing with us. I don't know who spoke.

"Where is the Praeses?" I said.

"He's a civil officer, not a military one. How will that help?"

"Anyone see either him or Constantinus recently?"

The same voice, but now it was ironic.

"Where *is* the Emperor?" I asked.

---

[31] A brimless pillbox-shaped felt cap.

"I believe he's in the Basilica," said Flaccus.

"He needs to be here!" someone shouted.

"If he were up here, I'm not sure the men would stay down there," I added pensively.

"Oh, shit! They're moving!" Someone shouted. "They're heading for the Basilica!"

And indeed, they were. No one had shouted any orders. I've seen this in crowds before and since... it's like they have a group mind, which decides together what to do.

One of the strangest things is that they did not just walk... or at least, they walked at the start, but they were soldiers, used to marching together. And as they moved, the steps grew together, as if centurions were shouting at them to keep time; until the crash of their hobnailed boots was regular and synchronized. If you've ever heard twenty thousand caligae striking the stones of a road at once, you know how loud the noise will be. It was, in a way, awe-inspiring. And it was frightening. The air was suddenly filled with birds, as they flew startled from their perches. I could not but help remember the time the starlings had wheeled in the sky at the wrong time, heralding the coming death of Constantius. If this was an omen, it heralded dark things.

I was not the only person to notice the resemblance. I heard someone mutter the word "sturni" behind me, and we all looked at each other. I was not sure all were starlings: most, I thought, were ravens, which made the omen worse.

I could not help the guilt in myself, when I realized that I, and the people who had attacked the payroll wagons, were the ones who had caused this. People would die today, because of us. Because of *me*. I remembered the old words "nothing worthwhile lacks a painful price", and tried to shrug it off.

"We have to follow."

Again, I have no idea who said that. It might even have been me. But this was how it was. The officers could not stay behind when the men set out on a path to mutiny. They would be seen as the enemy, and murdered piecemeal.

We followed, and the Praefectus Praetorio came with us. There was something rather pitiful about the entire command structure of the army following their men. But we were lucky. They could have turned on us. Now we were at the Basilica, and the shouting and shield-bashing had begun again.

Only now it was rhythmical: "Come out, Constantinus! Your army is here!"[32]

*This will not last long*, I thought. *They're going to smash their way in.*

Then I saw the doors to the Basilica open, and a man in civilian dress appear at the top of the steps, surrounded by a small group of military officers. I thought it was Constantinus, but then I saw it was the Praeses. I began to push my way forward. I knew the plan. The time had come.

I saw the Praeses shouting, trying to be heard. And then from all through the throng of soldiers, voices rose: "Let him speak! Let him speak!"

We had dispersed as many Amici as we could through the mutineers. And soon the calls merged into a rhythmical chant, "Let him speak!" and gradually everyone was shouting it. And then the quiet came.

"I am Lucius Castus Macer," he said, "Praeses of this province. I have come here not to tell you to go back to your barracks. For your cause is just and you should not return until you are paid!"

The cheers crashed out as the men heard what they wanted to hear.

The silence came, and he paused, just enough. He was very good. He knew exactly how to grasp a crowd in his hand, and make them eager to hear.

"Do you feel, men of Rome, that you have been betrayed?"

*"Hoc ille!"* they shouted in assent.

"Do you feel that Constantinus cares nothing about you?"

*"Hoc ille!"*

"Do you wish Carausius were here?"

For a moment there was silence, for this was a great and treasonous thing he was asking.

I shouted at the top of my voice, and I was joined all through the mutineers by the men we had planted so carefully.

*"Hoc ille! Hoc ille!"*

"Do you remember him, the Emperor who cared for his army, gave you his love and was foully murdered? Do you remember Carausius? Do you wish he were here now?"

A hiss started, and I thought that they were voicing their disapproval. But I was wrong. *"Sic! Sic! Sic!"* they were shouting. It sounded like a million snakes were hissing, but it was a hiss of approval.

"If he were here, you know you would be paid, don't you?"

*"Hoc ille!"*

---

[32] Exorīre, Constantine! Exercitus adest!

"Do you know that they did not kill all of Carausius's family? Did you know they missed a son?"

A low murmur swept through the crowd, a murmur of disbelief.

"Do you remember Carausius's son, Artorius?"

A man shouted from the far side of the square. "I remember him!" Others answered, "I do too!" And still others, "Me too!"

"I knew him as a child," I shouted, as loudly as I could. "Is he here?"

The Praeses answered. "Yes! He is here! Look behind you!"

We all heard it then, the measured sound of hundreds of hobnailed boots. We looked down the street, and marching up it were armed men.

"The Legion at Deva has come to join you! They call for you to join them! And with them is Carausius's son, Artorius! Look!"

They turned, and we all saw. Marching towards us, their standards high, were the men from Deva. And in front of them marched Artorius, in a plain robe and bare head.

"Here he is! Artorius son of Carausius!"

The cheers grew and became a flood of sound that overwhelmed us.

"Do you want him as your Emperor?" He leaned forward, his arms raised as he shouted, "Do you want to get paid?"

"Yes! Yes! Yes!"

"Raise him on your shields, and put the purple on him, and you will get paid!"

I knew the wagons were waiting, and to see them drive into the center of the unbelieving mass of men who saw that the promise was not empty. I have never felt so drained. I thought back to the coin Carausius had given me all those years ago, and its legend. "Expectate veni."

Yes. Indeed.

I walked up the stairs to the dais where the Praeses and the new emperor were now standing. It was a strange feeling. I knew him as a boy, and then a minor provincial official. Now? How should I deal with him? But I needn't have worried. He smiled, and embraced me. "I have no idea if I should be thankful to you or not," he said, "I am not at all sure at this moment."

"We have a great deal of work to do, Dominus."

I turned to the Praeses. "Where is Constantinus? He cannot be allowed to live."

He shook his head. "He fled the Basilica before the men came. I have men looking for him, many men. The city is sealed. We'll find him."

# CHAPTER 45

## Licinianus: Constantinus

I came home late that night to my sister's house, where I hoped to find rest. I had been out, like so many, searching the houses of those sympathetic to Constantinus, and scouring the streets to find him. The soldiers were wild. Any who they claimed to support Constantinus, they killed; and only some were guilty. The bloodshed was appalling.

I was now so tired I cared nothing for food, though a cup of unwatered wine would be welcome, I thought. I just wanted to take off my armor and sword and go to bed.

I was so bleary, in fact, that I almost missed seeing the fear on the ostiarius' face, and the wild faces he was making at me, as if he was trying to tell me something without speaking. But even in my exhaustion, I knew something was wrong.

I had no idea what he was warning me about, and I had no idea what to do. In the end, I simply went in. I could feel myself almost mentally shrug. What would be, would be.

I walked through the vestibulum into the atrium, and then, as I entered the tablinum beyond, I saw that the peristyle was brightly lit by torches and even lamps. And there were voices, and some were of men, but there were female voices too. Fear lifted me out of my tiredness. This was not normal. A peristyle would never be so bright at night except for a very special party of visitors. And those my sister clearly had.

I saw who they were immediately I entered, for all were standing around the body of a man who lay on the flags. It was Catigernus, and he was bleeding from a wound to his shoulder. Above him was Constantinus, in his hand a bloody sword, and with him three soldiers, all with their blades out. Helena was there, and two slave women holding Severiana's babies. And next to her was my sister, kneeling, trying to staunch Catigernus's wound, and Veldicca, looking like a statue.

There was now complete silence in the peristyle, and the sound of my hobnailed military boots on the stone was very loud.

"It is not the behavior of a good guest, sir," I said, "to walk into a house and wound a client and retainer of the owner."

Constantinus looked at me with contempt. "He tried to stop me. How dared he? I am an Augustus!"

"I fear not, sir, not any more. The army has deposed you and elevated Artorius, son of Carausius, to the purple. But I'm sure you're aware of that. You are being sought all through the city."

Constantinus had always had a short temper, and I thought from the fury in his face that he would strike me with his sword then and there. But Helena moved quickly forward, grasped his arm, and called out: "They have given us shelter, Constantinus! You cannot attack them! It is not their fault that this has come upon us!"

I looked around at the three men with Constantinus. I recognized none of them, but I could guess they were imperial guards. Those are often not the best fighters, since they rarely go on campaign. I knew I could take them, if the moment came, and the god aided me. This standoff could go on all night, I thought, and I'm already tired. Better to end it now. With great deliberation, I said: "You know our family's name, Lady Helena, I hope? It is Vindex."

An expression of confusion came over her face, and she shook her head in bewilderment. Then it came to her. "Oh no," she said. "Oh no!"

I nodded. "Do you think we would ever forget what your son and his friends did? Do you think we would ever forgive or forget the shame he brought on us? The misery he gave to my sister's life?"

"*You* were part of this? You and your sister?"

"You may wonder where the men who helped your son defile my family are. I can tell you…" and all decency fled me, in my hatred of this man, as I went on, "that one is dead amongst the Votadini. I cut his throat. The other? Apollinaris? I castrated him and hanged him from a tree. He died a criminal's death, Helena, and he deserved it. And now comes your son. I and my sister are Friends of Carausius."

"It was you who stole the money," said Constantinus, and his hatred surely matched mine.

I nodded. "I and many others. The money your soldiers are receiving this very night, and praising Artorius as they receive it."

It is not Roman to glory in revenge, but I have much Celtic blood in me from my Gaulish ancestors, and I am sure that they never hesitated to feel this emotion, exhilarating as it is, if only for a short time…

Constantinus looked at his men. "Kill him," he said, his voice low, but the murder in it very apparent. "And kill that bitch of his sister too."

Even his own men hesitated at that, for no man likes to go into a sudden fight. But then they came.

I saw how they intended to do it. One would come from each side, and grasp my arms. I was wearing armor, so a frugal stab under the ribs would not be effective. But with my arms held, a blow to my neck would suffice. I didn't give them the time. I dropped to a squat on one foot, and swung my other armored leg sideways, knocking the legs out from one of the guards. I lunged to the other side, and drove my helmet into the mailed belly of the man there. I heard his breath whoof from his body, and as he bent over, I drove my sword up into his throat. The god was with me, and the surroundings receded as I swung my sword hand in a low arc to smash the leg of the guard coming at me from the front. He screamed as the blade shattered his knee, and in a single move I pivoted up and down, and, reversing the blade, drove it into his neck, and down into his lung. He fell, blood pouring from his mouth. The last guard lay on the floor looking up at me, his mouth opening to beg. I drove my sword into it, and he died as the blade cut into his spine, for he deserved no mercy.

I stood, and the killing dream was still with me. Constantinus was next. I advanced on him slowly, hardly knowing what I would do, yet intent on doing it.

I heard Helena scream: "No! No!"

Constantinus's face was a mask of pure hatred. "If I die, then so will this bastard! I will have no child from this traitorous family!"

He turned on the slave girl holding the boy infant, and his pugio was out. He drew it back to stab at it but then he stopped, as if surprised, and looked down at the dagger my sister had driven below his ribs. It was perfectly placed, to angle up and into his heart. Her face was the face of a goddess, and I saw that her Dream had come upon her, just as it had all those years ago in Londinium to my aunt, for no woman born as a twin in my family can stand back as a child is killed, even if it is one she hates.

Constantinus crashed to the ground, his heart failing even before he fell. Helena was screaming like a madwoman, screaming and clutching at her face, throwing herself on the dying body of her son. But it was too late. The thing was done. It had started all those years ago with Carausius, when my aunt Flavilla saved a child. And now it was ended. I just needed to sleep.

"See to Catigernus," I said. "See to him."

I felt tears start in my eyes, for I was remembering years back, when in Londinium my aunt Flavilla had killed a man to save a child. And now I had seen my sister do it too.

I felt a chill. It had never before been borne home to me as thoroughly how much our family depended on our gods, and how powerful they were. I had seen my gentle sister strike as if she were a snake, and truly, just as her aunt had, all those years ago in Londinium. There had been in me an edge of disbelief when our gods had said we could have this vengeance if we would change the world. My aunt had saved Artorius. And now my sister had killed Constantinus. It was as if it was the same blow twice-delivered, for without one, the other could never have come to be.

And that was the source of the shiver I felt, for now I knew we were on the path they had warned us about, one that could no longer be changed. And it frightened me, for I had no idea what the future now held.

# CHAPTER 46

## Licinianus: Completion

It had been a hard eighteen months. Not everyone had accepted the revolt, for that was what it was, no matter how much we tried to claim it was just a "restitution". But then, every usurper claims that.

None of us had expected anything different. There were sporadic acts of resistance in the south, but those were put down with the aid of the northern troops. We even received a message of welcome from Galerius, though without an acknowledgement of Artorius's imperial status. We were all sure that he would be as friendly to us as he would have been to Constantinus; so we prepared for the worst.

What made things strange indeed was that we received a message from Gaul accepting Artorius's rule, even though we'd never asked for it. Hispania rejected it, clearly expecting us to ask for it. The irony was great. We had no desire to rule in either Gaul or Hispania. We were the Imperium Britannorum, and no more. We sent both a message saying so, which I'm sure they didn't believe, since the past – and Carausius himself – offered so much evidence to the contrary.

But there had been battles, if small ones, and I had been in more than one. I was so glad to finally get back to my home on the Oak River, for there lay all the reminders of a happy childhood and beloved people, though some of them were now amongst the shades.

Catigernus had recovered well. I'd gone to see him at the end of my last visit, to find him being looked after by his doting wife in the house we'd given him. He didn't seem too bothered by his large brood of children, though he had a stiff shoulder that was taking a while to come back. Indeed, his wife was in the process of adding another to the family, though she was getting well on in years. Numerianus, I understood, was still entangled with his Christian wife, still too afraid to tell her that he was not truly a Christian. Helena had simply disappeared. Some said she was dead. Others that she had gone back to her home in Bithynia. No one really knew.

I went from my cubicle and walked down the stairs to the gardens that my grandmother had so carefully laid out, long before I was born. They had been tended well, which in no way surprised me: my aunt Flavilla had loved her mother dearly, and she had made sure that their upkeep had been maintained.

I was still saddle sore. I had ridden in during the early morning, before the sun rose, and fallen into sleep very quickly. But the cool morning air was delicious, and I breathed it deeply.

"Licinianus!"

I heard noise behind me, the sound of women calling and laughing, and turned to see a little waddling figure coming from the house, falling onto his knees and staggering back to his feet as often as he fell. It was a toddler giggling as he clumsily ran, trying to evade the women who were after him. A woman pounced, and grabbed him up in her arms, laughing as she called him a naughty boy and cuddled him.

I knew the voice immediately. It was Veldicca's, and her mouth was opened in a smile as she saw me. She handed the child to a waiting slave, and walked quickly down to greet me.

"I heard you come home last night," she said excitedly in British. "I was so glad! There has been such fighting and killing! I was afraid for you!"

"You seem fully occupied with that child. It's Severiana's I'd guess?"

She nodded. "Yes…"

I knew from her expression that my sister's feelings towards Constantinus's son had not changed.

"It's sad," she said. "He's really a lovely little boy, full of sweetness and fun. I hope she'll get past it one day. He can't help who his father was."

"No. But she's a stubborn girl, my sister."

She nodded sadly, and called for a slave to bring my breakfast. I was grateful. I was hungry. I was thirsty. But what was uppermost in my mind was Veldicca, and how pretty she looked in a green tunic and matching earrings. I yearned to kiss her.

She put down a chair next to a small table along the path. "I told the slave to be quick! I wanted to get up earlier and have your breakfast ready for you, but I heard Laurentius making a fuss…"

"Laurentius? So that's what they've decided to call him?"

She looked down, then lifted her chin defiantly. "No one called him anything! You can't just call him 'the boy'! I thought that was ridiculous. So I started calling him Laurentius. And now everyone does."

"What do you call the girl?"

"She is Honestia, after your grandmother. I thought you would like that!" She looked anxiously up at my face, as if to reassure herself. "They are poor little infants! They are not to blame for what their father did! And if we bring them

306

up well, they will never be like him!"

At that instant, I made up my mind. This was a woman who had so much decency in her that she would give all of herself, to both her husband, and to her children. This was a treasure too precious to be lost.

I reached out to her and took her hand, kissing it. She reddened.

"Why Laurentius?"

She shrugged, as if embarrassed. "I just thought that I love the smell of bay leaves,[33] and his baby skin smells so good. So it seemed like a good name."

"Let's sit down, and eat together."

I knew what I was going to do, and the wishes of my family suddenly meant nothing. She poured two cups of wine for us, watered them well, for it was early, and we drank together. Then I broke two pieces of bread and gave one to her. We ate in silence at first, the kind of silence that only comes from happiness, both of us smiling at each other, as if at a private joke.

"Do you know," I said, "that at Roman weddings the bride and groom sometimes eat together a cake made from grape juice and flour?"

She looked at me, puzzled, her lips a little parted. "I've never seen a Roman wedding." Her eyes brightened. "But I did see a bride once. She was wearing orange!" The skin around her eyes crinkled as she laughed. "I would look horrible in orange!"

"I think you would look beautiful in anything. Will you marry me?"

She dropped her cup, and it clattered on the table, spilling the wine. I caught it just before it bounced to the ground and broke.

"I can't be your concubine, I can't be. It would be a betrayal of my father!"

"Do you care for me?"

She began to cry. "No! I don't *care for* you! I *love* you. I have for months and months!"

I picked up her hand again, marveling at the slender elegance of her fingers. I kissed it a second time. Can anyone know how wonderful it is to kiss the fingers of the woman you love until you've experienced it, just to smell the scent of her skin? "And I love you. I'm not asking you to be my concubine. I'm asking you to marry me, become my full wife, become a Roman matron – or a British one if you like – in every sense."

She looked stunned. "I have nothing! Everything I have your family gave me! Even these clothes!"

---

[33] Laurus in Latin.

Out of the corner of my eye I saw that Severiana was standing on the veranda looking down at us. She said nothing, but her head tipped as if she knew there was no option.

"Then let me give you one more thing," I said, "My love... and my protection for as long as I shall live. Become my wife!" I smiled with pure pleasure at the thought. "Even though you'll have to wear orange!"

"We've never even kissed!"

"I think I can fix that," I said, and did. And it seemed to me that Severiana, looking down, might have nodded. I hoped so. But I wasn't sure.

Suddenly I felt fear at the future. For I, my family, all of us, had made ourselves marked people, and by marrying this girl, I would make her one too. Emperors have long memories, and there were emperors still who would not forget or forgive what we had done.

# THE END

Milton Keynes UK
Ingram Content Group UK Ltd.
UKHW041046201123
432906UK00002B/49

9 781645 942184